Inside the impend  e
immediately to w e
wet cold spray act ,
and he brought his
the stick, and felt v ....us the
rudder. Everything, ... us the freezing fog, swirled.
He had no notion, apart from the dizziness he felt inside
his head, how deep the cloud extended beneath him. Arch
felt bird-like, turning like a bird, floating with the caprice
of the air and mist, it was protecting him, sustaining him,
gently upholding him. The words of the old hymn floated
somewhere into his head, he didn't know from where,
from schooldays was it, from the choir, he couldn't
recall . . .?

'If I take the wings of the morning, and dwell in the
uttermost parts of the sea . . .'

Then the cloud did break, at just below 500 feet. He
was alone in the sky and safe. Bickerton was gone off
crook, but alive, at least. No sign of the hostiles now,
thank heaven. The faithful pram, its instrument panel
demolished in front of him, had taken a terrible beating,
and the wings were wobbly, but the engine, unscathed,
flooded back into some kind of half-life, as he engaged
the Wolseley Vipers, and gently and patiently bottomed
out.

'Even there . . . thy right hand shall hold me . . .'

The Wings of the Morning

BY

PATRICK GARLAND

If I ascend up into heaven, thou art there:
if I make my bed in hell, behold, thou art there.
If I take the wings of the morning,
and dwell in the uttermost parts of the sea;
Even there shall thy hand lead me;
and thy right hand shall hold me.

PSALM 139. MORNING

THE WINGS OF THE MORNING
A BANTAM BOOK 0 553 40086 X

Originally published in Great Britain by
Hamish Hamilton Ltd 1989

PRINTING HISTORY
Bantam Books edition published 1990

Copyright © Patrick Garland 1989

This book is set in 10/11 pt Sabon by Goodfellow & Egan Cambridge Ltd.

Bantam Books are published by Transworld Publishers Ltd., 61–63
Uxbridge Road, Ealing, London W5 5SA, in Australia by Transworld
Publishers (Australia) Pty. Ltd., 15–23 Helles Avenue, Moorebank,
NSW 2170, and in New Zealand by Transworld Publishers (N.Z.) Ltd.,
Cnr. Moselle and Waipareira Avenues, Henderson, Auckland.

Printed and bound in Great Britain by
Cox & Wyman Ltd, Reading

Contents

PROLOGUE

The Goodbye Gate: 1916   9

PART ONE

1 Brontë   29
2 Recruits   62
3 Inns of Court   74
4 Soldiers Bathing   83

PART TWO

5 At the Good Old Carlyle   97
6 Mysie at the End of Winter   104
7 The Little Theatre in the Hay   109
8 A Patriotic Comedy   127
9 Mr Chancellor   137

PART THREE

10 Peckwater Barracks   153
11 Mysie in the Spring   168
12 Stunting   177
13 Mysie on Tour   185
14 Railway Cottages   192
15 First Blood   200

PART FOUR

16 Roman Landing   211
17 General Ascapard Makes a Speech   231

PART FIVE

18 Château de Bellinglise   249
19 Capité   260
20 A Witness along the Salient   269
21 November, 1916   283
22 Into Battle   293

PART SIX

23 Belgodère   317

PART SEVEN

24 Wolves to the Slaughter   439
25 Winter and Spring, 1917   449
26 The Train Station, Abbeville   452
27 A Funeral in the Forest   472
28 Captain Chevalier at Home   480
29 Eastward Ho! 1918   493

PROLOGUE

'One must first of all conquer the inner Schweinhund.'

GRAF MANFRED VON RICHTOFEN

The Goodbye Gate: 1916

For any young fighting man, returning at night to the Western Front and the trenches of that terrible winter war, the great London railway termini which supplied the Channel ports – Waterloo and Victoria, Blackfriars and Liverpool Street – were all Stations of the Cross.

Perhaps it was the generals who commanded it, but so it was elected on Sunday nights for a regimental brass band to play selections from the current variety concerts and pierrot-shows which had doubtless entertained many a young man during his leave; but, instead of brightening the occasion, at such times the cheerful music succeeded only in providing a melancholy contrast. Those enlisted men among the pressing multitudes with mothers or wives around their necks did, it was perfectly true, attempt to show some kind of appreciation, as if it had been for their benefit, but for the most part it was a hollow business. The jaunty rhythms, the brisk tum-ti-tum, the inept lyrics, seemed to deride their efforts to keep a brave face in front of their distressed families.

> K-K-K-Katie, beautiful Katie,
> You're the only g-g-g-girl that I adore . . .

With great puff and bravura the Royal Engineers' band was playing right there in the middle of the railway station, and the atmosphere around them was one of festivity, the shiny brass trombones and jaunty snare-drums putting a spring into the most reluctant step. Without its being Christmas-time, nevertheless it felt as if some vigorous winter feast-day was being celebrated and the civilians bustled about with extra energy. Porters wheeled trolleys with additional agility, just dodging women's ankles by inches, almost deliberately to show off their expertise. Because of the brass band, the rail-waymen were forced to shout above the noise, thus adding if anything to the confusion, and a small group of children, pulling away from their parents, stood in a semicircle, joining in with the words of a song most of them had been lucky enough to hear in the music-halls as a treat. So, life at Victoria Station took on the merry temper of an exuberant family party. Smoke filled the glass ceiling and curled around it and downwards, and strong naphtha flares swam about it, seeping orange and yellow dyes deep within, as if the steam were a cloth fabric. Sometimes this added an unpleasing, livid quality to the cheeks of people hurrying back and forth.

At this hour on a Sunday evening in October, the station was exceptionally busy, the booking-offices crowd-ed, and large queues of patiently waiting people bent under their luggage in lines at the barriers. Through the steaming air, flickering and suddenly dispersing, gaps would open up on another platform, to reveal a yet greater number of passengers passively standing. In front of them, or by their side, erect figures strode back and forward urgently, frequently seizing on some impassive silhouette as the victim of unexpected spasms of bad humour and abuse. There were further clusters of men moving at a different pace – like a frieze on wallpaper – each figure holding on to the one in front, shepherded by white indistinct shapes, but more solicitously, as if tend-ing children. What could all this uneven frenzy signify to a bystander, innocently walking in from London's com-panionable streets, in order to purchase his evening newspaper, or pipe tobacco? To what joyful purpose did all this energy, and noise, and rhythm, and urgency lead? In spite of the friendly, jaunty music, the playful atmos-phere given out by the raucous trumpets, and their ruddy-faced performers in bright uniforms, without a doubt the mood of everybody else was one of universal shabbiness, and heartache. The sound and the appearance clashed – where one was uplifting, the other was downcast. The vigorous music might have been assisting a public execution. And in a way it was. For this was a time of war, and these crowds of scurrying people were the cavalrymen, the foot-soldiers, the gunners and sappers, the artificers, the pioneers, raw recruits and old 'toughs', some wounded, some unscathed, all returning from home to the fighting lines in France. This was the Goodbye Gate at Victoria Station.

> When the m-m-moon shines
> Over the cow-shed
> I'll be waiting at the k-k-k-kitchen door!

Beyond the barriers, the ominous engines of departure waited in long corridors. Moisture gathered in oily beads on their carriage roofs and slithered down the sides. Within, behind yellow-lit windows, incoherent shapes pressed against the glass, bundles of men and equipment. The trains were so overloaded, soldiers had to perch on the netting luggage racks, and their khaki kitbags, blankets, rifles and helmets formed great piles outside in corridors, on the top of which more men swayed uncomfortably.

> Jimmy was a soldier bold,
> Katie was a maid with hair of gold,
> Like an act of fate
> Kate was standing at the gate,
> Watching all the boys on dress parade.

Sergeant Bickerton felt a pinch of cold without his fur-collared leather coat, on an October night whose temperature had swiftly and without warning dropped; he yawned and stuck his hands to warm them inside his pockets. A Guards sergeant-major stopped screaming at a line of mute squaddies standing at strict attention before

11

him, to turn his rage to the idle other-ranker but, not having the authority to abuse him publicly (as he belonged to the Flying Corps), tried by aggressive facial expression alone to wither the other man. Bickerton, after two years of battle in cold skies over northern France, was unlikely to be intimidated by a 'wooden-top' sergeant in a railway station and returned his gaze without enthusiasm to the brass band. The train was not due to leave for some while, and Captain Gendron, whose observer he was (and friend, in any case), was on the other side of the station, kissing his girl goodbye. Bickerton was accustomed to this and, opening his bronze box of cigarettes, prepared himself to wait, squatting on the kitbag between his feet. The tune was catchy, and Bickerton enjoyed the half-remembered song, as much as the familiar thread of smoke rasping between his tongue and throat. Bickerton was 'digging in' – a favourite phrase of his.

> K-K-K-Katie, beautiful Katie,
> You're the only g-g-g-girl that I adore,
> When the m-m-moon shines
> Over the cow-shed,
> I'll be waiting at the k-k-k-kitchen door!

Bickerton had known a recruit in basic training who stammered like that. Gunner Beecroft. They took him off guard duty because he could only stammer out: 'Who g-g-g-goes there?' The officer said grimly he posed a threat.

On the further side of the station, where the hansom cabs and growlers used to meet passengers coming back in cheerier times from the stylish resorts of Boulogne and Deauville, a party of walking wounded, with their nurses, held closely on to each other. Many of them were smoking, giving an odd appearance of comfort and repose, in the centre of faces wrapped in discoloured envelopes of bandages. Those unable to see, or feel, or speak, were assisted by the nurses. Small children, weary

12

of listening to the brass band, turned their attention to the wounded, staring at them the way children do, genially absorbed by any abnormality or terror. 'Oh, look, why are those men . . . ?' A senior male nurse attempted to shoo them away, discreetly, without disturbing the civilians. It was the soldiers, not the children, who embarrassed him. But the children, unembarrassed, resolutely stared on. One of the wounded men, horribly disfigured, blind even, appeared to be smiling, trying, by means of his smile, to establish contact with humdrum life roundabout. Bickerton watched with the same friendly lack of interest as the children.

'How you doing, old mate . . . ?'

'I'm doing all right now, mate – how're *you* doing?'

'Good to be home, mate . . . Got a regular blighty, friend . . .'

'Good luck to you, brother!'

But the few civilians who were there turned from him bitterly, with impatience, and the only ones who replied to his ghostly cheerfulness were other soldiers. The grin was all that remained of a face which had lost eyes, nose and jaw, and whatever he spoke was disfigured, unearthly. They moved on in their clumsy struggle, uplifted by the rhythm of the band:

K-K-K-Katie, beautiful Katie . . .

The porters on each platform called out, over the music, the destinations of each troop train, and the soldiers in great gulps poured through the barrier, chivvied and persecuted by their NCOs. A regiment of Scots Guards, in full ceremonial dress, with pipes, fifes and drums, marched boldly through the station on to their train, and the London Irish Rifles, dowdy by comparison, drowned the band by the vigour of their singing.

In isolated groups of four or five, gloved, unhindered by baggage, without rifles or bayonets, and, in place of heavy metal helmets, with peaked caps, the officers chatted: most of them, Bickerton noted, not for the first

13

time, identified by a collective habit of flicking the backs of their boots with the tips of their canes. They stood apart by manner as much as by dress, easy in each other's company, often conspicuous by their laughter. One little group appeared to smoke cigarettes in a characteristic manner. There were all the same, Bickerton thought, a similar breed. Several, accompanied by family or wives, might introduce a brother-officer, who would stand forward alertly and flick his cap peak with a gloved hand. Or even, to a distinguished elder, remove a hat and a glove to receive an extended handshake. Many of them were accompanied by their dogs and, as well as the trailing colonies of children, tribes of boxers, terriers, spaniels and, most frequently, labradors scuffled around the already busy station. Separated from all of these, Bickerton could just see, behind a newspaper-stand, his own captain leaning against the wall with utmost nonchalance, smiling and talking – even at this distance – in an undertone, as if it were possible he might be overheard amid such babble. His girl faced him, not looking at him, but touching his lapel sometimes, and appeared part of the time to be crying. Bickerton recognized her by the furtive wisp of her smile. It was the little soubrette from *Helping the Cause* at the Pleasure Gardens Theatre.

The captain had selected this corner, because it was a little less public than the main swirl of the station. And less noisy also. David 'Arch' Gendron had the gift – if it was a gift – no matter what the situation might be, of directing all his attention, his whole personality, on to whomever he was addressing at any one time. There appeared, amongst all the bustle, a pool of stillness round him. He was dressed for embarkation in his boots and puttees, wound up to his knees, and was wearing his usual double-breasted buff-coat with its junior schoolboy's scarf, and his forage cap bent over his right eye. He also carried his favourite walking-stick, with its bent handle, a present from his brother Chas, when both had first arrived in France the year before. His wings and ribbons he kept well out of sight. It was as if, around him, all the activity and tension receded, and Arch was involved merely in a casual exchange about arrangements for a rendezvous later on at some dance, or a theatre visit, or even the first beginnings of a flirtation. It was a gift, truly; Bickerton had observed it before, this amazing capacity to isolate himself from the confusion and violence around him. A man among men. He had witnessed it in Captain Gendron many times in air-battles above Béthune, when his stillness preserved them both in a sky swarming with vicious enemy machines. His smile, for example, was a patient one of reassurance and repose, nor was this the only occasion he had made use of it. But his girl was hard to convince, and reluctant to be reassured. To any passer-by, who had the time or the impertinence to stop and consider, their conversation might even have been the reconciliation of a lovers' quarrel, were it not that the same scene was enacted throughout many other shadowy corners of the same railway terminus, behind flower-sellers, and newspaper-stands, out of reach of the sergeant-major's commands, and the brass band's oom-pah-pah . . .

The young woman spoke with gravity, in an impulsive, nervous manner, her eyes shining, sometimes crying, and then wiping her tears angrily, as if they were specks of dust in her way. When she spoke, in her excitement she seeemed to run over her consonants, a curious kind of imperfection in her speech, as if what she had to say was too urgent for the words to catch up.

'Oh, you'll come back next month, Dazzle, promise you'll come back for me, won't you?'

His speech was slower, reassuring her. 'I always come back for you, you know I –'

She was too eager, would not let him finish – again tears. 'You'll not desert me . . . ' She looked like an angry child. 'And we'll go down to Puddledock again, and stay with Aunt Jane, and you'll stay in the apple-room next door to mine, and in the morning I'll bring you in breakfast . . . '

Now she was drying these tears, not with her handkerchief which she bunched up in her fist, but with the palm of her other hand.

' . . . and I'll undress, as you like me to while you're still sleeping, and I'll just creep under the sheet and you won't even notice I'm there . . . '

She wanted to hold him where he was by the force of her recollection.

'No, no Mysie . . . ' he said, gently putting her damp hand between both of his, 'please don't make it difficult for both of us. Come on, old woman.'

She was called Mysie by her girl-friends, short for Melissa. Mysie suited her. She was tiny of stature, strong in will, alternate in her moods, and capable of swift attacks of hysteria, which she used to enslave. 'Pretty as paint', her Aunt Jane said of her, in her own countrified way, 'but sometimes she could be a Madam.' It was necessary for Mysie to be deeply in love, even dangerously so, otherwise her moods tempted her to tease and abuse. She had been an actress for over a year now, and during the week appeared in a patriotic revue at the Pleasure Gardens, a small auditorium off St James's. But however much she might have been, in easier times, tempted to affect a softness or a vulnerability which would draw attention to her damp cheeks, and misted eyes, *this* time Mysie's weeping was authentic, her tears were genuine.

Too many leave-takings in the same corner of the station had taken their toll, every parting always appeared a final one. Against this show of true and affecting concern for his welfare, Arch could only provide a rather bluff and foolish defence. Partings embarrassed him, and he always begged Mysie to take leave of him in the little apartment they shared whenever he could get away from the Front, in Linden Gardens. There Mysie kept a canary and her aged dog called Apples, and her black cat called Music, and treated Arch with the protection, the dedication, almost the ceremony, many a young wife reserves for her new husband. He stared hard at her fragile beauty, and felt, as so often, the familiar stirrings of desire, when all that afternoon he had spent his time silently in her bare arms and gazed unendingly on her soft body. He wanted her then, at that moment, knowing well he could not have her.

Mysie gave everything she owned its special private name – and 'Dazzle' was her own nickname for him, entirely her invention, based loosely on the alliteration of his full name, David Archibald Gendron, and in part on his flair in the sky, his brilliance. At home, his two wild brothers found David inappropriate, Archibald too long, Archie too familiar, and settled for Arch. And Arch was what he came to be called.

The second hand of the large yellow clock-face jerked forward clumsily, and Arch noticed with a start that the minute hand was only four minutes away from eight o'clock. Behind the faint silver of Mysie's hair and its charming, rather ridiculous hat with an entire bird perched upon it, he saw the hesitating shadow of his observer.

'Here's Bickerton now, Mysie,' he said gently but with a note of firmness she recognized absolutely, 'I daren't be a moment longer. I have to be in Dover at dawn, and in France by midday.'

'But why shouldn't you leave from Hendon, like you did last summer, after we went to the races? You could, you know you could. You could always fly across. Oh, Dazzle, you don't have to report tonight. Please stay tonight at least.'

He was firmer with her now.

'You always promised, Mysie, you'd never hold me back. You know how much it tears me apart, you know I can't refuse you anything. It's so hard to explain without sounding a brute but, unless I can settle myself in at least twelve hours before I'm due to report to my commander, I remain unsettled all week. Things go wrong, you know, for a chap, low cloud, or the machines breaking down as

17

usual, or no machines, perhaps. There might even be new orders for me to fly on somewhere else. This was only forty-eight hours' leave. I promise I'll be able to get away for longer at Christmas. And then it will be grand. Hoppy Horner won't let me down.'

'But Christmas is a long way away, that's not grand at all.'

'Not so long as all that. Besides, you remember what I've told you. It is I who go back to a tent in the middle of a field. You go back to that lovely little room from which you can hear all the peaceful sounds of the street, and little Music to stroke. You go back to gossipy dressing-rooms, I go back to the rotten Front.'

Mysie suddenly remembered his naked body that she had caressed all afternoon, before the fire, until the cold air from the garden outside hurried them beneath the blankets, and she cried again.

'By going back twelve hours before, Mysie, it means at least I can adjust to my horrid new life, and leave your old comfy one behind me.'

'But twelve hours out of forty-eight is so many . . .'

'Bickerton's making signs now, Mysie . . .'

The observer was pointing with his finger to the yellow clock-face.

'It isn't fair. Now I wish you'd never come at all . . .'

'You don't mean that.'

'Yes, Dazzle, I do, sometimes.' She began to cry a little more. 'Not really, of course, but the wretchedness of seeing you go, of going back to that horrid room, no matter how cosy, full of everything except the one thing I really want, and to keep on doing that, month after month, for two years now, and no sign of it ever coming to an end . . . it's too hard for me . . .'

Arch's mouth felt dry. There were so many ways to love, it was never possible to find only one way.

Mysie seemed to give up, quite suddenly, and released him with a shrug of helplessness and defeat.

'Keep going, old woman . . . ' he said, without much confidence.

'Fly as fast as you can, Dazzle, my very dear,' were her last words in reply, 'and when you return – fly back like Hell!'

It was an expression he had taught her himself. The station now was a large dockyard, and the trains leaving the quays, like ocean-liners. Pale battalions of men stood in lines waiting to embark. Partings became more vigorous, more painful. The brass band seemed to be playing even louder in compensation. It was trying to drown out the misery of departure.

It was raining in the streets now, and a squadron of cavalry rode in, the troopers bending their heads as they clattered beneath the stone arch, and their grey capes spattered with rain. Arch wondered about his famous brother, Chas, riding with Colonel Norton's Horse. Dismounting, the grooms led the horses straight on to the platforms, and stowed them in the waiting transports. Without the benefit of their animals, the dismounted troopers looked faintly comic in their high-wound puttees and skinny-legged breeches, their top-heavy helmets.

Arch leant to one side to take his walking-stick away from the wall, and when he turned back Mysie clutched his neck with both arms as if she would wrestle him to the ground. Her tears sank into his soft brown collar, and the hairs of his neck felt damp. Her hold on him was painful, strangling him, so that he was forced to pull her hands apart. All this time she was silent, but her breast seemed to be shaken by impatient and convulsive gasps. Even his gentleness could no longer contain the violence of her sorrow and, with no further attempt to quieten or pacify her, Arch bent her arms back from his neck, and held her firmly against the wall. When he kissed her this time, he felt he had never kissed anybody so hard, and only after a long, long moment, their lips pressed together so tightly, neither of them able to breathe, did he feel her shoulders and arms relax. At last he was able to lean her gently back against the stone. Grasping his stick, he stepped apart and away from her, walking backwards all the time, never taking his eyes from hers. Then, without waving or making further sign, he turned smartly and swiftly on his heel, Bickerton struggling behind him, carrying the heavy baggage, and his own kitbag, and lost himself in the swirling crowd.

Arch strode impatiently through the barrier, past a line of new recruits to an infantry regiment. He did not return their salutes, but raised the hook of his walking-stick in casual greeting. Bickerton succeeded in dropping the baggage outside the compartment, but swerved ahead and opened the carriage door, to find the captain's reserved seat. The train was crowded elsewhere, but in the '*Officers only*' carriage the compartments looked comfortable and relatively exclusive. Neither of his two companions, subalterns in the West Kents, made any attempt to talk, or even smiled in greeting; one was immersed in a threepenny novel, the other staring darkly in front of him, not bothering to watch the activity on the station platform. This atmosphere of indifference was quickly shared by Gendron, who slumped into a corner and glared through the pallid yellow reflection, out at the dark track beyond.

He worried first of all about Mysie. He could picture her now, tear-stained, hardly able to see a foot in front of her, bumping into people, being shouldered from side to side as khaki shapes shoved and jostled her, floating against their unending brown tide. And then he imagined her pressed into the corner of a cold horse-bus (most of the motor-transport had been commandeered by the troops), and the yellow stains of London's street-lamps looming up out of the damp mist of this October evening, and hoarse shouting in the roads, and laughter from public-house doors; how long had she stayed there in that vile station, her back pressed against the wall? Had drunken soldiers tried to importune her? Was she still there? Or was she already on her way across the park to that wonderful low-roofed country house on the edge of London, with its long garden, where magnolia trees burst into white fire each March, and littered the pavements of old Kensington with their fallen blossom? Of course they only shared a small apartment but on summer nights they sat outside, often not talking, just listening to the sounds of the great fretful city.

They had watched a German airship from there, one night in June, when they were lying together on the balcony, and the sound of roaring wind made both of them look up; at that second, caught in the cross-beam of powerful searchlights, was the great silver sail of a marauding Zeppelin, silent and stealthy above Bayswater. Heavy artillery camouflaged under green nets in the elegant grounds of Lord Holland's house fired off salvo after salvo, and studded the sky with cloud-bursts, at first red and dark grey, and instantly lost in the night. The dirigible floated over them, and suddenly its engines started, and the sky turned into echoing, vibrating noise, and the great monster sailed higher, like some elaborate kind of fish, or, as Mysie said, a church tower blown over. It had succeeded in eluding the searchlights, which suddenly snapped out, and dropped a stick of bombs which exploded with a firmer and closer sound than the gunfire.

But what could Mysie be feeling now, he wondered. Their mutual loneliness comforted him, like shared grief, and brought her close for a moment.

'I knew there would be tears before night,' she had said, 'you were singing at breakfast.'

The sudden jerk forward, not the whistles and shouts of the train guard, returned Arch to reality. A few late-comers clattered in army boots alongside the carriage, and struggled with the door-handles. Bickerton squatted happily outside on a pile of baggage. He was still 'digging in'. He had lit a cigarette, one of those coarse cheap yellow ones he had brought over from France, and pressed his back, hunched up in its overcoat, against the

21

carriage door. Shortly he would be fast asleep. Bickerton
had long ago mastered the art of sleeping at a second's
notice. But with one eyelid faintly ajar – the other eye
seemed permanently asleep. Wherever they had been
together, manoeuvres, under canvas in winter, in slit-
trenches, in the open cockpit of his machine, Gendron
was used to his companion's blank features. He had the
look of a man whose eye winked in permanent confidence
over a secret of mutual concern. Bickerton was also just
about the best off-sider any man could wish to have on
board.

For Arch himself, the prospect of everything he would
face in France, and the tantalizing nearness of Mysie
(even at this minute, before the train gathered speed in its
wheels, surely he could run out, and find her still waiting
anxiously by the barrier), and the slow tide of all that he
had experienced, made sleep an unwelcome visitor. He
feared it, because under its influence he was in danger of
being caught off guard. And he was no longer able to
dream. In his nightmares, he would sit at the controls of
his machine in a cloudless sky, empty of anything hostile,
with the patchwork of fields and villages below him, at
his mercy, or at his pleasure, a feeling of incontestable
joy, when the slow hand of sleep would place its fingers
across his eyes, and, still in his dream, he would blissfully
fall asleep – and then wake, in a sweat of cold wet terror,
as the sky buzzed with countless enemy machines, and the
immediate air around was scarred with tracer, and the
sulphurous smell of cordite. His observer, wounded,
laced in blood, would stretch half-way out of the cockpit,
edging his body forward, not shouting, but pleading,
pleading in a gentle voice, low like a child's but heard
clearly above the noise: 'Oh, Captain, please wake up,
please wake up . . . ' And then he would see himself, his
hands slumped over the controls, in deep sleep, unable to
stir his brain to take the smallest evasive action.

It was too late now to think of bounding out of the
carriage back to the warm arms of his girl – not that he

had truly considered that anyway. The rhythm of the wheels soothed him, as the carriage clanked heavily over the bridge, the river-line snaking to left and right. The infantry officers leaned forward eagerly for a final look, as if to learn by heart every detail of that evocative scene. One of them, a young man, possibly on his first visit to France, not too long out of school, said in an undertone, 'Good-bye, London,' and then relapsed into silence.

'Would you care if I smoked a cigar?' asked the older man unexpectedly. Arch had hardly heard.

'I said, would you care if I were to smoke one of these cigars?'

He shook his head.

'Perhaps you would like to join me? I took these from Truscotts only this afternoon. A farewell whiff of the old city, you know.'

'Not at all, go on, I don't smoke myself, but it never bothers me if others do.'

'Much thanks. Much thanks.'

The young man seemed oddly affected in voice as well as phrase. Arch glanced at his uniform, and it confirmed his instincts. The officer had come directly from cadet school.

'We're on our way to Dainville, does it ring a bell?'

He shook his head. The younger man propped his ankles up on the seat opposite, and undid his jacket.

'I observe you're Flying Corps. I presume you get to covering a lot of the ground. My younger brother is with your people.'

'Whereabouts?'

'Near Béthune, I think.'

'I'm stationed near Béthune.'

'He's with the fighter squadrons. Pups, Stingers, that kind of thing. Is that your line?'

'No. I fly two-seaters.'

'Is that risky?'

'I suppose it is. Frankly, I never think about it.'

'My brother's name is Barker, "Golly" Barker. Does that ring a bell?'

23

'No. I don't think it does.'

'Do you go in for tennis?'

'Rather a lot, actually.'

'Then you might well come across him. He's called "Golly", and I'm Harry, his elder brother. Then there's the junior, he's called Freddy and he's joining us as soon as he's able. He's at school for now, though.'

'Isn't he going to stay on at school?'

'Heavens no, you don't know our school. That's the only consolation of joining up. At least one gets out of that frightful final year.'

Arch felt disinclined to pursue a purposeless conversation, and turned his head back to the window. The older brother of 'Golly' Barker went to sleep with his mouth open, and his fellow-officer smoked the cigar through, until he too fell asleep. As the train edged its uncertain way southwards to Dover, huddled in his corner, Arch reviewed the events of the last year. He felt the cold, as so often, and pulled himself deeper into his leather coat for comfort, even breathing into the neckerchief so that his throat and chin felt an extra glow. The West Kents Officer in the seat opposite him stirred.

'The food in France,' he drawled, 'is said to be heaps better.' Arch nodded and yawned.

In their house, he thought of Mysie now, stretched out before the log fire, as before, playing with her cat, Music, or reciting her quaint lines in a loud voice, laughing when he corrected her, and jerking her head angrily to herself, trying to din them into her brain. Mysie angry, her cast-down 'culprit' look, Mysie laughing furiously; but this was an illusion, he recognized. That image was two of them together. He knew precisely what she would be doing by herself, alone. She would be hunched as motionless as he was, the fire-grate unlit, dreading that awful moment of stealing between cold sheets, made more freezing than ever by the absence of her lover.

He remembered things. One evening they had decided to go early to bed, and the light of a bedroom fire had

24

silhouetted lasciviously her body as she undressed. He had lain across the sheets, chin on his hand, watching, not so much the disclosure of each corner and curl of her body in the firelight, but the gradual piling of garments on the back of the chair, her bodice, corselet, slip, camisole, garters, all weightless and warm with the electric thrill of her recently clothed body. In the shadow and light of the burning wood, in a gesture part coy, part unconscious, she took off her stockings and threw them lightly into the air. And he watched them descend slowly to the floor like snakes. Every surface in the room was covered with her skirts and underthings, and shrouded as if the house was to be abandoned for a long time.

'Mysie – I want to ask you to do something for me: stand as you are, between the mantelpiece and the fire, I wish to look at you like this: I shall always remember you like this for the rest of my life. Will you do this for me, please?'

She had obeyed him, guiltily, like a child, and stood as he asked, playful beside the light of the fire, bare, almost ill at ease. The flames altered in patterns the affective cadences of her body. And even when she finally walked back to him, holding her within his arms, Arch permitted himself a shy, lustful glance at her cast-aside clothing, over her white shoulder, not realizing that in months to come in France he would, without being able to resist it, summon up this picture – a celebration of Mysie abandoning herself to him – and an aching for every fugitive part of her again would spread throughout his body. She was profligate in her secret beauties. A sight of her he could only crave, and a scent which he could never recapture. For he never dreamed of Mysie now, he could only remember her when he was awake.

The train had left London's puzzling arteries far behind, and through the blackness, as it scuttled south-wards, even in the black-out the familiar names of wayside stations loomed up in front of him to tantalize. One such halt had passed in total anonymity (a cluster of milk-churns, some porters lingering about, smoking, the miniature tips of dog-ends, a station-master's face peering urgently forward) when the name, dimly reflected beneath a solitary gas-lamp, jolted him. It was the ordinary name of Wood End, a suburban station near Dartford, on the journey south. Dandenilog, the Jericho, Wood End . . .

PART ONE

*'At the tender age of sixteen years,
he began his wild career.'*

THE WILD COLONIAL BOY

CHAPTER ONE

Brontë

His earliest memories of Wood End were afternoons in January, with the barometer high in the hundreds. For this was Wood End in Victoria, a sheep-station forty miles' ride southward from Moonee Ponds. It was no more than a single street of wooden bungalows, some two-storey shacks, a Stand-Up bar opposite the Temperance Hotel, perhaps a telegraph office each side of a dirt track. Men sitting on the wooden steps of verandahs, their eyes hidden under the dark shadowy rim of their hats. A few horses would be gathered, necks tied to the balustrade, shivering gently against the attention of innumerable flies. And this monotonous wooden sign at the entrance – Wood End.

As the chauffeur, Goerstler, drove the long bonnet of the four-wheeler forward in the hot afternoon, and dust spread each side of the wheels, it was unusual for any of the seated onlookers to budge from their lounging position. On their journey to and from Little Brighton they barely indulged in a sideways glance. If you parted your mouth flies would settle and attempt to struggle through the lips. The car, a silver De Dion Twelve hp, usually provoked a little exchange of interest beneath the brims of the cabbage-tree hats, and sometimes an anonymous shout would mingle with the exhaust. The burnt-ochre dust lifted for a minute and collapsed again behind the retreating motor. Vehicles were rare enough in those times in the subcontinent, and an oddity in a sleeping station like Wood End. Town? – it scarcely counted as a settlement. At best, it served drinks to the stockmen. A divide the bullockies ran their mob of cattle through.

Generally, the De Dion Twelve would hold as passengers the three celebrated Gendron boys and their father, all on their way to watch the bicycle competitions held up-country at the McKenzie place. These were still popular, but had lost some of their earlier appeal, which had been enjoyed in Grandfather Gendron's time. In those days there were proper gentlemen riders, who raced on various high-wheel bicycles with solid tyres, while elegant ladies, fashionably dressed, with gloves and parasols, stood at the side of the circular sand track to applaud them. Among Arch Gendron's first memories of Brighton society at the turn of the century were the famous Italian and British teams who rode, sometimes as many as six to a single machine, circling round the hot sand track, spiralling dust and dirt behind them. After the contest, the young boys, Chas and brother Arthur and, if permitted, Arch, in sailor hat, would stand at the edge of a group of flattering ladies, and hover about the privileged circles of the champion riders, drinking iced lemonade. Sorley, Aston, the three O'Connors, and the great champion from Italy, Battistini, who always wore dapper suits and ties, and who appeared to have a faint fringe of sand engrained permanently around his features, beneath the eyes, around the ears, and just below the hairline.

Father-Sir (as they addressed Harry Gendron senior) would always be in demand, circulating the cool lemonade (in the evenings it would be something more substantial), jollying and joking with the gentlemen riders, most of whom he addressed on first-name terms. Of course, this was long before the terrible accident to his leg which left him lame. And it might even happen – to the great excitement of his sons – that Father-Sir might take off his jacket and, dressed in shirt-sleeves, waistcoat and trousers, with his high-buttoned, rather dandyish boots, would challenge Battistini himself, or Phipps, 'the tremendous Yorkshireman', or the elegant amateur, Sir John Weller, to a contest around one circuit. He never won, naturally, and it was all in good sport, but the 'old man' (merely in his middle forties) was not to be taken too slightly, he would end up giving the champions a good race for their money. Even in waistcoat and shirt-sleeves. Mother bore these frivolities patiently enough, a mixture of anxiety and laughter, begging him not to, and, at the same time, by the pleading tone of her voice encouraging her handsome husband with subdued admiration. And he was a much-admired man, there was no doubt of that.

One of the new-style Victorians, rich he most certainly was, oldfangled in countless ways, strict in religion, and with a preference for autocratic domestic life; but full of energy and new ideas, impatient to make and spend money.

He was also a fierce republican. Father-Sir learned his radical ideas all in the space of a July afternoon in London, in the year of 1901. A poor man who earned a sixpenny piece for loading the Gendron family baggage on the back of a hansom cab outside the De Vere Hotel in Kensington trotted behind the carriage all the way to Victoria Station to unload it on to the boat-train, in order to earn himself another. Father-Sir, on leaving the old country, could never forget the occasion, and often reminded his three boys. It had made a lasting impression.

Now he was one of the wealthiest men in the state, and he made his money from the country itself, sheep, railways, cement, minerals, racehorses, everything he touched, like the land itself, rich and unfathomable in the depth of its reserves.

'Good old Harry Gendron,' said the *Brighton Times*, 'as enthusiastic a sportsman and as good a fellow as ever lived under the Southern Cross.' To young Arch, the bicycle races at Wood End represented a carefree, even ideal period in his life, epitomized by the afternoon motor drives, with his mother and her companion in the back, father in front, in the De Dion, next to the German chauffeur, Goerstler, handling impassively the giant gear-levers, and hauling on and off the double-brakes with the strength of a labourer. They would drive along the lanes among the gum trees and eucalyptus (when Chas or Arthur were studying indoors with a tutor) on hot afternoons, in great storms of dust; there were no gravelled roads at that time, and they protected themselves in beige 'dusters' down to the ankles, goggles for the men, and gloves and veils for the ladies. Chas always said they resembled bee-keepers. On their return home to Brontë, these were collected by the maids and each afternoon fresh coats were laid out on the steam-chairs in the hall.

Arch's recollection years afterwards was of powerful contrast – sheltered rooms of stone floors, sun-blinds and shaded summer-houses, and beyond the walls of the garden a heat so weighed down that unless he made superhuman efforts to run about or ride or swim, he would suffer an aching longing to drop off to sleep. Australia was a country of hard-fought exercise. Schoolroom lessons were torture after lunch, and frequently the boys were ordered off to bed for a suffocating afternoon rest. But their bedrooms were shaded from the glare outside by striped and sun-faded blinds, and the wistaria bent its grey flowers through the open windows. The very first memory he ever had of Victoria was of an overwhelming scent during their afternoon sleep coming from a bank of Mrs Simpkins pinks that lay beneath their blinds. Not that they ever did sleep very much, but rested on white counterpanes in their underpants and shirt-tails with their shoes kicked off, and talked endlessly about sport – about tennis matches and cricket, riding and lacrosse and swimming and, above all, the cycle racing. They raced with the Old Timers Cycle Club, and rode to the Melbourne Hounds. Father-Sir built his own life firmly around sport, and that of his sons as well. It was a point of pride, and singled them out. All the old Ascendancy families who 'came out' had the same ambition – the Coghills, the Ponsonbys, General Groundwater.

Harry Gendron congratulated himself on having the latest, most advanced motor-vehicles in the old stables, not from his own vainglory, but for his enthusiasm in seeing modern up-to-date engines at work; and, when he gave his teenage boys the latest Douglas motor-bicycles to ride to school, he was offended when the headmaster refused permission. Not by school discipline, but because he resented any resistance to progress – 'The day of the horse is over, it's ended apart from sport and exercise,' he would grumble, 'for God's sake, let us at least admit it.' In his view, horses bit at one end, kicked at the other, and were painful in the middle. Even though he kept his own fine string of racehorses himself out at the Melbourne Trotting Club and won the Brighton St Leger in 1912. But racing was simply a sport, a hobby; motor-cycles were the real spirit of life itself, noisy and dangerous and new. He was obstinate and unbudging to the headmaster of the Grammar: 'If my boys don't ride motor-cycles to school, they won't turn up at all.' The headmaster at Haileybury (brother to the school of the same name in England) was not fool enough to lose the patronage of one of Little Brighton's more flamboyant families, and the Gendron boys were soon the envy of their schoolfriends as Chas and Arthur rode up to school each morning in a cloud of choking dust. Arch, as the youngest, raced them along the sand tracks on his black mare, Crow. So the boys grew up in a strange contrast of old manners and new attitudes. Constrained and disciplined at home, regimented in team games within school-hours, and yet required to face outwards, away from the Victorian suburb, and forward to the burning and bitter scrub.

Their days away from the regulated hours of school or family crammers revolved around sport. Perhaps that was typical of the new Australian too. To be sportsmen was the appointed thing. They went around the town in gangs, or 'pushes', arms slung loosely about one another's shoulders, proudly wearing their caps with short peaks and tassels, each proclaiming colours for cricket, and sailing, and swimming. And lacrosse, of course. Father-Sir promoted them all in the Brighton Wanderers lacrosse side. Cricket was the great enthusiasm, and naturally each one of the brothers was made founder-member of the new Melbourne Cricket Club, and many were the hours the boys sat in the pavilions, in their whites and blazers, watching the heroes of their day. Arch was introduced by Father-Sir one afternoon to the great 'quickie' J. J. Cotter, and Victor Trumper, the game's fairest stroke-player of all time. The cricket coach at school was no less than one of the Trumble brothers, and he taught the boys a stiff conformist game of cricket, which was already out of date, shouting at them whenever they tried to move their back foot, threatening to nail it down to the crease. 'Straight-bat it' was Hughie Trumble's despairing cry. And he developed in Arch a nimble wrist spin, to stand him in good stead.

The old man's democratic spirit worked in other ways. The house was full of Irish servants, several of whom had come over from Tramore when they settled in 1880. But there was never a word of nonsense about religious affairs. 'The Irish', said Father-Sir, 'are a murderous race, and do best out of Holy Ireland.' On St Patrick's Day, the entire household sported the shamrock, and they all proclaimed orange favours on the anniversary of the Battle of the Boyne. There was a between-maid, called Mad Maggie, who came from Kilcooley, and Dympna, formerly from Castletown, and a gardener called Hooley, who lived in a garden shed alone among his pots and graftings and seed-trays. This he seemed to prefer, while the boys avidly spent their time in his company, when the parents were travelling round the world, which a great deal of the time they were. Hooley always swore, and it was likely to be true, that in his younger days, he had ridden along with the Kelly gang, and had even been with them in the caves of Bendigo. For hours the boys would study with Hooley, who taught them Irish rebel history and wild songs, and how to play draughts, and on Sundays they would evade the eye of their tutors to abscond to the potting-shed; there, among the spades and scythes and garden-rakes, heady with the scent of hothouse plants, and wrinkled shallots, to settle themselves for a concentrated session of

34

draughts, and scrutinize the devious tactics of Hooley's game. And, of course, there was the German 'shover', as Father-Sir called him, Goerstler, to look after the Daimler and the De Dion, and to take the boys for Swedish drill on the croquet lawn every morning. Extra gardeners sowed the four acres of parkland, and vineyards, and hothouses, and anonymous housemaids lived in a separate wing of the residence, reached by a special back stair.

Of all the family meal-times, early morning breakfasts at Brontë were the thing. Father-Sir at the far end, Chas and brother Arthur on his right, then Arch on the other side facing the croquet lawn, with Mother on his right and cousin Nancy on his left. But pride of place belonged by right to Grimp, ninety-five years, one of the proper old Irish, and grandfather to the boys, hanging on determinedly for his hundred. 'Knocking up his century in ones, like Trumble,' laughed Father-Sir. It had been his ambition from an early age to outlive Queen Victoria (having been born the same year, in 1819) and one of his proudest days had been 22 January 1901 – after that he was quite happy, in his own words, 'to go to bed with a shovel', but he lived on and on, survived his ambitious son's frenzied decampings from Dublin to Toronto, from there to Melbourne, and now he patiently waited out his declining days.

'All I'm waiting for is my hundred years,' he used to chuckle, 'and then, that's it. I'll be going home.'

Even at this advanced stage in his life, or maybe because of it, he kept the eloquent features of an ancient Irish peasant. A broad-boned face, a large 'Dublin-grog' nose and, albeit fainter now, those formerly glaring blue eyes which, as Mother said, 'would look inside you and right out the other side', and white, white hair, falling almost to his neck. One of his final acts of defiance in a lifetime given to persistent rebellion – largely against English landlords and Roman priests – was to insist on keeping his hair, of which he had been so proud, uncut. His eyes still glittered with that brightness, almost low cunning, which earned him his title of 'the Fox of Doon' all those years ago, back in Athlone, but it was a long time since he had opened his mouth to express an opinion, or raise an argument. In his great age he had retreated into his own silence, complained of nothing, grumbled of nothing, reminisced of nothing. In a kind of genial daze he recognized his famous son, and his magnificent grown grandsons. Each morning he would walk from his rooms on the same floor, on to the verandah, in his impeccable white duck trousers, and vest, to take his place as the true head of the breakfast table, the mahogany fan revolving slowly above him, stirring faintly his white hair. And each morning, without fail, as they arrived, fresh scrubbed after their showers, the three boys would bend down and kiss him, with 'Good morning, Grandfather-Sir', and he would nod unsmilingly, and pat the backs of their hands in recognition and approval. Not even kindly and considerate Mother ever addressed a remark to him, old Grimp had long ago given all that up. Everything seemed to have deserted him, his sight was poor, his speech was non-existent, his hearing deficient, he had lost his enthusiasm for horses, his sentiment for the old country, his memory of the past quite gone, everything lost, except the affections. They burned steadily and passionately without diminution to his final hour. Four years before Father-Sir always maintained Old Grimp's last words of speech were in response to his habitual evening enquiry:

'Everything all right, old fellow?'

'Thank you, yes, my son,' came the gentle reply, as he lay in his bed, under the single sheet and the mosquito-net (at his age, he felt the chill even of an Australian night). 'I will just lie here quietly for a little while, thinking my thoughts, you know . . .'

And so he did. After that he kept his silence. At the head of the table, his final privilege eating with his fingers the food which Mother patiently divided for him into small portions, as for a bird, he resembled something of a retired sea-captain from a notorious whaler, the castaway of a thousand storms, and survivor of the tormented oceans.

When the three boys were already in Top Form at

Haileybury, the fashionable place to play tennis was Grundy's Green. There were spacious Victorian houses around St Kilda's set in large gardens with overhanging wistaria, and behind almost every one of them was a grass court of Velvet Bent turf. These tennis fields and croquet lawns were hosed with envious devotion by their Irish gardeners, and the English families who lived there spent their days sitting quietly on the verandahs in linen clothes, and drinking cold lemon juice, while a languorous and not particularly stirring game of pat-ball was enjoyed on court. The Gendron boys, naturally, because they had been carefully coached, were excellent tennis players. They were also, each in his own way, growing to be extremely handsome, and they were much in demand for social occasions off the playing-field. Charles Richard, the tallest of them, was immeasurably the handsomest. Tall, almost skinny, he went through life with the effortless confidence of the eldest son, accustomed to European manners as his parents always took him with them on the Grand Tour of the Continent which they liked to make every other year. His friends called him familiarly Chas. He was never really called anything else. He played cricket and tennis languidly, but with a good easy-going and flowing style. He was a superb horseman. For all this he remained miraculously unspoiled, and totally lacked any sign of vanity, and, while his first youth continued, was certainly the most sought-after eldest son around Dendy Street, adorning tennis parties and swimming picnics through the summer months, and decorating the evening dances with the same qualities he revealed by day, shyness, diffidence in manner, indolent conversation and unostentatious consideration for others.

The second son, 'brother Arthur', was irritable and awkward, where his other brothers were poised and at ease, and his red hair and sulky mouth might have seemed an expression of his angry and resentful spirit. As if he had been born outside his time, he was never able to give any shape to the frustration he felt. There was something

37

unhappy about him, something unexpressed. He was more shielded from love than his brothers, and deeply protected by them. He shone in the physical sports all the boys had to endure, more than his brother Chas, for instance, and yet his success gave him little pleasure, and certainly no relaxation. His bowling averages built up frighteningly on hatred and rage, and he pulverized other schools' polite bowling into humiliation; and, whenever it could be arranged without arousing Father-Sir's personal wrath, his schoolmasters tactfully dropped him from the Eleven.

'There is no particular need, young Gendron,' said the headmaster, 'to play as if you are determined – in a game – to destroy your opposition. Or, if you are so determined, then win with grace, and lose with good humour. Here, at Haileybury, there is no such slur as the intrusion of the professional. It is true of war as much as of the cricket field. You will eventually join your brother in the great European conflict. There you will soon discover that such an attitude as yours – albeit on the cricket field – may qualify you better for the other team. It may be said, and I do not wish to offend you, that it is the very presence of those characteristics which underlie the conflict itself . . . ' Not that 'brother Arthur' cared what the HM said. To real Australians-born, he knew, sport was life.

Arch, who was so kind to his gentle mother, and devoted to his dynamic father, was fortunate in sharing something of both his brothers' qualities, and developed handsome looks entirely his own. His eyes, if he had wished to, were dark enough to captivate, and his fair hair lay flat on his head like a small cap. It was certainly not academic distinction which set him apart, and in sport he shone, like his eldest brother, more in style than expertise, but his success with young women was uncanny. This success, however, aroused nothing but his indifference, and possibly that made him succeed even more. And yet, alongside this indifference, Arch possessed the one important gift of being able to switch his entire personality on to the favoured girl of the minute, whoever she might be – so that for a small period of time, long enough to secure her affections further, she truly believed no other person ever had existed, or ever could exist, for him. Even as a schoolboy, Arch had loved women from an early age, and recognized what many of his classmates failed to appreciate, that the art of making a woman like him was largely a matter of liking them very much first.

The exploration of innocence, or 'girling' as they called it, began early for the boys, because elder brothers soon paired off with other people's elder sisters, and the younger generations of each family did the same in imitation. On summer nights, when the heady scent of jasmine and bougainvillaea billowed about, at Brontë there would be picnics and singing parties. The eldest brothers would stand outside on the verandah, elegantly cool in their evening flannel suits, white or cream, or with their College blazers, high collars, and their hair carefully matted down with oil, smoking. Chas habitually would perch in his favourite spot, a corner of the balcony, both feet on the balustrade, hunched against the pillar, listening to the quiet murmur of conversation, which flowed, and sometimes rose up into laughter, and receded again, just like small waves curling over on the soft sand at night. He had just learned to affect a small bakelite cigarette-holder, no longer than a pencil stub, and he carefully manipulated the cigarette, lighting it from a silver lighter, bought with careful selection from Fribourg's in the Haymarket (a treat from Father-Sir) the preceding year. It was well known in the circles between Brighton and Toorack that parties were always *better* when Chas was invited. He would listen quietly, authoritatively, contributing little but his sensitive and eager presence, his eyes shining at the recounting of schoolboy exploits, the hunt for yabbies in the river, riding across the banks of the Yarra, sailing at the McKenzie place (Chas as a teenager had rescued young Chip McKenzie from drowning, thus earning the perpetual gratitude of the family) and, in moments of jubilation, breaking out into the war-cry of the lacrosse team.

This innovation of Father-Sir's, the war-cry of the First Side, struck calamity into the hearts of all their rivals. So much of Chas's style was owed to a careful reciting of the familiar, the working of old and friendly ground, always ready to move on from subject to subject at the risk of anything getting over-worn; but, above all, to his intuitive anticipation of any awkward corners, abrasive collisions, which in any young men's society were bound to happen. A large number of these boys were born and bred in South Australia, and long ago lost that chilly reserve which so set apart the 'new chums' who came to school there, and both distinguished and, in a way, disfigured them. So, the young men smoked and chaffed and gossiped on the balcony, following the surge and fall of discussion, stepping aside as Fobister, the butler, filled their glasses with chilled lemon or passion-fruit juice. Fireflies spun at the edge of the garden, with the identical red burn of the end of Chas's cigarette-holder.

Occasionally, as a special treat, a rare privilege, the old man would emerge from his smoking-room, holding the door apart, and a great wave of grey cigar smoke tumbled out, and, with arm extended, he would invite the First Side, his own chosen favourites, to join the adults for some Scotch whisky. This helped introduce them to the elders of Little Brighton society, the McCargs, old man Dendy, the Brickwoods, E. J. La Trobe. Shyly, backing aside for his fellow-athletes to take precedence before him, Chas would gesture the rest of the team into the distinguished presence, where they would smile nervously, blinking in the sharp light, after the peaceful soft greyness of the night outside. Then glasses would be pressed into their hands, and they would toast the King of England, whom they had never seen, and afterwards the Melbourne Cricket Club, and the First Side would stand nervously about in a half-circle laughing at Father-Sir's reminiscences.

They liked it when he grew excited about the old days

and the thrilling recollections of his friends, Spofforth and the immortal Victor Trumper (he would allow the Gendron boys to bowl him out in the nets at Brontë – God bless Victor Trumper!) and the creation of the lacrosse side, of which they were all founder-members. Then, as if terminating the discussion formally, Father-Sir would take up his walking-stick, and courteously shake hands with each one of the exclusive half-dozen, sometimes stopping to pat this one on the shoulder, squeeze another by the forearm, rather in the manner of a general inspecting a line of troops. For so they were, these young men, his Praetorian Guard, his Thundering Legion, the image of himself when young; and in later years – when so much had altered, and so sadly for the worse – Arch remembered those evenings, and the picture restored that room full of cigar smoke and laughter, and easy-going ways, and shyness, and confidence, and the stern tall young men, and Father, on his stick, reaching their shoulders, but towering above them in strength and determination and personality. 'A great sport, and an Irish gentleman' they called him. In truth he was their inspiration, and their driving spirit.

It was on just one of these magical evenings when the European war began, Father-Sir addressed them and, using the same vigour and passion which had succeeded so brilliantly on the lacrosse field ('an injection of good old Irish vim' he called it), he sent those same young men away to legendary British cavalry divisions, writing tirelessly to influential friends in London and Dublin to establish their welcome. He explained to them that evening that the twin spirits of sportsmanship and teamwork, which had driven them to victory on the lacrosse pitch and playing-field, were the identical qualities that had stared so defiantly back in the face of defeat, in those first months on the fields of Flanders.

'Teamwork counts first, passing the ball, thinking always – not of yourself but of the group – selflessly – not of how you are going to break through individually but always, first and last, the welfare of the other man.'

And later, as if at a hidden signal, the Brighton elders in the party would politely efface themselves – no leave-takings, no formal farewells, were necessary – those living nearby to return home in horse-carriages, those from further off to retire to one of the heavily net-curtained rooms, where the hot scent of the hibiscus hung deeply along the borders of the verandah; the Irish maids bustled about turning back covers, and lifting the sheets, or adjusting the draught ventilators, switching on the lazy ceiling fans.

This abrupt, but tactful, departure would leave the field clear for the younger ones, 'the brightest and best', to select their chosen girl of the evening; and, as Cousin Nancy sat at the piano, to play and accompany herself singing 'When the Sands of the Desert Grow Cold' or 'I'll Meet Thee in the Lane', they would find private corners in the empty sitting-rooms and lounge-halls, or wander away hand in hand towards the orchards where a canvas marquee was erected in the hot months of October to March. It was all a rather contrived affair, almost a routine. Chas would sometimes lead the proceedings, in his rueful way, and murmur discreetly: 'Well, then, ready to engage, lights off . . . ' and the lights would indeed be switched off, as if by signal, and each couple would settle back into the cushions for a long evening's hug and cuddle. Chas habitually went off with the eldest girl, Arthur with her sister, and so on. Of course, there were some exceptions – some pre-engagements excluded the familiarity of this rite, but not many, and this habitual pairing off took place through the tennis and swimming parties, unconcernedly throughout the summer. The younger boys scampered about the hallways in knickerbockers, Norfolk jackets, and golf stockings, and were tempted, when their own store of boisterous game-playing wore out, to switch on the light source at sudden moments, catching their older brothers and sisters in compromising positions. Generally the girls took the darkness as a signal to sit on their boyfriends' knees, and kiss and cuddle, for hours on end – and there was no shortage of company – but it never developed into

42

anything more serious than that. And later, invariably at the summons of Chas, a second signal would be given: 'Lights on – disengage' or some such, and after a last lingering kiss, or caress, each girl would gently remove herself from her boyfriend-of-the-evening's lap, and retire to tidy the slight improprieties to mouth and cheek and hair, and return again, smiling, full of ease and grace, to the verandah, where last good-nights would be made; and, with correct formality, each lady would take the hand of each young gentleman, who would escort her to the waiting carriage. Flares burned in empty stone urns at the end of Brontë's curving drive, and the light flickered against the wistaria which stretched across the ironwork of the verandah. There, Hooley would open and close the cottage gates, and wave them into Sussex Street. The Gendron boys (but not brother Arthur, who would have stamped off to bed in a sulk hours before) would remain on the balcony until their last guests had turned the final corner, generally the hard core left from the First Side, who stumbled into the dawn light, hands wound around each other's necks, pretending to be more drunk than they were. And then the boys would, as custom dictated, shake hands with one another, and depart to bed, sometimes preferring to sleep in the tent which Hooley erected every summer on the orchard lawn, while the sun crept subtly through the pale canvas, shrinking the radiance of the Southern Cross. On occasion, the boys would escort their girls home on the back of their motor-cycles, and the girls sat as elegantly as they could, which was in fact most inelegantly, side saddle on the 'flapper bracket', getting themselves into a small storm of dust and sand as they did so. But it was exhilarating; to ride fast and noisily through the quiet suburbs of St Kilda's at four in the morning, and a worthwhile price to pay for the retribution it invariably incurred at breakfast the next morning.

In each year, during the hot season, the boys would leave the city, and go off jackerooing to the sheep-station on the edge of the Simpson Desert, where Father-Sir ran an immense herd of 40,000 merinos. There the young boys lived a different life from the protective colonial routine playing tennis, and drinking lemon juice in Brighton. Father-Sir believed such rough treatment was the only possible antidote to an otherwise unmanly and slothful life, and without ceremony packed his boys off at the end of term to the Jericho to help the stockmen run sheep across an unidentified territory of scaly landscape known even on the map by the bleak name of 'Desert Country'. At 1,200 square miles, his land was the size of Northumberland. To turn from Little Brighton gent to jackeroo overnight was no easy task, but the brothers accomplished it with facility and friendliness. It was what they were brought up to do, and mornings found them at half-past five before sun-up, rounding up the brumbies for the station-hands, accompanied by swearing and cracking of stock-whips. The bitter landscape stood out on every side, monotonous, red and sharp. Treeless, spare, breaking in unending waves until a blue haze, almost a ghostly mist, gave it the impression of receding into a dark ocean.

'Damned contemptible country!' brother Arthur used to swear, squinting into the Simpson Desert. In reality, that edge of desert only merged into more desert, and the red sand wore gradually into their spirit, as it had been worn into the sweat-band beneath their cork hats, and the ridges beneath their eyes. But it could be green, and flecked with butterflies, after a solitary fall of rain.

Arch's best friends among the station-hands were two roo-shooters, of such absence of identity that only one of them responded to a name, and that was Ewie. His companion, a shrivelled dung-beetle of a Kerryman, neither spoke nor acted in any independent manner. All his life, he was known simply as Ewie's Mate.

'Oh! Here's Ewie's Mate,' the stockmen would say, without looking up from tucker. Everything they did, the roo-shooters did together. Their life consisted, as their name implied, of walking the wired outskirts of the Desert Country station, keeping under control as well as they could the rapacious inroads made by malignant kangaroos. From Ewie and his mate, Arch learned the desert philosophy, in the same way as Europeans of the earlier century did from nomads inasmuch as the desert had *no* philosophy: only an unending vista of monotonous despair with no manner of escape. The roo-shooters lived outside the station, and carried forty-fours in their saddles. Ewie and his mate, out of doors, dossed in an Indian-style tepee, in pegged-down canvas, with grasses stuffed in the apex. They made their own primitive dark bread in the ashes and christened it 'damper', and baked 'johnny cakes', which bushmen call 'bastards on the coals'.

For the most part what they managed to shoot, they cooked; kangaroo itself yielding little edible meat, except the tail, which they stewed into a strong soup resembling oxtail. They ate blackfella grub; bandicoot steaks, turtle eggs in sand; a special delicacy was porcupine, baked in clay, with 'rockers', a kind of sweet potato, which they washed down generally with billycan tea, always refreshingly hot, sugared and without milk. The stationhands preferred the vittles of their Chinese 'cookie', Mr Jiu. The two roo-shooters must have taken some kind of shine to the young jackeroo and seemed eager to impart the wisdom they had either learned, or, alternatively, not learned. Some things they understood, never having needed to learn them. The smaller but civilized world made no impression on them, they never made an effort to enter it, or share in its wonders or rewards. Ewie and his mate lived an odd, spartan existence, not even having resort to alcoholic binges with the other stockmen.

They passed on to Arch some of the legends they heard about the Dreamtime, and the days when a giant race of gods created the outback. All of this they had learned from the blackfellas. Silence was for them the most marvellous thing; for all its austerity, the landscape was ablaze with myths; in its vast depths, the gum trees, the eucalypt, and the deep, bitter scrub, it was listening attentively, waiting for you to pass, for your footstep to recede, in order to

return to its energetic, seething life. The blackfellas themselves seldom spoke; and when they sang their songs, and
danced their dances, and recited their poems, they sang
and danced and recited for themselves, never for one
another. All this the solitary, illiterate roo-shooters
absorbed and understood.

This, in their awkward, ham-fisted — but valuable — way
Ewie and Ewie's Mate passed on to young Arch, crouching
on his haunches before them.

These yarns, now, they learned from Crusoe, and Puttie,
and Old 'Peggy' Johnson (with his wooden leg), out 'bush'
north of the Never, and Cabbagie, who was songman for
all his tribe, and played the didgeridoo. Cabbagie was
what the blackfellas called 'nother kind', and missing six-
pence in the pound, but he held inside his strange head
countless old tales of Dreamtime; these legends he told
Ewie and Ewie's Mate over a feast of sugar-bag and ewelie-
worms late at night; the two roo-shooters then told Arch
across the 'damper', and years later, in the wet of Flanders
Plain, he was to remember them.

One night, Cabbagie slunk out of the shadows to join
the three of them, and shared their kai-kai and some
nigger-twist shag, pointing the stem of his pipe at Arch,
and grinning over and over: 'Poor bugger! Poor bugger!'
Which were the only two words of whitefella talk-talk he
had ever managed. Learned off a bullocky years before,
Cabbagie used the phrase in greeting to say 'hallo', and in
parting to say 'good-bye'. But Ewie and his mate spoke
fluent blackfella themselves, so they translated the strange
throaty smacks and mysterious images for the eager
schoolboy, sucking sweet fingers of charred strips of bandicoot.

That was the week the station ran 60,000 merinos from
Dubbo to Deaf Adder, and almost had a stampede on their
hands when the sheep got a whiff of water-hole from a mile
north. The rusty drought of a dry season had driven every
living creature underground, and at night the jackeroos
were frightened by the sounds the blackfellas made from

their hiding-places, calling to one another long distances, mimicking the howls of dingoes, and the hooting of wall-frogs, so that they could not distinguish which was real, and which the dream.

'So long, Cabbagie, good luck to you,' said Arch, when the man sloped off into the bush.

'Poor bugger! Poor bugger!'

Ewie and his mate spoke the native 'talk-talk' well enough so they could share Cabbagie's secret stories of the Dreamtime, and when the hands tried to ravish crow-bait up-country unawares (the *lubras*, already naked, frustrated their attempts by rubbing inside their groins with cinders and ash) the roo-shooters wished no part of it, and stayed inside the tepee. Besides, they knew, if you wanted that, the blackfellas would give it without asking, for a few tin cans of pilchards. Remote in their own customs, and in their taciturn seclusion, they themselves lived like white Aboriginals, belonging to, or following at least, no known tribe – unlikely to progress, uncertain to survive – absorbed only in their monotonous task of slaughtering the kanga; which, in its turn, devastated just anything it came across on which impoverished people could possibly subsist.

'Of such is life,' echoed the roo-shooters, recalling the last words Ned Kelly spoke before he kicked off, their fig-wrinkled faces parched and blackened under the Southern Cross. 'Of such is life.'

Arch, by now, had learned enough of running merinos, without wishing to replenish the experience. But, one day, on his return to Brontë, he found his brother's bedroom empty, the mosquito-nets tied up like a beehive, and the white bolster and bedspread drawn back. For one heart-clutching moment, he feared his superb brother Chas had been killed in some riding accident, and the household, his own mother, too overwrought to be able to tell him. It was not the case. Father-Sir called the two younger boys into his study, when they were cleanly shaven and bathed after weeks in the bush. They wore black-tie for dinner.

'Your brother Chas is one hell of a grand feller,' he began, 'and I regret either of you should have suffered a minute's anxiety on his behalf. But it was felt, that is to say, *he* felt, it was correct to carry out his duty in secrecy, to which his privilege as eldest son entitled him. I am referring, of course, to the war which is even now being fought on Continental soil, in which affair we — in spite of thousands of miles of safe waters between — cannot stand idly by. In the old country, it is the prerogative of those young men to recognize, some of them no more than schoolboys, an obligation which is given to too few to honour, and in their many thousands, even as we speak, the best of them are volunteering to do their flag immortal service. It is a duty, and a destiny also. I have recommended to Chas that he can partake in that sacrifice, and that, if he so will it, he had our permission to share their responsibility. So, he is going back home. Being the son I knew him to be, and that your mother (God bless her darling heart) has so brought up, Chas has enlisted as a commissioned officer in Colonel Norton-Griffith's Horse and after basic training in London's Cavalry Barracks will carry his lance with his regiment in France. It was his wish to depart swiftly, and with the least fuss. Typical of him, I am proud to say. To you all, in the native manner, he says: "nybingi", which as you know means "farewell".' Arch thought of Cabbagie, for a second, and could hear him laughing: 'Poor bugger! Chas. Poor bugger!'

It was their father's way of expressing himself, in these slightly rhetorical words; but the two brothers remaining at school could see the image of Chas before them, although now in shimmering cavalry no. 1 dress, with the same fixed shy smile, doing the only right and proper thing. And always with his own particular grace. It seemed to them at that moment inconceivable, whether the scale of a European war be bloody or restrained, that he would return without further honours and rewards.

'God save Victor Trumper,' were the last words Chas spoke, on his way to the boats, ready for coming home.

'Darling Father-Sir, we are both so proud of Chas,' they said.

'I shall read to you the letter your mother and I have telegraphed to Regent Street,' he said, and with the back of his thumb removed a lash from his eye.

'My dear old boy,
I just want you to know that at a critical moment of your life you played the game. If I did for you all I could twice over, it would have availed you nothing if you had not toed the mark. Dear old boy, good luck to you. Father.'

'I bet Chas gives the German socks!' grinned Arthur, and hugged himself tightly, pink in the face.

And so the eldest brother's room remained tidy, and his belongings packed (there were the golf-clubs and tennis racquets to follow), rather like a small schoolboy at term's end, boxes and trunks correctly labelled and stacked, ready for the school porter to load them. Goerstler had driven him to the dockside, alone, Mother was too tearful and only Hooley waited there to wave him off, as the ship steamed out of harbour. A fortnight afterward, on his eighteenth birthday, brother Arthur too enlisted with the Australian Light Horse and set sail for training in Cairo, without telling anybody.

In the days which followed, Arch missed keenly the unassuming presence of his eldest brother, and the abrasiveness of Arthur as well, and recognized that the pleasure of local sports was much diminished. This was true of other of his friends, and their tennis parties were played with far less resilience and verve. Picnics in the country were quiet, frequently adult affairs, and apart from solitary rides into the everlasting landscape of gum trees and scrub along the River Yarra there was little to do for these boys left at home. Chas and Arthur were by no means the only ones of their large, friendly, extrovert circle to have left for the 'big strafe' in Europe. Nearly all the old loyalist families had at least one son who had volunteered, and several luminaries of Brighton sporting circles – young energetic members of the Melbourne Cricket Club and the Wanderers – were cadets already in the recently recruited Anzac Brigade with good old 'Birdie' Birdwood. Chas wrote from time to time to his mother, and his letters were reserved, as expected, and whenever possible enthusiastic. But there was little sport to be enjoyed in London where he was posted, only a little shooting at weekends, a very few dances. Sometimes he stayed in the country houses of friends. Of Arthur, the only news was that his training in the cavalry progressed as expected, and he had been put on a 'fizzer' for speaking his mind to a drill-sergeant.

'There is no such thing as a *superior* in my country,' he was quoted as saying, and was frog-marched pretty smartly to the guard-room.

So Arch, left to his own devices, spent most of his time studying, and preparing for the day when he would be grown-up enough to follow his brothers to war. The nets were no good now, with Goerstler bowling underarm, and the fun had gone out of riding. Also, he perceived in this gigantic upheaval so many thousands of miles away, and so remote, an opportunity by which he could fulfil what had been for him for some years now an overwhelming ambition.

All his life he wanted to fly. The seeds of this unexpected passion were sown by a fellow pupil at Haileybury, who went by the unprepossessing name of Ogg. Bob Ogg had come to Australia from England at the age of twelve and, as swiftly as he grew into adolescence, at the same time so he grew to dislike every aspect of Australian life. Outdoor games, above all, he despised as wasted time. In turn, he was the recipient of the sneers of his fellow-schoolboys, who mocked his courageous attempts to sculpt. Filled with reforming zeal, 'Oggie' was not merely content to work at his own carvings, but tried and tried conscientiously to interest the rest of his schoolmates in the arts, especially sculpture. It was not a success, and their mockery of him, instead of encouraging him to share their enthusiasm for the beach and lacrosse field, made him resent their healthy philistinism, and scorn their efforts, as they did his.

Arch, in these lonely days, however, appreciated Oggie's company, and found his vision of things refreshing, even unexpected. Trusting in their friendship, enjoying even the protection of a determined, but not untypical, Australian boy, rugged and yet sensitive, Oggie slowly revealed to his new companion the curious byways of his mind. He flew, and indeed created with his own hands, the most elaborate kites, which he took down to the Esplanade and, at evening, floated high opposite the Marine Hotel. This enthusiasm had been promoted by his parents, when they had taken him with them to Bombay, and at dusk he had observed the radiant Indian women in their colourful saris, with their small children, apart on the terraces, flying the most elegant kites of intricate design and variety, so that the evening sky above the Indian Ocean was decorated by countless painted butterflies. It was an image of extraordinary beauty, which he had never forgotten, and when he followed his parents to the infinitely less magical Australia he brought with him several of his kites. Some of the plain box-kites he had constructed in his own workshops were head-high to the young men, and they sported with these on the beach, as off-shore the same wind puffed out the sails of the harbour yachts.

Almost as soon as Arch felt the string tug at his fingers, next the fragile wooden struts and sailcloth surface jerk upwards in long circling loops, and the tension of the wind suddenly slacken, or worse, vanish, and the twine loose in his hands, he sensed immediately the arrival of a new and profound enthusiasm. He had heard only rumours of the experiments with sails and wind that were being made, and at home Oggie had set out models of these frail lighter-than-air machines in his studio. Ogg was a strange boy, with a flair for eccentric design, but he was unduly gifted and his workbench was set out with these intricate toy models, which looked rather like elaborately built moths,

51

with their tiered wings, sometimes biplanes and sometimes triplanes. He had models also of original motor-cars, and warships, but it was the flying-machines which engaged his deepest concentration. They were often modelled on the lines of flying animals, not only birds or butterflies but also the flying-foxes of the outback and the bats. There were hornets and large bees kept in glass cages in their season, and the polished shell of a green-backed turtle, and the pinned wings, outstretched, of bower-birds. He kept as well a collection of stuffed Australian marsupials, and these curious antediluvian creatures from a forgotten era formed a remarkable museum of eccentric and ambivalent curiosities.

The ocean had always seen Brighton at its best. Most afternoons by the sea-shore, the two boys faced the sea along Bay Street, with their kites flapping away from them in sweeping curves, competing with quiet determination, as the twine played out into ever-increasing reels. Sometimes in a strong wind, they had a task to hold back a creation of their own, ten feet high, with a strong wooden frame, and the most expensive silk, which required both of them to guide its aerobatics in the sky. Their skills attracted a crowd. 'Go to it, Oggie,' passers-by would call. His interest in his son's new enthusiasm aroused, Father-Sir himself, 'shovered' down to the shore by Goerstler one afternoon, expressed real admiration for their creation, and stood with walking-stick upraised, following the delighted contours, spins and turns of the two skilful manipulators, who knew each other's movements as by instinct, as well as by practice. The experiment was a great success and Father-Sir financed the boys' endeavours, in his generous way, to help them create for the first time in Australia a machine called 'The Ogg Special', a structure – a form of flying wing – which could support a man. This task the two boys set out steadfastly to achieve, and for several months' absorbed work, which took Arch away altogether from the tennis courts, and the croquet lawns where lemonade was served, and the 'girling' sessions after lights out, and the smoking parties on the iron verandahs, Oggie and he engaged themselves intently in creating frame by frame, with the concentration of men working with matchsticks, a model of the first authentic Australian flying-machine. Poetic and light as a butterfly it may have looked on the drawing-board, but sadly clumsy and inanimate it turned out in performance, with its weighty motorcycle engine weighing it down, so that in spite of its flecked bat-like double wings it was unable to lift its own great weight off the ground. The wheels rotated, but slowly sank into the Sandringham Sands, and, unable to move from the tidemark where it eventually struck, the prototype was forced to remain just as it had ended up; in a few weeks, the off-shore winds had ripped aside all the fine silk that clothed the fuselage, and the struts frayed and wore away, until only the skeleton remained. There the Ogg Special stayed, a sad replica of a curiosity which never managed to get airborne, the disintegrating skeleton of a schoolboy's vision, like an early settler's frigate, rusting and collapsing in the basin of Port Phillip Bay.

In spite of their disappointment, neither Arch nor Ogg had been so naïve as to expect immediate success, and were philosophical to return to the drawing-board; and, after all, the experimental aspect was doubtless the area the boys preferred in any case. On his part, Father-Sir was perfectly prepared to redouble his financial efforts on their behalf, but the news from Europe was nevertheless eloquent enough, even at so great a distance, seriously to affect their lives, and both schoolboys were able to read in the newspapers accounts of an airborne reality in the skies above France, which made their efforts in experiment on a southern Australian beach futile and irrelevant.

School in Brighton for the three brothers, whose every instinct and muscle dwelt on playing-fields, tides and currents, off-breaks and backward passing, had been irksome at the best. The monotonous exercises in algebra and geometry, the inappropriate French and even more archaic Latin, seemed to them not so much a waste of life, but even an affront. But Father-Sir, himself a self-educated man of the old school, with democratic longings, informed and convinced in conventional Protestant reforms and attitudes, determined that his sons should enjoy the educational advantages he not only never had himself, but, through his prodigious fortune, was easily able to provide. It is true that, by his insistence on out-of-school games and competitive sport, and fresh air (which he deified as a religion: 'Let them worship God in the open air – what finer way is there to pray and worship God than that – the open air is a grand way to go to church without one half the trouble.'), for all his determination to baptize his growing sons in the fire of the South Australian desert in the outback sheep-station, Father-Sir remained at heart a strict conservative. At least, where education and manners were concerned. So, in their short flannel trousers, long golf stockings and Norfolk jackets, the boys sat in rows at narrow wooden desks, heads bent over their Virgil and Tacitus, struggling through *Persuasion* and Famous French Poets, perspiring through Euclid, while the tennis ball thudded monotonously in the school hard-courts outside. Long shades hanging down the tall windows kept the fiercest glare away but many were the times when the boys' eyes hung heavily over their form-books, and the droning voice of the scripture teacher sent them gently to sleep. Most of the masters came from public schools in England and several of them felt an aching nostalgia for the libraries and private snugs of their former university.

One of these tutors, a rather diffident young man whose academic career had never succeeded in fulfilling much promise, after being sent away ingloriously from a minor public school, partly from shame, and partly from genuine determination to carve out a new life, emigrated to Australia, and soon found himself in the position of English Assistant at Haileybury. With regard to the literary education of his boys, Father-Sir had little concern for the lack of the crammer's athletic prowess, but took another of his 'shines' to this young, earnest man, whose sensitivity towards English literature recommended him. His face was lean, and his sandy hair appeared grey, or lighter at the roots, his eyes had a tired look of one who read too much, too late at night, which indeed he did. For all his endeavours to start freshly in a new country, the truth was Mr Ffinch, as he was called, remained an exile, and yet it was this exile who gave to Arch the most remarkable nostalgia for a country which he never knew.

At night, while the tired expression in his eyes gave way to a new and inward rapture, Ffinch would fill his youthful pupil with a burning exhilaration over the remote antics and escapades of Roger de Coverley at the dance, Jonathan Wild at Newgate, Mrs Gamp and her friend Mrs Harris, Mr Twemlow's noble defence, Mrs Jarley and the waxworks, above all Uncle Toby and Corporal Trim, and the fortifications of Namur. This imaginary world Arch never tired of hearing about, and in his imagination, while the kookaburra ticked outside, the bower-bird whooped, parrots rattled in the tree-tops, and isolated gum trees stood on guard, his eyes dreamed fantastic pictures of this unknown northern city, half hidden in yellow fog, where lamp-bowls glowed, crowds massed and jostled outside gas-lit theatres, and long avenues of bustling humanity swayed back and forth to the accompaniment of raucous street-traders, and the rattle of hansom cabs. Through these thronged streets Doctor Johnson arm-in-arm with Boswell, Uncle Toby and Corporal Trim, Tulkinghorn and Herbert Pocket weaved their vigorous way, and in and out of their company, in endless good spirits, eccentric, jovial and outspoken, mingled Sam Weller and various members of the Pickwick Club. The taut alleyways of the Ratcliff Highway, Quilp's Wharf on the Surrey side of the Thames, Sweeting's Alley beside the Royal Exchange, the stale east streets of Shadwell Stairs filled Arch's imagination as he looked out at the fiery azaleas and flaming bougainvillaeas. The shades of bewigged lawyers scuttled under low-piered Inns of Court, and all year long abandoned fire-grates sprang into life as Ffinch filled the airless schoolroom with draughts under the door, and around the wing-backed chairs, and sent great flames roaring up the chimneys, and sweepboys to climb up afterwards when they were extinguished. White-pinnied maids flitted in and out briskly to heap more coals on top of them, and there was the busmen's shelter at Hyde Park, where the young mashers took tea and buns late at night with their girlfriends, all dressed to the nines, and joked with the cabbies – there were hansoms and growlers to ride and jarveys draped in gloomy benjamins to drive you, and in the alleyways dangerous footpads lurked to strike you on the head, and steal your hunter – Ffinch told the wide-eyed boy of the notorious rat-hutches about Wapping Wall, and the warren of Seven Dials, the piggeries at Notting Hill, where 7,000 pigs shared a handful of acres with 2,000 half-naked inhabitants. There was a goatherd with fresh milk at World's End, and Chelsea Pensioners in scarlet coats played on the bowling-green at the Six Bells. This evocation of Dickens's London so fired his imagination that he felt his blood thicken in anticipation at the very idea of walking those pavements, and he longed to be a scholar within those joyful walls, and belong to gentlemen's clubs, be acknowledged by manservants, rent a set of rooms in Lincoln's Inn with his own valet, who would tiptoe in with tea and toast on cold wintry mornings, lift the blinds to reveal the yellow fog swirling outside, and rake and bellows the fire, before splashing large jugs of steaming water in his wash-basin.

'London', said Mr Ffinch, correcting him, 'is by no means "the flower of cities all", as the poet describes, it is a monstrous sink of hell.'

And so, when that remote Continental war erupted on the other side of the world, instead of pursuing his studies in the local university, inspired by a craving to visit this grotesque city of smoke and seething, festering energy, with a determination and passion to fly, Arch asked for and obtained Father-Sir's permission to set sail for England. His parting present from Mr Ffinch was a thumbed-down copy of *Tristram Shandy*, and from his father a list of introductions to his own shirt-makers, and boot-makers, and wine merchants ('Boots from Lobbs, hats from Locks, and your burgundy from Pinks'). He was also presented with a warm letter of introduction to the secretary of the legendary Carlyle Club, where fifty years before had stood the distinguished premises of Almack's, in the Strand. Father-Sir's last words of advice concerned the barber:

'Ask for Mr Trumper in person – his father always shaved me, and *he* learned from *his* father, who cut Lord Nelson's hair the week before Trafalgar.'

But flying now . . . ? To partake in the new adventure of the rapidly formed Royal Flying Corps was quite out of the question without the distinction, first, of a commissioned rank. So Arch looked about for a regiment in which he might find a place. He did not have to look far.

'With the Horse Gunners to France,' boasted the recruiting poster, like a holiday.

He thought of enlisting with the Horse Artillery, at that time stationed on the Essex coast of England. Letters from Chas were still enthusiastic and friendly, complaining mainly about the excessive drill and discipline on the parade-ground, rather than the exigencies of battle-training, and speaking rather more of the pleasure of social life than military service. Of the war, there was little news, except reassurances that morale was high, victory certain and soon, and the standard well up. The two McKenzie boys had joined the same cavalry regiment, and there were other Dominion volunteers from Canada and New Zealand as well, and even two American troopers, and all were welcome, although the professional officers from England tended to treat them with a certain reserve. Chas's best schoolfellows had signed up eagerly for the Australian Light Horse, and Arch watched them slope off to camp in their familiar long-stirruped, slump-shouldered stance. He was present when the Brighton Wanderers Lacrosse Club elected Chas and the chaps of First Side as life members, and wished them safe return amid all honours.

And so, on his seventeenth birthday, his bedroom, like that of his brother Chas before him, took on the appearance of the last days of boarding-school, initialled tin trunks, and kit-boxes, and tucker-baskets stacked up, roped and labelled, and the iron bedstead left bare, mattress rolled over, bolster laid on top, mosquito-net looped carefully upward at the corners. Leaving home was still for Arch an adventure, and a beginning, nothing to be remotely saddened by. He could hardly sleep the night before the great morning came. The family stood outside the verandah, in the shade of the wistaria, to shake his hand. He shook hands also with his best schoolfriends, some of whom wore their cricket whites, as that same afternoon they were due to play against Toorack. Others were already in breeches and riding-boots, and their famous cabbage-tree hats. His gentle, retiring mother and his pretty young cousin Nancy he kissed. He shook his father's hand, and saw him leaning only imperceptibly on his walking-stick, dressed cool in a perfectly tailored English suit ('Never buy your shirts outside Jermyn Street' was another final word of advice), still smiling with a mixture of pride and even vanity. His father promised him above all to forward regularly all the scores of the Melbourne Cricket Club in summer, and in winter the lacrosse team results.

'If they slip to second place, Father-Sir, you cable me, wherever I am, and I shall return on the next available crossing to thrash them back up again . . . And when he gets back, try to make brother Arthur bat left-handed, I think it may solve his back lift. He'll never make a cricketer, if he keeps picking his bat up from point to second slip.'

Arch shook hands with Goerstler who wished him well, and Hooley stepped forward, with a quick look of anxiety at Father-Sir, who nodded his approval, to pin in Arch's buttonhole the last brown sprig of that year's shamrock, carefully nourished in his garden shed from year to year.

'May you always be your own man, but never lose your father's face,' he said, affectionately.

'God bless you, Hooley,' Arch answered, 'and good luck, always.'

'The luck of the Irish, Mister David,' he whispered, and winked.

He was wearing his school blazer and white flannels, appropriate, Mother felt, for on board ship. His evening clothes were wrapped in tissue paper on top of the trunk. He felt it right to wear his cricket-colours tie, with the faint hint of gold at the edge of each stripe. His mother believed he looked his best, with that sleek cap of bright hair curled on his head, and calm brown eyes.

'Oh, he is a handsome-looking boy, Father,' she whispered, as he stepped into the car. It had been agreed that leave-taking was to be confined to the front drive. Hooley loaded the baggage into the Wolseley, and it set off down the path. Arch took Father-Sir's seat in the front beside Goerstler, and as the great bonnet swept around the drive extended his arm from the window.

His little cousin rushed forward and held on to his out-stretched fingers, running along the dashboard. She was suddenly in love with him, as a child can be, in the space of an afternoon.

'Write to me, Nancy – and come on, old woman!' He squeezed her fingers.

'Goodbye, Arch, goodbye, goodbye. Goodbye!' she called. She felt her heart was breaking.

'Oh, he's a grand-looking feller,' said Father-Sir, 'a real Gendron, there's no doubt of it.'

The parlour-maids and gardeners gave him a cheer as the Wolseley rode down the azalea drive. Hooley stood on the running-board, and opened the lodge gates, and the great vehicle was gone. The young man was gone, the garden strangely and suddenly silent, the perfume exaggerated in layers of blue and green and wine.

On board, of course, the dear old Wanderers sent a cable, and so did the Dublin Old Timers from Phoenix Park. There they all were, straw hats in hand; three whole rows of them at the quayside, while the ropes strained and grunted, friends from Phillipstown and Tullamore, bicycle companions from Portobello and Strawberry Hall, standing in threes singing their hearts out in 'Coming Home'.

As the ship floated broadside out, easing itself into the harbour, at first huge and all out of proportion, long before it settled into the blue carpet beyond, twinkling and glittering, Hooley and Goerstler stood at the dockside, hearing the raucous shouts of the sailors levering the heavy ropes off the bollards, and lifting them awkwardly into the sea with a splash. Departure always takes an eternity.

'All clear on the bow end, sir.'

'All away on the starboard prow, sir.'

'Clear and all away on the port bow, sir . . .'

Hours later – with Hooley alone on the dock – the coastline flickered in an evening heatwave, and reddened like the approach of a sandstorm. At first a few faint darts of light were to be seen spotting on the shore, and then they vanished too, either in mist, or distance, or beneath the horizon. Arch remained, with other passengers, watching for the last light. From lower decks, the voices of hundreds of young men – all of them sailing home to enlist – came from the portholes and smoky saloons, and they were singing, of all things, 'The Wild Colonial Boy', a ballad Father-Sir discouraged, but which Hooley had taught them years back. So many young Irish men on this ship, he wondered.

> He was his father's only son, his mother's pride and joy,
> A credit to old Ireland was this wild Colonial boy.

And as their voices merged in harmony, not always perfect, David Arch Gendron knew for certain that this was all that would be left of that great secret behind the mist, in that arena of darkness his eyes strained through, an unknown country which he had enjoyed, but never seen,

60

or understood, or valued, or desired. He felt also that he had suddenly and without warning been transformed into a whole new identity, and his past life belonged to somebody else. It was his boyhood, not Australia, that he was leaving behind. David remained, but *he*, Arch Gendron, was *coming home*.

He had never thought of this before, never imagined such a thing, but saw himself now reflected for a strange moment as if between the dark water and the dark sky, in his blazer and cricket clothes, shaking hands again with Hooley in front of the iron verandah of Brontë. Touched the dry brown spray of shamrock in his buttonhole. The voices under his feet broke like a great wave, as they reached the conclusion and climax of their song, and had no more words to uncover, no tune to explore. The sea had little sound by now, there was no wind either, but from far away, behind the dark and empty quarter in that bland air, came, not just the vague impression of heat but, breaking like the bar, a curious inarticulate drone. Neither the surf on the shore, nor the engine hum, nor the finished song in echo, but the sound of heated minerals under that burned-out and bitter earth cracking and singing as they cooled. It was a curious phenomenon, but distinctive. An atmosphere as it were, which spread through and stilled the entire ship. Then it appeared gradually to abate, and Arch went below to dress for dinner.

CHAPTER TWO

Recruits

Too eager an expectation of a city, seen entirely through the eyes of literature and from the isolated distance of 12,000 miles, and seven weeks on ship-board, might have been impossible to uphold but this was not the case. That it is better to journey than to arrive is the saying, but in fact Arch's expectations of London were far exceeded by the reality. He arrived in the late autumn, and was delighted to discover Liverpool harbour dripping under punishing October storms, dour policemen standing impassively beneath their capes, blackened by rain, and the dock-workers scurrying under the protection of cardboard shrouds, if they bothered to protect themselves at all. He felt the cold intensely, had felt it some days before, at the approaches of the Irish Sea, but wrapping himself up in a blanket frankly enjoyed the tug of wind and driving rain on the upper deck, and waited impatiently for his first glimpse of a clammy pea-souper. He was not to be kept long in anticipation, and the very day of his arrival in a yellow fog-bound London, that same evening to be precise, found him standing with his back to the fire within the comfortable darkened walls of the old Carlyle Club.

The hall-porter had not disappointed him either, and greeted him with that curious mixture of surliness and intimacy he had been warned to expect from the British.

'Carlyle Club, sir, welcome – and don't leave the door flapping, if you don't mind, sir . . . the members dislike it . . .'

The porter, whom he later grew to know intimately,

was an oldish and generally cheerful man called Trowel, stage-doorman, until his retirement, at the Winter Gardens. Once Arch had made his closer acquaintance, he became for the young and inexperienced colonial visitor a perfect mine of information and gossip about that quarter of London, its pubs and pie-shops, club folklore, and its more striking members. Trowel lived most of the time in the porter's hall, a kind of sentry-box at the foot of the marble steps inside the main door, peering out at the pavement, anticipating with a nuance of judgement that could only be admired the arrival of a club member, fractionally before his hand went to the handle of the door. He was a fastidious observer of the club's complicated and esoteric regulations, and showed great good humour and sheer generosity in administering the regulations that were approved:

'Of course, I shall serve you with a glass of Scotch whisky directly, sir, and it is no trouble at all', or, just as agreeably: 'Let me set a further scuttle of sea-coal on the fire, sir, and we'll have you warm in a jiff', and implacable ill humour over the slightest infringement:

'I have told you, sir, quite firmly, that after 11.00 pm this club is closed to gentlemen's guests', or, 'The rule-book states very clearly, sir, there are no drinks to be ordered from the billiards room after eight o'clock on Thursday nights': a personal bureaucracy he justified by the expression, heard from his lips in a grumbling moment: 'Once you start giving the members what they ask for, there's no stopping them . . .'

He also professed he had the gift of second sight, and inspiration about the afterlife, which had afforded him, so he declared, a peace of mind he had not formerly enjoyed. This modest spiritual insight he was not shy to impart to the members, whose evening brandy and soda, or scotch and seltzer, might be disturbed by Trowel's direct question, accompanied by a fixed glare:

'I don't want to be rude, sir, but do you believe in the afterlife, sir? I do, if you don't mind my mentioning it';

63

or: 'It always surprises me, sir, if you don't object to the subject, that too many of the members leave God out . . .'

In Trowel's rather blinkered vision, his private and personal God somewhat resembled one of the senior members of the Carlyle Club. But it was from Trowel, in spite of his religious preoccupations, that Arch learned much about London life, and even of the local geography of Covent Garden, the Strand, and the chop-houses, dining-clubs and 'kips' which lay between.

London was a city which continually changed its appearance, according to the light. It assumed constantly a form of disguise. There were occasions when things were so altered by shadows that Arch could not even find his way. The sunshine sometimes sneaked out behind layer upon layer of cloud and sprang off the windows and tall roofs, casting an entirely new perspective among the grubby blackened buildings. Faded advertising signs ('Rooms at Four Shillings', 'Pills and Powders', 'Cures for Arthritis', 'Swan Ink') sometimes appeared as if magically, and one of these invited him to try 'The Cosy Dining-Rooms' in a side-street off the Strand, and between stairs which descended to the Thames. 'Full Meals – Two Shillings' read a signboard, and a fading rain-streaked arrow pointed drably down the brick surface, indicating, beneath a shop which sold seed-packets, an unenticing brown door.

Needless to say, it had been Trowel who had recommended the place, with one of his famous 'I don't want to be rude, sir' openings, 'but you'll enjoy a plain straightforward meal, not messed about, with a nice piece of white fish, or meat and two veg., followed by a suet.'

Arch remembered the recommendation and decided to explore. 'Good value at the price, sir, two shillings all in with a milk-tea, and tuppence for the waiter.' It was an easy matter to locate his brother Chas at his barracks, so they went together.

What Trowel had not explained, perhaps not even observed, but which became rapidly evident to Arch and his brother as they waited for the menu to be brought to them, was that the waitresses, some of them pretty and shabby simultaneously, appeared to be as available as the meat and two veg. The low-ceilinged room conformed instantly to his imagination of what a cheap London eating-house should look like, something out of Dickens's novels, with a low timbered roof, just above head-high, crudely painted ochre-yellow, with wooden partitions separating each table (almost like horse-stables), tall pillars at every corner, and bulbous, onion-topped balustrades. The benches were soberly cushioned, but worn threadbare and dirty, and some of the alcoves had curtains around them, from which, from time to time, couples emerged, shyly and red-faced, and the men hiding behind their hats. There were one or two young soldiers there, and one swaggered from behind the curtains brazenly, in red and gold, buttoning his jacket-collar and holding his belt over his shoulder. What astonished Arch was the sight of the girl, who followed somewhat meekly, casually brushing away crumbs from the deserted table with a rag, and hardly turning even to acknowledge the departing soldier. At the door he faced her and gave that curious suggestion of the jaw tilted a fraction upward which Arch had observed before in cabbies and street traders, a mixture of arrogance and intimacy. Watching the girl's reaction, he saw that she seemed to pay even less attention than before, a half-smile which she did not wish to intrude on the more important business of the table-wiping.

'I'm sure you can get a cuddle off the waitresses,' Arch confided to his brother, 'I've seen them do it. They take your order, and when you've got to the coffee stage they'll come behind the curtains with you.'

Chas was more reserved and less optimistic. His face crinkled in the familiar way.

'Well, the girls aren't everything they are at home, but they'll probably do.'

'Oh, this is grand, Chas, just grand. I'm so glad you got a spot of leave.'

'Not leave really, just time off. The White City isn't so far, and I can take the train. The colonel's a decent sort and, when I explained there was a chance to meet my kid brother from Australia, he seemed pretty reasonable about it.'

'Well, you're looking smart, anyway.'

And he was. He was in cavalry undress, with breeches and long puttees, and gaiters, and the give-away spurs on his heels dug into the wood and sawdust floor, as his legs stretched out. His flat peaked cap hung on the iron hook opposite, and the two young men sat in front of large plates of hot pie and chips. It had been the work of a few days only to bring about this meeting. A message left with Trowel at the Carlyle Club had been eagerly relayed to the new arrival, and Chas had come up from the White City, where his regiment was newly in training for future posting on active service in France. It was due to support the Ulsters on the Marne.

They swiftly exchanged family news, and gossip about their many friends from school and the lacrosse side.

'They sent a wire just as I boarded ship, bless their hearts!' laughed Arch, raising his tea-cup to absent friends.

'I think you'll find the Melbourne Wanderers pretty well represented in the Australian Light Horse,' said Chas, grinning, and leaning forward to breathe away the steam over his pudding. 'Thomas, McLaren, and Clarence have all enlisted. Father wrote to me, they are all in Third Brigade out at Table Top.'

'Any action yet?'

'All boots, belt, rifle and pack so far, Clarence says.'

'They're a boshter crowd, Chas. Absolutely first-class all the way.'

'Well, they were all Citizen Army boys,' said Chas by way of explanation. 'They were prepared for the show, unlike this country. Clarence wrote that when they arrived at Anzac, it was snowing – imagine it, snow. Most of them had never seen it before.'

The waitress came and brought their tea. Arch looked up at her and smiled broadly.

'What's got into you, Smiler?' she said, stamping the saucers down and swilling the tea in them.

'Now you've swilled the tea. Here, you've swilled the tea.'

'What if I have?' said the girl tartly, and steered sharply away, out of reach. She was fair-haired with prominent teeth, and her high, round breasts pushed out her black dress.

'This is my grown-up brother, Chas,' said Arch. The waitress seemed disinclined to move.

'What does he do, then?' she asked in a flat, uninterested voice. 'A jockey?'

'Too tall for that,' said Arch. 'And my name is David.'

'Well then, David . . . ' said the waitress, leaving the sentence unfinished on purpose.

A newspaper boy in the street sang out the evening papers monotonously, at intervals.

'So what is your name?' he asked, and felt himself blushing slightly.

'Never mind names, there's more waiting on your table if you've finished.'

'We haven't started.'

'Where are you two from anyway?'

'We're from Melbourne, Australia. The other side of the world.'

'Well, you're cheeky enough for it, anyway.'

All this time, Chas looked on silently, though with a great deal of enthusiasm. He stared at the waitress and, although she was busy and keen to get away to another table, where impatient signs were being made by customers, she could not resist looking back at him.

'You'll have me out of a job, if my guv'nor sees you trying to flirt with me,' she said, flicking her tea-cloth at imaginary crumbs. There were half a dozen diners at that hour, not more, mainly clerks, who looked as if they had come from the large insurance offices on the corner.

'Will you come out for a walk with my brother?' asked Arch. 'He's in the cavalry all the way out at White City.'

'I might,' she said, speculatively, taking the opportunity to look at him. 'What's the matter with him? Can't he speak for himself? Cat got your tongue?'

'I'd like to go for a walk with you, when you finish,' said Chas.

'Oh, that's later on.'

'Would you have a cuddle then, behind the screen?'

But that was a false move, too precipitate, and in a second she was gone, with a sudden wipe of the table corner, picking up expertly the only mustard pot to be shared jointly by all the diners. She wore a cheap perfume which reminded Arch of some unnamed summer flower which blossomed too heavily, mingling with the faint but unmistakable smell of unchanged clothes. The Cosy Dining-Rooms blended an aroma of grilled kidneys with stale scent. The waitress was a pretty girl, her hair combed up above her ears, and pinned in with a comb. Some stray hairs had fallen each side, and showed different colours, different shades, and left her small ears exposed. Slightly prominent teeth gave a sensuous appeal to her mouth.

'I'd like to kiss her,' whispered Chas. 'Do you think she'll let me take her outside?'

'She might, Chas, she might, I think she'd like to be your sweetheart.'

For a few minutes they concentrated on their meal, enjoying the perspiring comfort within, the noisy street outside, the sensation of cold fog beyond the windows.

A Salvation Army band was playing streets away, the old anthem 'Where is He born, The King of Judea', and wind gusted it through the door every time it opened.

'How do you get on with them all, Chas?'

'The Lancers? Grand. Grand chaps.'

'Did the Ducros give you an introduction?'

'They helped. There's been a bit of push here and there, Father-Sir will be pleased, I think. You see, Arch, almost from the day I arived in Liverpool, I could tell there would be some sort of show on, even if the chaps here couldn't. So I thought I'd get in on the ground floor before anyone else made a move. And I did.'

'You were lucky.'

'I suppose so. The other chaps call me "Flops"!'

They both spluttered into their tea.

'I say, this tea's budgie's piss, ain't it!' and Arch leaned forward eagerly; and, as he listened to his brother explaining, his mind raced ahead, to contemplate his own enlisting, and the splendid figure he'd cut in *his* uniform, but not the trim lines of breeches and peaked cap, and riding-boots with spurs, but the forage cap and leather coat of the fliers. He had already secretly ordered from Hall and Dance the thick but unmistakable buffy-coat with its fur collar which the pilots affected.

Chas said: 'Did you hear, Father-Sir's done his bit. He's raffled the brand-new Wolseley to support the Victorian Red Cross. Even the West Brighton Club is raffling tickets, and the Albany are putting on an auction. Five bob each! And she cost a cool thou' before the war! Still, now Goerstler's gone home to Hunland . . .'

'Father-Sir wrote to me that Victor Trumper hit 293 with a split bat in New Zealand.'

'There'll never be another Victor Trumper,' said his brother.

'Did Father-Sir buy you into Norton-Griffith's Horse, Chas? You fell on your feet, I must say.'

'Major Monck-Mason is more or less in command. A first-rate old buster . . . a bit fiery . . . but he saw fighting in Mashonaland and says he expects France to be a bit of the same. Most of the chaps don't want to be paid! Monck says it muddles up the accounts!'

The two men finished their meat teas, paid the waitress, and stole a kiss on her cheek, but received the wet end of a tea-towel for reward.

One overcast autumn afternoon Arch went out to the

White City and sat in bleak discomfort to watch his brother training. The regiment appeared an enthusiastic but disorderly bunch, and bore little resemblance to what he had expected a crack British squadron to be. But there was some tremor of exhilaration to be gained, when they formed into positions and the harsh cries of the horse-majors echoed around the empty station. A small group of young children watched them, from a vantage point they had discovered at the high corner of one of the stands. Their eyes sparkled watching the horses, well sweated by now, steam and smoke as they went through their paces. Arch observed that some of the children wore ankle boots, with neither laces nor stockings. They looked chilled to the bone under frail woollen jerseys.

'Stand to your horses – mount – wheel – wheel right ... Lean in ... leave the reins alone, and *do* sit up *straight*. Keep your shoulders back... lean in, for Christ's sake'; and all afternoon it went on like that, an unending, unvaried routine of abuse and commands, from sergeants and corporals wheeling in and out, not hesitating to tap irritably with short stubby crops at the faulty, wavering fingers, or hesitant heels, of their superiors. The recruits had discarded their jackets, and many wore crossed braces over their shirts; their noses and ears reddened in the cold. But never once did his brother show the smallest impatience, or dismay, and Arch felt a glow of pride at the discipline and determination these young recruits showed. He recognized that, when he first tried to conquer the air, the strain would be the same, the pressure as great, the humiliations as overpowering, and he vowed he would show the same determination and concentration to master his unruly machine, no less awkward and wilful, he felt certain, than the horse, and to gentle it in the air, with rudder and heel, wrist and ankle, just as his brother controlled and dominated his steaming horse. The colonel himself stamped up and down in one of the short British warms the officers affected, knee-high, showing his putteed and spindly legs.

He had a cavalry moustache, which gave him the look of a rat peering round a brush. His whole figure appeared top-heavy, as he blustered about instructing, ordering, yelling, whacking his ribboned ankles with his riding-crop.

Making no effort to introduce himself to the younger man, or even to ask the reason for his presence, he walked within earshot of Arch and without even nodding addressed him:

'First-rate troop of cavalry. Stick to the saddles like warts. What's yer name, and what d'ye do?' The colonel spoke in a curious mixture of clipped words and Cockney, his voice as private and special as his regiment, it seemed.

'Trooper Gendron's brother, sir, David Gendron, sir, and I have come from Australia to enlist in the Flying Corps.'

'Flying Corps . . .!' and the colonel let out a laugh like a scornful ass's bray. 'Dear God! What a waste! From Australia, too! Dear God in heaven! You should come into the cavalry p.d.q. Its a grand profession. I don't think a soldier's life can be beat anywhere. And I'll tell you one thing. There's talk of going to France to see if the Hun-article can be cut up, and no doubt they'll cut him up good and proper. But it's barrack-square and drill that counts. Do it right on the barrack-square and, when you face the real thing, it'll turn out right. Do it wrong on the barrack-square, and you're in a bugger's muddle. Take my word for it. I was in the Cape and I know. The farmers out there played cat-and-banjo with our best men. Cat-and-banjo. These Canadian and Australian boys are thundering good fellows, and they'll make the best soldiers in the world by the time we've finished with them. Even these Kentucky boys are smart as hell. I'll tell you about *horse*-soldiering. When these chaps get into the show in France, they'll be given a King's Commission and spark off in all directions, some here, some there. They'll end up Dragoons, Lancers, Skinners, Hussars, every bloody damn thing. Now – if they have learned their lessons here, and I pretty well think they have, they'll remember this! Never lose touch with your

71

men. Remember, *you* serve your men, your troops, and that is what matters. The troops matter. They're the salt of the earth, and they are the ones who will win battles. Take care of your men, and they will never let you down. Get the drill right on the square. And when flying-machines have learned how to do the horses' job, war in France will have a very different face from the one it has now. Good afternoon to you.'

Feeling himself summarily dismissed, Arch instinctively went to salute, remembered he was wearing a raincoat and cloth cap, and quickly resisted the impulse. The colonel was distracted suddenly by some infuriating imperfection in the seat of one of the young subalterns, and went off in the opposite direction, a combustible little man, yelling and gesticulating.

Arch had never felt the same passion to ride, or to undertake that strenuous kind of training, but he did feel the deep-rooted urge to serve and slipped away from the stadium absolutely determined to enlist as soon as possible. The next day, after a short luncheon without wine at the Carlyle Club, he walked to Adastra House, where he received a somewhat crusty interview with an impassive, granite-faced colonel in the Welsh Guards, who rejected him outright for the Flying Corps, and proposed that before he apply for a second time, he made certain of securing a commission in an artillery regiment.

'You'll never regret it, Gendron.' The Flying Corps, the Colonel said, could not consider a non-commissioned rank at that time.

However, in spite of this set-back, his dejection was not allowed to last long, and that evening the Ducros brothers wrote an impressive note-of-hand to a friend of theirs in the City, who had command of an officer cadet corps training at the Inns of Court. Arch's interview there went better than the previous afternoon's, apart from unexpected probings about his social eligibility. The officer, a balding man who was clearly younger than he looked and used glasses to read his notes, seemed friendly and well disposed, and was certainly impressed by the letter of recommendation from Sir Harvey Ducros. It seemed unlikely that he would be weeded out from his sedentary desk job and sent to the Western Front, from which the first, uncomfortable reports were already filtering through.

CHAPTER THREE

Inns of Court

The next morning, Arch tipped Trowel when he entered
with the lukewarm morning cup of tea, then left the
Carlyle Club early, to walk briskly and in good time to
report at Lincoln's Inn Fields, and the Inns of Court. It
appeared to him, with its chambers and quadrangles, to
resemble one of the ancient universities. Arch was to share
rooms with two barristers, both of them recruits to the
cadet force as he was, but versed in the manners and
mysteries of legal life. Arch, who persisted still in viewing
London life in terms of Thackeray and George
Cruikshank, was overjoyed to discover another secret
world thick in atmosphere, and regulated by unexplained
restrictions and rituals, all of which delighted his sense of
the unexpected. His companions were called 'Tusky'
Powell (on account of a prominent molar) and Cadbury,
and after a brief summary of the expectation of their
behaviour, and a perfunctory kitting-out, like his brother
Chas, Arch found himself exposed in the middle of a
parade-ground, being bawled at for infringements he did
not understand, in khaki overalls, with a peaked cap, and
a white band round it, signifying his lowly rank as officer
cadet.

And so, throughout that early autumn, while the first
attackers sought each other out in Flanders, and early
cavalry patrols skirmished in the fields and hedgerows of
the Marne, Arch was drilled and marched and brushed
and polished into a first-ranking officer cadet, in the
quadrangle of the Inns of Court, as unconcerned barristers in wigs scuttled back and forth with pink-stringed

bundles in their arms. Their drilling alone took place at the Inns of Court, that and lectures, of course, on discipline, on table manners, on war tactics, Clausewitz, Staff College, and the Orderly Room Rule Book.

The breaks and lunch hours were spent in the company of Tusky Powell and Cadbury, exploring the odd corners around Holborn and the Inns of Court. His days may have been wearisome and dull, but they were more than compensated for by the evenings which Arch spent at the McKays' elegant home in Chelsea, behind the Roman church, where he stayed. Father-Sir proposed in one of his letters that Arch should make contact with his cousins, the McKays, and he did directly he was installed at Lincolns Inn. Theirs was a country house in the west of London, hidden from the outside world by high walls, and with bay windows giving on to a large garden, which even in the untidy autumn had a certain repose and rural atmosphere. His bedroom looked out on the lawns, and he loved to wake early and hear the morning sounds percolate through the windows, still heavily blinded. First there would be the cock crowing from the mews, which kept its own chicken-runs behind Cadogan Square. Next the Household Cavalry bringing the horses down from Knightsbridge Barracks. And, later, various dogs barking, and from the secretive, secluded gardens of Lord Moon's estate the shrieks of the exotic peacocks and caged gibbon monkeys. Lord Moon retained through the war the last private menagerie in London.

The house itself resembled, in a way he had not expected in the capital, the style of country homes, single-storey, with large leafy verandahs leading on to the lawns, and huddled in wistaria and hung with ivy. Leaves cartwheeled across the grass and gathered in the borders in soggy piles, until the gardener raked them up, and built a large smoky bonfire below the tennis courts. But, above all, the house and its garden represented a secret country to the young Australian returning from drab lectures, monotonous parades and unexciting drill lessons. Tucked away behind its high walls, and protective hedges, only to be entered by a nearly invisible garden gate, the great private house lived a secret life of its own, in the swirl of London.

Inside, the McKays lived with great formality and reserve, seldom venturing 'out'. It was their talent to entertain, as well as their pleasure, and the warm drawing-room was frequently a calm harbour for the younger ones of their Melbourne friends, many of whom were at a loss for companionship, and discouraged physically by London's wintry weather. As old and close family friends, the McKays were only too pleased to welcome under their roof so eligible a younger son as David (as they were accustomed to address him), and they offered him a comfortable set of rooms, and his own manservant, for the length of his stay. Their only child, a daughter, Madeleine – called Maddy – lived with them, an austere and beautiful girl, knowledgeable about music and with a strange distant aura of her own, that made her seem, to friends and parents alike, aware at private intervals of an intense and unhappy life. There was little reason for this, other than it was so. Sometimes her withdrawal would be so marked in the friendly warmth of an evening's conversation, it was as if one of the guests had walked to the door and thrown it open. She gave the impression of leaving a draught, but defended her aloofness with a wintry, brief smile, as if to say: 'I know what I am thinking, and it is nothing to do with you . . .' It was accepted that Arch should accompany her on occasional evenings after training, and this he enjoyed, to the opera sometimes, other nights to dances, and even in a light-hearted fashion to the music-hall. Maddy had lived in Melbourne for a matter of four years, but knew and appreciated London life, especially the formal side of it, and so Arch found himself entering the fashionable drawing-rooms in Belgravia and The Vestry where the conversation ebbed and flowed around subjects of more general concern than the

76

parochial fortunes of the Melbourne lacrosse team, or the respective merits of the Brighton Tennis Club.

'Now, David, what do you have to say?' Maddy would ask pointedly.

At first, he had nothing to say, and took everything rather for granted, which was as well, since Maddy was one of those young women who had little enthusiasm for lack of poise, or any kind of social awkwardness; and as Arch 'got by', so to speak, by the readiness of his grin, his sheer good looks, and patient frown of concentration in whatever anybody was saying, everything flowed well between them, and they were accounted one of The Vestry's better-looking unattached couples. The stiff conventions of these Londoners, however, perplexed Arch at times, and he was greatly surprised when one winter's afternoon, having tea at home quietly with Mrs McKay, he rose from his seat to fetch some sugar from a table only two feet away from him.

'Stay exactly where you are, David dear,' said Mrs McKay, rather coolly. 'We have servants, you know, to do that.' With which, she put out her hand to the bell-pull, beside the fireside, and rang for a downstairs maid who several moments later, having climbed three flights of stairs, appeared and bobbed at the doorway.

'Oh, there, Fanny, will you take the sugar bowl and pass it to Mr David. I believe he would like some sugar. Thank you so much, that is all now.'

The cadet course drew wearily to its close and in spite of fruitless visits to Adastra House, and the writing of passionate letters, Arch was no nearer the Royal Flying Corps by the end of training than he had been before.

The atmosphere of the Inns of Court beguiled him, and twice a week he enjoyed greatly dining in Hall with the assembled barristers and judges (the cadets had their own table, and obeyed the rituals, standing when the judges entered, bowing their heads for muttered and unintelligible Latin grace, joining in the loyal toast, sconceing offenders of etiquette, and sharing the respectful silence for the fallen). It was discernible now that most of the younger lawyers themselves had left for the army, and the buzz of conversation in Hall was muffled and slower.

In the first week of November, abruptly, the course was concluded and the young cadets found themselves suddenly commissioned after an uncomfortable passing-out parade. A general lectured them, seeming to imply that officers for the infantry were needed urgently to replace the harvest of those heroically fallen at the front. First Ypres had not proved to be the success expected, nor had the assumed breakthrough taken place. The general, commanding with awkward candour, announced that substantial losses of vital men, 'with qualities of leadership', had brought about a genuine lack of such human supplies, and for this reason the intelligence and training course had been brought to a brief and summary conclusion. Commissions had been awarded, partly because the amount of training already undergone was enough, and because those so-called 'sought-after qualities of leadership' were allowed to have been there already.

General Sir Cather Blacker-Douglas was a commander of the old school, firmly blooded on the frontier against the Pathan and Garo tribesmen. He was a short-legged, large-headed man, priding himself on a sudden stare, an unflinching look to command authority, with a curiously flimsy moustache of the drooping variety, which contrasted with the rest of his aggressive figure, and reminded colleagues of Sir Edward Elgar. But his looks belied his opinions. He addressed the recently commissioned officer corps before they entered Hall for their farewell dinner that evening. The setting, an appropriate one, was the ancient Inns of Court chapel, and General Blacker-Douglas made immediate use of the analogy in his address:

'In the British Service, contrary to custom obtaining in many countries, in granting you a commission, the Sovereign presupposes your allegiance and devotion, in the

78

same way that a young man entering Holy Orders offers his allegiance and his devotion, both of which spiritual qualities are presupposed by God.'

And, after the slightest hesitation only, he repeated the final phrase again:

'Presupposed by God.'

This curious mannerism, rather like a visual tic, accompanied the remainder of his speech, and as the general showed no sign of reducing the length of his discourse Arch found the oddity progressively mesmeric.

'The Sovereign calls you,' he continued, 'his trusty and well beloved, and the possession of this commission gives you the right to be treated as an officer, and a gentleman. It is the admission to the knightly caste.'

He paused an instant.

'To the knightly caste. And as a British officer, I say *again* – as a *British* officer – you have adopted a calling with the express purpose of fighting in the greatest of all wars on the side of right and freedom, against the forces of tyranny, injustice and barbarism. Three things I wish to add – *esprit de corps*, discipline, humour. *Esprit de corps*, first. No man is infallible, and it may well be your superior has not tackled the problem in front of him in the best manner. All the same, back him up, heart and soul, and always remember a bad plan energetically carried out will generally succeed, but a perfect one not properly backed up is doomed to failure. Doomed to failure. Second – discipline. Smartness of turn-out, punctiliousness in saluting a superior officer, exactness in guard duties, all make for discipline. So, we have *esprit de corps*, and we have discipline, and thirdly we have humour. Do not be afraid of a little humour if it be to the point, and never forget, a good joke goes a long way to get over the road when it is long and uphill, and all the more so when it leads through a lot of barbed wire and machine-gun bullets. And good manners are perfectly capable of establishing friendly camaraderie without degenerating into familiarity.'

Assuming the general had finished, some of the front rank in the choristers' pews bent forward for their cadet caps.

'As you were – I haven't finished.'

The backs shot up again, arms instinctively straightened.

The general glared suddenly, as if he would have cut them down with a sabre where they sat.

'Learn to be cheerful under difficulties and at all times. Never grumble, and never forget, however bad things may be, they might always be much worse. Much worse. And remember this: play for your side, and not for your own bat. As long as the right side wins, it is of small account who made the runs. Point taken?'

Obediently, like choristers or schoolboys, the cadets in unison answered: 'Yes sir.'

'Good, good. Now then, there's something else I want to say, and I'm grateful that we are sitting in church at this minute, because this is the place to say it. Several of you young people have come to me, not necessarily here, but in the past, in other places, and they have said to me: With respect, sir, everything you have said we know already. What we want to know is: What is it all for? And I am going to try to answer your question. Before you go to bed at night always have a talk with Him, and you'll fire at the enemy ten times better. Ten times better . . . In addition –'

The general's voice took up a tenor note, and his face and eyes looked towards the rood-loft vaulting above them, as if he was, for a moment, spiritually uplifted, or in quest of inspiration. From far off Arch heard distinctly somebody singing quite loudly a music-hall song, possibly one of the younger college servants.

'We are fighting not only for all that makes life worth living in the country, for us Englishmen, but also for everything else which makes the world worth living in. If our victory in Europe should only be a partial one, without crushing once and for all the spirit of Prussianism

80

– which acknowledges no other right but might, and is for ever clanking its sword – we should be postponing the evil day. The war would have to be fought all over again, later on, and until this bloody business is decided once and for all, Europe will be an armed camp. The whole of Europe. An armed camp. Now if the result of this war is to be the raising of the national ideal and the national discipline, then in spite of all its horrors and its sacrifices it will prove to be a blessing, and not a curse. A man by no means unconnected with this City, and I refer to John Ruskin, has said these words, and I quote them with confidence in the house of God.'

The general bent his head over a small corner of paper, which he had for some minutes held in his hand.

' "I found, in brief, that all the great nations learned their truth of word and strength of thought in war. That they were nourished in war, and wasted in peace. That they were taught by war, and deceived by peace. Trained by war, and betrayed by peace. In a word, that they were born in war, and expired in peace." Expired in peace. War gives to the men who fight it high ideals. It brings splendid young men like you, men who to a man volunteered, often from far away in other lands, it brings them up, I say, against the realities of life. And brings them up harsh. I have already told you what we are fighting for – everything we hold sacred – and it is incumbent on us, not only for our own sakes, but for the whole world, present and future, using every force within us, spiritual, intellectual, and material, to leave no stone unturned to obtain victory. To obtain victory. Trusty and well-beloved officers of the Sovereign, you have my most sincere congratulations and good wishes.'

And, as he turned to stride urgently down the long stone floor of the nave, the senior cadet stepped out from the pews, and raising his cap volunteered three hearty cheers for the general, which echoed among the stone figures and sacred paintings around the high altar. When Sir Cather Blacker-Douglas's footsteps and the reverberation of the cheers had quite died away, Arch noticed the distant music-hall song still hovering in the quadrangle.

'All of this,' mused Arch to himself, though for the first time dejected, 'gets me no further towards the Royal Flying Corps.'

CHAPTER FOUR

Soldiers Bathing

He felt none of the tremendous pride of his fellow-officers at his commission. And, when he asked a further time to be transferred to the arm of his choice, to his dismay he was seconded to an understaffed Horse Artillery regiment, stationed at Shoeburyness, on the far eastern tip of Essex, at Foulness Island. For further 'technical training', so the word had it. This dreary prospect was reached two afternoons later, by a slow-moving train, past miserable weatherboard villages, facing the rain, and fishing-harbours in miry inlets. As the train halted interminably, Arch had ample time to observe from the rain-darted window the landscape which would shortly surround him. Featureless, expansive, where the horizon appeared three-quarters sky, and a limitless prospect of grey cloud blurring with grey water, it was broken only by pictur-esque (no other word describes them) oyster and shell-fish hamlets, clustered round the bottleneck of an estuary. Clouds of steam rose up, where the fish was already being smoked, out of doors, accompanied by a strong smell of burnt herrings, and baskets of oysters and clams being carried on the heads of fishermen in oilskins and black tarred hats. Women, with red shiny faces and hands, gutted fish-scales on to their black aprons. Eventually these villages petered out into tide-waters and disguised creeks, unbroken except by a tall finger-spire or, unexpec-tedly, herds of wild horses grazing at the far ends of sand-dunes.

At the point where Arch felt the only logical extension of this marshscape was finally under the sea itself, he felt with relief the train come to its ultimate halting spot, and wheeze and sigh, as the engines cooled, and the iron froze. If anywhere was the end of England, and the end of land, it was Foulness Island. At the far end, which he could observe from the station platform, he could see quite clearly a querulous and horizontal finger of sandy dune extend falteringly to the sea. A few level strips of pale sand broke the flat surface of the water about one mile out, and then it persisted into greyness again. An exhausted tide which barely quivered drenched the sand bar, and far, far beyond, a curious silhouette against the feeble sun, there cantered a dazzling troop of Horse Cavalry, towing limbers and guns across the splashing sands, and after that, a glitter of sun on water, one sidelong bar of light, metallic, bristling alert, almost hopeful. Above floated from every direction the light-hearted chatter of skylarks.

There followed many weeks of unspeakable dreariness and frustration. His commission seemed to Arch worthless in view of the unrelieved tedium of his duties, and the comparative ignominy of his role. The regiment, no doubt inspirited enough when plumed and frogged and spurred on Horse Guards, was undermanned and demoralized. Their wartime task was to test long-range artillery equipment, by firing behind sandbagged emplacements pointlessly out to sea. Sometimes, when the large shells failed to explode, which they frequently did, when landing nose-down in soft quicksand, it was the Horse Artillery's duty to ride out in carts (formerly used to collect seaweed) and explode them where they were, or to retrieve them.

This was the puzzling sight he had seen first arriving from the station, and this was how he first inspected his squadron, plastered with yellow mud, shivering in their discoloured battledress, with sleeveless leather jerkins belted round them to keep out as much of the cold as possible. It was only on occasional afternoons that they were permitted to use their horse skills in parade and

84

ceremonial duties, and even then, when called upon to appear publicly, it was largely to attend military funerals.

After Christmas the weather became even worse. Gales eroded the soft sandbanks, and tides of great savagery flooded the coastal villages. From early morning until last light, the Horse Artillery troopers slaved to resist the heaped waves, lugging sandbags in their frozen hands to bolster the collapsing seawall. St Lucy's Day came and went with scarcely a glimmer of light.

For all his lifetime, Arch regarded those weeks at Foulness as the meanest of his existence, and the monotony of them dragged out the days every bit as painfully as the actual labour and discomfort. He thought longingly of running sheep again in a desert country. The east wind ruffled off the estuary of the North Sea with stealthy determination, light and gentle in disguise, but razor-like, and these feathers of sea-breeze penetrated the soldiers' dampened khaki clothing day and night. Officers enjoyed little better comfort than the men, and nobody was protected from the unending sobbing wind. Later, when the worst of the weather abated at low tide, some of the officers played polo on the sands, and at this Arch felt more at ease, although the sport was ineffective.

The commanding officer had eccentric ideas, and seemed rather dislodged in his head, having come from the Indian Cavalry, and somehow assuming he was still there. A fierce cricket enthusiast, when one Saturday in January dawned with feeble sunshine, the colonel instructed all cricket players out on the sands at low tide, where they played a ludicrous game of wintry tip-and-run, with the colonel exhorting their efforts from the breakwater.

'I want this battery to be a happy battery,' was the Colonel's explanation, 'and when I see the battery at play, then I know more or less where they stand. Never waste time. Either work, play, or sleep, but don't idle, and don't loaf.'

Their breath froze on the air and, as the sun sank down

into the sombre blood-scored tides, a heavy mist rolled in from the mouth of the Thames, making the wickets invisible. At that point only, the colonel called the troop in enthusiastically:

'Bad light stopped play. Drawn game. Good show, Five Nine Battery.'

But it boded ill for the summer.

When the colonel heard, at dinner that evening, that Mr Gendron had been coached in the nets by the redoubtable Trumble brothers of the Melbourne Cricket Club, his enthusiasm exceeded all expectation.

'Why, that makes you downright indispensable, Gendron! Good show!'

Arch considered himself imprisoned by a life-sentence at Foulness, for ever consigned to collecting unexploded shells from the quicksands, and playing games of cricket on the mudbanks at ebb-tide. Shivering and dispirited beneath damp blankets, he thought wistfully of nights under the mosquito-nets at Brontë, and of the hopelessness of his predicament. He wondered, above all, if he would ever find the opportunity to fly. He felt himself as becalmed and beached as the famous Ogg Special, which was at that moment decomposing like a whale's carcass on the Sandringham Sands, 12,000 miles to the south.

It turned into an unendurable and tedious winter, sustained most of the time by drudgery on the artillery ranges, gun-greasing, arms drill, and the monotonous cleaning of unnecessary objects. Painting black coke white, for example, and burnishing fire-buckets a glowing grey. Arch accepted his posting to Shoeness with a spirit of abnegation, hiding his disappointment under conventional military obedience, and with a quiet assurance to himself (not always easy when on morning guard duty under a freezing sky, watching the East Coast fighters setting out on dawn patrol) that he was only biding his time, learning the disciplines and skills he would need in any arm. The 'objective' in army parlance was to stand guard on the giant coastal guns which overlooked the Thames forts, which in their turn protected the estuary to the Port of London. It was by this route after all that Admiral Van Tromp had stormed up the Channel through the front door right into the heart of England, his broomstick stuck to the prow of his flagship, and it was someone in High Command who advised that the Kaiser might easily try the same trick. In the winter of 1914, with his armies at the edge of the Low Countries, it was not an unreasonable proposition.

Shoeburyness itself was a promontory on the uttermost finger of Essex, a dead foreland deserted by all but a handful of wrecked cottages, the haunt of poachers, a few waterlogged duck pontoons, and wild geese. The army had requisitioned the island from its private owners at the start of the war, in order to turn it into a training ground for the experimental artillery, 'Ex-Peas' they were called, and what small contours it had ever possessed were now pounded and bombarded into flat, grassless plains. It was a featureless, despairing landscape, whose previous owners had abandoned the place to wind and sand for the centuries it stood in their occupation.

The only village on the island, oddly named Eerie, contained nothing but a wrecked manor-house, its stables, and what remained of a stunted Saxon church. Centuries before, the family, by tradition, bred horses for their Plantagenet landlords, and a wild strand of this original herd which broke free in Tudor times still ranged the lower part of the island, left to their own resources, breeding in limited but regular fashion over the years and retaining both their distinctive markings and untamedness intact. They were an odd race, certainly, hairy-chinned, long-tailed, quite short-legged, but above all unapproachable by man. Arch, who loved the unbroken brumbies from his days on the outback, nevertheless recognized that, for all its fidelity, the horse was a stupid animal, obstinate and feckless, unless dominated by whoever was on its back; but these animals fascinated him by their wilfulness, hostility, and fierce independence. When approached, far from timidly bearing off, as most animals will do, these island horses bunched together, lowered their heads offensively, and trotted arrogantly toward the intruder. They had been known to bite, and kick out when at close quarters, and any visitor to the island had been warned to keep clear of them. Not that visitors were ever welcomed, or invited. Maybe because of the island's seclusion, the feudal owners of Eerie were celebrated for their inhospitable nature, and discouraged guests or intruders. The family employed local wildfowlers in the capacity of casual gamekeepers, whose own traditional malevolence, and inimical dislike of 'foreigners', combined with their accuracy with the shotgun, soon put paid to unwelcome visitors. So, for generations, the horses had continued their grazing, mating and fighting life unobserved, and free from disturbance.

The isolation of the island, once the European war started, was further increased by the very fact that the only access to it consisted of a pathway which vanished quite beneath the currents as they came in, and only emerged at intervals as a muddy track, distinguished by the tall poles, at rip-tide. The only other means, by flat-bottomed punt, was indeed favoured by occasional wildfowlers and eel-diggers (something of a rarity in that part of the Thames) but they were generally warned off by the gamekeepers' effective use of the scatter-gun. Once the island was requisitioned by the artillery, however, it was a quick business to erect wire barricades each side of the channel, and a few dramatic warning signs to dissuade even the slightest attempt at intrusion. The waterway was patrolled by flat-bottomed pontoons, with machine guns mounted more to detect invaders than to deter eel-diggers, but the device served both purposes.

So Arch was, to some extent, cut off from the mainland and the outside world of warmth and companionship, in a sense marooned. The gunners called it 'the arse-end of Essex'.

And still more winter weeks passed – could it be January now, of another year? – and to improve their monotony, out on the marshes, away from the scrutiny of his fellow-officers, Arch decided to share the ground-down dissatisfaction of his men. Not in any sense to earn their admiration, nor their respect, but simply to distract himself from the unending tedium of it all. He shoved behind the limbers, when the axles slunk into the mud, hauled on the horses' heads, and took his turn kneeling beside the heavy guns, when the breech flicked open, and smoke spiralled out like fungoid breath, and he would time, again and again, their gun-drill, setting the iron monsters down, loosing the horses, running back and forth with the huge shells, as large as a child too old to carry, hauling back the reluctant breech, pushing the shell into the gawping barrel, clanging the breech-block into place, and pressing the firing pin. The sheer ecstasy of the concussion and the cordite excited him: the iron casing and emplacement shuddering and singing, the echoing boom of explosion following them from the other side of the estuary, the gust of smoke and filthy black pond of stink left behind, the levellers and layers bending their heads studiously over their gun-sights, and the howling, buzzing, whining vibration of the shells as they exploded in the wet sands miles away. Sometimes, while they reloaded, quite clearly borne on the sea air which appeared to gather it and retain it, cocooned, the gunners could hear an answering barrage, far off, moderate, but insistent and continuous like waves breaking. And through it all, invisible to the eye, perched on no branch, nor wading in a pool of tideless water, the unusual and eerie complaint of marsh-birds, plaintive and wretched as the gunners who nightly disturbed them.

One afternoon, hands in pockets, Arch watched a hawk pestering a wood-pigeon. The larger bird, cut off from the cover of trees, flapped agitatedly for height, but the hawk spiralled even higher. A second time the wood-pigeon avoided the predator's dive, and on each occasion the hawk lazily climbed. Finally, the grey pigeon could fly no further, and dipped aside, and the hawk fell upon its undefended prey, faster and stronger, ripping its wing feathers apart. The wood-pigeon, so energetic and vitally alert in flight, changed instantly to stone, and spun to the ground, as the lighter bird, uninterested now, flew upwards and along the ridge of the estuary. Arch watched intently, and twisted a thumb-pinch of feathers into his lapel, for some kind of superstition, for luck perhaps.

Another winter afternoon – was it March already? – the men out on the guns, greasing them, and the sun shining unexpectedly, Arch was exercising his great bay gelding Nagendra, this time across the dunes at Snow Hill. A warmer wind waved and flagged through the coarse goose-grass, shivering and inclining, bending it sometimes grey, sometimes yellow. There was an early beauty about it, the anticipation of a false spring.

The guards near the lighthouse saluted and waved as the horseman trotted by, and one had plaited some early marsh-flowers in his helmet. The bay twitched excitedly and demanded extra handling. Something nervous was in the air. Arch knew the gelding's ways in this weather, and held his mouth on tight rein. About them, and seemingly between the very hooves of the horses, twittered the larks. There was something truly exciting about such a glorious day. The wind stopped, paused. Sea curled softly on to the mud, with a stirring, slopping sound. There had been no gunfire that afternoon, the men were greasing the barrels. Some had stripped to their vests. Sometimes the horse sent a nest of larks bubbling into the sky, twittering with anger or joy. Arch wanted to have the solitude of the dunes to himself, and the eruption of the larks was a delight to him. His life at that moment was perfectly serene, containing nothing, longing for nothing, no war, no woman, no friend, no love. Everything was complete, secure and cherished, and alone. There was no fear, there was no love, but everything was suffused by an unfathomable joy. He could not account for the exaltation he felt, nor did he try.

Men's cries disturbed this, and as he rounded a particularly tall dune, obscured by waving spear-grass, he came across a sentry strolling beside some fifty young men, dressed in a uniform that seemed unfamiliar to him. Their song was new to him also but, as they marched by, the words drew his attention to their origin:

> *Zehn eiserne Riegel*
> *das ist ein Spass,*
> *die spreng ich als wären*
> *sie nur von Glas!*

They were, he realized as they marched by, German prisoners of war, who had been stationed in a camp nearby, also on the island, who worked on the estuary, and helped build dykes against the sea's erosion. He pulled his horse back to watch them march away from him. He ignored the officious salute, but nodded his head to the bombardier in charge, and smiled friendlily at the prisoners. Some smiled in return, or waved, and most of them called out to the horse, or to himself, compliments of the brilliant afternoon. What cheerful fellows they were, he thought.

'*Hei, Junge, das ist ein prächtiges Pferd!*'

Not far from him, a quarter-mile away perhaps, the sentry halted them and, while he watched, they undressed. This they did rapidly, for it was cold in spite of the wintry sunshine. And then they turned towards the sea, lapping the edge of the dunes, at its furthest reach, and with one accord ran into the water. The tide was so weak, the descent of the sand so imperceptible, they had to run far out to sea, in a long file, splashing the water beneath them, as if they were running across glass. Like small wings the salt water splashed beneath their heels, and glinted as the soldiers ran by, so that Arch from his position on the dune would swear they skimmed across the surface of the sea. Some of those in front discovered a sudden trough, which fell away beneath them, as a weak board may in an empty house, and the others, attracted to it, joined them and they began wading in deep up to their waists. Some of the stronger prisoners lay flat on the water and kicked their feet, partly to keep warm, partly for the freedom, the fun. Their waists and thighs shone with whiteness, their shoulders broke the spray. Wriggling their unfamiliar bodies, escaping from the chill of the sky into the sharper chill of the sea, and out again, finding it more frozen yet, they spun eagerly around like fish. Above this still the larks formed an ocean of excitable cries, and created a glorious background to the joy and radiance out at sea. The bombardier's boots pressed into the sand, and the faint wave of spume where the tide ended, and from time to time he yelled out to them; encouragement or abuse, it was hard to tell. Catching sight of the officer at a distance the sentry shielded his eyes from the sun, made brighter by the water, looking up at him. He was a young, fresh-faced youth, who had probably not been in the army long himself, and doubtless sympathized with the prisoners chafing under his charge. He had wished for a more active posting, but found himself, as did Arch, frustrated and cut off, on the wretched island. He had adopted island attitudes already, and sent his prisoners bathing while he watched them from the shore. It was against regulations, but it was fun, and he was young.

'Soldiers bathing, sir,' he cried out, 'permission to continue, sir!'

'Of course, Bombardier,' said the officer from his horse, smiling, 'let them enjoy the water. It's a beautiful day for March. Why shouldn't they?'

'Prisoners like it, sir, they're good Huns too – sticklers for hygiene and cleanliness, sir, and I doubt any of them'll swim for home, sir.'

'I doubt that too,' answered Arch. He felt a curiosity to see them closer, and waded his horse out to sea. His horse breasted the gentle swell boot-high, it came up no further than that, and his feet balanced on the meek rise and fall. The men were laughing, splashing one another, shrieking at the unexpected cold shock, and exhilarated by the sudden swift plunges as one, more impatient than the others, or more daring, suddenly ducked below, to haul another off his legs and backwards, spluttering and startled. The swearing was high-pitched, and explosive. Some were wrestling defiantly, encouraged by a ring of others round about, arms on one another's necks. A group further out had struck a sandbank and they were standing looking out to sea, singing out their hearts defiantly, like drunken men on a Saturday night. One or two, in the deeper part, swam steadily to a gentle breast-stroke, as conscientious as scholars. Some of the ex-Feldwebel were stout middle-aged men with side-whiskers, and they resembled bull-walruses, spouting and blowing beneath their hirsute cheeks, and one or two who obviously couldn't swim at all hovered frozenly round the edge, discouraged; when Arch steered his horse into them and the bay struck out with his forelegs, this sudden gigantic movement alarmed the men and they ceased their laughter and splashing, and turned for the shore as if checked.

'*Nein, nein, das ist nicht, meine Freunde,*' called out Arch in half-remembered German which he had learnt at home from Goerstler. 'Go on, swim, enjoy yourselves, why not – it's a beautiful day. *Schwimmen Sie weiter, und planschen Sie weiter, viel Spaß?!*'

Two of the younger men splashed forward and took Nagendra's bridle. He could see their whole-hearted admiration in their eyes:

'*Danke, Herr Offizier,*' they cheered. 'Three loud cheers for the horse-officer!'

And they swiftly surrounded him, naked, and yelling, and leaping to and from the sea, on every side of Nagendra, cheerfully splashing his jacket and tunic.

'*Alles ist gut, ja!*' shouted one heavily shouldered fellow, Saxon-faced, salty-cheeked, like the young Essex fishermen who frequented the nearby villages. 'Here there is no war. And there is the sea, and the sun shining, and we can enjoy ourselves, young men all together. *Alles ist Brüderschaft!* There is no war, and no hatred, only the sunlight. Sunlight and *Brüderschaft!*' And, grabbing the horse's bridle, the young Saxon turned Nagendra's sculptured head towards the shingle; on each side, sea water dripping from them, their naked bodies glittering in the sun, the prisoners headed for their clothes. Reaching dry sand, each man in turn shook his skin like a wet dog, and ran spiritedly down the beach, sometimes in pairs or threes at a jog trot, sometimes in pursuit of one another, tripping up heels, elbowing and shouting.

'*Brüderschaft* . . . ' Yes, he remembered that from the Wanderers, and the stockmen also. They had a word for it: Mateship.

Arch nudged the bay into an idle jog-trot, and the men on each side ran beside him to keep pace, for as long as they could keep up, one by one falling back. At last, only the strong Saxon boy had the lungs to follow, and with a friendly wave Arch clucked the gelding into a hand-canter, and finally a gallop, outreaching the Saxon's lope, until the prisoners and their calling and singing dispersed beneath the exaltation of the larks.

Returning to the Officers' Mess that evening, after scrubbing down the gelding and drying him off, Arch opened a letter from his friends, the Ducros. They had not been idle on his behalf. This letter contained two items of news, one serious, one heartening. His brother Chas had left London the day before to join the Queen's Bays fighting in defence of Messines with the 1st Cavalry Division; better still, his own request to enlist in the Royal Flying Corps had at last been granted. He was to report for training the following week at Peckwater Barracks, Christ Church, in Oxford.

At last he felt himself getting on some sort of terms with the war. Also, by now, he had found himself a nice girl.

PART TWO

CHAPTER FIVE

At the Good Old Carlyle

Some weeks before Arch had found himself alone in his own company, settled with the *Evening Chronicle* and a large Scotch whisky, thawing himself out in the members' alcove of the Carlyle Club. The precious corner resembled a private 'snug' in a respectable saloon. It was the first time he had really felt the value of a warm fire all winter. The club was deserted, apart from discreet visits by Trowel to attend to the welfare of the grate with renewals of sea-coal: 'I don't want to be rude, sir, but will you be wanting dinner?'

Encouraged by the coal fire, and the whisky, he felt himself drowning in irresistible sleep. His head must have slumped forward, and at that moment he woke dazed. He took a moment to recollect where he was – there was no sign of Trowel – and he found himself facing the slight figure, veiled, of a young woman. Half-asleep, his eyes open, he found no words.

'I'm waiting for Mr Legge,' a voice said. It was low, and timid, and had a slight catch of eagerness in it.

She had brought the cold in with her, about her cloak and shoes. Arch detected a scrap of white in one of her ears, which on inspection turned out to be a small twist of cotton wool, the kind that children use to relieve earache. He stood up, instinctively buttoning his jacket, as if before a drill-sergeant.

'Can I be of any help at all?' he asked. 'You seem to be a little unsure . . .'

'In this gentlemen's club', she half-laughed, 'I'm often unsure.'

'Is it somebody you have come to meet?' Arch interrupted.

'I think he might be perhaps in one of the gentlemen's bars. It is Mr Legge, I expect you know him. Captain Legge, an officer in the King's Own. He said he would be waiting for me. I worry that I am standing in a place I should not be standing in, you know, reserved for the members.'

She laughed nervously at the idea of breaking the rule, and at the inherent foolishness of it at the same time. Life was full of unnecessary rules in England, Arch had noticed, in the army, in clubs, in trains, in drawing-rooms, frequently directed against women. And the people appeared to encourage them most of the time, or certainly condone them. He remembered the Colonial Club back in Brighton Beach was the same.

'Well, I suppose I should tell you there *is* meant to be some sort of restriction about this area, near the fire,' he said. 'Reserved for the members, I gather. But I shouldn't worry about it tonight.'

'Ah, I suspected as much,' said the young woman, moving deftly out of the way as if to avoid a muddy patch of ground. And again, that bubbling, uncaring and musical laugh, as at a private joke. He noticed, too, she appeared to speak in a tumble of words, anxiously, and leaving consonants behind in her hurry.

'Would you mind telling me the name of your friend again?' he asked. 'The friend who arranged to meet you?'

'It's Mr Legge,' she answered, spelling the name out, 'he'll be in uniform, a captain, I believe, things change so quickly these days.'

'Wait here in the warm, and I'll give him a shout.'

Thinking that she could not know him really all that well, Arch walked down the corridor, to find a group of men in regimental dress standing around the bar.

'One of you fellows Captain Legge, expecting to meet a pretty young woman at the front hall?' he asked.

'Good heavens, you are a good fellow to tell me. That

must be my little Melissa. I must say I hadn't watched the time at all. I hope you kept her in good spirits in my absence, old chap.'

'There was little time for that,' Arch laughed.

'Actually', confided Legge, 'she's something of an actress, so you have to keep your eye on her.' And, putting out his hand, added: 'Now who are you, sir, so we can know what you're going to drink!'

'David Gendron, Royal Horse, out at Foulness, inactive and bored speechless.'

Legge drained his glass of whisky and slapped it firmly on the bar.

'Harry Legge, King's Own, "Sturdy" Bloom there's a Hussar, and so is Skevington, and these two gentlemen-rankers in fancy-dress Dragoon kit are Tiny Holmes, and Arthur Portarlington. Now, Jameson,' he said, addressing the steward, 'set up another order of whiskies, will you?' and, turning to Arch, he shook his hand. 'My God, but you're a splendid fellow, and it's grand to see you cavalry chaps in this club. There's one marvellous thing about all these fellows here.'

It was clear to Arch they had already drunk enough to create this atmosphere of fellowship and enthusiasm.

'The Carlyle is a wonderful bond, which doesn't stop at the edge of that carpet. It's far more than just a boring men's club – it's a way of life. It grows out across London, and spreads right through Sandhurst, and Eaton Hall; it disembarks when you arrive at Calais and Dieppe, and it marches with you along muddy roads, and it's still there, in heart, with you in those God-awful trenches and mudflats in France. And I know it because, believe me, I've been there, and I shall be going back to it. You see, you are not alone out there. It's a spirit, and it's called teamwork. That is the wonderful thing about the Carlyle Club – this spirit of teamwork.'

'And good fun, Harry,' added a subaltern in the Hussars, with a grave face and forlorn moustache.

'I should say,' said the third and older man who had an

odd habit of contorting his face, and combing his blond hair off his forehead with his fingers.

Two older officers in the scarlet hoops of the Yorkshire Dragoons nodded their support.

'It would be rotten without some fun,' said the one introduced as Arthur Portarlington, 'some of the time . . .'

To the surprise of Arch, Legge threw his head back, and bayed at the ceiling. The others joined in, and Arch was instantly reminded of the lacrosse field at home in Melbourne, and the Wanderers' war-cries. The four men then linked arms across one another's shoulders, and went into an old school war-cry. Jameson, the laconic barman, continued peaceably to rinse glasses; he was familiar with such horseplay. What terrific spirits these British officers had, Arch thought, always eager to let off steam, and indulge in sudden outbursts of excitable nonsense. Perhaps they were attempting to cram into their few fractured hours of relaxation almost more than they could logically sustain. His reverie was suddenly disrupted by the false heroics of Harry Legge, who had fallen helplessly into a club chair, hooking his legs over one arm of it, in a mock fainting fit.

'Good God, can you imagine,' he cried as he sprang to his feet again, smoothing his uniform and pressing down his hair, 'forgetting my companion like that. You fellows are enough to distract anybody. Put another round of that excellent whisky on my account, Jameson, will you? And don't let those Dragoon Guards put their hands in their pockets! Write it down, for God's sake . . . See you in the old pub next time!'

'Good hunting, Legge, old boy!'

And, beckoning Arch to join him, Harry Legge moved smartly away down the passage.

The young woman broke off her conversation with Trowel, who inclined his head in some form of bow, and turned anxiously to Captain Legge as he appeared.

'Oh, Harry – ' But Legge cut her greeting short.

'Say hallo to a fellow-officer of mine, will you, Mysie . . .'

'David Gendron, Second Lieutenant, King's Troop,' he introduced himself formally, and took the gloved hand offered to him, 'middle name of Archie, shortened by my brothers back home to Arch!'

'Mr Gendron of King's Troop, this young woman is called Melissa Bingham.'

He took her hand and then kissed her lightly on the neck.

'Stay and talk to Mysie, will you, David, while I grab my British warm. For somebody as delicate and fragile from the trenches as I, these London streets give me a chill. Look how well-wrapped up Mysie is. She might be joining our Russian brothers with the snow on their boots . . . what nonsense all that was too, by the way . . .'

And Legge wandered up the stairs, not without a little difficulty. The girl gazed after him hungrily.

Arch felt apprehensive to disturb her reverie.

'I had never met Captain Legge before – '

'Oh, call him Harry please,' she interrupted.

' – and he was buying me drinks and treating me as a friend with the best of them. He's a first-rate chap, isn't he?'

'This is the last day of his leave, you know,' she said, altering the whole tone of their conversation immediately. 'He seems determined to go out again. The men kept writing letters to him, and he decided to go.'

'Shouldn't he?'

'I asked him not to. He doesn't have to, you see. He was hurt so badly at First Ypres,' she said gently, as if trying to reduce the effect, like someone caught boasting about a medal. 'He could stay behind a desk if he wished. He's mostly in pain, you see. His hip-bone is all replaced now, it's made of something, some sort of metal.' She seemed so candid, awkwardly so, after so brief an acquaintance that it made him shy of her. 'But the men kept writing letters to him, they needed him, and he decided to go back.'

'I think it sounds as if he has a charmed life. He comes across to me like that, in any event,' Arch added quietly.

There was a silence between them.

'I understand you are an actress,' he began hopefully.

'Oh, I'm with Mr Chancellor, with the – ' gesturing to the doorway.

But, before he could answer, she looked away in the direction of the stairs, and her eyes glittered. Captain Legge took the giant marble steps two at a time.

'Here is Harry now,' she said with a kind of relief, holding her hand out. He held both their hands in his own.

'Among friends,' was his only response as, with a mocking salute, first to the marble statue of Carlyle, and then to the ghostly Trowel, accompanied by a Germanic heel-click, Captain Legge and his girl went clattering down the white steps, and the doors swung behind them.

It was only four days later that Captain Legge took his patrol into unsettled country in the Eastern Salient, beyond Polygon Wood, from which he did not return. Characteristically, a letter of resignation from the Carlyle Club had arrived two days previously, settling his outstanding account, and enclosing a generous gratuity for the servants.

Because of a dawn parade which he was earmarked to inspect, Arch decided he could delay his return journey no longer, and he walked through the dreary streets, damp with an almost-snow, until he reached Fenchurch Street in the City. He took the last train going east, huddled cold in a corner in his greatcoat, as the stations flickered past in a makeshift black-out. Small prospect, he thought, of any Zeppelins flying over London tonight. Sitting upright, his feet on the felt seat opposite, alone in the carriage, anticipating the familiar cold ache as he approached Foulness, Arch tried to doze. Dread of the glum discomfort of a week ahead, intermingled with curious memories of Captain Legge and his girl in the warm security of the club, prevented his sleeping. He found these days that he was beginning to think less and less about life back in dear old Brighton. His brother Chas had told him that he read news from home with a growing recognition of how foreign and how far away it all seemed. He dreamed about it sometimes, he said, as if it already belonged to the old days. What was new was France, and what he called 'the salient'. Perhaps this war would never end.

He awoke, as always, at the end of the line, when the guard rapped on the window of each compartment to wake the sleeping troopers. Groups of dazed men collected in the half-light of the station, dragging out their kitbags; there were some new recruits carrying rifles and walking in an untidy straggle towards the barracks, waiting to be bullied by the bombardiers. There was a smell of wet metal and fresh manure, and coal-smoke. One of the horse-sergeants was expecting animal reinforcements, and they came clattering and snorting out of their truck as he passed by, plumes of white steam coming from their flared nostrils, a pool of hectic noise and violence in the middle of this stale backwater. The horse-sergeant shouted and swore at the recruits and the nervous animals in equal degree and his abuse hung over the air like a shock-wave. Under the yellow glare of guttering station lights, the horses' heads looked disfigured, grotesquely enlarged, with their open jaws and flared, spraying nostrils; it appeared to Arch, walking back, that the beasts themselves were filling the night air with obscenities. Always, after week-end leave, he hated most of all that reluctant march back from the end of the line to the barracks, behind discouraged men and frightened horses.

CHAPTER SIX

Mysie at the End of Winter

At the first break of spring weather, a forty-eight-hour leave pass neatly pressed in his railway-warrant, Arch slipped through the back railings of Alma Battery, down the alleyway between the rows of sleeping billets, and across the iron foot-bridge to the station. An hour or so later he was in London.

The city was barely awake and Arch, enjoying the brightness of the morning, and the scarcity of passers-by, apart from a few newspaper-sellers, walked rapidly to the Carlyle Club. The gate in front was firmly closed, so he retired quickly to the Turkish Baths in Jermyn Street, where he sweated and shaved and ate kidneys and bacon.

Everything filled him with joy and anticipation for the first time in months. There was the prospect, above all, of learning to fly in Oxford, the equal pleasure of bidding an unlamented farewell to Foulness and, finally, the exhilaration of a short leave in his beloved London. Little appeared to have changed, except for the many windows blacked out and boarded up, small businesses in the seedier parts, cafés and tobacconists, evidently abandoned for the duration by their proprietors, and at times a brackish fragrance in the air of burnt cordite. Gaps in the rows of houses and monumental Victorian office-blocks revealed all too readily the reason: the Zeppelin raids had had a greater effect than newspaper propaganda had acknowledged. The Steam Baths had been active enough, mainly officers on leave from the front. But there was less of the old-fashioned camaraderie, he noticed, far less, and these officers sat apart most of them, eating breakfast silently, towels round their waists,

104

and absorbed in newspapers, some of them with an abstracted stare.

Arch felt no pressure to break the monotony of his casual stroll, as he stopped to watch the jarveys assembling in convoy along Piccadilly, bought a hot tea at the cabmen's shelter at Green Park, and then doubled back across Piccadilly to rest for a while in the quietness of a black and white Wren church and watch a poorly attended service of Morning Prayer.

'I want you all sweet, clean and ready to die,' said the padre in his address, before the Eucharist.

As Arch went out of the porch and into the bright sunshine, where the streets were now alive with morning traffic, the rector held his hand carefully within both his own, almost as some formal kind of benediction.

'Always a pleasure to welcome the Royal Horse Artillery. My son is fighting with them in Neuve Chappelle. Make good use of your leave, and when it is finished ride with your guns in the presence of God.'

Trowel was outside the Carlyle Club, buffing the brass door-handles.

'Very good to see you, sir,' he called cheerily. 'As soon as I've finished the front doors, I'll be right with you, sir. I don't want to be rude, but go into the back room, the one with all the newspapers in, you'll find a lovely fire already burning, sir.'

Mild as the morning was, the misery of the cold wind on the mudflats at Foulness seemed to have penetrated the marrow of his bones, and nothing was more inviting than the prospect of a whole morning devoted to newspapers, hot coffee, and a coal fire. So he fairly leapt past Trowel up the stone steps into the club, two at a time, and then up the main staircase. As he reached the top, he heard from below a cry from Trowel, waving to him excitedly at the foot of the stairs, clambering upwards, a letter in his fingers.

'Correspondence for you, sir. Arrived a week ago, would have sent it on to the regiment, sir, but expected you here before long, and never knew where it was you'd got yourself posted . . .'

The envelope was small, almost square, and the writing, in a backward sloping hand, not one he identified straightaway. Taking it with him into the smoking-room, he settled himself in an armchair and began to read. Curious, before tackling the small painstaking lines, he turned over the pages to discover who his unknown correspondent might be. The name at the foot of the fourth page read simply . . . 'Mysie'. He could not remember anybody he knew of that name, and examined the envelope carefully but it gave him no further clue. So he attempted to decipher the letter, and its tilted handwriting in brown calligraphic ink.

Dear Lieutenant Gendron,
You will forgive me writing to you I am sure when you understand the reason. Mr Trowel, the porter of this Club, was kind enough to give me your name, and to accept this letter. Heaven knows when, if ever, you will receive it — everything is very confused nowadays and badly organized. This war has a lot to answer for. We have been introduced once before, and this was in the New Year at the Carlyle Club. If you remember I was the guest of Captain Legge. Mr Trowel — oh, I must break off. I am so upset . . .

Arch put down the letter for a minute, as if he were in the very presence of the person who seemed to be so agitated and nervous. It seemed as if somebody was reading aloud to him, and could not go through with it. He looked at the page as a whole, without reading the words. It was geometrical in pattern, a complex equation of dashes, words underlined, exclamation marks, arrows, brackets, rows of dots, scribblings-out, evidence of every kind of haste and confusion, indecision and spontaneity; he could even hear the breathless catch in the the writer's voice, see the tears just brim into the corner of her grey eyes. He read on, carefully selecting his way around a miniature archipelago of watery blots.

106

I had to blow my nose then, but better now. Just a little cry. There, I'm more myself again. Oh, Mr Gendron, it is very hard for me, I have nobody I can talk to, or turn myself towards. My friends in the theatre (did I tell you I was an actress, I don't remember that I did . . . there, now, what a memory!) they only seem to be able to understand their own individual problems and, although friendly, have little time to spare for anybody else's problems. Wait, here's Ma with some hot chocolate.

(alongside, vertically in the margin, the correspondent had added: 'My Ma, who is my only friend and always tours with me.')

Where was I? – oh, I *do* remember . . . that evening I woke you to enquire if you could find Captain Legge, Harry was his *real* name he was in the King's Own. He's dead now, Mr Gendron, and for three weeks I found I could not stop crying. But what's to be is to be, so all the girls in the chorus with me say, the girls of number seventeen (*our* dressing-room), and quite a number of them have been in the same spot. Not that I want you to think I was his special girl, but we were friends, and *he* was always special to me. And always will be. They waited for the show to end, of course, and then Mr Chancellor told me – he was very kind and comforting, but the news hurt me very badly, and I remember I just sat down on the end of an iron-staircase, below the flies, and sobbed my heart out. You will be wondering now why I am writing to you, and I don't believe I know properly myself. But I feel lonely and alone and would like to talk to someone. Harry always used to meet me at 'the Old Carlyle' as he called it! He also called it his local – 'See you in the old pub' was his way of putting things. He would meet his friends there, but I never knew them, and worse, Mr Gendron, I think that several of his pals were killed the same night. One of the squaddies visited me at the theatre not long after, and he had his arm in a sling, He told me that Harry was wonderful to his men, and a lot more than one or two died in his arms. But he didn't die in theirs. He was on the wire for the whole night

107

and they heard him crying out all the time, but when a search-party went out he called to them: "Get back! Get back! There's a machine gun!", and they obeyed him, as they always had before. The next morning the line advanced, but it was too late. Oh! . . .

and, as if with a sigh, her letter broke off, and there were more blots and pouches of ink where clearly her tears had fallen. Then it went on:

I promised *not* to do that any more, I promised Ma, and I promised Mr Chancellor, and I *will* not let them down. Better now thank you. Anyway, what I was going to say was, if you are on leave in 'the Old Carlyle', and would like to say hallo, I am working just around the corner in Mr Buckstone's funny Little Theatre in the Hay, and if you were to leave your name with Mr Fenge, at the stage door (he's nearly always there by ten o'clock sharp making his tea), and ask for me – Miss Bingham, dressing-room seventeen (fifth floor, oh lord, those stairs, forty-three up and down ten times a day!) – I could get you a pass for the comedy. It might make you smile, and there would be a sweetheart for you afterwards, I guarantee, as we are seven pretty girls sharing one small dressing-room. You don't know me at all, but do not get the wrong impression. I am not a sad person usually, but these days I just can't seem to cheer up, and I'm sure I can make you smile. I used to be able to with Harry. So, no tears – I know boys don't like girls who cry. Your friend . . .

And several blank lines later came the faint back-hand signature he had looked at earlier: 'Mysie'. As Arch placed the letter on his lap, he looked behind him suddenly in the direction of the door. He felt certain that somebody warm, and light, and full of youth and joy had entered the room, and scented it with their presence. Yes, on reflection, he did recall the shade of a figure, but had quite forgotten the name. Short for Melissa, or some diminutive of Miss, perhaps.

CHAPTER SEVEN

The Little Theatre in the Hay

Fenge, tucked into his coal-box of a stage door, perched in schoolmasterly manner on a tall stool, was not a foreigner to reminiscence; a trait which Arch was to discover on many an occasion in the future, when he visited the famous Little Theatre in the Hay.

'Oh, yes,' said the shrivelled figure, 'Mr Buckstone's been seen in the backstage many a time. And in the pit. Not that I've seen him myself, but the showmen have, the boys on the limes, some of the company, the public even, yes, many times. On one occasion, Mr Buckstone was seen walking along the edge of the amphitheatre, cut off at the knees. Questions asked, no answer. No explanation seemingly. 'Front-of-House' comes round with one of these historical coves. Oh yes, he says, cut off where? At the ankles? At the waist? No. At the knees. Very like, says the cove, one hundred years ago, where them boxes is now, that was the back of the Promenade, and' – here Fenge leant forward, tapping the side of his nose, dropping his voice – 'the level of the auditorium then was twelve inches lower than what it is now.'

Arch had been waiting for about fifteen minutes, at first engrossed, later fascinated, by now slightly bored. And there seemed little possibility that Fenge would run out of anecdotes appertaining to the history of this curious theatre. It had an old-fashioned, comfortable air. Something about the place made it seem to inhabit a previous century, even another country. The door leading into it from the back-streets – unprepossessing and anonymous – gave no hint of the mysteries within. From the street it

109

looked exactly like any other exterior door. A laundry, perhaps, or the backstairs of a greengrocer's. A couple of pavement-sitters were nested beside it, draped for warmth over a grille from which the boiler steam issued, and there was a faint smell of carbon as one entered. Even the windows of dressing-rooms above were orderly, and symmetrical, and appeared more like the respectable windows of a dwelling, and not at all something so disreputable as a playhouse.

Arch had 'watered' and fed at the Carlyle, enjoying a cigar afterwards with some other Horse Artillery officers, and in the early afternoon strolled through the quaint little row of broken-down houses in Goodwin's Court, largely peopled by tailors and, he suspected, by the occasional street-women, before crossing the uncrowded square in front of St Martin's – a wedding was in progress, the bride's veil torn upwards by the wind, guests laughing, an oasis of joy, and confetti flying over to the fountains – and cutting through several side-streets to the back entrance of the Little Theatre. The front of it was closed by large nailed blue doors. A sentinel within gazed stonily back at him.

'What an inhospitable place a theatre is in the daytime,' he reflected to himself. Nobody guided him to find the unprepossessing backway in. Garland's Commercial Hotel, with its bronzed yellow sign, lay at right angles, and he noticed above his head, opposite the theatre, an entire storey of blackened windows and walls where some fire had recently ravaged the building. On the iron railings he read broad-printed playbills announcing *Soldier Boys and Girls!* advertised in red, white and blue lettering below as 'A Patriotic Comedy!' Then a list of names followed, and below them: 'Laughter! Songs! Ragtime!' He could not see Miss Bingham's name mentioned, and so, upon entering the stage door, enquired for her politely. He was answered with friendly familiarity, not at all the tone he had become accustomed to for the past few months:

'Lord now, my friend, bless me no, she ain't available, not by a long chalk. Didn't you know the first-house is on! Why, they're scarcely past the Celebrities Routine, and then there's Angels Tableau and Mr Dodgin's turn, you must know it – the Boy with the Obedient Feet! – a very handy turn, that – and Mr Chancellor's young ladies don't come down for Euphonic Sounds until just before the First Act Transformation. I'm just brewing up, so if you'll take the weight off for a few minutes, and set yourself down on that chair, we can have a nice little cup of tea. Then I'll get Cotterill, the call-boy, to send Miss Bingham down. Seeing as how you're on a spot of leave most likely, I'll bend the rules a bit, and you can have a bit of a talk with the young lady up until Beginners.'

The stage-doorman appeared to enjoy a most unexpected ease of manner and informality he had hardly met elsewhere, except at home in Melbourne, when having kitchen tea with the Irish servants. Fenge was respectful enough, but not afraid, not subservient. Rather self-confident, in fact. But, more striking than this, there unfolded before him, apparently, an entirely unfamiliar and bewildering vocabulary, a kind of local jargon, which was every bit as complex and unintelligible as that of the army. Strolling people's cant, he presumed. Like a cavalry regiment, the theatre inhabited a private world, apart from the common eye, even protected against it.

The tea was brewed, produced in an ancient mug, and Arch found himself hypnotically drawn in – at first, anyway – to the gnome-like stage-door-keeper's unending and ineffectual chatter. His cubby-hole was no bigger than a sentry-box, and much lower, in fact a step down descended into it, and Fenge sank on to a pile of what were once plump cushions, covering his tall stool, but worn so threadbare they appeared as wafer-thin as used envelopes. Other creatures seemed to inhabit this odd cave, a furry cat by the name of Ambrose walked pompously in and out, taking little notice of its other occupant, an ageing and decrepit theatrical dog called

Chant, from which emanated the unmistakable and deeply unpleasing rank odour of a stale kennel.

Arch listened patiently, but none too credulously, to the stories of the Little Theatre's celebrated ghost, its legendary past (the great Quipic died on-stage there in his dresser's arms), the haunting presence of its original builder in the auditorium, Bannister's popular comic appearances. Fenge went on to more recent proprietors.

'Eventually,' he told Arch, as from behind-scenes faintly there came the vulgar rhythms of a pit-band, increasing in volume as a door opened and receding as it closed, 'eventually it come into the hands of Mr Chancellor! You've heard of him, of course . . . Chancellor's London Players . . . Chancellor's Tours. Hold on, though' – and Fenge interrupted himself, listening intently to a brass fanfare – 'thought as much – that's the Donaldson Brothers – you know – "Sports in a Jungle". Oh, a very well-off gentleman, Mr Chancellor. He's the son of the late Mr James, or J.C. as the Profession knew him.' Fenge savoured the recollection for a moment: 'J.C.' He then appeared to dismiss the memory with a curt nod, as of a sudden awkward fact coming to light, debts unpaid, a scandal, something of the sort. 'So, young Mr Chancellor inherited the empire. Mr Harold. The Opera House, Leeds, the Pimlico Royal sort of thing . . . But this is the ruby in his crown. This Little Theatre in the Hay, Mr Buckstone's Emporium, as it used to be called, is the one he was always angling after. Yes, a veritable ruby. And, finally, he got it. And that's how he got me. Well, years ago now, before the old war with the Voortrekkers, in which, if you don't mind me saying, sir, I played my little part. A Mauser expanding in the knee, crocked the old leg, you know . . . ' he added, tapping it significantly. But happily, before the stage-doorman could carry Arch encounter by encounter through the African campaign, the swing doors suddenly burst apart and a young girl, incongruously dressed for a tennis party of twenty years earlier, complete with racquet, walked quickly through the narrow corridor, and threw open the stage door into the street.

'Oh, Fengie, I think I'll burst if I don't get a breath of air. It's stifling under the limes. All the girls are near fainting ...'

'An officer to see you, Miss Bingham,' said Fenge, quietly.

'Harry?' she asked questioningly.

The young woman turned, looked for one shocked second at Arch, who held his tea-mug in one hand, and cap and cane awkwardly in the other, and sprang violently into his arms, kissing him, and upsetting the tea.

'You *are* the person I want to see,' and then she stepped back shyly, aware that they had hardly been introduced. But the young man felt, for the second time that day, the intrusion into his quiet, plain life, the sudden rush of the morning, sunlight, the ground falling away beneath his feet.

'Lieutenant Gendron, I'm sorry, I must apologize. It has been so stifling on-stage, and the shock of seeing you, it's taken me with a rush. How do you do. My name is Melissa Bingham. Can we shake hands politely and start this all over again?'

Arch put cap, cane and tea-mug down on the ledge of Fenge's kennel, and shook the fingers of the hand which reached to him.

'Tickled pink,' she smiled. Then just as swiftly she turned her attention to the unprepossessing dog, falling on his neck like a long-lost friend. 'Oh, Chant, you dear old thing, I haven't seen you for two whole hours. This is the theatre mascot, Mr Gendron, isn't he a dear?'

Arch thought the rug of doubtful fragrance emphatically not, but nodded appreciatively.

'Why didn't you visit us in your usual way at the half, Chant?' she said, as if expecting a reply from this half-alive creature. 'You're a faithless creature at heart.'

'Is it First Act tabs, already, Miss Bingham?' asked

Fenge, confronting his stage-door clock incredulously. 'I didn't hear Gaudschmidt's Clowns go on . . .'

'Just,' she answered a little breathlessly, 'and I'm not a Second Act beginner. The house is a bit sluggish, that's why we're early. In fact I'm not on until after the Heliotrope,' she added. 'Can I take the lieutenant backstage for a moment, Fengie dear?' And, imitating a child's coyness, she pursed her lips, clasped her hands in front of her, and swayed her shoulders. This foolish by-play appeared to convince the door-keeper, as with many an equally insincere nod, wink, shrug, and wriggle he gestured the pair of them through the magic pass door, and into the bewildering world of back-stage. There, they nearly collided with a tall, anxious figure in bowler hat and tail-coat, who resembled the well-dressed secretary of a London club. This was 'Front-of-House' in matinée attire.

'Oh, Mr Vance, any business second-house?' asked Mysie.

'There is no movement on the sheets, Miss Bingham,' said Front-of-House airily.

Mysie looked a little crushed.

'Curtain down on Act One – curtain down!' called a dwarf, or a child, perhaps a little of each, in a dark Malabedeely suit and red scarf. 'There's tea and buns in wardrobe,' shouted the dwarf surprisingly loudly, 'and Heliotrope beginners in orchestra!'

The first impression was of wealthy people rapidly moving house. Builders and decorators or men dressed as such, all appeared to be strenuously involved in dismantling a vast glass conservatory at the same time as erecting not so much a house, but an entire Elizabethan street, with balconies, windows, doors, all of which were propped up, and braced from behind, by straps of wood. This furious activity was accompanied by the most unmerciful din, there was no one who appeared not to be shouting at one time or another, or hammering. Several well-dressed men not unlike tailors on holidays, or even bookmakers, with bowler hats on their heads and brown aprons round their waists were peering into the vast mouth overhead, and shouting instructions to further gangs of invisible workmen engaged in operations up above. Large canvases, with painted designs, came rushing down like topsails falling heavily on the main-mast, and up would go the nave of a cathedral, or a market square, to be followed by a race-track grandstand, or a railway station. It reminded Arch of a huge, helpless ship, spinning round and round, out of control, skipperless, rudderless, while ignorant sailors, disorganized, anarchic, pulled sails up and down, climbed rigging, swung booms, with neither instinct nor effectiveness. And a dozen captains wearing black bowlers ran about urgently, imperiously giving orders to one another where there appeared nobody to obey.

'Get back to your dressing-room sharpish, Miss,' one of these bowler-hatted captains snapped angrily, 'or Mr Chancellor will know about it.' Arch stepped forward, about to check such impertinence, but Mysie restrained him gently, laying her hand upon his sleeve.

'No, Arch. This isn't the artillery. This is the theatre,' by way of an explanation. Their own rules of discipline too, I suppose, thought Arch to himself, turning aside, following. As he reached what Mysie called 'the pass door' (why is nothing called by its proper name, he wondered, in this imaginary world), an apprehension of, if not quietness, certainly less than the customary din, approached him, and he looked back over his shoulder.

A voice, not so loud, but a little more authoritative, penetrated the hubbub.

'Bring in your sky-drop, Mr Greenhill. Thank you. Bring in your blue-washes, Mr Colby. Very nice. Call beginners for the Heliotrope number, Mr Marsh.'

And, as he looked, Arch saw to his astonishment, not only the restoration of order after so much confusion, but a strange pawky and unearthly beauty. In front of him stood a substantial row of overhung seventeenth-century

115

timber-frames; to the side of him a cobbled street, water-pump, and village stocks; but, behind them both, there loomed up the large stone interior of a manor-house, with minstrels' gallery, overlooking a courtyard, and, where the outside wall might have been, behind a transparent form of gauze, played upon by deceits of the gas-light, there stretched without a doubt the whole façade of Nonesuch Palace, with deer grazing, statues in the park, and dovecotes and stables, their coaches outside, and beyond that vistas of weald and downland, church spires, tall trees, reaching backwards to the faint rim of a descending sun.

'Seven minutes twenty-five,' a voice muttered quietly, to nobody in particular, at his elbow. 'The flies is still behind. Wednesday's first-house was down in nineteen.' And then shouting: 'Take your Iron out. Stand by, beginners.' And the door opened behind him and Mysie took his arm and led him away, just as music began, muffled, in front of the curtain.

She led him up a flight of scrupulously scrubbed wooden steps, with gas fishtails at every landing, holding her forefinger to her lips as they passed what appeared to be a private set of rooms on the first floor, like nervous schoolchildren tiptoeing past their teacher.

'That's where *she* dresses,' explained Mysie, in a whisper, and at that moment a file of the most brilliantly apparelled Elizabethan courtiers, all identical in white, with cloaks, and black velvet hats perched on their heads slightly at an angle, like forage caps, and carrying stuffed sparrow-hawks on their wrists, clattered noisily past, gossiping and giggling.

'Heliotrope, five minutes please,' said the shuffling dwarfish call-boy behind them, knocking at various doors. Along the next passageway, distinctly scruffier and dingier, they walked by what could have been mistaken for servants' lumber-rooms, or even small dormitories in a board-school, stuffy dens with coke fires burning, from which issued the smell of toast and rum and lemon.

'Care for a glass of b. and s., Mysie?' called out a man dressed as Gloriana, smoking a fat cigarette beneath a red coarse wig, and a batwing ruff. 'Good for the poor throat, you know.'

'Got my change coming up, Charlie dear – keep it warm for me before the Finale.'

Another open door was passed, revealing through floods of steam the drying-room, with rows of dripping white shirts and women's blouses lying in tiers on laundry lines from the ceiling.

'Don't forget to hand in your blouse, dear, if you want it on nice and pressed second-house,' a voice called out.

'All right, Glad, I'll get Queenie to bring it up when I've done my change.'

'God bless, dear.'

'God bless,' And as the door swung back, the voice continued: 'If you see Mr Fenge later, ask him to fiddle me up a bit of grub.'

Once again, Mysie turned round to Arch, who was beginning to feel decidedly underdressed, or at least wrongly turned out, stiff and formal in his breeches and long-jacket, boots and spurs. She stopped outside a door marked Number Seventeen, put up her finger warningly against her lips, and whispered, 'Now this will really surprise them!' And taking his hand in hers, surprisingly firmly, she threw open the door and advanced boldly with him into the room.

'Someone to see you, girls!'

There was an immediate outcry, as if someone had let a mouse loose in a classroom of schoolchildren. Arch himself was stunned, unaware of whether he was behind the scenes or, for all he knew, had been propelled on to the centre of the stage, in full glare of lights and the public. All round him was a frenzied activity of arms and bodies. He was in a low-ceilinged room, not unlike others he had passed, but larger, and shabbier, heated also by a smoky fire, in front of which various items of female underclothing steamed. Rows of white stockings hung across a clothes-horse. It was brightly illuminated by gas-light and electric bulbs, reflecting themselves off the dressing-table mirrors. At first glance the cramped quarters appeared to be shared by dozens of naked or semi-naked women.

'This is my new friend, Lieutenant Gendron, of the Royal Horse Artillery.'

'But we're trying to do our change, Mysie . . .' a voice wailed.

'You shouldn't bring your friends back-stage, during the show,' someone else complained.

'I'm so sorry,' stammered Arch, desperately ill at ease.

'We don't mind if you stay,' said another voice, just under his elbow, and he turned to see a dark-haired girl staring at him from inside a mirror, concentrating on painting an eyelid.

'It's not easy getting into Petit-Mozarts in seven minutes,' said another, nodding at a line of silver wigs.

The young officer realized that, although he had seen some women undressed, though not many of them, he had never seen them actually *undressing*, and rather enjoyed the sensation. There was an air of muddle about it. Not merely the startling flash of breast or thigh, which was obvious enough, but the revelation, for the first time, of the geographical landscape of women's bodies, of their shapes and contours, curves above all, the faint overhang of breast above a laced bodice, the way upper arms swelled out of shoulders, the firm breadth of back, the ridged backbone (unlike a man's) hardly evident at all, the gentle concentration of one girl on the mirror studying her eyelid, another, foot up on a chair, left shoe on, the other off, ungainly and enticing. His embarrassment had quite left him, nor did he feel aware of the actresses in an alien way. Seven to one, they had no fear of him, nor he of them, and he was at his ease, shy, but relaxed, and he accepted their offer of a stool beside Mysie's mirror, as she – rather more coy than the rest – disappeared behind a hanger of ballgowns to change into her stage costume.

Not all of the girls were as pretty as his first impression had led him to believe, but each had an allure of her own, and he enjoyed the coarseness of make-up, which brightened their eyes, and polished their mouths, under the burning glow from the gas-light. All round their mirrors were festooned postcards and favours and garters, and messages were scribbled on the glass. 'If you stumble tonight, it is because I am at your feet. Love – Port', he read to himself over Mysie's wig-block. No wonder he had imagined there were so many girls at first sight, for they were reflected and magnified a dozen times, even the room appeared larger because of it, and everywhere he looked he was met by dozens of matching heavily mascara'd, glistening eyes. While they changed, some were smoking cigarettes, some drinking beer. It reminded Arch of the friendly exchanges between the men he had grown so used to down at Shoeness, something he had not met before among other kinds of women in England, and he felt perhaps more at home with them, and happy for the first time.

Mysie's flirtatious chattering behind her mound of white ballgowns was interspersed with questions from her friends.

'Do you know Captain Collinson of the RHA? He's stationed out at Windsor.'

'Do you know Major Bamborough?'

'Do you know Pike?'

'Do you know a man called Trunky? He's a lieutenant somewhere . . .'

'Are you going back to France soon?'

'Want anybody to come with you?'

'I hope to transfer to the Royal Flying Corps . . .' Arch began, the first words he had so far uttered.

'That's *your* young man Harry?' somebody called, addressing a fair-haired girl, struggling with a white Mozart wig, like a Dresden doll.

'My boy's an observer. He's in France now. Hasn't been on leave for months. He says its freezing cold up there.'

'They give you warm leather coats, and furs, when you

fly,' explained Arch. 'I envy him. All my life I've longed to fly.'

'Then how did you get stuck in the cavalry?'

'Trying to get my commission. They won't take you without a commission.'

'Where are you stationed then?'

'Out at Foulness Island. It's rotten.'

'Fancy wanting to fly, and ending up on Foulness Island. That's no way to be a hero,' said Mysie carelessly and, brushing aside the flounces and frills of the ballgowns, took his hand. She was dressed by now in a boy's silver knee-breeches, and white stockings, with black buckled shoes, and a silver flowered waistcoat, and topped by a white wig, with sequins. Her powdered face gave her the dissolute paleness of a rakehell.

'Goodbye, Lieutenant.'

There was a chorus of giggling behind him.

'Can we join in your reveille?'

'Don't you dare miss your call, Mysie, you're on in ten.'

The noise subsided as soon as they closed the girls' door behind them. Mysie led the way up another side staircase. She had a child's body, and a way of gliding when she walked, covering the ground indiscernibly, her hands motionless by her side, not swaying left and right. Her hands and her full red mouth were the most expressive part of her, he thought, with that enticing hint of a gap between her teeth, just behind her upper lip. When she turned, her powdered clown's face was almost stern. She spoke rather gravely.

'I know a spot that's quiet. I truly want to talk with you. You weren't cross with me for taking you in the girls' room, were you? We're all such good friends . . . Do tell me you weren't cross.'

'Not cross at all, Mysie, I thought they were a grand crowd.'

'You'll get to know them better, if you can come here more often. We don't tour for months yet.'

She beckoned him into a room overcrowded with property-baskets and sewing-machines.

'Listen! We've got a few minutes yet.'

It clearly belonged to the wardrobe-mistress and her seamstresses, judging from heaps of discarded dresses and shirts, chemises, bodices, draped over every conceivable corner or hook. Arch was somewhat startled to see several brown rabbits eating odd ends of carrots and lettuce leaves, quite cheerfully nibbling, unafraid, and observing the limits of their territory by the door. Arch made as if to close it.

'Oh, no, they never go out. They belong to wardrobe.'

'Why does she keep rabbits in a theatre?'

It was a question that had clearly never bothered Mysie before, and she shook her head. She was perched on a tall basket, unaware of how defenceless and slight she appeared to him, her small feet in their black buckled shoes.

'You look quite like a boy in your knee-breeches.'

'All of us in Number Seventeen are dressed as Petit Mozarts. All the girls in Nineteen are dressed as little Nannerls. And then we do a dance routine to a very nice waltz-number. Mr Chancellor employed somebody from the Empire specially. It's called "Mozart in Paris" – it's a war-number.' She mimicked the French. 'And now, *Mesdames et Messieurs*, I present to you, Le Petit Mozart! Luckily it's my last change in the Second Act, and then we all get back into Red Cross for the walk-down.'

'Walk-down?'

'The Finale. You know, the curtain-calls, the bows. What we call the "who's best".'

Arch still looked baffled.

'When the people clap and cheer. The applause. The tabs. Going home time.'

'Oh, I see.'

'Do you?'

'Well, no. I don't suppose I do.'

From the distance came a regular thudding, rather

monotonous, like a precision barrage of distant gunfire, the fragments of some bouncing tune from the stage. Mysie, perched on the basket, looked him firmly in the eye. It seemed she had come to a decision.

'I did want to see you, David. By the way I can't call you Arch, like the others. I'll call you David, 'til I find something better. I'm pleased you read my little letter, and grateful that you came. Truly I am. There is a reason. You knew, of course, that I was very upset when I wrote. A lot of the time I was crying, and luckily Ma was there, and she kept me going with cups of tea and suchlike. And Apples of course.'

'Apples?'

She laughed, and nervily adjusted a silver strand of her wig.

'Oh, dear old Apples – that's my dog.'

'We have dogs at home – Father-Sir bred English sheepdogs, and used them on the station.'

'Apples isn't any kind of dog, really. He's just a fur rug, with an enormous appetite, but he's great fun when I see my Aunt Jane in the country, and we go rabbiting. What do you mean, "station", do your Ma and Pa live on the railways?'

'No, they come from Australia. Melbourne, in fact. That's where I live.'

'Australia . . . ?'

Mysie's eyes opened very wide, as she attempted to measure so remote a place.

'We have a sheep-station in Australia . . . as well as a house, of course,' he said timidly, not wishing to sound boastful.

'I've never met anybody who came from Australia, You don't speak Australian.'

'We speak English, like you do.'

'But what about your own language?'

'We don't have one. We came from England, you see, but a long time ago. Well, Ireland really. Twenty years anyway. Some came a little before that. Father-Sir, for example.'

'But where did you come from originally? We were taught at school that only black natives actually *came* from Australia. Oh, heavens, you're not convicts, are you?'

But this was only her joke, and just as Arch was attempting to justify himself she grinned broadly. Now she expects me to kiss her, he thought. We've been talking for three whole minutes, and she's taken me here to this funny little room with dresses hanging up, and rabbits on the floor, just to get away from the others, in order for me to give her a cuddle. He walked over to her and put his arms around her. And, just as he was expecting, she responded, by clutching him firmly and impulsively around his waist. But, when he bent to kiss her mouth, she moved her face away, and he could only find her cheek, near the line of wig. The mixture of cheap theatrical scent and spirit-gum both attracted and repelled him.

She spoke quite tartly, he thought, for somebody who had up to that moment so impudently flirted with him.

'No,' she said determinedly, 'you mustn't try to kiss me. I'm not ready to kiss you yet.'

'I thought that was why you wanted to be alone with me . . . I thought you took me to this quiet room just so that I *could* kiss you . . . '

'No, I don't want you to kiss me now,' she said firmly. 'I hate it when people try to kiss me before I'm ready for them. When I'm ready, I'll let you know. I might even kiss you first,' she added mischievously.

'I don't think I want to kiss you very much, while you look like a boy. It would be silly.'

'We think we look much prettier, when we're dressed up as boys. At least, Mr Chancellor always says we are.'

'Who is this Mr Chancellor? I keep hearing his name.'

'Who indeed? I wish I knew. Harold Chancellor. Mister Harold to the back-stage. Mainly he manages us, and produces these comedies. He's a wonderful man, so kind to all of us girls. He looks after us really, takes care

123

of us, sees we don't get up to mischief, and makes sure nobody tries to get up to mischief with us. But basically you know, in spite of what people think, they're very nice, respectable girls.'

'What *do* people think?'

'Well, that we're, you know . . . "fast". Well, being on the stage,' she offered by way of explanation. She nagged at the errant strands of hair in her wig again. More tenderly this time, Arch bent his head towards her, and just as delicately Mysie leant away from him. He stopped and smiled. She shook her head, still holding his hands firmly.

'All right. I promise. I won't try again.'

'You see, David, I don't want you to *have* to try.'

'But can I see you again?'

'I hope so.'

'Soon?'

'Do you go back to camp tonight?'

'Tomorrow morning, by the first train.'

'Outside the stage door, cross the road by the hotel, turn right towards the Haymarket, just a few doors down, there's a little alley – I can't remember what it's called, something or other Row, but it's very tiny, and quite easy to miss. There's a pub there the actors use. It's called The Volunteer but we all call it The Greasy Spoon because we have to eat their rotten fry-ups at matinées. I could meet you there after the second-house. Fengie will explain, if you can't find it. Just ask him for The Greasy. About ten-thirty by the time we've got all this mess off our faces. It can be quite crowded, and a bit smoky, but the actors use it, and at least we're always welcome. You might like to meet some of them, they're a very friendly crowd, it would make a change from all those boring generals you have to be with all the time.'

Before he could answer, a comfortable, elderly woman burst in, out of breath.

'Oh, there you are, Miss Bingham, thank heavens. All the other girls are on-stage nearly, and there's a hue and

124

cry for you all over the theatre. And here you are, sitting on a prop-basket as casual as you please, talking to your young man, and the call-boy's in no end of a tizz. Now hurry down on-stage — Overture and Beginners are nearly done, Heliotrope's on next, and it's the Mozart number any second.'

Mysie cocked an ear to the music coming from downstairs. She knew instinctively the place the orchestra had reached, and was quite unflustered.

'There's no need to panic, Mrs Horberry. And this isn't my young man, but Lieutenant David Gendron, on leave from the Royal Horse Artillery. A very important officer, and my cousin.' And before he could protest she had walked up to him, and whispered in his ear: 'If I agree to see you at the pub afterwards, I only agree on one condition. No kisses.'

Then she leant up to him on the tips of her little black buckled shoes, and kissed him discreetly on the mouth.

'Goodbye, dear Cousin David. Come and visit me again, when you're next on leave.'

And she was gone. Thinking of all the conventional girls he had known back home in Melbourne, and nice Maddy McKay, and some of the polite, well-brought-up English girls he had sat next to at London dinner-parties, sisters and girlfriends of fellow-officers, he realized this was what his brother Chas was always referring to as 'a flirt'. He looked forward immensely to seeing her again.

'Those girls in Seventeen will be the death of me,' Mrs Horberry was grumbling to the rabbits. 'Always wasting time with young men, and bringing them back-stage. In my day, young men wasn't permitted back-stage during the performance. Just because there's a war on, they think they can break the rules. I'll tell Mr Chancellor. Still . . . ' she softened, looking at Arch, ' . . . still if you're going back to the front line . . . From what I've heard from the girls, you young fellows don't have too easy a time of it, so I suppose a bit of enjoyment doesn't do too much harm.'

And, quickly losing interest, she turned her back on him, and began feeding carrot-tops to the rabbits.

Arch found his own way out of the theatre, descending the wooden staircase, following the volume of music as it increased, and bidding a cheerful good-night to Fenge at the stage door. In order to fill in the time before his rendezvous with Mysie later that evening, he thought he might visit the performance. So, remembering the make-believe world of the Mantalinis, the Infant Phenomenon, and Vincent Crummles (a world which, he realized, he had unwittingly penetrated), Arch bought himself a ten-penny seat for the gallery, and the second house.

CHAPTER EIGHT

A Patriotic Comedy

Soldier Boys and Girls! beamed the posters on the front-of-house. 'A Patriotic Comedy!!'

'Early doors, through the sides,' called out the manager.

The overture was playing when Arch reached his seat in the gallery, and the cheerfulness of the people about him, most of them eating and drinking, almost immediately lifted his hopes.

The gentle rat-tat-tat of snare-drums came from the pit-band. The spotlights along the edge of the upper circle dimmed on the curtain (a scene of old Hyde Park, in the time of the Prince Regent, painted with dreadful confidence), and a tingle of anticipation spread from one edge of the crammed gallery to the other. Craning forward, he could just see the glowing orchestra 'coal-box', where the musicians were illuminated by gas-light on their music stands. Right over his head, two arc limelights were ignited, and the acrid tang of magnesium mingled with all the other human smells about him. He leant back into the discomfort of his wooden bench to enjoy the performance, as the curtain rose on a medieval village square.

The subsequent entertainment attempted to tell a rather foolish story about the improprieties involved in mixed bathing, and it was called, quite plainly, 'Seaside'. Because the complicated musical numbers had little to do with the narrative, the action (what there was) moved its location promiscuously, so the audience was able to take in such leaps of the imagination as the old Brighton Chain Pier (with a full complement of bathing-machines, from which the girls issued dressed in saucy costumes) and the same

Elizabethan street which he had seen conjured into life back-stage during the earlier performance; this introduced a dream sequence behind a gauze about romantic love in 'olden-days-gone-by' and, with even more mystification, a transformation scene where the stage suddenly filled with white-wigged composers in satin knee-breeches. The excuse for this odd conversion into canvas-backed Rococo Vienna was justified by the outburst of an impassioned leading lady, addressed out front of the open house:

'Oh! how I wish I was back in *Vienna*, beside the Danube where I might have seen "le petit Mozart", walking in his beloved Vienna Woods.'

This last was given with such dramatic emphasis that a spontaneous round of exuberant applause trod hard on the heels of the last word, and quite covered the opening bars of a jaunty arrangement for saxophone (played by the pit-band) of 'Eine Kleine Nachtmusic'.

Arch sat back in his cramped seat in wonderment: all this was the most astonishing tosh. The musicians, in the confines of the orchestra pit, from his cockpit viewpoint in the gallery, bent their upturned faces towards the light like children before a fire. Their stringy necks stuck out from their stiff collars, reminiscent, thought Arch, of plucked chickens' gizzards. Their appearance was altogether of a seedy nature, belying the initial formality of black-tie and evening-clothes, and the sound their small forces emitted was raucous and jolly. One of them, cupping a delicate fiddle between jowl and collar, more resembled a pug than a violinist, and the conductor was a common, humpty-backed man, who pored over his score with all the unlikely concentration of a college professor. It was Mysie who told him later on that, whenever she was bored in the chorus line, she used to count the bald heads of the pit-orchestra.

At first it had taken Arch a few minutes to isolate the exquisite figure of Mysie from the identical chorus girls surrounding her, but a small characteristic she had, typically, of not looking altogether in quite the same direction as everybody else, singled her out, and the angle of expression in her eyes, turned slightly to the spectators as if to seek their approval, set her apart.

The performance ended in a rambunctious outbreak of cheering and foot-stamping, especially from his perspiring neighbours in the roasted gallery, what with the footlight-fumes rising from below, and the limes up above. This was called in the programme the Grand Finale. None of the entertainment seemed to Arch to have much to do with 'Soldier Boys and Girls', but when the curtain rose for the fifth and last time, and the leading lady had retreated finally into the wings bearing an armful of flowers, a most unexpected event happened.

Arch assumed he must have been dreaming, or, certainly, imagining things that were not there. He could not possibly be seeing them – surely not, and yet, all too evidently he was. Shadows of religious statues replaced the gaudy limelight; on every side, in stately descent were lowered galleries of tattered battle-standards. Then he recognized where he was magically transported – of course, this was the magnificent nave of the grand cathedral of Nôtre-Dame. The orchestra pit (barely illuminated at all now) resembling so many dutiful priests, played music of a devotional theme. Elgar, or the more audacious Parry.

Entirely by himself, on the now deserted stage, seemingly acres in breadth, stood the defiant, muffled figure of one of the ancient Knights of Malta. It was not a character who had appeared before that night, but the spectators seemed to be waiting for him. He was a mingling of the supremely noble and the faintly absurd – the fine white hair, and the long cloak, deep-collared, with its Hospitaller's Cross embellishing the black velvet drape about the arm, the arrogant posture, all these were grand; the martial music, the impressive shadows, above all the romantic evocation of an ancient cathedral, these, too, added to the sonority of the occasion; but there was something about the figure's actual face, a quizzical lift to the eyebrows, perhaps themselves slightly puffed, hence idiotic, and an impish twinkle in the eyes, lined with blue shadow, and red pips at the corner of the eyelids, which could not help but appear ridiculous – as if this quixotic figure, affecting gravity, was, on inspection, merely a kind of pantomime clown in mufti.

His voice, although resonant and sombre enough, was somehow too vibrant to be taken seriously. Beneath the eloquent tone and occasional selective gestures, the sound of a snare-drum could be heard playing Taps.

'A Gentleman of France,' announced the figure with emphasis, and then added by way of explanation: 'a Monologue . . .'

Rather like an auctioneer proposing an object of unusual value. He moved next from one patch of light, which promptly extinguished itself behind him, into a second oasis of flickering chiaroscuro. His fine cheek-bones were modelled by the restless light, but the mischievous glitter in his eyes shone out more discernibly than before. The announcement of the monologue succeeded, however, in hushing the excited house, and Arch sensed his neighbours prickling with anticipation, as the poem progressed. It was easily listened to, he felt, and was well spoken with quiet but slightly forced dignity. The story, for it was indeed a narrative which the cloaked knight unfolded, told of a happy young girl in a fourteenth-century Carcassone and her virtuous lover, evidently the 'Gentleman of France' of the title.

The last verse of this tragic story was emphasized by a gradual crescendo from the orchestra pit and, in a fanciful effect of the light, the tattered battle-honours were tinted with a golden glow, as if the evening sun had set dramatically behind them. The shrouded figure of the monologuist, no longer gesturing, lowered his voice by an octave:

> With muffled drums and measured tread,
> Back they brought their captain, *dead*,
> The chivalry of France.
> [Here all music ceased.]

In quiet convent walls dwells she,
So pure of face, so sad of glance,
She loved, for all the world to see,
[a pause of interminable length]
. . . A gentleman of France.

The snare-drummer paused over his instrument, head
bowed, like a man in mourning . . .

In the silence with which the poem ended, Arch heard
unequivocally the sound of snuffling and whimpering. He
had thought the poem effective, but untrue. Then there
was a fusillade of applause and even cheers, as the curtain
slowly, slowly descended, effacing first the head and
shoulders, then the cloak, finally the emblem of the Silver
Cross of St John as it swept completely to the floor. For
the first time that evening his neighbour at his right hand,
a dwarfish woman with an oversized hat, and breath that
smelt heavily of German sausage, turned to him. Her eyes
were rimmed with tears:

'Oh, I do love to hear that Mr Chancellor so – the
sweetness of his voice – I could listen to it all night long, I
really could!' and she blew her nose loudly, as the limes
splashed the curtain.

So this was the celebrated Mr Chancellor he had heard
about formerly from Mysie. He who was in command of
this touring engagement. Certainly, in spite of the rather
exaggerated manner, there was fine talent there; and Arch
respected the authority with which the solitary figure had
silenced so large an unruly public. But the entertainment
was not quite at an end. Or, if the entertainment was,
there were still further distractions in store. As the curtain
rose, unfolding the bright illumination, the large expanse
of the stage populated by one miniature man, an effect
carefully sought after by a skilful manager, the house rose
to him, and more flowers landed at his feet than ever
assailed a prima donna. Gratefully, with the right hand
positioned decently over his heart, Mr Chancellor bowed
to the boxes on each side of him (both unoccupied), and

to the applauding mass of public in the three-shilling stalls and dress circle. Then he stepped forward, and extending his right hand clear of the Maltese cloak besought, and instantly won, silence.

'Ladies and gentlemen . . . Young ladies and young gentleman . . .'

This was clearly a familiar form of address, and a further round of applause was forthcoming and, in the same way, hushed.

'This little monologue, often repeated before you by way of appeasing the public demand, is not only my own way of expressing on behalf of us all our deeply felt gratitude for your enthusiasm at tonight's little show, but also to remind us all . . . and I mean just as much ourselves up here, among the magic of the floats' – and he beamed genially towards the gas-lights at his feet – 'as those of you in the stalls and the royal circle, the amphitheatre, and yes' – looking upwards – 'our dear friends up in the gallery – to remind us all, dear hearts, of the boys we know and love who spend their days far from the cheery companionship we have enjoyed tonight, but in the heroic camaraderie of the front line. Whose local music-hall is a block-house, whose orchestra pit is a dismal slit-trench, whose little band is the sound of whizz-bangs, and weepers, and whose stage-illuminations are Very lights and Artillery flares.'

Chancellor seemed to be in full flow.

'In their fellowship of the heart, they have precious advantages which are concealed from ourselves at home. They enjoy the spirit of discomforts shared.'

Arch felt the old toughs in the line shared a little more than that. But, before Mr Chancellor could resume, a sympathetic ripple of applause echoed around the stalls.

'The army wants seventy divisions. You've heard Lord Kitchener's request. All volunteers. The British Expeditionary Force wants reinforcements, and it wants them now. So, let me address myself to those of you in the audience who have enjoyed themselves here tonight, and are single men. Is *anyone* proud of you? Are *you* doing *your* bit? And if you are a young man who goes home alone to a nice little house in Mill Hill, or Wimbledon Common, have you a *reason*, or only an *excuse*? There are three kinds of people in our war-torn world today. Those who hear the Call and *Obey*. Those who hear the Call and *Delay*. And there are the Others.'

From the stalls below in the darkness there rose up a comfortable rumble of laughter, and another outburst of approving applause. Encouraged, the actor enthusiastically elaborated his theme:

'I invite you all, in the years ahead, to ask yourselves in silence where you sit, how will you answer the great question: "Daddy, what did you do in the Kaiser's War?"' He moved one step closer to the stalls, and looked down into them.

'To those of you sitting by their sides, their wives and sweethearts . . . Is he to hang his head in shame because *you* won't let him go?' He lifted his head into the limelight. 'Young women, sitting here in front of us, you, in the circle, is your best boy wearing khaki? If not, shouldn't he be? If he does not think his King is worth fighting for – do you think he is worth *you*?'

Arch felt relieved to be dressed in uniform.

'If your young man neglects his duty to his country, the time may come when he will neglect *you*. Think it over – and ask him to JOIN THE ARMY TODAY!'

And, as he spoke the final words of exhortation, the old manager extended his arms outward to embrace not just the overcrowded auditorium but far more, the whole of London, roaring outside; behind him in place of the tattered standards on each side ascending firm and confident, there appeared – rising out of a trap-door upstage, like the sun – a golden burst of Imperial flags, their gaudy tassels hanging down, the standards of the Allied Nations. The actor then established himself in the centre of the stage, as the ovation which greeted this dazzling stage-effect died down, and, gesturing with a ghostly hand for the audience's attention, began to speak again; underneath his

133

voice, the three violins and banjo in the pit-band played a skeletal variation of 'Tipperary'. Then the girls (Mysie among them) re-entered as VADs in uniform and a column of six skinny children, dressed in scarlet, with miniature bearskins, to represent the Grenadier Guards, marched imperfectly across the stage. In place of rifles on their shoulders each carried a diminutive Union Jack, except for their miniature officer, who held upright, not a sword, but a defiant placard, which contained these five words: 'Our Dad's at the Front!'

The actor – with a gesture of classical reverence, offering them the freedom of the stage – turned back to the public, and spoke to an imaginary person in the middle stalls, as if singling him out: the drum beat its familiar rallentando.

> How will you fare, sonny, how will you fare,
>   In the far-off winter night,
> When you sit by the fire in an old man's chair
>   And your neighbours talk of the fight?
> Will you slink away, as it were from a blow,
>   Your old head shamed and bent?
> Or say, 'I was not with the first to go,
>   But I went, thank God, I went'?

The sunburst behind the flags glowed an even deeper red, and as if by magic the standards on their masts lowered their heads in humble salute. As the orchestra lifted in crescendo, the woodwinds playing the Irish fife and piccolo with vigour, the musicians standing at the conductor's behest, the play-actor bending forward to urge the audience to join in the chorus of 'Tipperary', suddenly, in the very act of rising, a voice in the gallery not many seats behind Arch, yelled out raucously:

'Why don't you go out yourself, Chancellor . . . !'

'You weak-withered old ram,' added a second voice tight on the heels of the first.

There was a dismayed hubbub of shushing and cries of 'Shame!', and the fat woman next to him said audibly: 'Oh, dear God in Heaven, it's those rotten Irish . . . '

The orchestra, shaken, slithered to a halt, and seizing the opportunity in the silence the same voice – it was true, there was a strong idiom of a County Cork accent – yelled out again:

'I'm talking to you, you long-haired intellectual! Why don't you go out yourself, Chancellor, if you're so enthusiastic . . . '

To Arch's surprise, and unashamed delight, the actor walked to the edge of the footlights and stared up at the anonymous gallery, shielding his eyes dramatically from the limes with his half-raised cloak.

'Now lads, you know I'd be out there with you, if it wasn't for the old leg . . . '

Arch was by now enjoying himself thoroughly, a great deal more if truth be told than during the performance, and he felt himself taking part in a splendid, improvised London ritual; although around him there was consternation. This was barnstorming of the first order. The heckler in the Gods was warming up:

'There's a hundred thousand Irish joined British colours and you've got an internment camp for Sinn Feiners erected there in Bala, Wales, putting men away without trial . . . '

'Directly contradicting the Defence Regulations . . . '

The heckler had produced a ginger-haired compatriot sitting beside him, who, while supporting his friend, rationed himself to providing the pedantic details of the issue. Down in the stalls there was a fair degree of muddle, the three-and-sixpennies already reaching for their top hats and fallen programmes, and the blinded actor trying without any success to locate at least the direction from where his tormentor was shouting:

'You're a rogue and a vagabond, Chancellor, I'll say that for you. You're very eager to hand the stuff out, but not so keen on volunteering yourself . . . '

This was entertainment indeed for a winter's night.

A large shape in rough moleskins, a row in front of Arch, stood up, blocking for a moment the stage-light before him:

135

'Why don't you rotten Paddylanders shut your rag-boxes!'

A further voice, rather elegant, and Belgrave Square, came to the defence of the two Irishmen, from the other side of the upper circle:

'Now then, they've got a perfect right to speak – they're good Inniskillen men . . .'

'Get orf with yer 'alf-crown voice!' came the withering reply from the obscure and aggressive shape.

'Wonderful to see our boys of the service up there enjoying themselves,' said the play-actor from the forestage, not having altogether heard distinctly, or understood the drift of the argument.

'Free the Sinn Fein boys that you have illegally interned in Frongoch Camp in Bala, Wales!'

'Men of Ireland,' shouted the lonely figure on stage, by now hopelessly adrift as to the actual contention raging up above on every side, 'the safety of your homes, the sanctity of your churches, the honour of your women, can only be secured by defeating the Germans in Flanders . . . Join the army today, and prove that through your blood flows the Irish blood which made the traditional fighting Irish famous throughout the world . . .'

And the rest was drowned by an outburst of guffaws and abuse.

'Balls off, Chancellor, you old faker,' called out the sprightlier of the two soldiers.

The lamps faded, and the stage-figure groped in darkness towards a faint candle-glow from the wings. Then the curtain folds entangled with the cloak of his retreating figure, and in an uproar the lights of the auditorium slowly went up.

The gilt cupids and Ariadnes, whose naked blushes had been hidden so discreetly in the dark, as the chandeliers revealed their charms stood transfixed in all their shameful vulgarity.

CHAPTER NINE

Mr Chancellor

'Inspiring house – cathedrals of laughter – a tidal-wave of merriment,' mouthed the face half-buried in a brimming jug of grey froth.

Whether he had credulously misunderstood the interruption, or whether he was rather hard of hearing, it was evident, when Arch later met Chancellor face to face in the public house, that something of the same confusion prevailed with him. Mysie was still in the turmoil of Dressing-Room Seventeen, but Mr Chancellor included him like an old familiar:

'Marvellously encouraging – the reaction from those boys in the service, way up in the gallery. It does me so much good, my hearts, when I feel The Word comes across. One worries about it sometimes, you know. I mean it hardly counts as legitimate comedy in the show, does it?'

They were standing close to the snug bar of The Volunteer in the habitual corner Chancellor occupied after the evening show. The saloon was crowded with late-hour drinkers, some of the company from the theatre, and some rather muddled French sailors from the Port of London.

Extending his right-hand, with an amiable 'Do I know you, sir? I'm glad you enjoyed my front-cloth number,' Chancellor involved the young officer in both the intimacy and the jargon at the same time. 'It's an effective little piece; now let us both imbibe a flagon of the Greasy Spoon's coolest huffcap.'

Seizing Arch eagerly by the arm, the distinguished

137

actor-manager, no less flamboyant for the replacement of his Maltese cloak by an overcoat of an unpoetic beige, greeted him effusively as somebody he had met on a previous occasion. 'How wonderful to see you again, among our little ensemble, dear heart!' And promptly ordered up a tankard of black Old Ale, which he recommended as 'the local brand of warm piss' and thrust into his hand.

'Octave, draw me a pint of owl's water!' he winked to the servant behind the bar, and then, once it had arrived, swimming on a drenched tray, with a pretended splutter: 'Potman! Take away this budgie's void. Remove this fraudulent bats' pizzle.'

Chancellor's warm, unexpected personality, soon attracted around him a cheerful circle of hangers-on, whom he alternately entertained, harangued, or abused, in a high-spirited fashion. His face, Arch observed, still wore that rather droll expression, as of a circus clown's wiped clean of its greasepoint, thus adding a comic suggestion to almost everything he said, whether aiming for a humorous effect or not. Chancellor's face looked as if it was made up, even when it wasn't. There was still a greasy line around his forehead detectable just under the hair, and that looked to be false. Among the company, it was known as 'Chancellor's rug'. Here in the snug the actor-manager was at ease, secure in his friends, in his authority, and in a flood-tide of eloquence. His voice, deep and commanding within the gas-lights, was sharp and high-pitched beyond them, attracting the ear of the crowded public bar:

'Celebrating the thirty-sixth year of inconstant employment in the business, since starting out "play-as-cast" in '79 . . .'

He was in mid-flow already, engaged in a debate with a small character man, whose white goatee-beard and fussy bow-tie gave him the look of a French schoolmaster. And all about him, muzzy or sober, the enchanted circle laughed as a further round of drinks was ordered across the bar. He liked distributing, but not necessarily paying for, largesse. For greater emphasis, Chancellor's hook-like hand perched affectionately, but firmly, on the officer's shoulder-bone.

'Stay to hand, dear fellow-student, the night is yet youthful, and we'll teach you to drink deep 'ere you depart . . . And ginger shall be hot in the mouth, too!'

Mysie who had by now arrived with a girlfrend from Dressing-Room Seventeen claimed special friendship with Arch, stepped close to him and tucked her hand through his arm. Chancellor smelt the top of the officer's beer.

'What's this you're drinking,' pointing to his tankard, 'sow's ullage?'

'Now, now, Mr Chancellor, don't you mock our brave boys . . .'

'Out upon you, for an arrant bawd!' exploded the old actor. 'You peevish, self-willed harlot . . . !' and then, placing his right hand across his heart, 'Mock them, dear little Mysie, what are you talking about?' he asked in pretended horror, looking about for reassurance. 'Mock our wonderful young boys?' he gasped. 'Could you believe me capable of such a thing, my dear?' Without waiting for a reply he rushed on. 'No, of course you couldn't.' And calling to the barmaid bent over the beer-handles ordered: 'A full-flagon of Father Whoreson for the gallant foot-soldier.'

And then, to delight his audience, affecting a theatrical pose of make-believe, he turned to the barman, laconically wiping a glass on a dirty napkin.

'God gi' thee good-den, honest Squire, wilt thou exchange for a particle of honest profit a modicum of civility and attention!'

Unsmilingly, the barman replied: 'Fourteen shillings to you, Mr Chancellor, counting the oysters and beer on Friday night.'

'How sharper than a serpent's tooth it is, to have a thankless potman,' Chancellor grimaced, opening a small, dirty purse, and extracting the precise sum. Adding rather ostentatiously a threepenny piece, and shaking hands with his immediate circle, gesturing largesse to a non-existent gallery and with a 'Goodbye, hearts!', Chancellor left the crowded room backwards, with the air of a great emperor abdicating his throne. Indeed, the room, still thronged with enthusiastic drinkers, seemed that bit the quieter from his departure, and more shadowy. One or two bystanders had actually applauded.

Mysie steered Arch away from the main bar to a quieter table in the snug.

'He's a wonderful man, Mr Chancellor, and such a laugh in the pub – I can't think how he gets the energy. He's always working us to death, and himself too, I shouldn't wonder.'

One of the plain wooden Jacob chairs was already occupied by Mysie's best friend from the theatre.

'This is my friend, Flee,' she said, introducing the small-boned, dark-haired girl, whose large brown eyes Arch saw in the pub lights were heavily made-up.

'Is that really your name?' asked Arch politely. 'I mean, Flea, like the insect?'

'Of course not. Not Flea. It's Flee-ee! Felicity properly, but you know the Theatre. Mysie started it, and it stuck.'

'This is my friend, Arch Gendron, I call him David,' Mysie said.

'Tickled pink,' said Flee, with a sharp smile. It was obviously a saying from Room Seventeen.

Arch asked the girls what they were drinking, and after a few moments returned from a conspiratorial hatch-window with two schooners of Old Brown and Gold.

'It's nice and cosy here, isn't it?' said Mysie, agreeably. 'Better than the saloon.'

It *was* rather cosy, he agreed, sitting down with two attractive girls who drank strong sherry and smoked cigarettes.

'Do you girls always come here after the show?' Arch enquired, and Brown-eyes answered for them both:

'Most evenings. Unless we get invited out, don't we, Mice?'

'Well it's generally the whole gang of us. And it's nice, too, to have a place we can meet our boys when they're on leave.'

'Have you got a boy of your own then, Flee?' enquired Arch.

She coloured slightly and looked down at her sherry glass, circling the rim with her forefinger until it whistled.

'Oh yes,' she answered softly, 'he's out with the cavalry in France. We write every week.'

'I've got a brother in France with the cavalry. He's a lieutenant.'

'Might be in the same regiment – mustn't say where though!' and they both laughed. 'You never know, do you?'

'Somewhere in France is all they say,' added Mysie, 'never more than that.'

'Well, here's to both of them,' and Arch lifted his glass.

'My boy used to be in the company, but when it started he enlisted right away. He's an officer now,' said Flee.

'But you're not engaged?'

'Well, not strictly speaking, no. But in a sort of way, more or less, yes . . . ' Brown-eyes did not sound very convinced.

Mysie answered for her: 'There's an understanding, isn't there, Flee?'

'Oh, that, definitely, yes.'

There was a small moment of quietness between them and an outburst of raucous singing swept into the snug. It was getting late and loud. Mysie spoke up, as if gathering her courage:

'Flee's lonely, David. So if you've a nice friend in the

141

Horse Artillery, we could make up a four one evening after the show.'

Flee's brown eyes stared at Arch with the round solemnity of a child lying over a broken toy.

'Is *he* in the company also?' Arch enquired, looking over to the further bar, beyond where the French sailors were involved now in some kind of fumbling dance. By himself, on a bar-stool, sat a young man, conspicuously apart, with tense shoulders, taking rapid sips from his beer, an object of unease in a roomful of high spirits and warm humour.

'Oh, Wilbraham,' answered Mysie, resignedly, as if in explanation.

'He says he has lung-trouble,' said Flee, 'but it doesn't seem to stop him dancing.'

'Or drinking,' added Arch, noting a semicircle of spirits-glasses.

Arch felt a twinge of danger from this young man, for all his aloofness. He seemed to have inside him a kind of rage, bottled up, and with difficulty stoppered; even where he sat by the bar, there was this space all round him, an impression of panic in a crowded room.

The two girls sat drinking quietly, leaning close, whispering some little intimacy, and separating with a grave nod. Arch noticed the first lines of anxiety beneath Flee's large eyes, and close to her brow, on the left side, a short circular scar. Flee looked respectable enough, even homely, but something in her mouth and brown stare betrayed her. Yes, thought Arch, she *is* available. But to whom? To him? Arch was unconvinced this so-called cavalryman even existed. He looked at Mysie too, giggling over some secret to her friend, and wondered what romance lay in her life, eager to be betrayed. Or perhaps the girls were just lonely, in the same way he was. Loneliness was an aspect of love, neither very important, nor very passionate, but always there. In any event, a cautious assignation had been made and, politely shaking hands, Flee rose and left the bar.

'If you bring any officer friends to the show next time, try not to forget me!' she said, and to the potman, an old familiar, 'To-byee, Harold, and God bless.'

'Now we're by ourselves, David, there's something I would wish to explain to you.'

Mysie's face was grave as if she was about to tell an unhappy fortune from the beer-stains.

'Your friend Felicity seems a nice girl,' Arch said, not entirely certain he wanted Mysie in a serious vain at this particular moment.

'Her life has not been very easy,' explained Mysie, 'her mother and father died when she was young, and Flee was brought up as an orphan by an aunt who kept a little school in the country. When she was sixteen she ran away with one of the local farmer's boys and they were happy. Going to be married, probably, but the war came on and he went out early. And was killed at First Ypres. And it makes her sad.'

'And she feels lonely now?' he asked lamely.

'Of course, and she's not the only one. None of us in Seventeen are much good without somebody to think of or care about or write to. There's not too much point in doing all those idiotic things Chancellor makes us do, even though *he* believes in them.'

'They were heckling up in the gallery tonight, you know. Mr Chancellor didn't seem to get the hang of it.'

'Oh, they often do – I don't think he pays too much attention to how the public react. Just as long as they respond. He's in a dream-world, most of the time, our Mr Chancellor. Besides, he's half-deaf. Just as well.'

'What is it you wanted to tell me?'

'Something between the two of us. A secret thing.'

There was a slight disturbance behind Mysie's shoulder; one of the French sailors had deteriorated from exuberance to aggression, and Harold the potman was attempting with difficulty to extricate him from the public bar. There was a fracas of sorts. The nervy young actor called Wilbraham came over and, ignoring Arch totally, asked Mysie if she was thinking of going home. The muscles at the side of his jaw flicked stubbornly, like those of a shy horse.

'Can't you see I'm talking to a friend of mine at the moment?'

'Well, when you've finished talking to your friend — there's a lot of drunks about, and I think you should go back home with somebody.'

'Perhaps this officer will escort me — let me introduce you.'

And, taking his sleeve, Mysie attempted to turn the young man round to face Arch.

'This is Wilbraham, he's the juvenile from the company; I'd like you to say hallo to Lieutenant Gendron of the RHA, soon to be posted to the Flying Corps.'

But the attempt at friendship was a failure, and the tense young actor, ignoring the other man seated at the table, not even turning to acknowledge him, shoved his way through the back bar. Mysie shrugged, not thinking the incident of importance: 'Poor Wilbraham, he's always upset over something. He's so tense and nervous. The truth is, he has a soft spot for me, and he gets jealous.'

For the second time, Arch felt that intuitive twinge of unease over this difficult and taut young man.

The barman called out 'Time' and swung a ship's bell.

'This secret you have for me . . . It'd better be quick, as they've called Time now . . . '

'There's nothing so important about it. But it is special.'

'To do with you?'

'Perhaps to do with both of us, if you'll accept it.'

'Of course I will. Any secret is safe with me. Besides, I mix in the army world: your world of the theatre is quite different.'

'Give me your hands then.'

He laid his hands on the table in front of her, and Mysie lowered her voice as one of the potmen came over to clear their glasses. She placed her hands on his.

'I wrote to you because I wanted to. I needed a friend. Not for any other reason. Harry Legge was very close to me, and he looked after me. And, when he was on leave, I looked after him. But, before him, there was somebody else too. Like my friend Felicity – and we were meant to get married. But I lost him, too. Ashley, he was called. Ashley. He was with the East Surreys. It was night patrol. Wiring. He was shot in the face.'

Arch was about to sympathize, but she cut him firmly short.

'No, it isn't for that I told you. It's been something I've had to understand or forget, or pretend never happened. But the thing is, I cannot be alone now, I just can't be. And the girls in the theatre, well, as I wrote to you, they don't understand other people's problems. Flee does, but she's in the same boat as me. Flee has had the same rotten things to put up with. I think we are both very lonely. Lonely for life, if you can understand me.'

'Yes, of course, I *do* understand.'

The bar had emptied entirely by now, and the potmen were stacking chairs noisily on top of the iron tables, to leave the floor clear for sanding and sweeping, but no attempt was made to eject them. The landlord passed them with a broad conspiratorial wink. Unmusical singing from a distant street filtered through the curtained windows. 'One of these days you think you love a brunette . . .'

'I suppose,' sighed Mysie, 'at other times, there was a better way of doing things, there was more time. I've always liked you – I liked you this afternoon, you were a surprise, and I was glad I wrote that stupid letter . . . When I met you that night at the Carlyle Club, I liked you. David, forgive me for telling you, but I knew Harry was going to die – I don't know how, don't ask me, but he knew also. You don't have to mention these things. Do I make sense to you at all?'

'Some. Not pleasant sense – but some. Yes.'

'Oh, dear.' Mysie looked guiltily down at her beer-glass. 'Now I've made you dull.'

'No, go on, *please*. You haven't made me dull.'

'I would hate myself if I gave you the wrong impression. It's friendship I'm talking of. Not other things, although I know these days other things take place. If there is such a thing as love, it will have to wait until this war is ended. I do not think I can bear to love any more. Friendship is much safer and much better. Don't you think? That was my secret, anyway. Can you keep my secret?'

'I would like to share it with you, Mysie. I should enjoy being your friend very much, Will you let me accompany you to your home? I don't have any girl of my own so far, if you want to know.'

As an afterthought, she said: 'Are you always known as David? It doesn't terribly suit you.'

'That's what the other chaps call me. It was my brothers called me Arch at home. It seemed to stick.'

'What's your middle name?'

'Well, Archibald, but don't get any ideas that I'm called Art, or Archie, for that matter . . .'

Mysie thought for a second, mouthing his initials together and pronouncing them in different ways to herself; then she asked: 'Would you mind if I called you Dazzle?'

'Not terribly. I might if you said it in front of my commanding officer!'

She roared with laughter, too sudden a laugh, he thought, too noisy. But full of life, certainly.

'So we are going to be friends then?'

'It looks as if we are.'

'Yes, that's what you look like to me. Dazzle.'

Mysie clapped her hands in delight. He noticed, not for the first time, that her laugh was quite delightfully coarse. She could appear impudent and virginal at the same moment.

'I knew we would end up friends. You know, it's so strange but the people you like for ever, and the people you like most of all, are nearly always the ones you like straight away.'

'That seems unfair.'

'I know, but it's true – fairness doesn't enter into it. That and so many other things.'

Full of life, he thought. Yes, that was it, beautiful, delicate, flirtatious, and coarse.

The landlord at the far end of the saloon bar began to turn down the gas-lights. The older of the two potmen scattered a handful of sawdust on the floor near them.

'Now we really *are* unwelcome, Mysie, and this time I'll make sure you get home safely. Besides, that dreadful Wilbraham fellow may still be hovering outside, or those drunk sailors.'

Arch helped her on with her coat, and together they faced the stern gust of cold air as the door swung open.

'Good luck, girlie,' called the landlord, 'and you too, young man, all the luck you need. And take care of her, she's precious, our little Mysie.'

'God bless, Harold. See you tomorrow night.'

'If we're still here, Mysie. And good night to you, sir.'

Mysie lived in the old quarter of Notting Hill Gate, in one of the cobbled lanes not far from the farm, and near the gate itself, and as the growler made its way along the wide thoroughfare, beyond Bayswater and the silent park, the lateness of the hour brought one or two curious glances from muffled passers-by.

Mysie curled herself in her brown cloak and leant her head securely against Arch's shoulder. They remained happily in silence for the greater part of the journey, the sound of the wheels cutting against the uneven surface until they reached the quieter sandy paths near the toll gate. Shadows of the fretworked branches of wintry trees flickered across their faces, as the cab passed each gas-lamp. Flares outside the Clarendon Hotel emblazoned the interior of the growler with momentary light.

'Tell me about the flying, Dazzle,' asked Mysie. 'Tell me why you want to join the Flying Corps.'

'All my life, Mysie, I've wanted to fly. There was this

schoolfriend of mine who invented a machine. Oggie. He started me off somehow – it was like a bug. I think it must be the single most wonderful thing in the world, flying, finer than scoring a hundred runs at the Melbourne Cricket Ground. Or swimming in the Pacific back home.'

'Isn't that terribly dangerous?'

'It is sometimes. When it isn't we try to make it so. You get smashed up and scratched on the shingle, and sometimes, when you're lying flat, another wave will topple over you, like a brick wall, just when you're at your most defenceless, and flatten you, and take all the breath out of your body. And that's how I think it must be in the sky – the earth and clouds all upside-down and your kidneys inside out, and your brain spinning, and most of your stomach inside your mouth, and your eyes full of water, and a great rushing noise in your ears . . . that's what I think it must be like when you fly.'

'But the enemy? The enemy up in the sky with you?'

'The sea was the enemy there, and always so much mightier than yourself. But I never think of an enemy, Mysie. The Hun, you mean. I suppose you'd treat him like a fox, watching for you in the sun, watchful and sly and crafty, and always waiting for you. I suppose it's that I'm after, a feeling of danger. A menace. A death-adder. Something that keeps you bright . . .'

'So you have this feeling of loneliness too. And an urge to run towards it.'

'I have my brothers, whom I love, and my friends. And there's always Father-Sir, and Mother, and old Grimp, my grandfather, even though they are so far away, and I love them too. But, yes, I do feel what you say in a strange way. It's hard for me to describe it. My aloneness brings me a sense of danger, I suppose.'

Abruptly she pulled away from him, watching him at intervals as the shafted light switched on and off his face, long periods of shadow, fleeting impulses of light. He worried that she had grown suddenly afraid of him, and withdrawn.

148

'Have I frightened you with what I said, Mysie? I never meant to scare you, you least of all. You seem to have gone away from me for a minute.'

Her voice was reassuring and calm. How slight she appeared inside the cab.

'No, Dazzle. Not at all scared. The opposite, for once. I want to see your face.'

And, to stare at him more intently, she framed his cheeks between her hands, ungloved, and slightly chill. She felt – and it made her cold in her blood to feel it – that she had ceased now to be his friend, and never could be such a person again.

'You are different from anyone I have ever met. Anyone I have ever seen. I think you are the first man I have known who has no fear. Everybody else I've known has been brave, loyal, and full of hope. And life. But they all knew fear, at some stage, and you are different from them.'

'Mysie,' he answered her gravely, 'I have not had to face fear.'

The growler turned neatly into Linden Gardens and drew up outside a grey-faced lodging-house. In the past, it had advertised 'Theatrical lodgings. Always reasonable terms to the profession.' The landlady had known the Business, and enjoyed a long acquaintance with Mysie's Ma.

'I'd ask you in, Dazzle, but it's too late now, and I share the bedroom with my Ma. And Mrs Mildred is so respectable. Will you take the cabby back again?'

'No, I want to talk to you a little longer.' He leant towards her.

'But not to kiss. It isn't the time yet. But I like you, Dazzle, and I will see you again. You have only to come to the stage door, and ask old Fenge. He knows you now. And I want you to meet Flee again, and Chancellor, and meet my dear Ma, who's wonderful, and Apples, my dog. There'll be so much for you to do in London, on your next leave, and it will be something I can look forward to.

149

It's wrong, I'm sure, to talk about oneself, and one's good points, if there are any: but I'll tell you one thing about myself which everybody says, and that is, you'll never have a more loyal, more trusting girl than your Mysie, if you make a friend of me. And I don't think there's anything more important than that. Do you?'

The jarvey's loud voice, uncomfortably intimate, broke in on them from the jump-seat.

''Ere, guv', either kiss the girl, or don't kiss 'er, it's all one to me, but don't sit there all night long, for Gawd's sake: I want to get back to the Garden afore mornin' — I've got me flars to load up . . .'

Mysie giggled, hand up to mouth and Arch was forced to smile also, thinking how every last detail of their conversation had been so effortlessly overheard. With a formal gesture, half-mocking, Mysie held out one hand for him to take, pressed it, and, opening the cab door with her other hand, was gone. At her doorstep she turned and waved and in a second had disappeared inside. The growler turned in the road, and clattered eagerly towards the toll gate. Horses, as well as their masters, know the fastest way home. Arch, sinking back in the cushions, felt the aftermath of the peace Mysie had spread throughout the journey, for the whole evening, and dozed lightly until the jarvey brought him to the gates of the Carlyle Club.

A faint glimmer of dawn, no more than a trace, brushed the streets, and out of the market a familiar pungent breeze of vegetables flavoured the night. It was coarse and heartening, and reminded him of Mysie's laugh.

As he ascended the club steps he looked up and above the roofs of Covent Garden. To the west the sky was black, but seared by red clouds, as if beneath them a fire was blazing with unearthly rage.

PART THREE

CHAPTER TEN

Peckwater Barracks

In a firm hand on a blank sheet of paper Arch inscribed the first entry of the journal he intended to keep up, every day, for a few minutes at least, in an old aircraft log-book:

> March 16th 1915
> Reported at Oxford for training, Royal Flying Corps.
> Quartered at Christ Church. Rooms in Peckwater.
> Good quarters and good Mess.

The university was deserted in those days, or so it appeared to him. Monastic life went on, privately among the more ancient professors, and the college servants, but nowhere was there any sign of young men, on tow-path and playing-field, or noisily breaking through the quad-rangles. Lieutenant Gendron and his fellow-officers were billeted in Peckwater Quad, to his eyes a sunless block of sombre stone on the east wing of the college. But his rooms, which he shared with a brother-officer from the Royal Garrison Artillery (the Flying Corps tried to keep the regiments together), were snug in a weary run-down way, and a decrepit manservant had done his best to heat the place by lighting a faltering fireplace.

The mattresses were rolled up on the iron bedsteads to air, and it seemed that the military had done its best to add a kind of cheer to the spartan existence, formerly tolerated by scholars but unacceptable to officers. Faded engravings by Hogarth and Gillray stained the walls, there was a Nollekens bust under the window, and the carpets were trodden down at the edges and stained with wine and tea. Smells of ancient cooking penetrated the rooms and, when Arch threw open the windows to invite in the fresh March air, a damp mist from the River Cherwell filtered through behind the grey curtains.

The second officer, in riding-breeches and stockinged feet, introduced himself as Harold Skilbeck, recently garrisoned at Mortlake, against Zeppelin attacks. He had not long ago left Sedbergh, 'a God-awful place', he added with some emphasis.

A row of Latin grammars and several other classical textbooks, Herodotus, Pliny, Livy, upheld the scholarly interests of the previous resident, and a worn Burke's Peerage propping up a doorway gave a clue to his style. There was an armorial emblem in the butler's pantry, and a handful of monogrammed silver forks. Certainly the college scouts regarded the invasion of the military with dejection. The staircase servant assigned to look after Gendron and Skilbeck was a despondent figure, to be addressed as Civil, with a face so permanently moist that it looked sometimes as if he threatened to melt altogether. His temperament was as liquefying as his appearance, and even the smallest command seemed to bring his eyes to the edge of weeping. After showing the two officers their set of rooms, he asked tearfully: 'Will you two young gents be wanting anythink else, then?'

Arch noted the drip at the end of Civil's nose, courteously inviting permission to drop.

'I don't expect so, Civil,' answered Skilbeck for both of them, looking out at the quadrangle below the window.

'I have my room then, sir, just beneath the staircase, and if you will be needing hot water, or coals or suchlike, you have only to call for me. Tobacco and spirit-wines likewise, sir.'

'We'll get our own hot water, Civil, if you'll just show us where it is . . .'

'Oh, no, sir, that would never please, sir. Hot waters and coalfires is most of me duties, that and bed-making, sir. My former young gentleman, Lord Eu (which he

154

pronounced to rhyme with 'true') 'never did anythink for himself, sir, it's not in college regulations, sir.'

Civil's determination to serve contradicted the extreme misery with which he pursued his task, and Arch did not know whether to feel sorry or grateful, for the modesty of his domestic duties. Certainly as trained soldiers, he and Skilbeck would have preferred by far to look after themselves, but with a tactful nod of his head Skilbeck signified to Arch that they were probably better off accepting his offer.

'Of course, the Welch Regiment's stationed at Jesus College and those young gents ain't so well off as us down here in The House, sir. There never was baths installed, not for the commoners there wasn't, seeing as they're only up eight weeks.'

'Any prospect of such a handsome luxury here?' enquired Skilbeck, without budging from the window-seat. 'A bath wouldn't come amiss before grub.'

'Oh, surely, sir,' said Civil with watery fervour, 'one for this quadrangle, and one for the main quadrangle, and one for New Buildings. Very luxurious, if I may say so. Quite an innovation for College, seeing as how it's done without for five hundred years. Some of the older servants don't hold with it, sir. They was always used to carrying the water up for the young gentlemen so they could have their baths in their rooms. Very comfortable it was, now, with a nice coal fire warming you up.'

'My people always insisted the army was very good about hot baths after drill,' added Skilbeck to Arch, 'so they'll approve . . .'

Civil continued tearfully: 'Lord Eu, God rest him, was very pertic'lar for a bath in front of the fire, after a day out with his beagles, and a well-warmed bottle of claret. Always very partial to that, sir.'

'Where is Aldred Eu now?' enquired Skilbeck. 'I believe he was once at school with my brother.'

Civil visibly reddened.

'Lost at First Ypres, sir, in last year's Michaelmas term,

sir. His lordship went over with the Rifle Brigade, sir. We lost a lot of our young gents that week, sir.' Then he added: 'The same week the Oxford Volunteers paraded on Balliol Cricket Field. Three hundred veterans of the South African war.'

Arch thought for a moment Civil was going to disintegrate entirely, but the older man rallied, and said with a gentle passion, 'Forgive my rude way, sir, but if you was to stand here, sir, where I am now, and to look across, sir, at those windows.'

Arch stood beside him and Skilbeck turned his head idly.

'Well, sir, in all those windows, there's not more than four young men what stood there looking out last summer, that's still alive today. They've all gone. Mostly on the Marne, sir. The lists of German losses was posted regular on Big Tom gate, sir. We used to have a lot of Vons before 1914.'

This did not strike Arch or his companion as a profitable subject to pursue, and tucking a clean shilling slyly into his hand Skilbeck opened the door for Civil, who backed away bearing under one arm a battered set of Latin Glosses.

To celebrate their new sanctuary and toasting a certain camaraderie, Arch and Skilbeck broke open an old bottle they had found of Dolamore's College Claret. The evening light, the last of it, enflamed their glasses. And afterwards, with a half-turn to the empty windows facing them, they lifted their glasses to friends in absentia. A ray of watery sun, which had edged out in the final half-hour before darkness, caught several glass panes opposite, and reflected the bleakest of acknowledgements. Skilbeck tipped his glass. He was a pale reflective figure, spare-framed, fair-haired, resembling an aesthetic Master of Foxhounds.

'I can't pretend Civil fills me with deepest confidence, can you, Arch old man, so here's hoping for ourselves. All the luck of the Irish.'

Later, dining in Hall, Arch was impressed by the dark oak room, the candelabra dripping wax, and the tall portraits of college dignitaries on the walls, dating from indulgent-faced Plantagenets, in their pomp and vanity, to the more austere divines of the present age. These varnished faces bore a racial similarity, he noticed, to the gathering of clergymen and students in their canonicals, and furred gowns, at High Table. Bent over their plates, they muttered together about academic scandals. Secluded in their own world, they paid scant attention to the warrior-élite below them, who in turn grew oddly subdued, not daring to disturb the scholarly praxis; a far cry from their former mess-halls, which resounded to cries and yelps of bravado, ritual sing-songs and idiotic pranks. A solemn Latin grace of some minutes was spoken before and after the dinner, and this further repressed whatever bubbling spirits may have been imminent. No one was in the mood for a bit of bread-throwing, as at the Inns of Court. Before Lights Out, the new Corps cadets trooped informally into the Long Hall, where they were addressed first of all by the College Magisterius, and later by their commanding officer, Major Treadaway, a breezy veteran of the Cape War.

The Magisterius was an old but magnificent divine, renowned among the established clergy for his scholarship concerning St Jerome, and his penetrating authority on the controversies surrounding the Nicene Creed. A Latin Principal of venerable distinction, scrupulous to the last minutiae of ancient Roman rustic life in the colonies, these modern times, and the recent conflicts on the continent of Europe, had left him remote, and his absent-mindedness was notorious both within college walls and in senior academic society. The Magisterius addressed the young officer-trainees with small regard to their comparative absence of classical education, and none at all to their unfamiliarity with Rome. It was his convinced intention, he explained carefully, speaking in pedantic tones, to disregard the turbulent events of the Western

Front and the strenuous energies expended so wastefully in the Ypres Salient, and to embosom instead the fresh intake of youth in the same manner as he would welcome a new generation of undergraduates for Hilary term.

The officers, one after the other, rose to their feet, and in answer to their Latinized names stepped forward obediently and inscribed them in the College Register, as they were pronounced, in Latin. They then bowed, and were bowed to in turn by the gowned masters before they returned to their seats. Each was presented with a violet leather-bound copy of the University Statutes, and instructions in classical Latin that these laws were to be obeyed. The old Master bent over his task, meticulous and precise, carrying out the roll-call without emotion, but once they were all seated again looked round him, staring uncertainly at the light through his half-lenses.

'It is not likely that from this hour we will have a great deal to do with one another. Your duties and mine share little in common weal. I will, however, on behalf of myself, and my distinguished fellow-pedants, and of this ancient House, allow myself one personal word. It is with an ancient language that the lawcourts, school-halls, and temples, as well as garrisons, of this city were honoured by the pacifiers of our barbaric Celtic wilderness. These men and women, far from their homeland, short of stature, dark of face, energetic, resilient, law-abiding, friends of domestic comfort, enemies of refractory pathways, practised their alien accents in public thermal and triclinia, stable and senate, hippodrome and odeum all over a countryside which had long been abandoned to the payment of wergild, mistletoe-worship, ritual sacrifice and tribal war. It was an oppressive landscape not greatly remote from the one in Hither Gaul you are about to confront. The culture, obedience and legality these Latins sought to spread, the land-bridges they struggled to build, the security of an absolute Authority they for a magic moment succeeded in establishing, at its height extended to one-ninth of the Known World – Rome. All of that

158

noble endeavour faltered eventually, and declined – those extended frontiers of pride crumbled and fell away – those legions, eagle-proud, armour-clad, reeled back and retreated, finally withdrew. Walled cities were deserted and men built pig-farms from their stones. But they left behind them, let us never forget, remnants of a legend far more imposing than anything they had wished to achieve in reality. The myth of Rome. A presence more tangible than a hundred years of colonization. Your role today in Flanders, and the lowland continent, is the same as theirs – a challenge against a barbarian horde no more to be admired, no less to be feared. Your possibilities of failure to uphold such ambitions are as equal, as fearsome, as inevitable. Therefore, support the vision of your ancient, stern compatriots, and adopt their austere ideology: *Eheu fugaces ... Ave atque vale ...*'

The effect was electric. There was silence for only a suspended moment, and the seated rows of khaki-clad men thundered their applause, stamping their boots. Not many of them had followed his drift, but the sound was splendid. The Magisterius raised his hand.

'I would like to conclude these few personal reflections of my own, by referring to your consideration these lines of a young gentleman from this House, who was looking forward to devoting himself to the profession of literature. When foreign hostilities began, he joined the University OTC. He served for a year in the Oxfordshire and Buckinghamshire Regiment and went to Belgium in November last year. Walking down a quiet village street, a fragment of stray shell struck him, the wound though slight turned septic and he died aged twenty years. These words, from a poem he wrote in the spring of that same year, may be of comfort to you. They are to me, who has the unhappiness of teaching so many young and splendidly alive gentlemen.'

The rows of faces, eager, unsure, and sometimes tired, stared at the Magisterius, who spoke from memory, without indecision, and holding lightly in each hand the sleeve of his embroidered gown.

'*Anglia Valida in Senectute*,' he announced formally, 'by a former undergraduate of The House.'

> We are old, and worn, and schooled with ills,
> Maybe our road is almost done,
> Maybe we are drawn unto the hills,
> Where rest is, and the setting sun.
>
> A little while and we are gone:
> God knows if it be ours to see
> Again the earliest hoar-frost white
> On the long lawns of Trinity.

There was a silence. Then he added: 'He refers of course to Trinity, Oxford, off the Broad, and its fine gardens. Not to the similarly entitled college in Cambridge, which is quite a different place.'

There came something very like laughter from one corner of the Long Hall, which was not entirely the effect the Magisterius had intended, and in some confusion the old professor left the room to muted applause. Some officers stood in respect, and when they had resettled themselves on the benches the commanding officer rose.

Major Treadaway's message was somewhat different in its point of view.

'It may be all very well for one of these schoolies to give you what he believes is the right sort of address as if you were a riff-raff of students training to be college deans, but you're not – you are all perfectly ordinary young men with a job to do for your country, and looking up to us to teach you how to do it.'

The major – a veteran 3rd Sherwood Forester who had begun in the Cape as a cadet and fought two first-rate wars – had been gassed and wounded on the Mons Canal and won both a DSO and an MC. He looked squarely in front of him as if on a parade-ground before a brigadier-commanding. His single eye, a pale, metallic blue, hardly

160

looked to left or right. His single arm lay along his whipcord breeches. He paused rather dramatically, and poured himself a glass of water.

'And teach you we bloody well will.' He drank one mouthful from the glass, and carefully replaced it. 'The last troop of soldiers quartered here, in this very Hall, were men of a very different stamp, with a tough job of work to do, and they were the men of the New Model Army. Sitting here, like you, more or less where you are now. Christian men of your own age, if not altogether your social class. But, unlike you, just starting out on a new and terribly exciting adventure, these were the battle-stained veterans of Edgehill, Winceby and Roundway Down. Far from being veterans, you men are starting a long trip into the unknown sky. A long trip, and a dangerous one. And you're going to need a lot of courage. A lot of what we in the Flying Corps call "bottom". Bottom may be called old-fashioned, and there's not a man of you here who hasn't heard about it, but it's going to have to see you through a lot of rough work. You are going to be taught on this course how to handle a machine, how to tackle the morse code, and how to fire a Lewis gun. But the one thing you cannot be taught is how to tackle fear. I say this, that if one of you finds out that blue funk has got the best of you, and you are about to buckle under, then think of the other chap. Think of the team. Don't think about yourself and how much of a funk you're in. If three of you fellows meet three Huns in the air – and this is exactly what you are going to do . . . many times . . . if one of you gets in a funk and doesn't do his bit, then he'll let the others down, and not only will you yourself be killed, but all of the others as well. So remember the team. This stuff you read about, and all of this,' (he gestured indifferently at the ribbons on his breast) 'this hero stuff is all very well, but it's a lot of tommy-rot, let me tell you. It's devotion to duty, and to your job, and to the team, and the discipline of that team, that is what it's all about. Now it isn't all work, don't think it is. Play hard, and fight hard, that's what will win the war. Personal glory is no passport to paradise.'

Treadaway stopped gazing at an imaginary distance between the rows of seated recruits, but looked pointedly with glaring eye to his right, almost as if he had suddenly discovered a dirty cap badge previously overlooked.

'I wonder how many of you really think they are going to outlive their own generation.'

Surprisingly his voice was gentler now.

'War is no great adventure, believe me. Most of you will be bored to death or scared to death. But, if war is cruel and pointless and a wicked evil, it's there because it's got to be won, and there's no better use of any man's life than to give it eagerly and efficiently in the cause of stopping this unending slaughter. Whether in the trenches or at sea or in the air. It's a war of men – determined men, strong men, generous men, who give up their own lives for the sake of not only their friends, as the Bible asks us to do, but for the sake of the nation – and weakness and funk has no part of it. And I suggest,' concluded the major, staring out again in his parade-ground fashion, 'that if you think more along those lines, than along the lines suggested by our well-meaning headmaster friend, you'll enjoy a better war.'

And, on those uncomfortable last lines, the major collected hat and gloves and cane, in a pincer-like movement of his left hand, and with a short 'Good luck to you' left the room.

'I assume that's to cheer us all up before Lights Out,' muttered Skilbeck.

The next day Corps training began in earnest, and a monotonous business it was, with no sign of an aircraft. After melancholy Civil had woken them, and presented them with a basin of lukewarm shaving-water, and after a breakfast of greasy eggs and sausages, the two young officers strolled across to the lodge, outside which they were collected by motor-bus for machine-gun training.

Models of the machinery had been set up in class (the former Examination Halls, a large fussy Gothic building with the stale smell of scholarship about it) but what struck almost all of the novices was the extreme youth of their instructors, little older than themselves. And these were battle-veterans, some of them wounded. Their own training instructor, or 'improver' as he was called, was no more than twenty-three, and he was missing two fingers of his right hand, and had a large circular scar across his right cheek. Some of the other pupils had served already in the trenches on the Western Front, and one of them was sitting next to Skilbeck, who asked his neighbour if he was a veteran. The question had been prompted by the irregularity in the officer's training-dress, of a battered and worn-down Sam Browne. The reply was courteous.

'It belonged to my brother. He was six months with the Flying Corps, and claimed seven victims. He was shot down last month by Immelmann.'

Fledgling officers without battle experience were known dismissively as 'Huns' largely because, flying the undependable Farman Pushers, the cadets frequently accounted for more deaths and casualties than their enemy did.

'You Huns fall in over there,' was the customary order at the end of a technical lesson from the improvers. Lectures and drill continued for all of the first week, on taking off, on landing, on dual control, on machine-guns, on wire-splicing, on map-reading, on the morse code, on dodging anti-aircraft fire, called 'Archie', on reading cloud, on military history, all of which Gendron and Skilbeck relieved by lengthy dog-trots along the oozy banks of the Cherwell, watching the young boat crews loosening up, until they were drawn into the next intake. These boys must come from a nearby public school, Arch reflected, but it revealed to him what the old varsity once was like. He became aware, quite suddenly, that the staircases, chapels, quadrangles, side-streets, public bars, even the covered market and the river-banks were all devoid of sounds. There were people but they were silent people. The city reminded him of the Melbourne Cricket Ground late one night after an eagle match, devoid of spectators, vast, littered and lifeless.

'Do you notice how quiet it all is?' he suggested one afternoon to Skilbeck. 'It's like a wood where no birds sing.'

The abandoned college house-boats, elegant water-bound follies, presented a melancholy sight, as they lay heavily in the reeds, swathed in the thin mist, and Arch imagined the excitable, keen-voiced drinking parties he had heard so much about, Commemorations during the lazy summer months, and the nightly balls. Subjected to strict college discipline, and Lights Out, Gendron and Skilbeck amused themselves after hours by visiting local brew-houses, The Bear in Bear Lane, The Stickleback on a bend of the river, The Duragon Arms, which they enjoyed for their snugness, and huddled over draughts or dominoes in a back bar, indulging in a little mild flirtation with the barmaids. It was Skilbeck who introduced him to Best Boys bitter. Their favourite haunt was a plain little public house, a spit-and-sawdust job called The Old House at Home, mortared into Christ Church walls, where the old college scouts and bedmakers assembled for their nightly grumble. Once they saw the scarred improver, Dyson, there, and he informed them coolly that the public bar was not the place for officers and gents, least of all Huns, and that the lowest form of human existence was 'a trainee novice in the Royal Flying Corps'. But there was no rank in The Old House. He offered them sour half-pints of Best Boys, all the same. But it was Civil of all people who was responsible for the most agreeable of days when he told them of a particular public house on the river called The Rose Revived. Very few people out of college service knew about it, as 'The Rose' existed on a minute island called Salome, far up the Cherwell, which could only be arrived at by punt.

So they chose a dazzling Sunday afternoon to explore,

when they were both excused guard duties. It was a long walk through the mist, past the Parks where football was playing, and across two chain-ferries. The day had an unusual hint of spring in the wintry air. They arrived opposite the island of Salome and, after a half-hour's fruitless enquiries at local houses, managed to unearth a grumbling ferryman, who agreed, but grudgingly, to row them over for the noble sum of a sixpenny piece. He also promised to row them back after an hour. The Rose Revived was the most joyful of the many oddities Arch had discovered and enjoyed about peaceful English life, as it seemed nothing other than a private home, formerly belonging to the lock-keeper, now run on severe lines by two spinster sisters; it stood alone by itself on its own island in the middle of the river, protected by fields, miles from the road, and yet with its sign outside, proclaiming its identity by a paint-faded, old-fashioned cottage rose. The only drink sold there was beer, which the old ladies climbed into cellars beneath to bring up in fat white jugs.

Arch ordered two half-pints of Best Boys from the less forbidding of the old sisters, who was dressed in yester-day's style, with a striped apron over a dress of black bombazine. She wore glasses, compressed her lips in a thin line and looked for all the world like a headmistress respected for her severity.

'There's no Best Boys here – it's all home-brewed. Proper hops and no lumps,' came the irritable reply. Her hair was drawn into a tight bun at the back, and bobbined together. Stern-featured, like her sister, no trace of a welcome, or even a smile, escaped from her clenched mouth.

'Twenty steps down to collect, twenty steps up to carry, it's quarts or nothing,' she said. So Arch hurriedly altered his order, and with an unforthcoming nod the sour bombazine figure disappeared down a ladder into the cellar below.

There were no other guests at that time of year, other than one lonely eel-fisher in the parlour; a shrivelled coal fire was lit in a back room, and when lunch-time arrived there was no sign of the ferryman to row them back. In answer to their timid request, plates of game pie, and winter greens with a few cold potatoes, were brought over to them. A quart jug stood on a mat, brimming over with froth. The beer had a dark bitter taste, and a glowing red colour in it when held against the fire.

The bird-like 'Who-whoo' of the ferryman from the other side of the water disturbed Arch's reverie.

'I see you young fellers is practising to be flying boys,' the ferryman said, prodding the nose of the punt in with his pole. 'I've got a lad of mine out there with the Ox and Bucks so I knows a bit about it. He's had a bad time of it though. He's been over to a hell-hole called Hooge, and got shot at with the camping-parties. Terrible place he says it is. Says the mud comes up above your ankles day and night, ten days on end, he says.'

Skilbeck had joined them on the bank.

'Rats is there too,' muttered the ferryman gloomily, 'rats as big as pigs.'

The friendlier of the two maiden sisters, empty quart jug in hand, stood outside the gates of The Rose Revived. 'Come back in the summer,' she called. 'Summer's best for the beer . . .'

The two young men waved from the punt as it spun gently in the current, and the island receded from view. On the bankside, Arch tipped the sad ferryman generously, and shook him by the hand.

'We wish your son all the luck in the world. By everything we hear the Ox and Bucks are a fine mob, winning through all the way.'

The man seemed to look up to them, as if they were on a private mission, going on to France to do a personal service for his son. It both moved and surprised Arch.

In bed that night, worn out by the week's tedium of the machine-gun manual, the impenetrability of morse code, the chill from the river and the glum prospect of another day's basic training, Arch fell swiftly asleep. His last thought was of Mysie's sweet, upturned face, and walking with her in July across the solitary lawn and the song of the river trickling past.

It was in these unpromising spring days that the ugly Examination Schools down by Magdalen Bridge were turned into an officers' hospital, and the wives and daughters of the dons volunteered as British Red Cross nurses. The walking wounded paraded in their pale battalions.

One morning, Arch walked down Catte Street to purchase some pipe-tobacco. An officer looked to be in distress.

'Can I give you a hand, old fellow?'

An invalid captain of the Buffs, shivering or weeping, quite incapable of crossing the road. Arch and the nurse helped him to sit on the pavement where the officer wept into his hands.

'He's shocked, that's all,' explained the nurse, ' – he's shocked. Can't you *see* . . . '

It was the first time Arch had heard the word.

CHAPTER ELEVEN

Mysie in the Spring

All of April that year belonged to Mysie. That part of him, at least, which eluded Flying Corps duties. When Arch was not actually with Mysie, he was travelling to see her, or planning to see her, or thinking about her, or writing letters to her, or just dreaming of her. Some nights he would escape from his training squadron, and take the train to Paddington, and wait for her to leave the theatre, surrounded as she invariably was by her actor friends and other admirers, old men in Daimler cars, holding bunches of flowers; she would spy him on the other side of the street, standing apart, framed in the lamplight over The Volunteer. Then, quickly, she would detach herself from the excited group surrounding her, and rush over to him, and throw herself into his arms. She preferred to see him in uniform, and the singular flying-coat he wore, and its masculine fragrance of leather mixed with machine oil. And he loved the smell of her, that special perfume, slightly cheap from theatrical make-up, and the arcane scent of her clothes worn through the day. They were not proper lovers, but loved one another tenderly, and part of the novelty was always a part of the joy. The special delight for Arch was that Mysie would abandon the cheery circle she was among, just to be with him and his loneliness, and his longing for her. And in the eyes of her actor friends her Dazzle was of course something of a hero, a celebrity – as Chancellor used to say, 'our famous Mascot', or 'the Eminent Aviator' – and he relished their affection and easy-going friendship.

'You are one of us,' the actors would say, embracing

him in their generous and private world. Sometimes Mysie would be sitting with Chancellor himself who always welcomed Arch, taking his outstretched hand firmly and affectionately.

'Give me yer hand, in faith,' he'd call out. 'Give me yer worship's good hand. Always pleased to see you, *dear* old heart, our Eminent Aviator,' he would add. And to Harold, the cordial potman: 'Waiter, bring me some owl's water . . .' and everyone around would relax and laugh. As for The Volunteer, a seedy low life public house, Chancellor christened it 'The Codpiece and Plackett'.

These theatre-people, thought Arch, were unlike anybody in London, anybody he had ever known, certainly in the Mess, so much funnier, so full of life and joy, and humour, and so prodigal in their affection. There seemed no end to it. He felt himself drawn in as if to a rarefied and unusual tribe, whose laws, rituals and privileges were a secret mystery withheld from outsiders. Gypsies, Romanies, Aboriginals. And he revelled in the luxury of belonging to them. It was as if they made him a special place. As he entered the backstage, for example, minutes after the curtain fell, always the rosy face of Chancellor would light up:

'Aha, and here is our famous war-bird! Now we can call our company complete,' and good-humouredly he would tuck Arch's arm in one of his own, and march off to the pub.

'It's been a profitable week – the first round on your manager, hearts,' he would say to his cronies. 'I will say one good thing about the war, it makes a full house.'

Faces flickered in the gas-light, and the public bar would be crammed, and somewhere in the back bar an Italian concertina-player would be playing, and in their hearty camaraderie for a few hours at least Arch would forget the monotonous routine of morse code and Lewis guns, wind-speeds and firearms-drill, and all the irritation and triviality. It was the closest he felt to the traditional

169

mateship of the stockmen or the Wanderers, and if he felt at times restless at the conviviality there would be Mysie's eye to catch, through a dozen perspiring faces, her hand to touch, the rise and fall of her breast to watch from the other side of the snug; to see her flirting with officers on leave simply delighted him, or her easy carelessness with some of her fellow-players, that casual exchange of kisses – sometimes, she would hurl her arms around one of her actor friends, and kiss his cheeks repeatedly, ruffle his hair, hang on to his hand, and slyly wink at Arch behind his back, sharing with him alone the exclusive world of their love. Her kisses for him were different. When she caught his eye, they were alone in an empty room of their own.

The only one of Mr Chancellor's merry company for whom Arch felt the slightest unease was the tense actor he had observed before, Wilbraham, who never succeeded quite in joining the friendly group, but stood apart. To appear interesting and unloved, Arch sensed, was a kind of pose for Wilbraham, and the young flier felt an instinctive mistrust. It puzzled him. Once, for the sake of conversation, he asked the actor why he was not in the infantry. They were at the bar one evening before the show, drinking some Best Boys at the counter, and found themselves sitting side by side.

'Is that anything to you?' came the abrupt reply. Later, feeling he had gone too far, Wilbraham made an attempt at apology. 'I hope you didn't imagine I was deliberately being rude, Gendron, but so many people ask me, it touches me on the raw.'

'Not at all,' said Arch casually. 'I was enquiring out of interest, merely, not out of curiosity, because I assumed there must be an obvious reason.'

'Well, there is frankly,' said the young actor, 'I'm asthmatic. When I was a child at boarding-school I was taken home because I suffered from asthma. And, although I know I look well, I still do suffer, every night, almost. Not on stage so much, Doctor Theatre, you know, but the army has exempted me. A pity quite frankly, as I always fancied myself as a gunner. I envy you, Gendron, you may not believe me, but I do. It's rotten walking round in civilians, like a slacker.' He turned back to his bitter, the subject closed, and Arch did not again refer to it. He observed though in Wilbraham the trace of suppressed panic. Not only envied because of my fitness, thought Arch, but because of my girl also, and intuitively he always kept up his guard whenever Wilbraham approached them. By contrast, Chancellor included Arch constantly in whatever social life his players were involved in. He was always made welcome on every occasion, professional as well as private, and warmly implored to resort to that most inviolate of hermitages, 'backstage', as if it were his own Mess, to make use of the Green Room and dressing-room, until he was as familiar an intruder as the workmen who operated the oxyhydrogen lights, or the showmen stationed high up in the flies. He was a patient spectator at rehearsals, if his leave coincided with the odd professional hours of the actors, and he preferred to sit in the anonymity of the back-stalls or the wings, waiting for Mysie to finish, rather than his Carlyle rooms.

One afternoon, in the empty auditorium, he was surprised to find a solitary woman sitting somewhere towards the centre, in overcoat and flowered hat, a large handbag on her lap, evidently at her ease, but formally dressed, as if an early arrival for a performance. She seemed both respectable, and out of place.

'Are you the new juvenile?' she asked confidently, raising her voice a little above the awkward squeak of violin, and rasp of trombone. Arch was in his customary Flying Corps buff-coat, fur-collared and imposing, so the question was not unusual to somebody familiar with theatrical costume. Probably she thought he was dressed for his part. In this world, even soldiers were mere make-believe. He was also rather flattered at being casually mistaken for one of the company.

'I'm a friend of Miss Bingham's,' he explained. 'Mr Chancellor kindly permits me to watch rehearsals. I'm with the Flying Corps, but on a day's leave just now.'

'Aha,' replied the woman in the hat, 'then permit me to present myself. I'm Mysie's Ma, and you must be young Mr Gendron, of whom I've heard a great deal.'

'And I've heard of you, Mrs Bingham.'

'Oh, don't call me Mrs Bingham, I'm Mysie's Ma, everyone calls me that at Chancellor's.'

At which point the grey-green curtain, unlit and drab, swung down to dust the floorboards, and after muffled shouting behind the drapes, and energetic discussions in front of them, some sort of overture began. Arch settled himself behind Mysie's comfortable mother in the pit, and waved cheerily to Chancellor as the latter wriggled through a gap in the curtains and let himself cautiously down into the auditorium from a set of treads leading off the stage.

He leaned over and squeezed the younger man's shoulder reassuringly.

'So glad our little Mysie is under your wing. We all love her very much. She's a good girl, dear heart, as well as a pretty one, but she doesn't always know her way. They're all good girls, basically, but, I mean, look at them up there. What sort of life is it for them? I'd like to see our little Mysie settled down, as soon as this rotten war is over. She likes you, I know she does. That's her Ma, sitting in front. She went on once at an hour's notice for Viggie Todd in *Seaside Girls*.' And he bustled off to attend to the pit-musicians.

'It's wonderful, isn't it, the way he brings it to life.' It was the voice of Mysie's mother. 'He's something of a magician, our Mr Chancellor.'

Watching the stage, Arch found nothing at all magical in the obvious and mechanical set-dance going on before him, and the tune and melody, though catchy, struck him as wooden and absurd:

> Look, the soldier boys are marching,
> And I can no longer stay,
> Hark! I hear the bugle calling;
> Goodbye Dolly Gray.

Mysie's Ma conversely, seemed most affected by it.

'Oh, it upsets me so much, that song. Her daddy went to war singing that song, and I never saw him again, you know.'

Arch appeared surprised, so she continued by way of explanation.

'Murdered by those rotten Boers, he was, while serving with the Hampshires. My little girl was no more than seven years of age. We've grown used to it by now, but old songs bring back memories, don't they? I remember the boys singing that all the way to Waterloo Station. Primroses in their pith-hats, and wild flowers in their gun-barrels.'

Ma seemed a nice, comfortable body, diminutive, in her rather elaborate hat, somebody who had once been extremely pretty, even flirtatious. He looked for a sign of Mysie in her, and saw a hint of her 'cross' look. When the rehearsal broke up, the girls in the chorus, out of breath and bubbling with high spirits and excitement, crowded about Chancellor, patient and schoolmasterly, while the orchestra solemnly wrapped their instruments in velvet bags. The showmen dismantled the settings of what looked remarkably like the façade of Windsor Castle, effortlessly lifting cast-iron gates and a vast portcullis in their arms. Mysie, still in stage clothes and straw hat, slipped unnoticed behind him, and placed both her hands over his eyes.

'Guess who?' she cried, before hugging him round the neck, and cascading powder on his fur collar. She pointed out a small morose figure, changing out of his oversized shoes. 'Oh look, Ma, there's Mr Fickling, the low-comedy merchant. You must meet him, Arch, he's something of a "boulevardier".'

For a little while, she sat with her mother, going over the intricacies of her costume, contending with her emotional agitation about the tune.

'Oh, Ma, it's only an old song. Don't get worked up.' And, turning to Arch: 'Did you like the routine? It's very good in the show. It comes after Alice singing "We Don't Want to Lose You", and goes straight into the Finale. Then Mr Chancellor does his monologue – "Gentleman of France". Mr Chancellor always has good taste. You do think it's tasteful, don't you, Dazzle? And they say the boys love it. But this waist is all wrong, Ma! I can't breathe in it at all.'

Mysie's mother was immediately all anxiety, fingering the coarse silk.

'Tell wardrobe to let it out, dear. You can't go on stage restricted like that. It'll upset your bloodstream, and they'll have to replace.'

'Oh, Ma . . . !' Suddenly, in one of those swift changes of mood which was her way, Mysie put both her hands in Arch's own. 'Have you very long with me, David, this evening?'

'No, Mysie, I have to get back to Oxford for supper. There's some novice Huns coming in, and the improvers have to take over two fresh machines. They're sending us down some of those tight little Sopwiths, and we've got to discover how to take care of them. They have a nasty trick of climbing up their own tails, if you don't watch them. They need careful handling.'

Artfully, Mysie sent her mother away behind the scenes to find somebody in wardrobe to take out some of the stitching from her dress.

'We haven't got much time then,' she said, and taking Arch's hand led him confidently out of the auditorium, into the quiet foyer and ante-rooms behind.

'There's so much noise going on down there,' she said. 'I know somewhere quiet. Let's sit in one of the boxes. We can talk. I'm not on until after the Park Lane medley.'

'I know somewhere quieter than that,' Arch said.

'Where?'

'Somewhere up there behind the gallery.'

'Up in the gods?'

'Right up in the rotunda. I went off exploring and I found a funny little set of rooms up there. It must have been a manager's office, in years gone by.'

'All right, but not for long. We haven't practised the Finale.'

Sure-footed in the wilderness behind the scenes of the playhouse, Mysie soon found her way in, and out of, and around, pass doors and stairwells, arriving suddenly at the short ascent of stone steps which led to the old apartment. She swooped with eagerness on the playbills, explaining the identity of some of the vanished attractions. Charles Kean, Tarleton and Bannister. They found themselves in a confined sequence of small rooms, scarfed in dust, and filled with ancient furniture. The private suite of an old actor-manager, perhaps, with kitchen, bathroom, a brown-stained tub still in place, and a Johns lavatory, whose throne faced the open door.

In her quaint costume of an earlier time, Mysie did not look one hair out of place among the jumbled furniture and curiosities of the room. When she turned towards him, he felt for a short second that she was a ghost he had stumbled on by chance. So much of life was in that fleeting moment. There was still the smell of greasepaint, a strong masculine flavour, on her skin and hair, and the subtle stain of rouge on her neck-collar, and her cuffs, and at close quarters a smear of greyish powder rubbed off on to the edge of her chemise. The relief from the hubbub below, their own excited chatter, and hurried footsteps, suddenly overwhelmed them. They stood, motionless, sensing each other's closeness, within touching distance, but not touching, hands near, but not holding, scenting one another, each feeling the gentle trace of the other's breath.

'Now,' Mysie said finally.

She ventured into the next-door room, and called him, not shyly, nor with fear.

A bed stood there, grotesquely, with an undressed mattress, and horsehair bolster. He had not expected this. She had not expected this. The door remained open. It led behind to a small dusty office, and a shallow flight of steps. At the foot of the steps was the auditorium, and on the stage, even now getting ready to sing, twenty or thirty people. The call-boy would be searching for her in empty dressing-rooms, calling her name in vain down the corridor. Anybody might burst in at any moment: 'Miss Bingham, on stage please! Miss Bingham, your Finale call!'

Arch, with precise fingers, unbuttoned in one steady movement her theatrical costume, and opened out the whole of her dress to look at her. She faced him, her eyes never leaving his own.

'Will they hear us?' she asked, staring intently but not moving away.

Arch did not answer, nor shake his head. His leather flying-coat, with its fur collar, was already unbuttoned. It was with merely the slightest shrug he removed it and laid it across the bed, the work of a moment. Arch grasped her by each wrist, stretching her on his coat, still without kissing her. Taking her completely, his right hand placed across her mouth, he restrained the imploring cries.

'Oh! Dazzle . . . Dazzle . . . oh, yes . . . Now.'

Into the cupola under the theatre's roof drifted the chorus from the rehearsal far below on stage: 'Hi! Hi! Never say die! I'm one of the Deathless Army.'

She was crying a little, and wiped her eyes with her knuckles. Hours later, in the empty theatre, the actors long gone home, listening to the mice scuttling in the flies, they lay awake with one another. Mysie had missed the Finale after all, and did not care. Arch would have to walk to Paddington, and take the milk-train back to Oxford.

'You are the captain of my heart,' she whispered.

CHAPTER TWELVE

Stunting

Abercrombie, popularly known as Apple Crumbleby, spoke up first.

'God in heaven! They're trying us out on "pushers" – who's in charge of recruiting around here?'

'Dear God,' stammered Skilbeck, as they stood outside the canvas hangar in the drizzle. 'This is some sort of toy.'

Helplessly out of scale, dejected in the middle of the large grass space, looking like a collapsed sewing-machine, lay an old Henri Farman Shorthorn. It seemed discouragingly unsure, like two schoolboys' box-kites, braced together with wires. Captain Dyson, the improver, was little more prepossessing than the machine, as he stood to one side, attempting to look nonchalant with a cigarette in his hand, and the early traces of a recently grown moustache on his upper lip. He was well known, in his tent, to read Virgil's Georgics in the original Latin for relaxation.

Rumour had it that the Flying Corps, in its first year, had killed off even more instructors than pupils, and certainly little tolerance or life-expectancy was given to either. The other type of improver consisted of the no less disheartening sight of a former cavalry officer, recently invalided out of the Western campaign in the trenches, but still determined to keep his eye in at the enemy, and uneasily accepting a teaching role. Some of them were embittered by the prospect of fresh youth with sanity and limbs and morale intact, careless of their safety and heedless of their vulnerability, having already lost part of their own. Nobody questioned these officers' bravery, or their steadfastness in continuing an individual battle, nobody for a moment criticized their indifference to physical pain which discomforted them, but that they were frequently indifferent to life itself was beyond dispute.

Dyson was no stranger to this eerie philosophy; especially difficult to accept, as he was a mere twenty-two, and had been badly wounded in the shoulder at First Ypres, and wore his MC with distinction. In addition his face was scarred around the chin-bone by a machine-gun bullet. Just inside the range at Streaky Bacon Farm, Dyson was honourably 'pingoed' the day before Christmas.

'Good morning, gentlemen,' he addressed the yawning and shifty cluster of Huns. 'Whose turn is it to take the Rumpty up first? Any volunteers?'

And there never were. It was a well-known proverb at Peckwater that basic training accounted for more British corpses than ever the Germans did.

The Rumpty, as the men christened the Shorthorn, was as alarming in the air as it appeared on the ground, and could only be flown up daringly on days of exceptional smoothness. Dyson called it a 'vicious little beast'. This spring day was not such a bland one, and so for the morning they hung around the stick-and-string machine in clusters, examining the controls, taking turns in the flying seat, turning the engine over and running it along the ground. Finally, Dyson decided to take it up himself, and to their admiration he succeeded in lifting it clumsily into the air with a great deal of buzzing and revving of the 75 hp Renault engine, and after making a shaky circuit of the meadow managed to bring it as gently down again as anybody could achieve. The hours of theory and desk work were over. Here was the thing itself. Each cadet knew he had to achieve personally four hours' solo on one of these Farman Shorthorns before moving forward to Avros or Sopwiths, and the prospect filled them with unease.

But this was a new world for Arch, which excited him and absorbed him. All that his brother Chas felt about horses, and had tried to explain to him back in the Never, was everything Arch felt about machines. The smell of pure castor oil, the high-pitched, spluttering, kicking noise, the particular jerk and bump and swing of the rudder, became for him the new sensation he sought after. As he stood in the small circle of awed cadets, in front of the precarious, as if unfinished, fuselage and wire machinery, a sort of inept bath-tub with its childish pram wheels, he felt a great thrill and remembered plainly the first time he had visited his friend Oggie at home, and the tingling exhilaration of following him to his private gymnasium in the centre of which, instead of the more characteristic wooden horse, squatted their 'Ogg Special'.

Suddenly Captain Dyson was addressing him.

'This is a spiteful, vicious beast, Gendron, so for Christ's sake keep a cool head, and don't get into a blue flunk. If she stands on you, wind up, tail up! Now get in.'

The Rumpty was an oldfangled 'pusher', with the Renault engine set directly behind the pilot's head, so that if he had the bad luck on landing to hit something, or came in too fast, if whatever was in front of him did not kill him, the weight of the engine and its propeller behind would finish the job. What was really surprising was that the 'pusher' got off the ground at all, and turned and manoeuvred with any degree of predictability. But it did, and Captain Dyson knew perfectly how to adjust to the bumps and blasts of wind and draught. When his turn came, with the improver sitting behind him, Arch began to feel, however clumsily, the insensitive rudders and obstinate joystick respond. His illusion of flying had all been one of speed, of floating effortlessly in the sky, side-slipping and wheeling, curving and swooping with the assurance of a sparrow-hawk. He thought the business of the air was to discover the currents and pockets of wind, to examine the contours of the earth's face from on high, to seek the blind spots of the sun, to circle elegantly

179

like a bird of prey, to bounce about upon the crests of the clouds. In fact, in the Rumpty, he soon discovered the alarming knack of remaining airborne in a machine which lumbered along so slowly that even to be lifted into the air at all was a terrifying experience. It was the most insubstantial experience of his life and, when the instructor behind him wheeled on the stick, it was so agonizingly slow he felt he was back again on his motor-cycle, and by some terrible error had taken a hill-curve too wide, and swung out dizzily into the sky from the corner. It felt as bumpy as driving over a ploughed field. Dyson shoved the stick to the right, the left wing tipped up crazily, and Arch felt his stomach leap up into his gorge. There was a vile taste on his tongue. He shut his eyes, and clutched the edge of the cockpit. Captain Dyson was yelling something, whacking him on the shoulder with his walking-stick, and trying to make himself heard above the Shorthorn engine. In front, Arch felt his ears block up, his eyes too, and deprived of sight and sound, and with a devastating itching in the soles of his feet, helpless in the cockpit, he sensed their imminent plunge to the ground, and waited for the frightening impact. The left wing tilted sharply down. He felt a violent levelling off, then his belly returned to him, and his eyes reopened. He saw the grass of the airfield flattening out to engulf him. The noise of the engine cut back and, as his ears cleared, he heard a perfectly calm voice talking to him unconcernedly above a gentle whisper in the wire struts.

'Keep the needle at forty-five – pull back throttle – cut engine – lose height – keep nose forward – now bum on! – if you get a cut-out at take-off, for God's sake, push her nose forward, keep bumming on – don't try and turn back. You'll get straight into a spin, and it makes one hell of a mess. Added to which, it mucks the machine up, and we haven't got all that many to spare.'

Captain Dyson added emphasis to his instructions by knocking his stick regularly on Arch's shoulder-blades.

The engine broke into life again, and the Rumpty hovered over the green grass for an instant, and after several clumsy bounces came to a standstill. Arch sat, itching with sweat, gripping the stick to conceal his shaking hands.

'Good show, Gendron,' was Dyson's only remark. 'Like I told you, flying's perfectly simple if you just obey a few simple rules. Make friends with your machine. Come along, Skilbeck, get over here.'

His first flying lesson was over, and within two days he was taking turns with Captain Dyson to circle the aerodrome, sharing the controls.

It was not a craft he was ever to enjoy, or dominate, it was not intended that he should, but the crudeness of the training period gave him an acute sensation of being heavier than air. He had learned perhaps the first lesson of war. The politics and the strategy were of supreme unimportance. What was going on, from first to last, was simply the unjust, disorganized, fortuitous selection of survivors, in varying degrees of fear, danger, or chance. Training was one of these. Skills were required, alongside instinct to withstand it and, of course, luck; 'The more you fly, the luckier you'll be,' said Dyson, 'and remember – any fool can fly fast, it's flying slow that matters.'

Of those cadets flying solo in front of the officer commanding in Port Meadow the next week, only a few had had as much as five hours of solo flying, and several of them not more than two. But word said that there had been a great German push in the area of the Somme and that pilots were in grave demand to support the Front. So the colonel commanding and his little group of aides stood in the field with their short British warms, tapping canes against their top-boots, set apart from the cadets, who clustered in nervous groups around the hangars. The first one got off all right, zigzagged for a bit, but instead of circling the aerodrome went straight on. The instructors had to explain to the CO that, although he had courage and flair, this trainee only knew how to take

181

off and land, but had no experience of turning. The CO commented dryly (as the cadet disappeared into the grey distance) that he would land eventually in Wales, and to let Command know where to collect the machine. This grim pleasantry was shared by the officers. The second man in another Rumpty made an expert take-off, and went into a skilful series of dives and zooms, but failed to circuit the field.

'Why in hell's name doesn't this bugger come round?' enquired the irritable major.

'Because he knows how to fly, but not how to land, sir,' was the instructor's reply.

'Hasn't anybody bothered to teach this officer?'

'We got a bit of a wind-up on the day we were giving him instruction, sir, and never got round to it.'

At that moment, after a long turn, the little hunch-backed Rumpty came coughing in, and the inexperienced pilot made a not altogether disastrous landing, taxi-ing to a standstill just short of the hedge. He was congratulated by the knot of officers on his success – or survival. The pilot in the next machine was inept at landing-technique, came in too fast, failed to level off, and bounced on impact a fully sixty feet up in the air. Sensibly he did another circuit, after switching on the motor again, and after four more attempts smashed the undercarriage. The machine flopped forward, rather slowly, like a drunken, overweight man falling into a flower-bed. The pilot was told he would probably make a splendid observer.

Arch got round easily and Skilbeck made only a slight error in landing.

At the end of the afternoon a nervous pilot called Yearsley, who had once worked as a stable-hand at Newmarket, got the idea into his head that joining the Flying Corps was something like a steeplechase, and that a Rumpty Shorthorn was a mechanized form of horse. He never settled correctly. The stable-lad taxied out to the far end of the field, and ran all the way back, leaving his lift-off far too late. Perhaps out of sudden nervousness he

182

recognized his mistake and, instead of switching off, and turning, and repeating the whole thing, he snatched at the stick, pulling it right back. The Rumpty could not conceivably respond to such sudden pressure, stuck its nose up straight into the sky, stalled, and hung on its propeller. Then it did a tail-slide right back to the ground.

'Chute mortelle,' affirmed Captain Dyson.

'Stupid bugger,' said the major, scowling at the pyre of grey smoke, 'those machines are damned hard to replace – what an arse! Well, bum on.'

The ambulance, 'the most hard-working machine on the airfield' Captain Dyson had once grimly jested, bounced over the field at full speed. In the distance, by the hedge, there was no further movement from the collapsed concertina of flaps, struts, wires and wings. Arch was reminded of when he and Chas had been out in the Bush shooting birds – of that electric quiver of flight, the sharp sudden shot, the powerful impulsive movement instantly crushed, and the object spinning impatiently to earth, crumpled, and shorn of all its effortless vitality.

'Are you the officer's improver, Dyson?' snapped Major Treadaway.

'I am, sir.'

'Then all I can say is, he don't seem to have improved.'

'No, sir. Understood, sir.'

Major Treadaway called the small group of highly rattled young cadets to stand to attention before him. His solitary eye glared, and his left hand fidgeted with his swagger-stick, like the restless twitching of a cat's tail.

'I want to say to you all one thing, and one thing only; there will be no cessation of activities on the airfield this afternoon. Solo-flight instruction is to be continued as planned on Battery Orders. Carry on, Sergeant-Major.'

Captain Dyson had been standing watching earnestly, as if willing himself to be crouched behind the trainee, correcting the faults of stick and rudder, advising, instructing; but, when he turned to the men, his reaction was curt, and different from what they had anticipated.

'Should have kept the nose forward and lifted clear. Remember this, don't jerk on that stick, any more than you'd jerk at a horse's mouth. The Rumpty can tell an inexperienced hand, and will work you off in a short second. As you saw. For a riding man, that was a pretty poor display.'

And he stalked off irritably in the direction of the commanding officer's tent.

'Back to Virgil's Georgics, no doubt,' muttered Skilbeck under his breath.

The rest of the training period at Oxford continued monotonously, with Arch and his fellow-Huns graduating from Farmans to Avros, and being directed from airfield to airfield, as they progressed. It was a special day of celebration for them to put up their wings. By the end, Arch knew the sound of his engine like a blind minstrel stroking his harp; and could side-slip his Avro with a gentle dove-like descent, and glide – engineless, brakeless – inside its own hangar. It had taken time, but Captain Dyson had helped them tame the vicious beast, and eliminated their fear. Not of the enemy – that was to be tried in combat – but at least the machine was not a vindictive savage which sought the destruction of its master. He taught them 'bottom', as promised, and the art of airmanship. He taught them the feel of the rudder with the feet of a trusted church-organist. That the Avro and the Sopwith were mechanisms of principle and dignity. That they could be mishandled and ill-treated, like dogs. That they were equally nice-tempered and reasonable and loyal, if cared for. They obeyed an honest book of rules. Far from being rebellious, the flying-machine was as respectable as a maiden aunt. He taught them a kind of love.

CHAPTER THIRTEEN

Mysie on Tour

Mysie finished *Dolly Grey* and was with her new musical play *London Bridge*, a touring show; while he was at Peckwater she had written to Arch from various sea-towns of the English coast. Her Ma was still at Linden Gardens minding Apples. She was bored, Mysie wrote, actresses spent a large portion of their time being bored, and often irritated by the inadequacy of their accommo-dation, the mediocrity of the audience's response, or the tedium of fellow-performers. Most of them, she told him, were either boring or drunk. Some of them, boring and drunk. She appeared more weary of Mr Chancellor than before. Wilbraham was growing more and more 'obstro-polous', as she put it. The latest show was a trivial comedy with propaganda songs and dances added, to cheer the hearts of war-workers, and to encourage recruitment. It was the sort of thing Arch privately disliked, home-front patriotism, but as Mysie had no prospect of understanding what it was she was perform-ing or relating it to her life, or the war, it was of little importance to him. In her letters, she wrote affectionately and sweetly, enclosing small sentimental gifts, a curl of her hair, a pressed flower, a postcard of lovers, a lacy corner of her nightdress. She worried endlessly about his safety in the Rumpty. She also wrote flirtatiously, with shy attempts to provoke his jealousy, about one of the actors who was trying to pursue her, of an admirer here, of a rich industrialist there, of presents left for her at the stage door, of bouquets of flowers delivered to her digs. Sometimes she would write directly:

My sweet heart.

You tell me about the nice rooms you share with your friend. Have you ever thought of sharing a room with me, I wonder? I am so quiet, you would hardly notice my presence, it would be like sharing rooms with a ghost. But I should like it too, and be cheerful to bring your hot water at night, instead of that horrid old boy-scout, as you call him, with a drip on the end of his nose. And later, how much I would like to curl up close to you, as you sit by the fire, and lie between your knees watching the fire. You could read to me, or speak to me about your life in the Desert Country, and your brother Chas. How is he, by the way, have you any news? One of the girls here has a friend in the cavalry, but of course she doesn't know where he is. It sounds a far worse time than you're having at university. It must be nice to be a scholar there, better than being an airman, better than being an actress come to that. I am lonely for you, Dazzle, come and visit me soon . . .

And so, one day, just for fun, he did. She was staying in Brighton, elegantly for once, at the famous Marine Hotel, and performing a musical comedy on the Royal Pier. Knowing that she would be sleeping the morning away, Arch flew his Avro down before luncheon from the grass track at Port Meadow, over the chalk hills on a gentle day, and landed an hour later on Brighton Beach, not far from the pier. There seemed not to be an appropriate two-acre field or garden to hand. The tide was far out and nowhere looked more suitable or inviting than the edge of the sea. The day was bright and glittering. It caused great excitement along the promenade, this arrival of the machine. The Jollity Boys on the sands lost their audience entirely, and the youngsters came running behind the slipstream as Arch taxied in for a classic dead-stick landing. This little gathering of urchins formed an escort behind him as he walked up to the hotel beyond the pier, cheering him as he walked. He left the donkey-boy as guardian by the machine, defiantly holding on to Arch's fur-lined flying-helmet.

Mysie was, exactly as he guessed, still in her bedroom, and on receiving the news of his arrival from the hall porter finished her dressing hurriedly, and ran down the staircase. She was brimful of happiness, her words tumbling all over one another in their fervour to escape:

'Oh, Dazzle, this is exciting. Did you come by train, or have you a car? Are you on leave? Can you stay? Did you come on your motor-cycle?'

'I came by Avro, as a matter of fact,' he said, with some confidence and not a little pride. 'It seemed the obvious thing to do. I had a free day at the airfield, and the use of a machine. Technically, I'm still in training, but I can go out solo, and it's all counted as experience. An extra couple of hours notched up, actually.'

'By Avro? I can't believe that! Oh, Dazzle!'

'Well, Mysie, I just have.'

'Where did you leave her?'

'Well, you can see her from the windows of the hotel lounge.'

And excitedly Mysie ran, half-skipped, to look out, clapping her hands with the thrill of it, and crying with laughter. She looked so pretty that morning, her face was not made up, she had been caught unawares, and was only just dressed. She smelt so fresh, the tiredness of the night before showed slightly, and a small brush of theatrical powder still rested on her cheek.

There on the sands stood his machine, the tidal line behind it, and an admiring throng of spectators several deep around, as if it were a beach-side attraction, like a pierrot-troupe or a Punch and Judy show. They had lunch together, and a watery sun came into the dining-room. Arch was handsome and confident in his uniform. His dark yellow flop of hair, tidily brushed, Mysie said, 'was like a fair-haired cat, sitting on top of his head'. The new assurance he had gained in his flying added to his frank open face. He felt relaxed in her easy company, as much

187

as her vanity was flattered by his glamorous presence, 'a flying officer' in uniform – quite a rarity – the attention of most of the diners. An elderly man even approached their table, and offered his compliments and admiration of the young man's achievement, likening it to a deed of medieval chivalry. And, suddenly recognizing Mysie from the entertainment in the theatre which he had seen only the night before, bowed and allowed her also her small moment of triumph. She extended her hand to Arch, and smiled fondly, wrinkling her nose at the same time as winking both eyes, a little way she had. He took her hand.

'My best girl,' he said.

It was a painting in her mind come true for Mysie – the valiant aviator, and his girl, having lunch while on tour at the seaside – and how she wished fervently the entire company would come in and catch her. She thought it just like a romantic scene in a play. Time: the Present. Scene: at The Marine Hotel. But she liked him too, and his nice neat uniform, so different from the commonplace cavalry officers the other girls encouraged, his soft, handsome face, and the sudden surprise, and the machine on the beach, made her suddenly amorous. Their meal was not quite finished, but she whispered:

'Come up to my room, Arch, I want to sit on your knee and kiss you . . .'

And, throwing down his napkin, he rose quickly to follow her up to her bedroom on the second floor. The manager observed the move, from his desk in the foyer, and quietly went on with checking the keys. They haven't so very many hours together, he thought, let them enjoy themselves.

From the window of her room, Arch could see the machine sitting where he had left it, and the tide safely out. The shingle reflected a little of the sun, and the crowd, less interested now, had moved away, apart from some small children who examined everything in detail. The donkey-boy seemed to have appointed himself the

188

leader, and delighted in keeping the others at bay. The room was pleasant, light, and the curtains blew back from an open window, and a smell of the sea came into the place. The bed was still unmade, and the soft white nightgown she wore lay at one end. Other items of her toilette lay untidily about, and her colours tray with its lipsticks and rouges, and powders, and hairpieces occupied the dressing-table in considerable disarray. This unguarded carelessness endeared her to him in so many ways, and almost immediately she caught sight of herself in the mirror, expressed dismay, and began combing her hair into place. Arch stood behind her, and pressed her back against his chest, placing an arm just below her breasts, feeling their slight pressure against his wrist, and their soft rise and fall. She was still fresh to him, with a most appealing softness. Mysie let her head fall back on his shoulder, and stayed there for a long time. Breaking away with a suppressed giggle, she took his hand, and led him to the largest of the chairs.

'Quick, quick, we haven't much time . . . ' And she sat him down, herself on top of him, tugged his neck nearly strangling him, and kissed him long and hard.

'There,' she said, as if having bestowed a reward, 'I felt like that, didn't you? Oh, I have missed you, Dazzle, every evening and every day, and I wish we were nearer one another and always able to be like this, don't you . . .? I would like to kiss you so hard all over your face, that nothing would be left. Only scraps.'

But before Arch could properly answer, as he was busy kissing her and fussing with her bodice, a sharp rattle at the door, followed by a persistent knocking, itself immediately followed by the entrance of the portly French manager, put a stop to anything he might have said. Or done.

'*Monsieur, monsieur l'aviateur*, please be quick . . . the boys have run up to the hotel to say the tide is on the turn, you must fly away soon or your machine will be drowned in the sea . . . '

189

Arch sprang to the window. It was true.

The idea of apologizing to his colonel for leaving a brand-new Avro abandoned on the sea-shore, like some kind of mechanical sand-castle, which had been washed away, suddenly loomed as the most appalling prospect, and, grabbing Mysie's hand, Arch thanked the manager, and ran down the stairs. The boys were there in an excited rabble, invading the foyer and cheering him as he made his escape. He sprinted down to the beach. There was just enough time, though he had cut things fine, and the edge of the grey water seemed to be advancing visibly. Mysie ran a few paces behind the manager and some of the waiters and housemaids behind her, all eager to watch the sport.

'*Courez, monsieur, courez . . . C'est vite fait. Avertis une catastrophe . . . !*'

The tide lapped only a few feet away when he reached the machine and, climbing into the cockpit, with the aid of the donkey-boy at the propeller, he soon made contact with the engine, and as it spluttered mercifully into life the crowd, by now numbering about thirty or forty, staggered back. The propeller swept shingle and spume up the beach towards them, and his last sighting of Mysie was as she turned away from him, to shield her eyes. He was in luck. The grit held his pram-wheels firmly enough as the machine ponderously taxied away, and there was a friendly supporting sea-wind to tug him off as he headed into it. He made a slight drift, his prams splashing the water's edge, but by then he felt the wind lifting his wings, and his speed was sufficient not to allow him to be waterlogged. As he floated upwards over the Brighton promenade, he decided – just for fun – to make one turn more, and approaching the bystanders at full throttle – as they used to on the airfields when they were confident enough – played ducks and drakes along the sands and skimmed as low as he dared to touch wheels once or twice at intervals along the water. Some of the boys threw themselves flat on the ground as he ran towards them, clearing them by inches, and even above his engine he sensed he could hear the hint of a cheer. Mysie ran in the opposite direction along the very edge of the sea-line, so that he passed over her once again, before lifting up into the sky; he could lean out to wave and she was standing ankle-deep in the water, both hands held crazily above her head, waving with joy and fun. She stayed there, long after the Avro had become a speck in the sky, as the crowd of schoolboys began to disperse, listening to his engine, which took for ever, before that too was submerged by the gentler sounds of seagulls, and tide lapping, and the occasional motor-car along the sea-front.

He flew all this way just to spend the day with me, she wondered, watching the tidemark erase neatly all sign of the tell-tale tram-lines on the shingle.

And her eyes burned deep into the hole of grey cloud, where his machine had disappeared.

CHAPTER FOURTEEN

Railway Cottages

'Always stick your nose down and go in hard' was one of the valedictory morsels of technical advice from Captain Dyson, after the Oxford Huns passed out from Peckwater. Those who were going to flunk anyway, had already flunked, and Arch, his good friend 'Apple Crumbleby' (to everybody's surprise) and Skilbeck, all were awarded their wings the very same morning. This was an event to celebrate. First, they ceremoniously flung their much-detested 'Hun' helmets into the Cherwell, off Folly Bridge, and as they watched these symbols of repression float soggily down to the depths, and fitted the new tight headpieces on to their skulls, this was the beginning of their great adventure. Apple Crumbleby and Skilbeck found themselves assigned to the Sopwith Zoo at Nancy, Arch to the 10th squadron of two-seaters at Béthune.

'Into battle, and – here's to it!' they said, and swiped open the college champagne bottles with their sabres.

'Give me Pups every day,' said Skilbeck, 'no tricks and no vices.'

The next day was hang-overs, long heads and noses, and vows of eternal friendship, most of which were forgotten by the time the train arrived at Paddington. But Arch's farewell to Skilbeck was entirely genuine, and tinged with real sadness, as they had shared the miseries and triumphs of training closely, and witnessed their first flying casualties together; all of these things created some kind of bond. How glad they would be to realize that in time to come, they would both be flying together along the valley of the Somme, during the great 'offensive' of 1916.

Leave was offered, and gratefully accepted, and Arch grabbed his forty-eight-hour pass and took the underground railway to Leicester Square. The curtains all over London were already 'coming down' by the time Arch arrived back-stage at the Hay, and Fenge gave the – by now – well-known flier details of where Mr Chancellor was in the very act of giving one of his celebrated 'lobster-nights'. These were occasions of festivity at his own 'assembling-rooms', as he called them, in Railway Cottages, a row of terraced villas next to Cleaver Square – an area, according to the actor-manager, sympathetic to 'theatricals'. These much-vaunted occasions turned out to be, as Mysie warned him, rather subdued affairs, mostly consisting of Chancellor's monologues, and family sing-songs with Mysie's Ma at the piano.

Innocent they might be, for a young man about to be blooded in France at any time, but they did not lack humble affection, and Arch – who had attended these affairs before – was quite happy to perch against the piano, Mysie beside him, with a mug of hot chocolate in his hand. It would hardly have suited Skilbeck, or the languid Abercrombie, whose tastes were more provocative, but for the moment, it suited Arch. Besides, he knew he would end his evening in the pale arms of Mysie, and that was enough for him.

Chancellor had seldom been in more eloquent form.

'Here's to you, David, and the success of your wings. God bless you, my dear, dear boy.'

Arch grinned. Secretly he'd hoped to show off his bright new uniform, with the white wings already attached. Chancellor extended his hand; he was dressed in what he fondly described as his 'lobster-night' togs, which consisted of an old, velvet dressing-gown of hopeless squalor, and on his head, incongruously, a smoking-cap of Victorian vintage, formerly belonging to the comic actor, Oddwell. From a large ruffled and indeed ravelled sleeve, his tenacious hand grasped Arch around the wrist, and propelled him 'centre-stage' as it were.

'Give me yer hand, faith, give me yer worship's good hand.'

'I never appreciated you knew one another, Mr Chancellor,' smirked Fickling, currying favour.

'Know one another . . . ! The good lieutenant and I?' – and folding Arch into his extended arms – 'Sweet knight, we have seen the seven stars.'

And using this as a cue for the traditional Friday night sing-song, 'Tune up, Ma!' he commanded, and the little party went instantly into a version of 'We Don't Want to Lose You, But We Think You Ought to Go' – such a popular feature, as Mysie explained, of their previous show *Helping the Cause* at Stoll's in Charlotte Street.

And then everybody sang 'Tipperary', which Mysie's Ma bravely strummed out on the piano, just anticipating the singers by calling out their next line. Then the time came when all the company clapped and stamped and entreated the newly graduated flying 'ace' to sing them 'one of the Flying Corps songs' – an ordeal Arch had never yielded to before – but on this occasion, because the tune and the words were still buzzing round and round his brain from the previous night's celebrations, he found himself singing the Huns' version of the best-loved song in all the world: 'D'Ye Ken John Peel . . .' although, as he explained, the words *were* a little different.

When you soar in the air in a Newport Scout,
And you're scrapping with a Hun, and your gun cuts out,
Well, you stick down your nose 'til your plugs fall out,
'Cos you haven't got a hope in the morning!

And he conducted them all in the chorus, which they swiftly got up:

Oh my batman woke me, woke me from my bed,
I'd had a thick night, and a very sore head,
And I said to myself, to myself I said,
'Oh, we haven't got a hope in the morning!'

This went down well with one and all, and further mugs

of chocolate and purchases from the local pie-shop were handed round. The sing-song ended with the patriotic anthem, and standing in a circle, holding hands, Chancellor conducted everybody in a tearful version of 'Auld Lang Syne', even Wilbraham conquering his diffidence, and joining in.

'Another of Chancellor's monologues, or another mug of chocolate, after last night, I'll crash in a dead-stick landing. It's France for me tomorrow. Mysie, can we creep out without offence?'

'Of course we can, Dazzle,' she replied, 'I'll fetch my things. Don't say goodbye.'

Mr Chancellor saw them at the door:

'I won't give you my blessing, old son, it might bring you bad luck – but I'll give you a penny. Here . . . ' Somewhat puzzled, Arch accepted it. 'The loveliest thing I ever heard on any stage was old Bannister as Costard telling the little boy: "And I had but a penny in the world, I would give it thee – to buy gingerbread . . ." Here you are, old son, and don't trouble yer heart about our little Mysie – we'll take care of her for you.'

And Mysie reached up on tiptoe to kiss her guv'nor's faintly carmined lips.

Then rather like two children, they slipped away out of the back door of Railway Cottages.

'Is he going to France to die?' asked Mysie's Ma, somewhat tearfully, over the cocoa-mug.

'To die is easy,' answered the old actor comfortingly. 'Only comedy is difficult.'

In her tidy little sitting-room in Linden Gardens, to cheer them both, Mysie had lit a coal fire, although it was warm enough outside to do without it. But they felt the cold between them.

'We'll drink a little toast together, Dazzle, I've got a bit of Christmas port left in the larder. It'll warm us up.'

And she trotted with borrowed cheerfulness into the

parlour, where all of a sudden she found herself crying unutterable tears. There, Arch discovered her, when minutes had passed and she did not return. He held her so tightly, tighter than he ever had before, he almost squeezed the breath out of her. She calmed herself, and then they went back to the table, and sat up to it, like a respectably married couple out for a celebration in their first restaurant. Mysie set down the port wine and the two glasses, and accidentally (perhaps he felt nervous as well) Arch touched her glass with the neck of the bottle, and it sang.

'Oh,' cried out Mysie, 'mind the poor sailors . . .'

'What do you mean, Mysie?'

'If a glass pings, try and stop it at once. If you don't, a poor sailor dies at sea.'

Arch rested his forefinger lightly on the glass-edge to stop the ringing.

'There, that's better,' she smiled.

He had noticed before, she was always so superstitious about almost anything. He asked for the salt, an ordinary enough request: 'Oh, help you to salt, help you to sorrow,' she'd say. Two spoons meant a letter – crossing on the stairs (at the Hay she'd prefer to run all the way back to the top again) was bad luck – and blackthorn should never be brought into the house. Taking the glass sadly to her lips, without raising it, as she usually did, in an imaginary unspoken toast - 'Happy Days' or 'Long Life' – she sipped with the timidity of a sparrow.

'Come along, old woman,' said Arch, stroking her bare wrist, 'are things so very bad?'

'I think they might be when you feel very happy, Arch,' she used his proper name for once. 'You're so thrilled about your wings, and as for me, how will I ever feel happier than this? I feel so happy right now, it breaks my heart.'

Both of them sat there in silence for a second, not complete silence, because Apples was enjoying some magical rabbit-hunt of his own, dreaming and whimpering excitedly to himself.

'You see, even Apples is happy.'

Set back from her, Arch took away his hand and looked intently into her eyes. It was not so strange she was always superstitious about the sea.

Even her own Ma had always maintained 'there's something of the sailor about Mysie – well, you know, "here today, gone tomorrow" sort of thing. Sometimes, I think there's something unlucky about her. Sailors are always meant to be unlucky, aren't they?'

He loved many things about Mysie. Her soft voice, and the gentle tumble of her words all pouring out on top of one another, her white-golden hair, which he called 'silkworms', but Arch loved best of all her harsh sailor-blue eyes. Even on stage, he could pick out Mysie in a chorus line, not by her long legs, which were just like all the others, or her hair, which could be disguised under a wig, but the unmistakable blue of her eyes, periwinkle-blue, St Andrew's blue. Tonight they were a field-gun grey, as if the colour had been drained out of them.

'What are you thinking now?' she asked, quietly.

'I'm wondering if everything just happens, all in one year,' he replied.

'All of it?'

'All our happiness, all our youth, all our pleasure. Just one year. And that it might never happen again.'

Watching her closely, like a rare and infrequent bird, Arch noticed her face turned to one side slightly, and he recognized her sweet, purposeful child's expression, like the young girl she used to be. When she turned round, she had reverted to her normal self again.

'Now it's my turn to ask what *you* are thinking?' he said.

'When I was a little girl in Puddledock on Midsummer's Eve the whole village used to walk up on the Downs. As far as you could see, there were a million tiny glow-worms. A million, maybe even more. And the whole side of the Downs would glow, as if it was candle-light. One night, on the Chart with my old Aunt Jane (I was only a little girl then) she picked them up, these glowies, as we called them, one by one, very gently, like a moth's wing between her fingertips. And she set them all round my straw hat. Right round the brim, so it made a little circle of light. It was the prettiest thing you ever saw.'

There was perfect silence between them for a while, then Mysie sat so lightly upon him, he hardly felt aware of her weight; and she kissed him so timidly he felt her breath on his mouth, but scarcely her lips, and *that* she called her 'glow-worm', and when she tickled the surface of his cheek with her eyelashes, *that* she called her 'butterfly'.

Mysie's thin shoulders seemed too narrow to support her full, completely spherical breasts, they almost seemed disproportionate, white and perfectly tipped at their bud. He could hardly bear not to touch her, and learn by heart her geography by the inside of his palm – eyes closed, and with the softest part of his mouth. Arch and Mysie together cursed all those wasted days and nights they had known one another and *not* made love – even the very first of days, when he had driven her home. Unexpectedly, there was a sudden squall of seagulls outside the curtains, tussling and shrieking in the tree-lined square.

'Seagulls this far inland?' Mysie wondered. 'Means perhaps a hard winter.'

They were able to talk together peacefully for some time, before the hour of Arch's departure struck.

'This is the nicest thing to happen to me since picking raspberries . . .'

She was smiling at the recollection, even in the dark.

'At Puddledock in the summer, you have to crouch down among the stalks and the suckers to pick the best ones, and mint grows there for the shade, and you can smell the heavenly lemon-mint in the shadows, down there among the raspberries where you find the very ripe, fat ones, and then tiptoe away, with a tiny, tiny, pinprick of blood on your finger, just there . . .'

And she showed him, sure enough on her finger, a

scarcely perceptible spider's speck of blood which she had drawn from the corner of her lip – a pale raspberry pink.

Thereafter, on her way to and from the theatre, out for an afternoon walk in the gardens of Holland House, if ever she heard the sound of an aircraft above her head, Mysie always looked up and waved furiously. Arch had told her once about his improver – Captain Dyson – who was flying a desperately wounded observer back to the airfield near Béthune, himself bleeding to death into his boots, struggling for home: and a French farm-girl, all unknowing down below, waved to him. And he lived, and wanted to live, and so did the observer, simply because of the wave.

CHAPTER FIFTEEN

First Blood

'How do you get along with wild birds, young Gendron?' asked the commanding officer, a cheerful figure in informal rat-catcher, shooting-cap, walking stick, Bedlington terrier at his heels. He had introduced himself as 'Medlicott, Michael, Major, but go easy on the Major, will you, we're all friends here, and I don't like the sound of all those Ms . . .'

'I'm more accustomed to jackasses and bush-boys, where I come from, sir, but I enjoy the home-grown variety.'

'Good for you, and a little less of the "sir", sir, if you don't mind. At least, when I'm in civilians. We try to keep things going on a more or less home basis. Just follow me a moment, I'll show you one or two surprises we've got for you . . .'

Arch found it difficult to recognize the authority of his new commanding officer in the bearing of this compact, housemasterly figure who led him round the back of the single-storey gatehouse, which served as office of the 10th Squadron, his new home.

'Our squadron bluetits are just hatched – look at the little beggars, up there on the roof, fluttering their wings – that's because they're intensely ratty with me as I'm disturbing their feeding process . . .'

And the major pointed up to a line of straws and feathers alongside the lead gutter, from which issued an outcry of enraged twitterings.

'Go to it, my little darlings . . .'

Still twinkling away, Major Medlicott led Arch back to the 10th Squadron office or, as he called it, 'my den'. The

10th Squadron was stationed in a certain splendour in an old rural manor-house near Béthune. The building itself was somewhat run-down, had been a château, now was more of a farmhouse, and went by the name of Capité. Although its fortunes had somewhat faded, nevertheless it retained something of a former dignity, like a retired ceremonial horse finding itself somewhat unexpectedly doing the milk-round.

'I think the best thing now is for you to meet Bickerton,' he announced, 'Bickerton – your observer – your quick-firer. How many hours have you done "solo"?'

'Only eight.'

'Dear God – sending out more Fokker fodder, are they? Never heard of anything so irresponsible. I tell you, Gendron, the Hun – and I say it with great respect – has got some murderous bastards flying up there these days, and you'll need every bit of practice we can give you. Bickerton's a grand chap – as rough-edged as they come – but something of a legend here. He can bring a machine down with a single burst. He puts the bullets in by hand – I've seen him do it. He'll take good care of you. "Let the dog see the rabbit", that's his philosophy. There he is now, just coming from the armoury. Over here, Bick!'

Major Medlicott called out to a slender man, with more the build of a jockey or a groom, in blue dungarees, who was carrying on each shoulder – not unlike a snake-charmer – two bandoliers brimful of machine-gun bullets.

'Bickerton – this is David Gendron, who's joined us from Peckwater. He's not done very much on his own, but he got a splendid report from Dyson, sounds like a bit of a rascal, and knows how to glide a Rumpty right into its hangar on a dead-stick . . .'

'Handsome,' was Bickerton's monosyllabic reply. But he held his hand out in greeting. Arch thought he must be a few years older than himself, but it was hard to tell.

'Captain Dyson your improver?' he asked, once Major Medlicott had bustled away to steal breadcrumbs from the Mess for his bluetits. Arch said he was.

201

'And who was your guv'nor?'

'Major Treadaway.'

'That old dug-out?'

'He gave us a pretty hard time. Tough but fair.'

'Very fair.'

'I think he managed to get through to us that there was a way to handle the machines. That they shouldn't start handling us. That you could get the hang of them. You know, tune them, tinker about with them, learn their ways.'

'He told you that, did he?'

'Well, yes, in a way he did . . . It worked for us.'

'Handsome,' said Bickerton again, when Arch explained how he gained, finally, his wings.

'Everybody get through, did they?'

'No, one or two bailed out. Well . . . smashed.'

'Chute mortelle?'

'One or two. Three, as a matter of fact.'

Bickerton whistled softly, but not happily, at the news.

'Three. What a pair of balls . . . !'

This reflective expression, as Arch was to discover, was another of Bickerton's favourites. He was a man of few sentences, and those he had he liked to recite from time to time, as if to amuse himself. But as stockmen used to say of good horses, Bickerton was a 'cow-wise' character, to put it mildly. It was not the overalls he wore, they were practical enough, even though unlike his fellow-fliers' garb. In fact, Arch discovered Bickerton dressed even more eccentrically when in the air, usually pulling his breeches and flying-jacket over whichever pyjamas he happened to be wearing; and when flying low, he liked to sit on a flattened steel helmet underneath a rubber cushion. But it was not the costume, it was the look of him, which so startled Arch the first time they met. Unless he was very much mistaken, Bickerton, his quick-firer, his first-line defender, his pair of eyes, was blind in one eye. A one-eyed observer seemed unthinkable.

'If us two is going to work together,' Bickerton recommended, 'then it's what I call a bit of a thinking-out job. So our best shot is to sit down over a nice cup of tea, and talk it through.'

Which was precisely what they did, on a pair of canvas stools outside the tents. And while they chatted, tin mugs of 'gunpowder' in their hands, and Arch explained about his training, and what he thought about things, Bickerton laced and unlaced his cartridge-belts, making use of a neat little nail-file he carried in his top-pocket, wearing down the superfluous metal around the base of each bullet.

'Each one made "by hand",' was Bickerton's explanation of his task, 'like Chelsea chocolates. That's the secret. Or, one of the secrets. And,' he added, 'when we run into hostiles upstairs, make sure you let the dog see the rabbit.'

Arch leaned forward on his stool, to get a good look at the other man, to make sure his own eyes did not deceive him. No, it was unmistakable, his right-hand eyelid hung down low over the eye, making his left side squint. And, when he winked at you, he did so with his one good eye.

'You want to treat your machine they way you'd treat your own horse,' he advised. 'Gentle, like. Never push it flat out, never kick the rudder, unless you have to . . . Get the feel of her nose, just like you would your horse's mouth, get the touch just right. Learn to fly by the soles of your feet. That's the trick of it, or one of the tricks. And one more thing – run with your luck – and remember, the more you know, the luckier you get . . .'

Well he had had that lesson before, from Captain Dyson. By the time they had drunk their tea, Bickerton, so far as Arch was concerned, sounded like a veteran.

Together, so that he could feel the difference in weight, and sense the 'touch' the observer spoke of, Arch took up the two-seater Bristol, a ponderous machine which depended absolutely on Bickerton's expertise in defence, as it had virtually no evasive potential at all. Patiently, Bickerton took the battle-inexperienced pilot through the techniques of landing, climbing, rolling and dropping bombs – something of a hit-and-miss activity.

Their first contact patrol together was to go over the

sugar factory at La Bassée, which they did without incident, dropping two bombs, missing the factory, but hitting the railway yard, and then returned. Enemy Archie caught them flying home at 2,000 feet and Arch made his first effective dive when a heavy gunburst of shrapnel exploded near them and holed the machine. What Bickerton called 'a coal-box'. Arch's heart lurched, but he remembered Dyson's advice, put his nose down hard, and dived at a throttled-back 120 mph. A piece of steel flew into the magazine carrier, and one sliver whipped through Bickerton's coat.

'Now you know why I wear a steel helmet on my arse,' was his comment after they had landed safely, and examined the damage. But it was a confident start for a beginner. Gradually, the solo flying hours notched up, and Bickerton approved his pupil's progress. Before long, the contact patrols (interspersed with early-morning riding and tennis matches – the major once ordered him to land by the local hospital, to ask to borrow their roller for the tennis court) became daily routine; sometimes Arch took an artillery officer up with him in Bickerton's place, for observation, and sometimes he would photograph Hun positions over Loos; and, to relieve the monotony, sometimes the two of them flew low on their course back to the airfield, and strafed the Hun trenches, dodging rifle and machine-gun fire. Once over the brickstacks they dropped dangerously low and paid for their sins by a tail-full of 'woolly-bears' on the Kaiser's birthday.

News from home was less good. Father-Sir had sent the copy of the *Sydney News* with the terrible report that Victor Trumper died in June.

'This war hits us all hard' wrote Father-Sir, 'and the losses in the Dardanelles are bad enough, but Victor was a top-gallant. Your mother and I went down to his funeral at Waverley. Tybby Cotter and Warny Armstrong were there bare-headed. Victor always played for the man at the other end, and Hugh Trumble said he made any wicket look like jam. Fourer after fourer. In Shakespeare's fine phrase,

Victor Trumper was as proper a man as one shall see in a summer's day.' Morale dropped to sea level at 'the dear old 10th', and almost cost Arch his life.

One morning, having flown up to 6,000 feet, his favourite flying altitude, Arch lost his path in heavy fluff, and succeeded in ditching his fighter escort at the same time. With Bickerton vigilant behind him, Arch flew the ponderous two-seater out of a shy wisp of protective cloud, peered down to check the altitude and, unbelievingly, saw below him, a few hundred feet away, perfectly placed, an undefended Fokker triplane. His first Hun? A sitting partridge? This was too good to be true. He must be on training exercise. Or was it a trap? There was no time to consult with Bickerton, seconds were precious before the Hun looked up and spotted him. But for a clumsy old 'flying pram', as the Bristol was often called, to bring down a single-seater, now that would be a prize. Arch could catch him in his dive, front on, with his forward Vickers, and if he missed it would give Bickerton a burst with the Lewis guns as they crossed. A frantic switch of the eyes up, down, no, the Tripe was totally unprotected, there was no fighter escort with its familiar scarlet markings. Nose down, and IN. He was tearing the wings back and even now the Hun did not seem to have spotted him. Dare he risk a further second or two before pressing the button in his gloved hand? It might be his first kill. He dared, and it was a fractional mistake, for the Hun must have heard the downward shriek of the stout Wolseley, and sideslipped. But not fast enough. Arch's burst sent a spray of bullets across the dashboard and nacelle, and to his exultation a plume of black oil-smoke began to pour out of the stricken fuselage. His only error, by delaying one second too long, was that poor old Bickerton had been denied the chance of putting in the finisher. The Hun machine turned on its back, a dead fish already, rolled over hopelessly and spun out of sight.

Arch, almost academically, watched the enemy machine plunge down. He was levelling up and flattening off, turning casually for home, when Bickerton's fist banged him heavily on his right shoulder. He turned his head and switched off to listen above the howling wind on the struts.

'You daft bugger, he's still coming after you – you didn't get a clean kill! Switch on, and give me a burst at him. He's coming back at us . . .'

The triplane had indeed somehow miraculously recovered, though it still trailed the tell-tale plume of thick oil-spray. Instead of being the persecutor, Arch was now the target. The Tripe, even when winged, had greater velocity, and was trying to gain, *was* gaining altitude, tucking itself into precise order behind his tail, fractionally below in the dreaded 'blind spot'. Arch was almost distraught with rage at himself, even shame, he could hardly think. He cursed the ponderousness of the Bristol, hearty and bullet-free though it was. Then his senses cleared a little, just enough for him to realize that he must give Bickerton his chance. It was a faint hope, but their only one. 'Let the dog see the rabbit' fumed in his brain. The observer had to trade with the Hun on a man-to-man basis.

He dived into a bandage of low-lying cloud, just as the triplane fired its first burst, through the propeller, splattering the glass faces of the instruments. The dashboard erupted over Arch's hands. At the same instant his sleeve, as he struggled to reload the Vickers gun, tugged the emergency engine switch upwards – inexplicably, it seemed, the steady Wolseleys spluttered and died. All hope of presenting a no-deflection shot for Bickerton had vanished: he was done for now, on his first engagement, and the machine hung in his hands, a dead weight.

'Please God, we don't burn up,' he prayed, but a quiet voice behind him said, 'Switch on!'

He looked up, saw to his amazement, the switch was indeed *off*. Switching on, he heard the engine cough twice and crackle into life.

He hit the vapour, trusting to find cover, but to his misery discovered it was only wafer-thin and that he was out in the open sky again. He heard also the familiar toc-toc-toc behind him, and knew the triplane was still there, leaning on his shoulder.

The sound from Bickerton's double Lewis at aft was low and menacing, like an organ stop, like the thumping of a drum. He counted up to eight of them, and the hail of lead from his tormentor miraculously stopped. Leaning out of his cockpit, Arch saw the Fokker spiralling giddily away, wrapped in a white cloud of gas. He pulled the stick back slowly, checked the rudder flap, and swung smoothly into the patch behind the stricken machine, just south of the smoke-plume. Flying up and under, he fired the Vickers full out. The air seemed full of acrid tracer, cordite and oil fumes. Above the wreckage in the air, he side-stepped, held the wing steady, and Bickerton ripped a mouthful of tracer into it. At first he thought nothing had happened, until he saw, by the nose, a tiny red flame flickering shyly forward, almost too timid to emerge. Then the hands of fire seemed to run all round the Fokker, as it plunged headlong, caressing it on either side, swarming up the tail, and consuming everything in their grasp. And still Arch hounded its progress, flying alongside and below, and still Bickerton, every time it came into his sights, emptied burst after burst . . . The Hun observer had dropped from sight. They had taken the eyes out of it. The triplane was blinded and at their mercy. At 2,000 feet from the ground, the burning figure in the pilot's seat struggled on to the rim of his cockpit and, arms horribly outstretched into the air, covered with fire, like Icarus, he leaped into the emptiness and nothingness, and spun down and down and down. It was the single most terrible thing Arch had ever witnessed. Bickerton was firing still at the somersaulting machine, until it detonated, the wings tearing off in one direction, the engine, a flower of yellow flame, in another. And only then did the relentless toc-toc-toc-toc cease.

Arch's boots and leather sleeves were shredded badly by machine-gun bullets, and there were glass splinters in his lap, but he was miraculously unscathed. The dashboard was ruined. As they landed at the airfield the engine faded during the run-in and the undercarriage was crippled badly; but at least they had arrived home.

Arch jumped down. His head spun, and he clutched the wing with both hands to keep himself upright. He dreaded Bickerton's wholly justified reproaches but wanted to thank him for saving his life. No words came.

'We were in a right three-and-fourpence there,' was all the observer found to say.

His one good eye appeared more screwed-up than ever.

'Still, we gave them a right bladdering. The old bollocks would have been quite pleased with you.'

'Pleased? *Pleased?*' Arch could hardly believe what he was hearing. 'I made a proper bugger's muddle of it. I should never have gone in, on an old pram like the Bristol. I made a right balls of it, it's lucky we're alive – '

'Oh, yes, you should. Only thing is: if you want to be a proper tradesman, never give a bloke a second chance. Still I reckon you learned that.'

Bickerton began to walk back in the direction of the armoury to refill his cartridge-belts. He seemed quite unconcerned. Arch called to him:

'Bickerton! Thank God you told me to *switch on*.'

'When?'

'Up there – when we were being attacked by the Fokker. Thanks – I owe my life to you.'

'I never said anything,' said Bickerton.

'You never said anything?'

'No, there was too much on my mind. I was digging in.'

'But the switch was *off*. And *you* said "*Switch on*".'

'Not me,' said Bickerton, and continued on his way.

'Somebody said "Switch on",' insisted Arch.

He stood there, holding the wing. He felt his hands and legs beginning to shake violently. He feared the other officers would see him. His whole body seemed to vibrate.

'Hey, Arch,' said Bickerton, grinning over his shoulder. 'You'll do.'

The observer continued on his way to the armoury, and failed to see Arch being helplessly sick all over his boots.

PART FOUR

CHAPTER SIXTEEN

Roman Landing

Arch Gendron had met Lord Portarlington before at the Carlyle Club, of course. The first occasion, with Captain Legge, was forgotten, it had been so brief. They had been reintroduced one evening later that summer by Chas who messed with him in France, and they enjoyed a glass of shooting port together. It was the end of an extremely pleasurable leave, a week before Hodson's Horse were marched up the line to Venges, and Chas with them – all destined to play a part in the great summer break-out. As they were leaving Lord Portarlington said to Arch:

'Look, do come down to Roman Landing, if you have the inclination one leave. If I'm not there myself, abroad or something, there's bound to be my mother or servants or somebody, and it's such a pretty place. I'm told the house is very pretty too. Come down and visit.'

Naturally, Arch did not think of inviting himself.

On a third occasion, quite by chance, Trowel had made an introduction in an empty club, with tumblers of hot whisky on a cold night, beside the anthracite fire.

'But look here, Trowel, I know Mr Gendron very well, and we talked horses for hours last, when was it, July or August . . . ? This ridiculous war muddles up one's sense of time so much.'

Arch had heard countless opinions of the war by now, but this was the first time he had ever heard anybody describe it as ridiculous. He thought to himself, I'm going to enjoy this officer, as he looked at Portarlington, with his light foxy hair that fell back from a high brow, and eyes permanently screwed tight, so that in order to see he held his head at an angle as if to prevent its falling forward. Though he had the expression of somebody so bored by daily events that he seemed permanently half-asleep, around his mouth there was invariably the hint of a grin.

'Look here, you really must come down to Roman Landing, I insist . . . '

This time Arch felt it would be impolite to decline. His brother assured him that Arthur Portarlington found the incessant company of young cavalry officers tiring, and was worn out by their horsy ways, especially when off-duty.

'There is a limit to the infinite fascination for manège,' Lord Portarlington complained, 'I mean, you know, horses are truly very stupid animals, and the only people who find them clever are cavalry officers – and I suppose, in relation to other cavalry officers, they are!'

The journey was complicated, as the estate itself was located on a peninsula of private land in an obscure corner of Sussex, between the retreating sea and the last collapse of a gentle range of downland called The Quells. It was a solitary place of bird-call and salt-marsh, penetrated by channels, or ripes of green, reflecting water. Local farmers called it the flow country. To reach Roman Landing, Arch had to change from the familiar L.B.S.C. line at Regnum, on to a single-track private railway. This was in fact the only way to find the private demesne of the Portarlingtons; a signpost in the railway station expressed this baldly: 'Private railway to the Manhood Peninsula only.' Cut off from the rest of this protruding tongue of flatland Sussex and standing by itself, as aloof as a lighthouse, and as isolated, Roman Landing dominated the Manhood. Tradition said that it was the oldest inhabited house in England.

At forcible times of the year, February or full moon, the ripe-lands were in danger of being segregated from the county by fast-racing neap-tides. Centuries ago, it had been a forest. By now, there was little left, natural or man-made; even the tide-mill had ceased working some thirty years before, fallen into dilapidation, and pulled down. No house, but the iron mill-wheel remained. A single row of coastguards' cottages faced the Channel, and Lord Palmerston's rusty defence-forts out at sea.

A curious trick of the light, trapped between The Quells inland and Sheep Island offshore, appeared to magnify ships, fishing-vessels, and the fortresses themselves several times over, and made them look menacing and strange. It was an illusion of the haze but, on those days when a sea-fret swept up from the south, before they vanished altogether, the naval forts in the Channel roads loomed up outside and threatening, like a haunted medieval city.

The down-line bent southwards and headed east in a long curve, and from his rattling carriage Arch noticed the muddied banks of sea-dykes and, to complete the inherent sadness of the scene, a grey heron, which lifted its ghostly wings and flapped away at the train's approach. Every kind of marsh-bird nested there: partridge, lapwing, waders. At one moment he imagined he saw in the distance, indistinct, like a ghost story, a castle from the mysterious world of Mortmere outspread with keep, buttresses and fortified walls – but it soon disappeared behind a row of pale poplar trees. Last year's leaves remained on the branches, overdue to fall, but sandy and lustreless. The blue boughs of the hornbeams and the ashes sagged. On every side, the identical grey sky, the flooded fields of sea-arrow, populated by motionless cows standing as if reflected, ankle-deep in water, all contrived to remind him of his dreary service in Foulness and the bleak landscape there. A flow country indeed. The winter oppressing the absent spring. Occasionally, he passed an outpost of the local defence force, barbed-wire coils, a solitary sentry with fixed bayonet gaping vacantly out towards the sea, cement pill-boxes, reminiscent of the salient on the other side of the Channel.

Inland again, painted sunblinds, jaunty front doors, and bright south-facing balconies boasted a courageous gaiety, that masqueraded as a seaside town: a spacious hotel facing the golf links, open for the out-of-season enthusiasts, included a solarium that captured at this hour the last winking rays of light in the drab peninsula. Beyond it the miniature railway line worked its way past two farms, rough grazing land, the relics of the abandoned mill, the Canal Bridge, and at last the diminutive train station itself; this consisted of some sleepers piled up on top of each other, and roofed in corrugated iron. It looked unprepossessing enough. But there was the sign sure enough: 'Roman Landing' all by itself, a milk-churn bay, and one wooden seat for private passengers with time to kill. As he expected, Arch was the only visitor. The last few miles or so had rattled and bumped over Lord Portarlington's private grounds, and this inadequate platform and shelter was his lordship's private station.

'I'll handle those bags, sir,' a voice interrupted him, as he stood on the bare platform, alone but for a short, rather goofy-looking boy.

Certainly Arthur Portarlington lived, as he had promised, in a remote and unexpected place, but of the 'pretty little house' there was no sign. The landscape of scrub and tamarisk was so bare and featureless, it reminded him of the worst parts of his native Australia, that dreadful sombre space, unbroken by hedges, ditches, and intruded upon by occasional stringy-barks, and little else. Assuming some kind of vehicle would be waiting to meet them, Arch was charmed to find that, in the place of Lord Portarlington's Daimler-Benz, there stood a small brown and white donkey, hitched to a shabby farm-cart. In the back of the cart, the goofy boy had already stowed his bags.

'There's a cushion up the back, sir,' called the lad, and swung himself up. The lean wind made Arch pull across the lapels of his fur-lined flying-coat.

The boy, who revealed his name to be Apps, worked, he said, on the estate, and kept the horses and the donkeys; it was no chance that a cart rather than a motor greeted Lord Portarlington's guests, for 'my lord won't keep'us Daimliars on the estate, and likes to lett'us livestock work the war'; all the vehicles (there were several) had been sent to

214

the front except one. Before 1914, it had been a tradition that the Portarlington chauffeurs played the Manhood second eleven every year at cricket, but so many traditions had collapsed after that devastating autumn.

'It's disused, sir, been disused ever since the war began, and small chance of us ever taking up again.' Apps referred to the canal. Moorhens spearheaded towards them, and once a large brown rat slipped clumsily into the water from the bank. The whole region, according to Apps, looked likely to fall into extreme neglect. The place was rural, exclusively, no kind of industry for miles, just wildfowlers and a saw-mill, eel-fishing; the farms lacked labourers because of the Kaiser's war.

'My father and grandfather worked on my lord's estate, on the farm, so to speak, but they're in France by now, and I'm due to go in a couple of years . . .'

'If it goes on so long, which I doubt,' said Arch optimistically.

'Not according to our dad,' returned the boy, in between emitting strange prutting sounds to encourage the donkey, 'he says it's going on till the duration.'

It was not a long ride, for, after following a circular sweep left-handed away from the setting sun – a cluster of fire and curling cloud wrapped up ready to explode into the sea, streaking out in all directions – the canal recrossed again, and a footpath overtaken, the cart turned awkwardly from the gravel to an uneven strip, heavily ridged by farm vehicles, and lurched its way between a file of straggling alders. This track appeared to ascend a gradual incline, and as the patient donkey reached the summit, with the effect of a blow, it so took away his breath, Arch saw spreading before him the fortified walls of the castle he had witnessed mysteriously from the train.

Perhaps the moat had dried up centuries before, and the drawbridge was now a permanent causeway, but remnants of the old portcullis still endured and, as they passed through it, opened out on to a large grass courtyard, with steep walls at each side, and turrets at every corner, and there were dogs barking and leaping up to reach them, young Apps standing in the cart whipping them off, and calling, 'Get down, you sods, get down,' and a cluster of ageing servants and grooms and young stable-lads, as well as Lord Portarlington himself in white breeches, walking down the steps to greet him, and the lights in the braziers on the walls flickering into life. They shook hands, and Arch thought his friend's eyes were more crinkled up than ever.

'I'm so glad our little train delivered you safe and sound, Gendron, dear old chap, it has been known to have the most inconvenient derailments from time to time . . . '

'I thoroughly enjoyed it, and young Mr Apps here was a most entertaining carrier . . . '

'Well done, you,' said Lord Portarlington to Apps, who was already unhitching the cart from the donkey.

'Now, Lucking, mind the bags, will you . . . '

'To the Tower Room, sir.' For a second, Arch hovered uncertainly. 'The girls will take those up, sir, you just go on ahead with his lordship.' While the butler organized his bags, Arch followed his host up the stairs into the Great Hall. So this was the celebrated 'demesne', of which so much had been spoken. It was curious his own brother had said nothing of the place being a great medieval castle, more like a village than a manor-house, although he quickly recognized that, in spite of the impressive battlements and the imposing keep, the fortified exterior was largely a ruined shell, and the domestic apartments protected within, as if inside an egg. All the same, looking backwards over his shoulder as he entered the guard-room, he had the impression of being a toy soldier inside a child's fort.

'We'll have a drink directly,' his host suggested, 'and then I expect you'd like to bathe and change. It's freezing cold down here, in spite of lighting up the fires, but the place has always been full of draughts; my father never would have it heated up. It's more of a tithe-barn than a home. The oldest house in England, they say: I say, the

216

coldest! We have to make do with pipes and things, but I hope your bedroom will be warm enough. March can be a cold bugger at best. I've put you in the Rawmere Tower, which looks out to our little island and, provided the wind keeps down, you should have a good night's sleep. Better than under canvas anyway, and there's a coal fire up there, I imagine. Lucking will take care of you; he's a bit old, but what can you expect, the uselessly old and the uselessly young, that's all we've got left.' By now they were in a small wood-panelled room, a library of sorts, just off the Great Hall.

'It's why I pray for this beastly war to end,' said a voice in the corner, almost hidden behind the high wings of a large-backed chair, 'the servant crisis is so ruinous. I would have imagined the Germans feel the same. You'd have thought sensible people would have come to sensible arrangements.'

'My mother,' said Arthur Portarlington, 'Lady Rawmere, she's frightfully old and dreadfully deaf, so you'll have to yell. Hope you won't mind that, as I've sat you next to her at dinner.'

'Please forgive me not getting up, it's terrible being so inactive.' The old lady seemed extremely small.

'A friend of mine from the Carlyle Club, Mother, Lieutenant Gendron, of the Flying Corps.'

'Please don't budge, Lady Rawmere,' replied Arch, taking the tips of the fingers outstretched beneath pale pink gloves.

'It *is* a bother,' answered the old lady, 'and the bother is this osteo-arthritis I seem to be afflicted with. I can't ride any more, I can barely walk, can't go to morning prayers, well, I can't say I mind that, and I can't stand for more than a minute. Hence my chair.'

Portarlington waved generally in the direction of a side-table covered with decanters and glasses.

'I can't keep a man around endlessly pouring out drinks, and overhearing every single word one says, so please go ahead and help yourself; everything's there, I think; I'm

217

drinking dry sherry. It's fractionally less disgusting than that stuff we get at the old C.'

Arch went over and helped himself to a large whisky with water.

'This is Lieutenant Gendron,' Portarlington yelled again to his mother.

'I know. I heard you before, there's no need to shout.'

Lady Rawmere seemed to be convulsed among the cushions, her elbows balanced on the two arms of the purple chair, her fists clenched as if expressing some argumentative point, their fingers stretched outwards. He could see they were dangerously knotted inside the gloves. Her face was dusted so heavily in white powder, some of it had discoloured her dress. Arch could see she had been at one time a beauty.

'I've met your brother, haven't I?' she shouted back. 'I remember him being the most marvellous horseman.'

'He's in France with Lord Strathcona's Horse.' Arch bent over her, to keep in range, shouting as if against a gale. There was still a disfigured beauty there, beneath the powder and the arthritis, which in its day had bewitched Ashley Rawmere, before he, also, declined with the century.

'I can't go on riding, you see,' answered the old lady, 'that's just the trouble. It's so hard when you've been active all your life. It doesn't seem fair.'

'I hope they don't cause you too much pain,' sympathized Arch, 'I know how terribly painful arthritis can be.'

'Well, the doctors keep giving me things to help, but they don't do much good, you know, drugs to deaden the thing and all of that, but I won't take them if I can help it. Even if it does cause me pain. The trouble is these pain-pills or whatever they are make me feel stupid, and I can't bear that, I'd rather suffer than be stupid, wouldn't you?'

Arch wondered whether he would. It was not death, but wounds in battle, that troubled him. He sipped at his whisky, and it stuck in his throat.

218

'Don't talk to me about my wretched daughter,' she suddenly announced. The rather fierce-looking Sealyham in Lady Rawmere's lap looked alert and self-centred.

'Doesn't do her duty by a visit,' explained Lord Portarlington, 'lives on the estates in Ireland.'

'Not that she means any harm by it, I know she's got things to do, hunting five times a week and all of that. Arthur does what he can, but he's overseas most of the time. This wretched war. Doctor said it all depends on what you eat, so I don't drink coffee now, and I don't eat green vegetables, but it doesn't do a great deal of good. Still, one wears on, I suppose; you may see me leaping about, Arthur, before I die, but I doubt it somehow.'

'Alcohol, I suppose,' put in Arch diffidently.

'No, that I absolutely do refuse. Nothing is going to stop me drinking, except *death*,' the old lady replied with emphasis.

'Mother's rather defiant about that sort of thing,' Portarlington explained. 'She was the finest horsewoman in the West Sussex, and went out regularly with them until last season. It's extremely hard for her. She was Master of the Rawmere right up to the war. Conrad – you'll meet him over grub – frequently rode with her. Had all the hounds put down last year, she was so disappointed. God, I hope I won't end up old.'

'Well, we all tend to want what we don't seem to have.' Arch added more water to his whisky to deaden the sting.

'I don't want old age, and I don't think she does either.'

'Somebody mentioned grapes,' muttered the old lady, 'but I can't imagine them doing anything for you. Imagine life, eating nothing but grapes. You'd better ring for Mrs Juniper to help me into my things, if we're not to be late. You know how long these old fingers of mine take me.'

Portarlington, in his stockinged feet, pressed a bell by the fireplace which sounded deep somewhere in the castle. The stone corridors carried the echo.

'I could do with a pair of carpet slippers,' he said vaguely.

219

'Are you giving us our places, Arthur, for dinner – or are we all just going in hugger-bugger?'

'I'm going to do places, it's probably simpler. Now, I'll show Mr Gendron his turret-rooms first. Arch, you bring your drink with you. Always so comforting in the bath, I think.' And with a courteous bow to his mother, he led the way into the Great Hall, which a patrol of the New Model Army had occupied when they invested the castle after the Siege of 1644.

The housekeeper, Mrs Juniper, came bustling in, full of anxious concern: 'Oh, my lady, put your feet up, you look so *jaded*!'

Climbing the wide wooden staircase out of the Great Hall, Arthur Portarlington paused and gestured vaguely to a spiralled stone turret lit by a guttering torch on a wall-bracket.

'You'll find your rooms up there, old chap, if you follow the rope banister. Just climb to the top, and you'll probably discover Lucking has set your clothes out ready for dinner. There's a bath next door, and just come down when you feel like it. Grub's up in an hour. There'll be some sort of dreadful gong, but you may not hear it in the tower. You'll not know the guests but they're a splendid mixed bunch. Better than a crowd of horse-officers anyway. Most of them have just ridden over for dinner, only a couple of house-guests this week-end mercifully, so tomorrow the place will be to ourselves. I've asked a couple of locals over you might like to meet, General Ascapard, Captain Chevalier, whom I'm sure you'd care to know, one of the friars from Amberley, well, he's a house-guest actually, and a couple of other people. Should be a cheery group. Anyway, it's nice to be in the country, one seems to breathe and sleep so much better. I always feel London's like the war . . . so crushing somehow . . . so entrenched . . . don't you?' And, without waiting for Arch to answer he turned into what were presumably his own quarters beyond the main stair.

When Arch stooped to enter the turreted room after

crossing a short stone-flagged court, he found to his delight a succession of vaulted rooms in what might have been the former armoury. It was from here in earlier days, looking out over the easy approach from the marshes, that the retainers of the old recusant family had vigorously withstood an eight-month siege against the New Model Army. Sir William Waller accepted Captain Tarleton's sword, on behalf of the loyal garrison, 'pinched with famine as they were'.

Arch explored his quarters at leisure. Fires burned brightly in each of the rooms. On the double-poster bed, he saw his evening clothes already laid out. He decided not to linger by the view; the sky beyond the turret windows was already shadowy, and he would have to wait until the next morning for the surprise of the countryside below the castle walls. He stripped quickly and sank into the hot scented water, reflecting on the eccentricity of his journey, the private train, the picturesque arrival by donkey, and the warmth of his friend's welcome. He allowed his thoughts to reside happily on Mysie, and her familiar frown, and the alternating timidity and eagerness of her embrace. He wondered how rehearsals were progressing with Chancellor. He wished Mysie was with him now, undressing and bathing in another part of the castle, and dreamed indulgently of seeking out her bedroom late at night. He found there was something erotic about country-house weekends.

Dressed and checking his appearance in the pier-glass, Arch walked from the cosy bedroom into the chill turret-yard. There was no wind and the shadows flew back and forth from the light shed by a pair of flambeaux. He paused and decided to walk around the four sides of the turret-square to see what it must have felt like to be on sentry-go in old times, a retained archer, perhaps, a royalist trooper. The New Model Army must have marched over the damp fields from the road to Regnum, which would mean from the direction of that vague, golden glow over there, he assumed. Out to sea, all was thick darkness, nothingness, except far in the distance the swinging light of a fishing-boat. He was startled by a quiet, unfamiliar voice. Caught in the cross-fire of flickering light and shade, in a corner of the embrasure, which somehow intensified the vision, he saw a medieval monk draped in the robes of the Dominican White Friars with a prayer-book in his fingers.

'I can only apologize for the shock,' said the figure contritely, 'but I thought it better to speak out than remain silent. One forgets the impression one is bound to give to the world outside. For one who spends his life in a medieval cloister, I am by now fairly used to ghostly friars! I know you must be Lieutenant Gendron, as our host has warned me about you, and I am Father Leodegar, a grateful guest. From the Dominican house at Amberley. We are due to descend any minute now for dinner, I expect the gong, but I could not resist a short turn along the battlements. Not just to suit my monastic mood, truly, I like to come up here, especially when invited on a stormy night to dine, so that I can observe the dramatic massacre of the waves below.'

Arch, laughing, took the monk's hand warmly and then turned back with him to look out again at the darkness.

'I've always admired the histrionics of Arthur Portarlington's domestic hearth, and teasingly claim part-ownership, as these estates and lands all once belonged to the see of my abbey. "*Jour de ma Vie*" is a blazon shared by courtier and cloister. But a long time ago, I'm afraid. Arthur's greedy ancestors were opportunists of the worst sort, and finding themselves close to the Protestant shoulder at the right time succeeded in disinheriting Holy Mother Church when her stock stood, frankly, somewhat low.'

'Were they Cromwellites?'

'Wicked radicals, certainly, but opportunistic, as I said, rather than religious zealots. The divisions of State and King provided them with their profit, I'd say. Later they cut great inroads against the murderous Irish, and increased their estates over there. You know the way the

222

English acquired their land – simply by taking it away from those it belonged to. I believe they still exist all over that benighted bog-land, in Offaly, Rossmore and Athlone, but sadly run-down. Port tells me, since the old duke's time, the Rawmere acres are mainly shooting-commons now. The treacherous Irish threaten to burn down his house he tells me, from time to time. But then, seeing us occupied elsewhere, they would.'

Arch was about to mention his own Irish connection when the echo of a gong trembled up the spiral staircase and out to the battlements where they stood.

'I hear him saying ha-ha! among the trumpets!' said Father Leodegar mysteriously, gesturing towards the sound of the gong. 'Time for dinner, I think,' he added. 'The Port battlements arouse a positively medieval hunger!' As they carefully made their way down the spiral staircase, 'You'll enjoy the set-up, I'm sure,' continued the monk, 'and some of the guests. General Ascapard is a most interesting character; he fought in Kabul, and I hope you'll take to Count Zehnder, who visits us at a difficult time from so far away.'

'It sounds a German name, but I don't imagine it can be.'

'Not really, no, although I assume naturally there's German blood. No, Count Zehnder is an old friend, and a frequent visitor at Roman Landing. He comes from German Switzerland originally, but has the right as a neutral to "to and fro", you know.'

'Seems odd, in the middle of a war,' responded Arch, as they strolled side by side down the wooden staircase into the Great Hall.

'In a way I suppose it is rather odd,' answered Father Leodegar, 'but I believe it is always important to look at things from another angle. To keep one's mind open for an alternative point of view. Heaven knows, we stand in need of it.'

The young flying officer noticed how different this kindly monk appeared from all the stuffy C. of E. padres he had met on church parade.

'I gather I'm next to Lady Rawmere,' said Arch, 'but I hope we'll get a chance to talk again.'

'Ahah, Lady Rawmere . . .' smiled the monk, 'I suspect that's the penance due from a guest on his first visit.' They both laughed. 'But you know, she's quite wonderful, and dreadfully keen on our work . . .'

But, because Lord Portarlington came up at that very minute to introduce them to his other guests, Arch could not enquire as to the nature of the 'work' that Lady Rawmere encouraged and Father Leodegar pursued. Their host introduced them airily to General Ascapard, by the doorway.

'Leodegar to rhyme with dredger, is it?' the general asked with some ferocity.

Just before dinner Arch had an opportunity to exchange a few words with General Ascapard when the butler asked them both what they wished to drink. Arch deferred to his senior officer.

'What day of the week are we?' enquired the General testily.

'Saturday, sir.'

'Saturday, is it? Well then . . . a large glass of Irish whiskey.'

It seemed as good an excuse for a whiskey as any.

'Come over here, young fellow,' commanded the old man, 'you look ready for a bit of tug-jaw.' But his grey eyes were brightly shining underneath a hedge of white eyebrows.

'Gendron – Gendron – rings a bell somewhere. Just back from Franz, eh?' he enquired, as if there might be something reprehensible about the place. For his age, Ascapard was astoundingly upright and tigerish.

'Yes, General, I'm seconded from the Horse Artillery to the Flying Corps.'

'Any future in that? Cheers. God bless you . . .' and he gulped at his glass.

'I believe so, General.'

Arch sipped more warily at his own drink.

'I doubt it, young fellow, but I don't wish you ill. The whole business in Franz is such a buggers' muddle – a few jabs with the kukri and the bayonet and this lot would be over in a month . . .'

And, before Arch could disagree, the general whirled round on a second footman, as if to cut him down with a sabre.

'Look here, slip another Irish whiskey in there, will you, I seem to be carrying an empty glass in my hand – and don't ruin the thing with putting water in it – I like to see the colour of my whiskey' – and with a hint of a wink – 'like warm brown pee . . .'

'I believe with respect, General, much of the future of the war will take place in the air . . .'

'Flying battles? Heaven help us if it does, but look here, Gendron, we're here to amuse ourselves, not talk *war* all the time. There'll be plenty of that once old Count Zehnder gets up on his lofty nag. Do you like riddles? Here's one for you, it isn't difficult. What is a blind pig in two letters? Children love it. Not difficult.'

The general's change of tack was too sudden.

'Good heavens, I'm hopeless at these – pi, is it?'

'On the right lines – no, I'll put you out of your pain. P.G. – take the eye out, do you see!' And he exploded with a sudden gunfire of a laugh. 'Tell the flying boys that when you get back to Franz! Children love it!'

The gong reverberated a second time, elaborate and far off, and the men made a corridor each side of the door, as Lucking ushered Lady Rawmere into the dining-room.

'Now,' said Lord Portarlington, 'if you sit here, Mother, we'll work from there . . . General Ascapard, please . . .'

Father Leodegar pronounced a tortuous Latin grace, and a thick soup was passed round in a silver tureen. Almost at once a man in the brilliant regimentals of Skinner's Horse turned to Arch, who was sitting on his right hand.

'Look here, we haven't had a chance to meet – I'm Chevalier – old school chum of Arthur's . . . You must be

225

Arch Gendron. Saw you locking horns with Andrew Ascapard at drinks – ferocious old dug-out, isn't he? They say,
when he was hunting man-eaters in Sikkim, the odds were
four to one on Ascapard.'

'I can't say I'm very used to approaching Chiefs of
Staff . . .'

'Oh, he's not Staff, my dear,' said the precocious cavalryman, 'he's above all that – the word is, he has the ear of
Kingy. Heaven alone knows how: I gather they play complicated war games together with lead soldiers – you
know, fighting the Battle of Ramillies all over in that
ghastly billiard room at Sandringham. Keeps the King
occupied, I suppose, and out of the field marshal's hair.'

'Plays toy soldiers with the *King*?'

'Or so I've heard,' came the airy reply. 'I always think
the placement is so important, don't you, Gendron?' he
said affably. 'I remember how touchy the French are; one
evening at the Mountjoys, old Dolly Foljambe turned up
her plate in a terrible huff, and stormed out . . .'

'Turned up her plate?'

'Well, it's the sort of thing the French sometimes do, you
know,' explained the captain, 'and rather to my surprise
Admiral Geyral next to me said quite coolly, "*Oui, elle a
raison, Dolly est très mal-placée.*"'

Arch turned his attention to the man on the far side of
Captain Chevalier. There, without a doubt, was Graf von
Zehnder, far younger than Arch might have imagined,
rather precise in an unaffected way, monocled, courteous
but confident, eminently a diplomat with the precaution of
selecting the perfect word ('Have you had time to examine
the harquebus stanchioned within the Rawmere Tower?'
he had enquired at their introduction earlier) and not at all
the Hunnish figure Arch might have anticipated. Apparently he was important 'behind the scenes'. On Arthur
Portarlington's left sat the poet Conrad, in a worn dinner
suit.

The soup was coarse and brown and lumpy on the
tongue. It was not, so far, one of the better dinners Arch

had enjoyed in England, even below the Carlyle Club standard – which was never very high.

'Fruit from the Portarlington orchards, vegetables from the kitchen gardens, cream from the dairies, pheasants from the plantations, preserves from the pantries, butter from . . . where would you say the butter came from, Lucking?' asked Arthur, playfully.

'Suet substitute from the village shop, my lord,' came the reply.

The guests laughed in sympathy with the embattled butler.

'What, no butter, Mr Lucking!' asked Lady Rawmere. 'What is our gallant navy doing?'

'Tumbril-talk from Lady R.,' mumbled Captain Chevalier. But the butter appeared to be the only noticeable shortage, the soup the only disappointment. Everything else was in abundance, not lavish, but robust. The wines continued well, and Arch observed that, in spite of the war, there was no lack of fine Mosel or claret. Portarlington preserved an admirable cellar. Quails followed the soup. The wood-smoke mingled with the burning wax; long shadows fell on the diners' cheeks, lengthening their pale faces, as they sat beneath the chandeliers. In the cavernous grate in the centre of the hall huge branches spat and sparked. On the stone chimneypiece itself, Arch made out the motto of the Anglo-Norman family: '*Jour de ma Vie*'.

'Recently returned from Franz?' called across General Ascapard.

'Setting out again fairly soon,' Arch reassured him, and the general seemed satisfied for the minute.

'Is Lord Medmenham still dead, does anybody know?' Lady Rawmere enquired in a vague, uncertain kind of way. 'He certainly was, I don't know whether he still is . . .'

Arch's attention was riveted by the glittering eye of the general.

'When did you say you were going back to Franz?' Some sort of facial stroke had paralysed the pale eyelids, and

227

Arch felt himself transfixed by this seigneurial stare. The disconcerting result of his palsy was that when he blinked, his left eye remained unblinking, and stared in front of him like a fragment of glass.

'At the beginning of the week – I'm flying two-seaters.'

'You were a gunner officer, you told me. King's Troop, I assume: well, good show for that. As for piloting as the war of the future, I don't doubt it,' said the general sympathetically. 'Marvellous young men, full of the right sort of spirit.' He turned to his hostess. 'You should tell that boy of yours to get away from those horses, dear Lady Rawmere, and follow the example of this splendid young man. He's quite right. The future might be in the skies: I can see the brand new morning of a magnificent aerobatic warfare. I wish I was young again. Musketting's finished, in my view. This trench-bound slaughter in Franz is nothing but a scandalous, monumental, purposeless waste. A waste of time, money, and of youth. And youth of the finest. Youth that is irreplaceable, and is not being replaced.'

'Youth is inexhaustible, surely,' argued the Dominican.

'And it has the flower of death in its mouth,' muttered Ascapard.

'I should be sorry to see the decline of the horse,' Lady Rawmere replied.

'To say nothing of the lance,' Captain Chevalier concluded, creating a short silence.

'Well, maybe . . . ' Ascapard turned to his right to help himself to some chicken-jelly which Lucking thrust under his nose, 'but all I know of horse-officers is farting, swearing, and playing at cards.'

The kitchen-maids carried in crisp pheasants on a silver tray, half-cold already after the journey along the castle corridors.

More moderately, in the middle of the table, Father Loedegar was extolling the monastic rule, and deploring the present-day reluctance of novices to join the order.

'But, after all, what can be expected? We are all involved in this terrible war, and until the time comes for swords to

228

be turned back into ploughshares, and helmets once more into hives of bees, how can we reasonably expect young Christian boys to forsake the fields of battle?'

'There is new inspiration in the air,' agreed the general, 'and it is drenching the fields of Franz.'

'You know that the losses are devastating. Devastating.' This from a serious Portarlington. Conrad spread a finger of salt on a circle of claret. He had kept silent most of dinner.

'On both sides,' Arch ventured confidently, 'there's bound to be a break-out in the line soon. I think the cavalry will settle it at last.'

'I doubt it,' said General Ascapard, 'I see no reason to imagine such a thing. There's no sign of it.' His blue eyes glared in defiance. '*Is* there any sign of it?'

'We all know the atmosphere of secrecy we are in,' said Arch boldly, 'and I can hardly be precise as to detail, even among good friends, but my brother is held in reserve with several brigades of cavalry for that precise moment the German line breaks . . .'

'Your brother is presently at Zonnebeke,' broke in Captain Chevalier, without a smile, 'holding a section of the front between Ypres and Sanctuary Wood. He and the rest of the Ninth Lancers are no longer in reserve, but dismounted, holding the line as best they can until relieved by the Sherwood Foresters. The strategy of the swift punch-through and the cavalry charge beyond the lines, followed by general outflanking along the entire Hindenburg Line, was abandoned some weeks ago.'

Arch was astounded that this cavalry officer, who had seemed so young, and frivolous, should know as much, and in such precise detail. He felt immediate anxiety about his brother. Portarlington relieved the tension.

'You mustn't misinterpret Charlie's information as anything underhand. He's at the War Office, and it's his job to know these things. He could tell you the disposition of every Allied cavalry regiment up and down the salient if he wished to . . .'

'And most of the Boche as well, frankly,' smiled Chevalier. 'No, I wished, Gendron, merely to make a strategic point, not a defeatist one. Please don't be unnecessarily alarmed.'

'This is the sort of thing General Ascapard wants to talk to us about later on, over the port. I think it will be of special interest to you, Arch,' continued Portarlington, in his easy-going manner, 'and something from which we can all feel reassurance.'

'Of which,' Father Leodegar gestured gently, 'almost every one of us has need,' with a glance towards the taciturn figure on their host's left.

Arch had been told only a little about Conrad by Chevalier. He had, it was said, been knocked over by a shell and spent time in Craiglockhart. Some sort of crisis had taken place, almost a working-off, and, after a return to health, a deep-seated bitterness and anger had been replaced by a passionate quest for some new way. It was no longer possible to return to the earlier light-hearted mood of the dinner-party.

The pheasant was cleared, and the cheese set upon the table.

'We follow the French style at Port – *fromage, et ensuite le dessert*. Heaven knows why,' said Portarlington.

'You do know why, Arthur,' corrected his mother, 'Kingy always insisted. But, if you're going to be so serious all of a sudden, I am going to take this woman off.'

The gentlemen rose in anticipation, as Mrs Juniper appeared – as if at a signal – to draw back Lady Rawmere's chair.

CHAPTER SEVENTEEN

General Ascapard Makes a Speech

Lord Portarlington tapped his madeira glass lightly with a fork.

'Now I think Andrew Ascapard wants to address us for a few minutes. This should be of special interest to you, Arch, as you are a new friend of ours, and we feel, if any of all of this', he gestured vaguely around him, 'is to take hold, we shall have to find support from the new young class of officers coming in. I should tell you all, Lieutenant Gendron's older brother is a frequent visitor here to Port, and stands absolutely shoulder to shoulder with us. The room is yours, General.'

'Now you'll see what I mean,' mumbled Captain Chevalier in an undertone. 'Andrew Ascapard is a man of ferocious appearance and a somewhat murderous conviction.'

Arch looked round at the guests, one after the other, as they shifted their chairs back from the table.

These faces of the past, of individual strength of character, of survival, and of continuity: so much to admire, he thought to himself, as the purple port-wine, 'the Englishman's wine', ascended into his brain.

The plain workaday countenance of Father Leodegar, for example, of such remarkable beauty. The sardonic lift of Lord Portarlington's head, his sandy hair flopped back, growing out of his head so exactly *right*, soft and filled with different blond lights, ash-grey and white, streaked with sand. His eyes, in their perpetual screwed-up gaze, half-mocking, half-grave. Restrained, courteous, and ironic, looking at him, even as the general droned away, watching to see politely, assiduously, how well the young flier responded to this new philosophy. Perhaps most interestingly of all, the poet, Conrad, never following the face of the person he might address, or who addressed him, but sitting with his hands politely folded, his dark countenance strained with buried fear, and the points of his jaw-bones tensing under the skin. What provoked him? The prisoner of his dark conscience, his horror-stricken experience, his craving for revenge, the love of, and horror of, and certainty of, death? Did he long to share it with all the dead men who drowned him in his sleep? And the general himself, white-haired, hoarsely whispering now, his grey sharp eyes, and small paintbrush moustache above a mouth which hardly opened. Everybody, in the shadow cast by the candles and the draught that fretted them, leaning forward to catch his words, spoken urgently, quietly, unemphatically, like a prayer.

'Only when the harvest is on fire can we accept that this is the supreme moment for us to try – with all our energies – to save it.'

Arch listened out of courtesy, but he did not really hear anything. He could not understand it, in any case. He wanted to fly most of all, and not much else – that and, second, to lie in bed with Mysie. That was all. To return to Brontë, to show his wings off to the First Side, to see dear Mother, and darling Father-Sir, and Grimp get his hundred, and then play cricket and lacrosse again just like before. Innocent enough ambitions in a young man. Ideas foxed him. He sat forward, putting on a frown of extra concentration to compensate for the lack of interest he truly felt, passed the port as it revolved, and looked above him at the magnificent hammerbeam roof. How dark and uncomfortable it must have been in those days before electric light. That tall roof disappearing into shadow, and those stone walls, now blanketed in tapestries and hangings, and ancient ancestral portraits. He remembered the few family pictures at home, the Protestant aunts, and respectable grandfathers, from their substantial homes in Offaly and

Athlone. Waistcoats, signet-rings, and watch-chains, mostly lawyers and doctors. Here the wealth of counties and cathedrals populated the smoke-blackened faces of the family, some with the characteristic tilt of Lord Portarlington; pale, disdainful, rich, remote. And here, around him, the monuments to the historic patronage and influence of the Portarlingtons and even more ancient Rawmeres. Ascapard beat on relentlessly.

'Of course it is vital, absolutely *vital*, to defend the frontiers of our rank, before the dangers and forces which imperil it from without, and torment it from within . . .'

Above his white head, the walls were hung with ordnance and trophies which had belonged to Sergeant Pride, when he had made of Roman Landing a Roundhead garrison, following the siege of Regnum, and the occupation of the cathedral. Their horses had splashed and mired the retrochoir, and troopers disfigured the head of Lazarus in the east transept with their fowling-pieces. The scandal was, while the men scavenged, the captains obligingly looked on. A similar mythology lay behind the burden of Andrew Ascapard's address. It had infested the anger of West Sussex against the Commonwealth for a hundred years.

'Everywhere we see the rise of a new and rapacious bourgeoisie, rich with new wealth, with a new kind of material violence, immersed in a racial struggle to wipe out the traditional ruling class, and humiliate the domestic one still in their care. Not just here in England, but all over the world. In the continent of Europe, in Franz, the Prussian, the Junker, the Polonais, the Rus . . .'

Along the wall facing him, Arch counted up to twenty-four buff-coats, helmets and gauntlets above, twelve iron breastplates and pistol-holders below. His back was to the large Sussex dog-grate and before him extended the armoury of Skevington's Horse. Cuirasses, crossed lances, carbines, bandoleers, drums, holsters, plug-bayonets, pistols and powder-flasks.

General Ascapard continued in his emphatic whisper.

'. . . a group if you like, a social class if you wish, an élite if you *insist*, who call upon their right to survive intact. Free to enlarge, not trapped and suppressed and taxed and stamped upon like a marauding animal, but as a *man*. To protect and preserve unravished values and privileges and obligations, above all, *obligations*, generously built up over nine centuries. The spirit of idealism and self-sacrifice is inherent in this, and decisions relating to it are matters of deepest conscience and of the most personal conviction. You know this, Conrad. You've written about it, and written plainly and well.'

Conrad nodded a long time. 'Yes,' he said, 'I think it is possibly wiser, even safer, to remain loyal to an old attitude, than to adapt to an untried liberal idea.'

'This has been always a deeply held precept of the Church.' Father Leodegar filled the silence, addressing part of his remark towards the young flier, as if he was the one most in need of persuasion. 'I have always, within the limits of my obedience, deeply reproached the reforms of our late Pope who failed and failed profoundly to turn back the clock of Catholic reformation by a single minute. Naturally, one's incipient Englishness in this case rises above one's spiritual convictions. My own rather poverty-stricken definition of faith . . . ' he smiled apologetically, hands outstretched, at Arch, who nodded sagely and uncomprehendingly in reply.

'So,' von Zehnder summed up, 'the military and the Church. What is the view of the nobility?' And he turned expectantly to the head of the table.

For the first time, Lord Portarlington spoke at length.

'The great families are in decay. The ancient dynastic families, I mean. So many of the old estates are under the hammer, occupied by the regiments, voluntarily given up to field-hospitals and asylums. Paultons, Bretley, Cassiobury Park, Philippines, Weirdale, your own estate, Conrad, Old Nineveh, their windows shuttered, their chandeliers bagged. After derequisition, with the original inheritors either killed or impoverished, worse, the great fortunes dispersed, the lands abandoned by the labourers, the gardens over-grown and rejected, what will happen? What can happen? Emmets, in Sussex, is now a camp for prisoners of war. Weirdale, in Kent, was bombed and burned to the ground by a Zeppelin. The magnificent beech wood at Philippines was set on fire and, because the tenants were volunteers to a man with Lord Lamb's Light Horse, the flames swallowed greenhouses, orchards, and the finest rhododendron-drive in Berkshire. Think for a moment of the loss: this dreadful demolition which confronts us afterwards, this tumbling-down, worse by far than occupation by enemy troops, the involuntary selling-up and auctioning-off of fine sets of Gobelin tapestries, matchless carvings, fireplaces, por-ticoes, and escutcheons. The hammering-down of walnut bookcases, exquisite paintings, rich carpets, canopies of state . . .'

'I have this vision,' continued Conrad, hands stuck deep into his pockets, feet stretched forwards, tilting back, 'of empty, desolate, shuttered and ruined houses all over the shires.'

'It is the same predicament for our friends over there,' added von Zehnder, 'the same quest for justice, humanity and dignity. The same pleas for tolerance. A common ideal of a united and self-reliant European mission.'

'Hence our deepest wish, in this time of dreadful division, to extend the hand of friendship and chivalry towards our brother in blood.' General Ascapard had finished his peroration and, rather like a formal chorus in a baroque opera, each of the guests appeared to address the newcomer in turn. Arch could not help but wonder what Chas would have said in his place.

'As Lothar said to me only last week at Schweidnitz: "*Blut und Erde*, surely that counts for something."' Von Zehnder looked around him for reassurance. 'What the world craves is two powerful nations that could share it, and run the thing the way it should be run. Germany and Great Britain are the only nations that could do it.'

'The family of mankind in all its simplicity,' added Father

Leodegar, 'against the absurdity of this bloodthirsty combat. The only supreme evil is Death. The only wickedness is War.'

Arch regarded the faces about him, agonizing that he could find nothing to say by way of return. But he could not understand their view, or share what little of it he did understand. Father Leodegar in particular. What on earth did he mean? Was he against the war? Or *for* it in some curious way, as a kind of cleansing process? His face was sympathetic, kindly even, reminding him for some strange reason of a boy he had known at school who – when the headmaster read to the boys on Sunday nights – always brought the book, and knelt with it, at his master's knees; putting him in mind of a page at the feet of his chosen knight.

'International conscience at last is up in arms. Hence, our good friend from the other side of the Alps,' continued the general, smiling thinly, with a courteous salute of the wrist towards von Zehnder.

A fractional hesitation in the flow of words allowed the count room to reply. He spoke carefully, choosing his words strictly, as if to offer his proposals with gentle diffidence.

'The modern world which confronts us,' he began, 'the one, above all, which *will* confront us after the fighting dies down – I say *after* the fighting because I believe it to be merely a façade of several far greater conflicts beneath an agitated new century – is due to enslave itself to something called egalitarianism, a steadfast decline of ancient spiritual values' – and here there was a nod in the direction of Father Leodegar who grimaced unsmilingly in agreement, breathing on his fingertips – 'and social eruption'.

'*Un âge des bousculés*, in a word,' added Captain Chevalier, lightening the tone.

Nobody at the table disagreed, or agreed, nobody even turned.

'The familiar democracies, the traditional fiefdoms, the monarchies, are candidates for corpse-fatigues,' continued

236

the count, using the old familar argot of the salient, 'a ceremonial parade of the walking dead.'

Ascapard, almost, seemed to explode.

'Dear God in heaven, there are decrepit, broken-down republics in Italy and Franz, and a ghastly Hapsburg collapse imminent in Spain . . . '

'Small hope of redemption there,' agreed Father Leodegar.

'What a harvest of degenerate jackals!' growled the general. 'From the effeminate seepage of Neuschwanstein to the sexual dalliance of Mayerling. Aristocratic blobs. And as for those ugsome haemophiliacs around the Winter Palace, the sooner they get kicked off the better . . . '

'Andrew Ascapard at his most bloodsome,' Chevalier muttered under his breath.

'There's no prospect of that, General,' interjected the count, 'you can be assured the Rus is inured to centuries of dog-like obedience to Tsar and ikon. They'll never lift their hand against the status quo.'

Arch had never heard such radical convictions so vehemently held in polite society before: least of all at a country-house party. His experience in Officers' Mess and on airfield had not led him to expect such things as opinions. He was more at ease with Manfred's Flying Circus than these violent minds. He wondered if they represented the 'liberals' his father had warned him about at Brontë. Von Zehnder was confidently correcting General Ascapard about modern Russian developments in the political theatre.

'Don't believe it, General. With respect, the raving ideas in old Petersburg are anarchistic, nihilistic even, and doomed to the familiar catastrophe; they have been defeated already, so there's no hope of optimism from that quarter, I'm afraid. Anybody of any intellectual aspiration is held inside Tobolsk or exiled to Sakharov. In the field, Tsar Nicholas's armies are destined to defeat, even now, as we sit here agreeing over our port.

My confidential friends, the Dukelskys, assured me of that, last week-end at Trebetzky. The German war is quite lost in the east.'

'Truly?' enquired Portarlington, his screwed-up eyes suddenly opening like a blind.

'Oh, it's a disaster. The Rus is so poorly officered, he's in total disarray. At the siege of Lodz, I was told Prince Volkonsky refused point blank to shoot armed deserters, and took the risk of being reprimanded himself in front of the Grand Duke.'

'I think we're cousin-connected in a vague Balkan sort of way, not by blood, mercifully, but by marriage,' Lord Portarlington interposed, 'not that it has much to do with things, but possibly à propos.'

'There has to be some beacon of inspiration, of enlightment, from somewhere else. There *has* to be. The general is right.' Count von Zehnder turned again to Arch and seemed to speak directly at him and him alone. 'He doesn't believe anything can happen in England. The climate is too stodgy, the people too, well, glum.'

'Blobs,' interrupted the general, 'I think of them all as lame-brained benighted legions of blobs.'

Father Leodegar said with complete simplicity: 'As I walked through the wilderness of this world, I dreamed a dream. These are the generations of the earth when they were created, in the day that the Lord God made England and heaven.'

'Amen to that,' said General Ascapard.

'Our old friend, Bunyan, modified a little by me,' added the monk.

'Would General Ascapard care to sum up?' asked the count.

The old man spoke in a merest whisper, like the rasp of a key in a rusty lock.

'An irresolute and irretrievably vacillating working class: all its traditional strength and solidarity hammered out by the industrial revolution. Can't blame them for it; there's no energy left. Not in this country. It's an oppressed social caste, bled-out, worn-out, worked-off, idle and permanently discontented. The workers are lazy, and the men who should lead them exhausted . . . '

'When they're not already spent,' interjected Conrad.

'Precisely, Conrad, mown down like a field of untimely reaped corn. Green, and blind; the whole set-up is on its back. Any chance of leaders of a modern, invigorating society, a society for the properly named twentieth century, slaughtered like grouse in tens of thousands, hundreds of thousands, on the Western Front. A vile, mechanical beastliness in the trenches; idiotic generalship, inadequate supplies, incompetence and insane, old-world strategy . . . Everything noble and heroic and worthwhile, wasted. All some sort of frightening, unimaginable error. A malevolent bugger's muddle. And our conclusions must forcibly lead us to assume some *body* is planning this. Part of a universal racial conspiracy. The wholesale destruction of privileged descent, cutting across frontiers, carving through boundaries. Some mute, inglorious Moloch. So we have to look elsewhere.'

'Elsewhere?'

'Out of all this inhuman industrial expansion, with its corresponding contraction of old rural traditions . . . ' Arch's brain floundered to grasp what von Zehnder, who had picked up the thread, was now saying. 'The civilized tribes of Europe have to address themselves to some form of survival. Not of the fittest, perhaps, but those fit at least to survive. To the new territories, perhaps, the recent colonies, to the dominions.'

At least Father Leodegar had not lost his familiar smile of reassurance. The monk leant far across the table and placed his hand over the young officer's own.

'*We* think, some of us, that you and your brother Chas, for example . . . ' his voice, curiously, wavered and sounded thick, 'so many of our own young men, Harry Legge, Arthur Portarlington's younger brother, Eddie Horner, you see, scattered like chaff . . . we think *you* will survive.'

Arch looked about him, close to panic. He had not

thought before of *not* surviving. It seemed every pair of eyes was fixed upon him. Leodegar was still addressing him.

'Our prayers are invested in you. Won't you join our little order, perhaps? So that we can all stand shoulder to shoulder when the time comes, so that in this way, at the least, this dreadful war can truly merit the adjective we all seek for it – *Great*.'

Only Conrad, rocking back in his chair, a napkin dipped comically into his shirt buttons to catch the shavings of walnut-shell, had his eyes closed. But he was the one who spoke.

'To put you in the picture, Mr Gendron, Father Leodegar here, General Ascapard, Arthur, von Zehnder, and I suppose myself, have tried to salvage a small group of young officers from the wreckage of the Western Front known for their loyalty, respected for their fighting spirit, their "bottom" if you like, to resist what we interpret as the inevitable erosion of freedom, and the eventual collapse of patrician authority. Call it the survival of the men of an outdoor spirit, if you like. Somebody has to take this thing on. Were there to be, and there might, an Imperial catastrophe – '

'There will be, there will be,' growled the general.

' – somebody has to resist the Visigoths at the gates – and so, we have invited a few people, informally if you wish, to create perhaps a nucleus of those who might survive and serve. The lovers of outdoor life and manly sports and the English countryside. We call them the Sons of the Morning after Reginald Heber's much-loved hymn. Harry Legge was one of them, your brother Chas is a second. Your compatriot, General Birdwood, a third. We hope to persuade you to make a fourth.'

At that minute, Arch knew, absolutely and irretrievably, that he was out of his depth, and had no way of swimming back. He had nothing to say or think, and their gaze, their intense *need*, gave him feelings of profound unease.

'But how should I survive? I agree, it's not something I've given much thought to, why should I? I do my best each day, and turn the engines over, I make friends with my machine, and I ensure I've got the best observer I can fly with . . . the guns in good order.'

Conrad smiled, and Arch felt the sympathy which emanated from him.

'We don't know why, Gendron, but, as the war goes on and on, you get a smell of these things.' And then he added, jokingly, 'Don't yer, eh! Father?'

'Of course, of course – it's only an idea. It's not a club or a monastic rule! But what do you think? Aren't you with us, or what? We think you're right on the mark.' And gravely: 'We need young men to lead us. And them, the people of the new country . . . '

'The *Volkesgemeinschäft* . . . ' said von Zehnder, in conclusion.

They continued to look at Arch as if they wanted something extra from him, which he was not able quite, not prepared, to give. He had liking, and duty, for them, and loyalty too, but they appeared to demand his love as well. He could not offer them that, as it was involuntary, and he felt for the only time how a young girl might feel with the young man whose devotion outweighed her instinctive response. Mysie had told him once how difficult it was to go through life being loved. Not that he had understood her.

Arch felt himself in the presence of a sacred family rite, which he was incapable of understanding, or of worshipping. Aware that everybody was looking at him, he struggled to find something appropriate to say. Anything. Nothing came and, in the tension of impending silence, he was grateful that Conrad at the far end was speaking, but in a voice so quiet it was seemingly to himself, as if musing aloud. It was some kind of prophecy. He drew with his finger a second ring of red from the claret glass.

'I see within a shadowed space – this circle of fire – a crowded amphitheatre of light and dark: of searching lights, and wild banners; and fires. I hear exalted music reaching into our deepest soul, our deepest loins: and, all the time, I hear this voice, this insistent voice, harsh, strident, this madman calling over the North Sea.' He broke off and turned to the monk: 'How can you explain it, Father? This passionate voice, threatening me, urging me, prophesying: rise up, England, arise! Like a sword surrounded by a fire . . .'

'Amen, say I, to that!' whispered General Ascapard.

The monk did not answer, but closed his eyes and then, in a short, fierce, unexpected gesture, looked up, his fists clenched as if imploring a miraculous sign. There was silence. The fire whispered. The wax candles glimmered.

Later, in his own room, listening to the wind, Arch's brain whirred with the excitement of the evening, and the mysterious marsh journey of the afternoon. It had been one of the oddest nights of his life; what extraordinary people they all were. He must write to tell his mother all about it in the morning. On crested paper, too, with the family motto – '*Jour de ma Vie*'. But his dream was of Mysie, naked.

The following morning, Arch was up and about early. Two superannuated foxhounds in tow, hunching his shoulders against an inimical wind, he set out across the flat countryside, the thin ice between the furrows splintering in fragile scraps and reflecting the colours of the rainbow. Port was proud of its desolation, great masses of light, the horizon, three-quarters sky.

Walking determinedly in a south-westerly direction, he saw Conrad moving towards the wet slipe, on the other side of a ploughed field. Calling to him, his voice carrying in the breeze, Arch clumped across the furrows in a jog-trot, and Conrad, who wore nothing over an old hacking-jacket to protect him from the freezing fog, patiently waited until the younger man caught him up.

'Good hunting country,' said Conrad, while Arch regained his breath, 'well-hared fields, going light to middling, thin flinty clay over chalk, just the right ticket.'

Their boots, sinking into the tacky surface, seemed to double the weight of their feet.

'Let's just draw this field, why don't we? It should take us to the sea, or what Lordy calls the sea. A slop-country, I call it. Mudflats and sea-arrow mostly.' And stealing a battered hunting-pipe from his shirt with a grin all his own, Conrad set it to his lips like an enchanter. His music drove hounds crazy with excitement. 'Come along, Ransack — come along, Pitiful, get on, on to 'im, get on — on to 'im!' He had a huntsman's echoing voice.

'Look — you shouldn't take what went on last night too seriously, you know. I mean Lordy's all right, but the general's mildly dotty, the count's a Hun-lover, and as for that fellow disguised as a priest . . . well.'

'I must say, I didn't feel myself altogether on their scent,' answered Arch, cautiously, 'I'm more of a battler myself.'

'Just as well, really. Stick to it,' replied Conrad. Arch had his first good look at the man. His face was strangely drawn, as if under some terrible strain; the beauty of his thin features was ingrained with the heavy sun of Salonika, and coarsened by the horizontal rain on the Western Front. If ever there was a veteran of the world's wars, it was Conrad. His spare body hardly filled out the country clothes he was wearing, but at the extremity of his frayed jacket he had red, raw, housemaid's hands, with thick fingers, and calloused skin. They were the hands of a rough ditcher, exposed to all weathers. He had the face of a dreamer, and the limbs of a gamekeeper. A symbol of fortitude to the home front, Conrad persisted in remaining a decent rifleman of the old foot mob.

'Coming through all this scot-free . . . ' he ruminated, 'although I don't anticipate getting out of this world altogether alive, I'd like to make some sort of mark until we break, I admit.'

Conrad trudged on in silence.

'Oh, I understand what they're getting at, Gendron, you know. After the upheaval . . . the restoration of what they remember of the "Old England" if it ever existed. I mean I'd go down fighting for Glastonbury. For Aspatria, House-steads, and Uricon. I cherish the fragrance of that lost pagan world — but not, I suggest, Turnham Green, Balham, and what the queen used to call "dear little Bognor". Most of the time I'm in a bright funk. And, when I'm not, I'm convulsed with a vile disgust for everything to do with battle – but never once have I lost my faith in the fact that we are fighting a spiritual war. And the Fritzies do too, I assume. But I never cared for the field marshals. French I regard as a perfectly rotten bugger. And Haig a murderous buffoon. And I won't believe in God. Why should I? Oh, with one exception. When that soldier died in Salonika. Private Homewood. Shot dead while he was asleep on the sandbags. I put paid to the bastard that sniped him. And then I found myself praying to a God in whom I do not believe. What kind of a warrior does that make *me*? The mad sabreur, I suppose! But that was the only time I came near it. That apart, the old gods do best for me, thank you. Oh, yes, I'm scruffing to the death for Wooden England.'

'Oh, I believe there's a God all right,' said Arch, 'but not necessarily fighting on our side. Not on the Germans' side either. I think he'll come in on whichever side looks like winning. He's the God of fair-goes; that's what we have to do, Conrad, I'm convinced of it. We have to fight like hell. To make our own luck. Help out our mates.'

'Perhaps,' said Conrad, thoughtfully. 'We certainly take different points of view, Gendron, but I'm glad we're fighting on the same side!'

'Oh, there's no doubt about that.'

'Ever been hit?'

'Oh, yes – scratched about a bit. Blood in the boots, you know. Nothing serious. Been lucky. Grand full-back in defence – my observer, Bickerton.'

'You Flying Corps boys are lucky. We've got no defence, not in the line. Just a matter of keeping your head down. And not even then. I got smashed in the leg when I was going over with the gardeners of Salonika. I'm in a lot of pain.' He mentioned it in the tone of one commenting on an overcast morning. The two hounds were snuffling after the tired scent of a long-departed hare.

Arch knew it was the wrong moment to look at his

244

companion, or to express sympathy, and so said nothing, and faced the estuary, at whose edge they had arrived. The undertow of the tide sounded like a subdued ripple of applause.

'A field where the plough has never cut,' said Conrad, gently, staring at the water. 'Every spring, radiant clusters of golden saxifrage. This morning, while I was standing here, looking across to France – hidden behind that cloud – but that's where it is, straight ahead – I had a strange . . . what . . . experience? Vision? I don't know, some bloody thing. Just standing here, perfectly still, looking out. At first, it was the curl of the shingle, nothing more than that. A few marsh-birds in the saltings: not even the boom of the sea. And then I heard, or imagined I heard, or *dreamed* I heard, the tread of marching men. But it was quite unmistakable. I even heard them breaking step to cross a foot-bridge. They were walking in the rhythm of the combers, here on the shingle. The sun is generally up at that hour of the morning, but I felt cold, as cold as frozen fog. As they curled and circled white and frothy, so pretty and substantial – you could stoop to pick them up, couldn't you – the waves formed . . . It wasn't my imagining it, I promise – I don't *imagine* things any more – but, round and as soft as small pebbles, as white as the salt-spray, these skulls rolled out of the shingle to lie at my feet. I was standing among the skulls of the ghostly dead. And the monotonous marching feet of the waves. The dead regiments in France were shuffling out of the sea. Breaking step. A column of rout.' And then, as if making a decision: 'Should I go back to the Salient? I think these dead men were speaking to me.'

'You're wounded, Conrad. You're crook. You can't go back.'

'The leg's hard up. But I'm not worked-off yet.'

'Yes, but all the same . . . '

Arch thought he saw something obscure in the western headland of the ten-acre field, concealed now by a moving patchwork of fine rain, but could not decipher it. Whatever it was lay just on the edge of vision.

Fists in their pockets, jacket collars tweaked up against the wet, heads tucked slant-on to the wind, Conrad and Arch returned to the fortified manor-house across the ruffled plough. For a final time the foot-soldier took out his stubby hunting-horn, and blew for Home. 'Come along, Ransack! Come along, Pitiful!' Widgeon cried out, side to side.

'My God, Conrad, I wish you were one of us with the good old Tenth. They could use a man like you – and I'd like you to meet my best mate, Bickerton.'

A new wind slanted a faint, purposeful rainfall in the direction of their faces. The broken-coated buckhounds nosed along in front.

'Bickerton? *He* sounds a bit of all right!' Conrad sounded more himself again.

'One of the best is what he is. They don't come better! Bickerton's my eyes and teeth.'

'He's your quick-firer, eh?'

'Bickerton can bring a man down with a solitary bullet. All he thinks about day and night is putting that little lead-ball dead centre. He's a tradesman.'

They trudged onwards through the plough, fighting against the rain, which gritted their teeth, jacket collars turned up. Father Leodegar, from his cosy spy-room in the turret, thought he had never seen a sight more optimistic of promise: the two young men talking cheerfully together almost in their shirt-sleeves, unaware of the vile weather battering all round them. He was to remember it long in the future. Conrad was less enthusiastic: 'Slop country!' he muttered, through the teeth of the wind.

But Arch sensed a hint of spring in the sodden air – or, if it was not in the fields or the sky, he felt it in himself, deep inside, warm and musical. Or just the sound of the earth, perhaps, sucking feverishly like a young colt.

PART FIVE

CHAPTER EIGHTEEN

Château de Bellinglise

At night came terror, which had not been there before, and the ever-vigilant fear of falling. The noise of battle, which had begun on Midsummer's Day, roared as barrage contended with barrage, miles away, a bestial surf pounding on an obscene shore. The Big Push was imminent. Major Medlicott ordered Arch and Bickerton out of the air and replaced them with Fielding and Edwardes, two fliers who had shared rooms at Peckwater, the same time as Skilbeck. Arch had graduated to single-seaters by now, which were faster and better-aimed. He was a captain, after a successful raid on the Zeppelin sheds at Fish-Hole, but he missed the steely companionship of Bickerton. Even the Hun was wary of them. They were experienced veterans in this section of the front line and had flown on patrol many times, and accounted for several Hun machines. Bickerton stayed in the armoury, perfecting his double Lewis, while Arch mastered the Sopwith Scouts.

'Fancy an afternoon at the nets, young Gendron, keep your eye in?' winked the major. 'Hear the swallows in the rafters! God's messengers, bless their hearts. Brighten up any war!'

The afternoon was warm, and birds sang gaily in the trees, offsetting the bombardment to the west and north. While he was sitting outside his canvas tent, whitening his buckskin boots, Arch saw the figure of Diviani, his lugubrious mechanic, coming across the field towards him.

'A telegraphic just come in, Mr Gendron, sir – thought you should get it at once, sir.'

'More flying?' anticipated Arch eagerly, jumping to his feet.

'From your brother, sir, the cavalry captain, sir.' Diviani had met him when Chas visited the Flying Corps Mess in the spring. Arch's heart quickened for a moment; obviously Chas was in good shape, that was the main thing.

'He asks if you'd find time to visit him, sir. The regiment's stationed out the back of Beauquesne, sir. It's been dismounted.'

'Where are they?'

'Here's the address, here, sir. I wrote it down directly, sir. Bellinglise. Glad to hear good news of him, sir. There's been no end of strafe up the line at Verdun. Sergeant Mayhew brought first casualty reports in, and they say the French have lost thousands.'

'Bickerton and I were on contact patrol. From where we could see, it seemed a bit of a shambles.'

'The Flying Corps lost a lot of men it can't stand to do without, sir, in my view.'

Arch replaced the whitener in its container and took stock of the situation: clearly, his vantage point from the air informed him, there was a substantial build-up for forty miles along the Somme Front. While the South African mob were taking life easy behind the lines at Auxi, the rest of Kitchener's army were securely dug in along a front line which began at Arras in the north, and reached down to Albert in the south. Evidently the cavalry had been pulled back from the line, and were standing to, for the break-away, behind the defences at La Bassée. The Church lads were dug in at High Wood. Arch knew the Château de Bellinglise well, having enjoyed mess dinners with the Queen's Bays when they had billeted there, and taken part in occasional tennis tournaments and swimming parties. But that was before the build-up. Clearly, a show was in the offing. He took one of the squadron's spare hacks and rode out leisurely towards the Forêt de Bellinglise.

'It's a great day for riding,' said Diviani, waving him off, 'enjoy your rest.'

There was a whole summer's afternoon ahead of him. Arch lazed along, scarcely bothering to trot. It was a gentle corner of Picardy countryside, narrow country lanes passing scattered cottages, and isolated farms, where women paused at their washing to wave to the solitary horseman, and the yoked oxen stood at the harrow, heads lowered, muzzles watery and dripping. Sometimes the towers and turrets of a freshly requisitioned château craned above the branches, or a ruined gate leaned awkwardly on its hinges before an overgrown avenue. The fashionable homes of a local aristocracy in the seventeenth century, these manorhouses had been largely forgotten by their proprietors and, shadows of former glory, had declined into the demesnes of local farmers, even to the extent of being divided up into holdings shared among the peasants. Lines of whitewashed sheets and black dresses testified to the new ownership; the tiles and windows were untended, cracked or half-hanging.

The distance was not so great, he was early, and the afternoon hot, and as he passed a lake, with an overgrown temple at the water's edge, Arch decided to have a swim. Striped dragonflies hovered. His large clumsy-boned horse grazed nearby. As he dried in the sun, he must have dozed off, until he was disturbed by the metallic clatter of a squadron of horse. An astonishing sight met his eyes as he rapidly dressed within the ruined walls. Bearing lances with their pennants bent backwards, a force of turbanned Sikhs had trotted their horses up to the water's edge, and without dismounting, reins held slackly, permitted them to drink from the lake. They presented an electrifying sight, their banners, bright uniforms and white turbans seeming even more dazzling after the inescapable khaki and fieldgrey of the battleground, to which Arch had grown accustomed. Seeing a uniformed officer, the subahdar dismounted instantly and saluted.

'Are we trespassing, sir? I hope not,' he asked politely. 'I have this squadron here seconded from the Doghra Lancers, and we had just been exercising in the forest. I hope we are not so irresponsible as to have strayed on to private land.' His English was as smartly turned out as his dress, and the accent imperceptible.

The horses snorted and sipped in the trough of the lake.

'On the contrary, Subahdar, I am merely a visitor here, just as you are, and may be trespassing every bit as much on the owner. But this place looks pretty well abandoned to me. The temple's in a fair mess, as you see.'

'Ruined grandeur, sir.'

'I'm on my way to visit my brother, who is an officer with Strathcona's Horse at the Château de Bellinglise. He is with Fourth Squadron out at First Wing. I believe the Bays have invested them, or whatever the word is.'

'Then when you are ready, sir,' said the Sikh, 'we will be proud to escort you there in person. I am subahdar commanding the Doghras who are, in turn, seconded to Strathcona's Horse, and we are all messing together. Perhaps I am acquainted with your brother – how does he call himself, sir, may I enquire?'

'Captain Charles Gendron.' Hardly had he mentioned the name before the dazzling subahdar replied in some excitement:

'Captain Gendron is a very good friend of mine, I can assure you of that. So, you see, even in Flanders, sir, the people meet. I am honoured to make the acquaintance of the brother of so esteemed an officer. And, the more so, in our glorious cavalry of the air. Well, good heavens, sir, we are ourselves, all of us, your brothers.'

Arch remounted his horse, following the Bengalis as they re-formed, and clattered on down the country lanes. He felt shabbily dressed in comparison with the shimmering Doghras.

'There is your destination, Captain, and my compliments to Captain Charles.'

The Château de Bellinglise was a bright eighteenth-century building in splendid condition, with shuttered windows, overlooking formal lawns in the French style, which sloped down to a lily-covered lake. He perceived at a glance that the careless disorder associated with his flying world bore little resemblance to the meticulous discipline of a first-rate cavalry mess. In the gardens, a line of neat canvas tents housed the Doghras, and the house itself shivered with spit and polish. From one of the corners of the gatehouse a fox mask grinned down at him. As he followed a smartly turned-out sentry in epaulettes and spurs, he observed various mess-servants in the dining-room, with ceremony and precision marching out with the Mess silver proudly on display, like battle-honours. A trooper, glittering as bright as a jewel, saluted.

'Captain's compliments, sir, but he's finishing a polo game, and offers you hospitality of the Mess until his return, sir.'

A second orderly ran up.

'Mr Gendron's guest for dinner from Ten Squadron, Royal Flying Corps, please to come this way, sir – you'll be expecting to dress for dinner, sir . . .'

It was the last thing Arch would have been expecting. In fact, he could not remember dressing for dinner since Peckwater. The Yorkshire Dragoons clearly went to war in some splendour.

'The captain has set aside a clean set of dining-clothes, sir, but if the fit isn't to your satisfaction, I'm sure we can accommodate you, sir.'

Shown to a room, and presented with his own mess-servant, Arch was left to his own devices, and decided to take a walk in the gardens. The sun, by now low in the sky, painted dark shadows against the neat French hedges, and a pleasant murmuring of grey doves added to the harmony of a perfect evening. The Château de Bellinglise was untarnished by the war.

Dragonflies of darting beauty strafed the surface of the lake.

'Hey! Wait there . . . I'll walk down to you . . .' His

brother Chas, top to toe in white polo kit, his bandy legs elegantly encased in leather boots with spurs, was calling down to him from the gravel terrace. The two men faced one another, pink in the face, almost embarrassed. They were not sure what to do. Shaking hands seemed a little tame, and they could hardly kiss as they were used to at home in Brontë. So, separated by a few inches, they simply blushed.

'Well, this is grand, Arch, you're a trump to ride over.'

'Wouldn't have missed it for worlds, Chas, old fellow, the Bengal Doghras gave me a king-emperor's escort.'

'They're a splendid sight, aren't they, absolutely mustard. Wait until you see their charge. They're invincible.'

'You're looking swell. Your man says you've been playing polo.'

'Well, a little work-out against the local Hussars. Buggers actually beat us, surprisingly. The old man looked a bit savage about it. Now listen! Marvellous news from home, I've just received my letters. Father-Sir raffled off his Daimler for a cool two thousand and gave the lot to the ANZAC Hostel in Brighton. You remember the Terminus Hotel on the Promenade? Well, that's the new hospital. And Uncle Jerry's padre-in-chief to the brigade. Bonzer news, what!'

'And Mother?'

'Mother's grand, and rallying round the distaff-side with lemonade parties and sewing-bees. Father-Sir says the Brighton ladies group have raised a fortune for the field ambulances. Worth an entire division he claims! Cousin Nancy's joined the local Red Cross, and getting involved with "Parcels to Gallipoli".'

'And how's dear old Grimp?'

'That's the best news of all. He's notched up ninety-seven runs this year, and the Wanderers have proposed a charity dinner to raise funds to celebrate his century. But, the trouble is, this lot'll be all over by then. Grimp *will* be disappointed. Father-Sir promised to raffle his

254

racers. Oh, and better still, Arthur's coming over. It's all in Father-Sir's letter, brimful of good news.'

'Brother Arthur? Is he still with the ALH?'

'Yes, they've chucked it at Anzac Beach. Johnny Turk's thrown his hand in, it seems, and good old Birdie's moving the entire show to help out on the Salient. It'll make all the difference. They love a fight.'

'What's Arthur's news? Any action out there in the Aegean?'

'Very little he can say – plenty of bathing, apparently, between shrapnel raids, and the weather not all it's cracked up to be. A bit of cricket on the beach. He doesn't say much apart from that, but you know brother Arthur.'

'You always have to read between the lines. Anyway, it sounds as if the Turk's keeping him out of trouble.'

'It'll be splendid stuff to see him again over here.'

'Any news of Hooley?'

'Fa says he's helping out with the grass-mowing, you know, the pony side of it, now the gardeners keep enlisting. Oh, and Goerstler's fit and well. With the other team, of course. Father-Sir saw him off on the steamer, and he wrote home to say he arrived in good shape at Bremerhaven. Mother sent him a food parcel, as he says the blockade keeps them short of decent grub. He's transferred into a motorized unit, of course, because of being mechanical, but he couldn't write any more than that.'

'Well, naturally. Poor Goerstler. I hope he don't come up against our Flight.'

'Shouldn't think so, Arch. Besides, it'll not go on much longer now, this push should finish the match, once and for all.'

When he thought about it afterwards, sitting in his reformatory-type mess back at Capité, Arch was sure that the food at Bellinglise was about the best he had ever eaten. The resplendent Doghras were in attendance, and made the most loquacious speeches in reply to the colonel's toasts; but Arch found that a little eccentric, especially when they all stood up to toast the King-Emperor with wineglasses of water. It bothered him, especially, when his brother supported the Doghra colonel's prognostication that the military solution lay in the much-spoken-of 'wearing-down' along the Somme, followed by a sudden breakthrough which would open up the German lines, said the colonel, 'like a whore's thighs', and leave the flanks unattended and wide open for 'rolling up'. When this great assault took place, the Hun capitulation would speedily follow, and the war end within a matter of weeks. It was only with some diffidence that Arch suggested this might be an oversimplification.

He remembered only too plainly General Ascapard's vivid phrase: 'the Bays' youthful seed-corn was harvested on the Messines in 1914 . . .' And here they all were, two years later, eager to ride with the sower once again.

'I can assure you,' declared the colonel, Lord Adversane, 'that after four hundred years of hard battle experience, the Cavalry '– These old dug-outs were always the same, thought Arch, experience counted for so much more than expertise.

'In any event, Captain Gendron, if you would care tomorrow morning to ride out to the edge of the Forêt de Bellinglise with your older brother, I can promise you a sight you will never forget to your dying day. The Doghras are practising their Field Discipline.'

And, shortly afterwards, the regimental silver was removed by the servants, and the glowing candelabra extinguished.

Arch rose, as promised, sharp the next morning, set out to the open-air amphitheatre where, before the Revolution, the old vicomte had enjoyed exotic firework displays just beyond the Lac de Bellinglise, and waited with Chas. A frail summer mist, anxious to disperse, hovered about their horses' necks. Beside them, on his fine grey mare, sat the silver-haired colonel.

In the middle distance, a tender filled with orderlies

256

drew up, and shirt-sleeved men ran out smartly to where a haystack stood in the corner. This they proceeded to dismantle, setting down dumpier stooks of hay at distances a few yards apart at the end of the recently mown field.

Everything at the double. Then the same group of orderlies, on the rapid command of a sergeant, raced back again to take their places in the tender, which promptly drove away, leaving the non-commissioned officer behind.

Almost before he became properly aware of it, Arch felt the presence of an immense force, spread out under the fir trees. Almost furtively, two squadrons of the Doghra Lancers had assembled beneath the camouflage of the branches, their hoofbeats muffled by the mattress of pine needles and sand. Their officer on the right flank fired a high blue flare, which appeared to be a signal to the distant sepoy on the other side of the field, for he sprang into action and rapidly set fire to each haycock in turn, with a loping, running movement. The word of command appeared to be spread by a whisper, or by intuition, for as mysteriously as these cavalrymen had arrived, so mysteriously they threaded their way through the forest fringes, and on to the edge of the field. A series of smoking pyres spread from stack to stack, disfiguring the far hedgerows.

'Now, young feller, you shall see,' murmured Lord Adversane gently.

The Doghras looked magnificent with their high white turbans, their scarlet and gold tunics, the broad sashes fluttering about their waists like pennants, and their white pantaloons inside black leather boots, set off by gold spurs.

'Lancers . . . Forward! Trot on . . .' came the word of command from Lord Adversane.

The only sound was the infrequent clink of sabre against harness, the more startling clang of stirrup scraping against stirrup. The last vestiges of morning mist gave the illusion of giant centaurs. Now the subahdar pushed his mount on to a right-hand canter, and the jingling sounded again, louder, but, because they were riding away, at the same time receding into the distance. And then, the fire-raiser having thrown away his last brand on to the final haystack, there was a guttural cry, and the leading squadron sprang forward into a gallop.

'Now, Doghras . . . attack,' said Adversane quietly.

The Doghras' lances remained pointed to the ground, almost lazily. The second squadron stretched forward to challenge the gallop of those in front, and the ground thundered and shook, the stubble crackled and split, and without a word of command – on an instinctive signal – the points of the lances came forward and up! The sun was out now – streaking across their breastplates, and along the bangles on their wrists, and catching their spurs. And, behind them, came two more squadrons of Bengalis, this time armed with sabres, already breaking from the trot to the canter, the canter to the gallop. And then, with the most terrible unearthly cry, the lines furthest forward opened and extended left and right and the bugles from the boundaries trumpeted.

'Squadrons forward to the attack! FOR-WAAAARD . . .!' This was the subahdar. And the front line was among the haystacks, cutting and prodding and stabbing amid the smoke, and the husks raised by the horses' violent hooves.

'German cavalry! Deploy to the right!' The legion swung as a single wave.

'Ride like hell, boys! God be with you all!' This was Adversane, standing at full reach in his stirrups, waving his huntsman's cap towards the piling barrage of dust. The bugles blew again.

'Deploy to the *left*!' And, with one movement, like the most glorious of swimmers, the four squadrons wheeled in one perfect, flowing movement, in the opposite direction.

—'Go at them, Doghras!' called out Lord Adversane. 'Give the Hun everything you have!'

'Enemy cavalry in front! Draw swords and lances! Doghras, *CHAAAAARGE*!'

Moments later, the horses and their riders had stamped and lanced the haystacks to mere ashes. All that section of the field was blurred and powdery with dust and smoke, and the air smelt of ash. The squadrons, impeccably led, wheeled and skirmished, and swung their lances left and right, tips catching the light, as the sun blazed through the shifting mist. The Doghra subahdar rode smartly up and presented his sabre. Lord Adversane returned the salute.

'Bravo, Doghras. Magnificent stuff! You have acquitted yourselves brilliantly!' And, turning round in his saddle, he addressed Arch, who sat his horse open-mouthed: 'You may live a hundred years, but you'll never see a charge as brilliant and as beautiful as that again!'

The subahdar wheeled away, and trotted back to the re-formed columns.

'No, sir, I don't suppose I ever will!'

'And all funded by the maharajah! Makes you think sometimes. I begin to question all this Staff nonsense. Time was when private regiments took the field. Can't help wishing it was that way again. You see a different spirit today. Still – magnificent show all round. And a great inspiration for our own boys. Good morning to you, and God speed to you both. No less to you, Captain Gendron. I wish the Flying Corps well with all my heart!'

'Thank you, sir, and for all the marvellous hospitality you have shown me. I shall never forget it.'

'Well, you'll see the effect of all this shortly.' And, hauling his own mare about, in order to trot back through the Forêt de Bellinglise, Lord Adversane said: 'Magnificent things brewing up – all along the Somme. You know, I feel certain this could be the final break-away we've all been waiting for.'

CHAPTER NINETEEN

Capité

Arch had been hard at tennis since early morning. It was 1 July, the anniversary of the Battle of the Boyne.

Long before the war, Capité had belonged to an aristocratic family of insubstantial means, with more affection for the place than income to keep it up. After the Franco-Prussian war the graceful manoir – well suited to the petite-noblesse – had deteriorated, degenerating into a nursing-home, next a village school, finally a dairy farm.

The airfield, once pasture land, lay to the south of the manor-house. Now the Flying Corps officers shared the same straggle of outbuildings with a robust Flemish farmer and his large family, who kept pigs in the salon, green hay in the old ballroom, and chickens under the staircase. This untidy domestic atmosphere was enhanced even further by the rabbit-warren of thick-set, ugly, but cheerful, peasant children – low-browed and flat-nosed – who ran wild about the place. The friendly squalor of Capité was a long way away from the grandeur of Bellinglise. Both headquarters were paradise compared to the uplands of the Somme.

It was not possible to find proper fish-netting for the tennis courts out of mess funds, so the officers employed the Flemish urchins around the house to field their tennis balls at a few spare centimes a game. It was a warm July morning, ankle-deep mist clearing at dawn, and by seven o'clock the sun was already causing the two contestants to perspire, even though their game was desultory. Arch's opponent was an old friend, Sisley, with whom he had drilled at the Inns of Court; now he was flying with 10th Squadron.

The pipers of the Tyneside Scottish were turning up around the hills at Tara ready for the whistle. Only a few minutes to go.

Sisley had been involved in several dangerous stunts, and had already won his DFC for returning to base with his machine enveloped in flame, landing, and then rescuing his bullet-creased observer. With characteristic modesty, he had insisted on filling in his daily report of the successful hits his bombs had made on a strategic junction behind enemy lines; this had without doubt impeded an advance of supplies in ammunition and men towards La Boisselle. What the Flying Corps called 'pinning the enemy down'. Sisley had handed in his photographic report of the damage, recorded the positions of new Archie batteries which had hit his machine on the return flight, praised his mechanic, saluted the colonel, and promptly fainted. It had taken several months for his burns and wounds to heal, but they had done so, apart from a slight disfigurement around the mouth, which gave him a perpetual grin. His tennis arm was in no way impaired.

At Thiepval, the Sheffield Pals were lying down in front of their wire: the 36th Ulstermen were preparing to celebrate the anniversary of the Boyne, the best way they knew.

During their fifth game, as the two fliers tussled at deuce, and the Flemish boys burrowed for missing balls in the rhododendrons, the distinct walk of the major's batman was observed advancing towards them. He had been Mr Medlicott's manservant in Bexhill-on-Sea before the war, and served on. His arrival and sense of purpose swiftly broke off their game, and after a brisk shower the two pilots presented themselves before the major in his office. It was 7.30 in the morning, and the guns along the forty-mile front had miraculously silenced.

'There's a bit of a show brewing up in the region of

High Wood,' was all Medlicott said. He stood before a large map of the battle front, and with his hand out-stretched concentrated on a specific section already covered with blue, red and black arrows. This disclosed a hinterland of the Somme basin, from Gommecourt Salient, south of Arras, to the anti-aircraft batteries at Péronne, an undistinguished upland region, lifeless, apart from the frenzied military activity on every side of it. The river itself looked like the central artery of a long-dismembered corpse, where all veins and blood vessels were centred – it was in real terms the principal human drainage of a profligate system of gutters, all pouring their life's blood into it.

The major was habitually a phlegmatic man, given to understatement, ill at ease among heroics, but this July morning both junior officers felt an unfamiliar but sup-pressed nervousness. So much, in fact, that they were expecting to be carpeted for some misdemeanour. But Medlicott turned from the map, moved behind his desk, and gestured to them to be seated. He bent down to pat the Bedlington closest to his swivel-chair.

'I must tell you both, here and now, at the outset, that if either of you wishes to avoid what is in my opinion something of a wild-cat scheme, the proposal which follows does not, repeat *not*, constitute any kind of order. And if it is the two of you whose names have been forwarded to me, it is simply because – out of the lottery of life, which seems to guide most of our steps – both of you have already been noticed by your king for actions which are, to put it mildly, not to offend you, a little out of the ordinary. Which is to say, whether you like it or not, you've both succeeded in distinguishing yourselves well enough to get called up for a jaunt which involves a great deal of risk. Let me explain to you the position, so you know exactly where you stand.' The major rose suddenly to his feet, distracted for a moment by a scene outside the window.

'I am asked if you will agree to fly on contact patrol in a

liaison stunt with the army along the Salient during a major push. That, in a nutshell, is the business. This is not the simple matter of going for a roll. Not by any means. And it isn't a tea-party. Look over this, will you.'

And he walked to the blackboard where another map on a larger scale was pinned up. The brightly painted flags, pointed in different directions, festive in colour and design, indicated the positions of military strength at various points along the line. Arch, leaning forward, saw the region represented around a small town called Albert, circled in red crayon.

'The intention with this one is that the Allied forces, working together on a wide and united front, in order to ease the stranglehold von Falkenhayn has upon the French at Verdun, and to prevent the transport of highly trained Hun divisions to the Italian or Russian fronts – where they have obtained some singular successes – will invest the enemy-held positions on both sides of the River Somme, here, and here, and along here. To pierce Hun lines right in the middle – bash through – and outflank. The Big Push, so long awaited. Please God, we're not all climbing Fool's Hill.' So this was the 'break-away' hinted at earlier by Lord Adversane.

Medlicott indicated precisely with his fingers, tapping the surface of the map.

'The main assault will be carried by the British Fourth Army, under Sir Henry Rawlinson, supported by Allenby's Third Army on the north, and in collaboration with the French Army, stationed here, in the south, with Sir Hubert Gough's Fifth in reserve. I might add – and naturally this is all strenuously "out of bounds" stuff – that Sir Hubert's army has already been called with some degree of confidence "the Army of Pursuit". It contains, as you see, several squadrons of cavalry, horse artillery as well as mechanized troops.'

'Including my brother Chas,' interrupted Arch, 'he's with Strathcona's Horse at First Wing.'

'I'm glad to hear it,' said the major, 'because it makes

my job a little easier at least with you, Arch, if not with Mr Sisley – it helps to signify a brother in the air is supporting the efforts of a brother in the field.'

'Thank you, Major,' said Arch.

'Oh, this little show has been brewing for a long time. In fact, I'm not breaking security when I tell you that the sheer mass of artillery and manpower surpasses in weight and numerical strength anything up to now imagined in modern warfare. It makes the earth – I do not deceive you – *shake*. The High Command is determined on these banks here, left and right, to deal such a blow against the German that he will either break in half, or bleed to death. It's the hammer against the Hun. According to dear old General Rycroft, after the bladdering the Gunners have been giving them all week, there's nothing over there bar the caretaker and his dog!'

Sisley spoke up for the first time. He had been quietly taking in all his superior officer had to say, reflecting on it, even jotting down a few notes.

'Where do we play our part, sir?'

'Communication, Sisley. The most vital link between the men in the field, and the strategy from Command which places him where he is. It will be the Flying Corps' job to keep Brigade Headquarters, Division, and the Fourth Army all informed of the situation of our own troops, the position of the enemy, the state of his defences, the movements of his reserves, the disposition of the battle, everything which pertains to the bloody matter in hand. Take away that knowledge, and a carefully planned victory could turn into a shambles. Grant it, and like an all-seeing eye you can follow the ebb and flow of battle, even dictate it, if you wish. For months I've had this vision of the Flying Corps sharing the responsibility of war, hand in hand with the infantry, instead of being relegated as I feel we often are to some sort of casual "support", held in vague reserve, dividing our energies between tennis tournaments and dining in a neighbouring officers' mess. A vague kind of chivalric

264

passage-of-arms in the skies. Going for a roll, and indulging in a scuff with Manfred or Lothar. With our fellows selected for the new job of contact patrol, the idea is that, by picking up and delivering their messages, by reporting in good time any indications of the enemy massing for counter-attack, and by dropping ammunition and supplies where they are needed, we will be rendering unsurpassable material aid to the foot-soldiers in the field. I also fervently believe we shall be able to partake in the actual battle itself by confronting the German infantry wherever they declare themselves, and dispersing their machine-gunners by aerial bombardment whenever they hold up our advance.'

'But, in the heat of battle, what kind of communication are we expected to make?'

'Two proposals have been put forward in the wisdom of the home side. For some time now, in preparation for the show-down, War Office have been experimenting with various schemes in full co-operation with the infantry. First of all, the assault troops were to be fitted with metal discs sewn on to the backs of their uniforms. These discs were clearly visible from the air. War Office Staff thoroughly approved the notion, until some bright subaltern from the Lancashires observed that the Huns would be equally delighted with an accurate idea of our position. So that one went by the board.'

The major chuckled to himself. He had led the two fliers into something of a trap, as they had accepted his brief with gravity up to that moment.

'No, the straw-haired geniuses we like to call "War Office" have now come up with a much more acceptable idea. They're not entirely lacking in the upstairs department. After a great deal of argie-bargie, Staff propose two separate methods. You might care to write these down. First of all, as the infantry go over the top into Advance, they will light at clearly stated intervals a series of coloured flares. These flares are to be placed securely in the bottoms of shell-holes, so that they can be read by the

Flying Corps, but not by the *Jagdgeschwäder*. They will indicate our troops' advanced positions. Secondly, there will be a code of letter signals, and this will contain all that is necessary for you chaps to read. That is, if they taught you how to read at Oxford . . . !'

The major walked over to another blackboard and, pulling at a cord, let down a third chart with a sequence of letters marked alongside a set of instructions. They contained headings like 'Lengthen range', 'Held up by wire', 'Raise barrage', 'Lower barrage', 'Reinforcements wanted', 'Enemy resistance at . . . ' and 'Enemy retreating at . . . ' and so on.

'These signals cover pretty well everything you could possibly require. They will be displayed on the ground, laid out on a large white panel, and will, it is thought, prove a good deal less clumsy than any attempt at morse, which is easily misunderstood in the heat of battle, and might lead to dreadful mistakes, the one in trying to transmit, the other in trying to interpret. Number Ten Squadron is detailed to the Fourth Army front, and we will be flying Nieuport Scouts for the exercise. It is your job, first and foremost, in the few days before us, to fly over the trench system in the sector between Thiepval and Fricourt' – he indicated the section on the map – 'and read it like a book. In fact, it is no exaggeration to say, you should go up and down that sector until you know it blindfolded.'

The major returned to his chair, sat down, and looked at the map firmly, avoiding their eyes.

'However – there's a catch. There usually is in this sort of scrap. Those trenches in that sector stand opposite the German centre. In other words, the Hun's crack brigade. These are the veterans of the Marne, and First and Second Ypres. Stubborn as merry hell. They are not going to give way gladly, without a bit of a set-to. In fact, they'll scrap like the devil. So let us not imagine that this is going to be any kind of picnic. Low-flying over the trenches, and let's face it, you'll have to drop down to 300 feet, is not milk and honey. You'll have to bottom out pretty damn low, because there'll be no end of smoke and all sorts of filthy stuff drifting about, to say nothing of Archie, in order to read your signals. And I wouldn't wonder if the Hun used gas. That means flying back and forth for an unpleasantly long time, in an atmosphere of extreme discomfort. When the German barrage opens up, as we all know, there's a devil of a lot of woolly-bears and coal-boxes contending for a poky few yards of worthless acres. The other day, one of our chaps disputed the right of way with an eight-inch shell, and there was little left to tell the tale. Granted that the risk of being shot down from the ground or being hit by passing shell-fire is no light one, recognizing that you two have the best eye for the country of anyone in the squadron, you won't mind if I approach you . . . '

Major Medlicott paused, looked out of the window in the direction of the tennis court, and turned to face them, levelly and with great seriousness.

'You see, if anything were to happen to either of you on this jaunt, I should never forgive myself . . . '

Arch spoke for them both.

'I don't suppose, sir, it is any more frightful than it sounds. After all, those poor devils on the ground are going to need every bit of support we can give them. And if we can make their lives easier by keeping in touch with artillery in Command back at base, then you can rely on us.'

He looked at Sisley who smiled firmly, as if words were unnecessary at such a moment.

'If you don't mind, Major, we look like having our hands full for the next few days and, as some other devils seem to have bagged our court, we would be glad to finish our game.'

'Sisley speaks for me, sir,' added Arch.

'We were even, at deuce, sir,' said Sisley, 'and Gendron and I don't go in for drawn games.'

'Get off, the pair of you,' the major laughed, and

267

gestured them out of his office, 'when ruffians like you two stop thinking this bloody war is just one long game, the German flag will be half-way up the Eiffel Tower and they'll be selling *Bratwurst* in the Champs-Elysées.'

And, from dawn to dusk thereafter, the two pilots were in the air, pausing only to refill their tanks and to load up with ammunition, patrolling the lines from Thiepval and the trenches around the River Ancre, where later that same week the Sixteenth Ulster Division fought itself to a standstill and lost the glory of its men. It was the cruellest week of a jealous year.

CHAPTER TWENTY

A Witness along the Salient

That first morning in July had entered like a ghost. Up the line at Thiepval the ground quavered, and the sky vibrated like a cello-string.

But, about Béthune, the air was soft and light-headed, and most of the aircrew had been up at dawn, and gone for their customary run around the edge of the lake. The château of Capité trembled in the distance, its windows winking in the morning sun. As Arch stood in the aerodrome, there was the familiar smell of fresh-mown grass, and of paraffin oil. The machines under their canvas camouflage were lined up for inspection. They looked sturdy on the ground, pugnacious with their upturned noses, jutting outwards, and yet vulnerable, almost too delicate for the tremendous task which lay ahead. Hardly a solitary 'messenger' in the sky, just a gentle scarf of grey here and there. After midnight along the Somme the unending tidal wave of gunfire, with its monotonous drumming, had ceased. The week-long bombardment had erased the last trace of opposition.

There was expectation in the air, as well as the scent of grass, lark-song, and a brilliant July morning. The struggle for mastery of the Somme was beginning. Hares were leaping in the middle of the field. As if in celebration of the morning, gunfire in the south appeared to grow less and less, swallows dived to right and left with a swift tearing sound, and the British Fourth Army went over the ground along the entire Somme Front. It was a magnificent advance.

* * *

By the time zero hour arrived, most of the Scouts were high in the air, in position over the Allied front line. As Arch and Sisley climbed into their machines for 'contact patrol', the siege gunners reopened the engagement and rained down shells in screaming torrents on the German trenches. Chalk fountains sprayed the sky. Flying at a mere 500 feet, taking a west and east section, Sisley and Gendron swiftly discovered, just as the major had warned them, that the air was impenetrable with thick, acrid yellow smoke. The artillery were laying a barrage of such density that it could remind Arch only of the worst of London pea-soupers. Visibility was counted in fractions. In their days of reconnaissance, that area of the Somme, seen from the air on a June afternoon, had presented an upland valley of unspectacular dips and rises, with the river easing its way between. At higher altitudes, the observer leaning far out of his cockpit, one eye ever watchful for the Fokker spiralling out of the sun, would have seen a wide expanse of brown-green country, and been reminded of the South Downs of Sussex, but lower, within range of ground fire, might have observed the ground pitted and scarred with white chalk, criss-crossed in every direction by trenches, disfigured with heaps of rubble, and sawn-off forests, trees snapped short and splintered, the earth brutally ravaged.

Under the appalling bombardment the whole bending landscape with its curves of hill and valley seethed and twisted from the most terrible devastation. A carpet of smoke filled the sky in a thick wedge from Gommecourt in the extreme north right down to the Somme. Even from the exposed cockpit of his machine, with the engine revving, Arch could hear the guttural pound-pounding of the Allied artillery as it shattered the entire front line. The ground below his nacelle appeared literally to shudder and vibrate as these hammer-like drum-rolls echoed from battery to battery. Through the yellow scab, chunks of upended earth hurled themselves skywards, breaking up into spray like violent waves against a sea-wall. Between

270

the yellow and black smoke of the heavy artillery, and fractionally in front of it, smaller mushrooms of white smoke announced the opening of the field artillery barrage, and the blast made the ailerons on the wings bounce and dance. Furthest in front, miniature volcanoes of earth and smoke spouted upwards as the heavy fifteen-inch shells from the rear exploded, each creating its personal circle of destruction. Secure above it, Arch knew no human being within such a fire could possibly survive, and he felt convinced that the war was at that very minute drawing to its last outburst of explosive contest.

He flew to the end of the line which was his to patrol, observed no appeasement to the devastation and, turning in a wide arc, began his flight back to base. He looked in vain for Sisley, stuck somewhere in that yellow fog.

To his surprise, however, the grey columns of smoke, which outlined the fringes of the forward artillery range, of their own accord so it seemed began to edge their way forward, followed in turn by the white puffs from the field-guns. And, as the smoke-screen pressed further forward, like a menacing cloud of poisonous gas, Arch, by descending a further 200 feet, saw clearly the bunched men of the British Fourth Army scramble out of the assembly trenches where they had been hidden, into the advance. They were, from the air, an impenetrable brown and grey mass, like columns of wedged rats, with the occasional glitter of a bayonet showing up against the dullness. But they walked steadily forward, never once breaking into a run, wave after wave after wave. For the first time, then, the yellow fog which spread ahead of them faltered, and the air cleared momentarily. His machine ceased to bounce, and Arch flattened her out, easing down as low as he dared. From his vantage point, like a hawk wind-hovering, the conflict below looked to him like a game of toy soldiers. The drumming halted, and his ears cleared, except for the familiar buzz of the engine. In the short time it had taken for his machine to reach the correct level for observation, the sea-wave of

271

grey uniforms had reached the further trenches, or most of them had. Suddenly serious gaps emerged, the unending line was torn about, like a valuable garment ripped in several places. At one point, Arch saw isolated soldiers tangled helplessly in a maze of wire, imprisoned there and unable to cut their way through. In another quarter, like a mountainous pile of game after a successful shoot, hundreds of men lay sprawled on top of one another. He heard the staccato, unmistakable stammer and stab of machine-gun fire.

He recognized then, with shock, that at no point in the line had the deadly barrage succeeded in penetrating the barbed-wire entanglements; that the British line was in danger of being held entrapped by it; and that, in freshly defended nests, German machine guns were emerging from their dug-outs, which had been tunnelled beneath the danger level of the shellfire, and were setting themselves into position for counter-attack.

Saul slew his thousands, he remembered, and David his tens of thousands.

From his eagle's-eye-view, Arch could see where the ceilings of the German dug-outs had survived intact, and the enemy reinforcements doubling out of them in formation, their dirty grey uniforms and *Pickelhauben* easily distinguishable.

Now it was the moment of action, and Arch brought the Scout down to a mere 100 feet, blasting his klaxon horn, scarcely audible above the greater noises beneath his undercarriage. Officers lit their flares, and Arch quickly marked the advanced position of the infantry on his trench map. Fricourt had fallen to the East Lancs, and some sections of 24th Brigade had pressed through stubbornly to Contalmaison in spite of hideous losses. In the direction of the Ancre, the attack was nowhere near so successful, and the conflict around Thiepval Wood was ruthlessly entrenched. As he reached the end of the line, dodging and weaving, Arch swung around right-handed, in order to drop the crucial information to the signallers.

Sisley, behind him in his single-seater, burst suddenly out of the fog, hammering away at his machine-gun.

Six or seven times that day, the two machines zig-zagged backwards and forwards, up and down the line, absorbing fresh information, being peppered by ground-fire, only returning to base to refuel, and to taxi out again, back to the ever-rising smoke and yellow dust which made observation more and more difficult. Sometimes the machines screamed down to below fifty feet, trench-hopping, in order to pick up signals, risking the howitzers; but, as the long afternoon wore on, the messages from the ground – at first so optimistic – took on a bleaker and more beleaguered aspect. One final time, Arch and Sisley manoeuvred their clumsy Scouts up and down the line, their klaxons shrieking over the din. In Hell-Fire Corner, the artillery barrage of Allied Command held up a desperate advance.

'H.H. *Lengthen range*' came the despairing cry of the front units of 34th Division.

'N.N. *Short of ammunition*' was the signal from the Black Watch, pinned down at Arras.

'Z.Z.' repeatedly came from the troops to left and right, '*Held up by wire.*' And in the section viciously contested between the Bavarian centre and the Worcesters and Gloucesters: '*X.X., F.F., P.P., Held up by machine-gun fire – Enemy offering strong resistance at Mametz Wood. Reinforcements wanted.*'

Over Mucky Farm, the Anzacs were shoved in to plug a huge tear in the fabric, and Arch could see clearly their reserves marching forward all around Pozières.

By the close of that first dreadful day on the Somme, as the two machines, battered, with several struts torn away, ribbons of canvas stripped by gatling guns, limped home to the airfield, the fliers were done in; the day, which had begun so full of anticipation, seemed already doomed. Not all official flight reports were checked, but Sisley and Arch preferred to reserve to themselves the horror they had witnessed, which, only now that it was ended, could they begin to assimilate, realizing as they did so that the outcome was still in contest, and that the omens were looking conspicuously black. There seemed to Arch nothing but demolition and catastrophe the entire breadth of the salient. He thought constantly of his brother Chas, waiting expectantly in reserve with the Yorkshire Dragoons for that spectacular breakthrough which had never remotely looked like taking place at any part of the front line. He wondered about the Doghra Lancers. And his brother Arthur at Half-Way House.

Brigade plans changed and a directive came next morning, ordering the machines out of the sky. The Somme breakthrough had collapsed, though the onslaught was to continue for months. As quickly as he could, Arch commandeered a tender and drove to the Château de Bellinglise for news of Chas. It was obvious to Arch, if not to the men in the trenches, that the show on the Somme had turned into a dramatic reversal, even some kind of catastrophe. He was terrified for his brother's survival. Could any man or horse survive what he had witnessed from the air?

Remembering those defiant Bengalis from his previous visit, their dignified manoeuvre in full dress, Arch worried also how events had fared with them. As the vehicle drew into the neat gravel courtyard of the Château de Bellinglise, there was small sign of the Indians, and none at all of the Bays. Tents by the side of the grass appeared to be full of wounded or sleeping men. The flaps were ajar and, within, rows of cots could be seen. No sentries presented arms now, no mess-servants showed him the way to his room, or solicitously offered to lay out his evening clothes. The rooms in the summer heat were shaded and empty, and Arch shivered as he walked from empty billiard room to deserted library. The soles of his riding-boots echoed as he walked. Finally, he forced an explanation out of an orderly in the kitchens, who informed him the entire regiment had been taken up into the line, and promptly dismounted. This man was sitting on a stool, disconsolately sipping at a can of tea; it was as if he had been hit by a stun-shell, and he spoke as in a dream.

'The lads were marched straight up, sir, and into the reserve trenches, just dressed as they were, in bandoleers, boots and spurs. They're holding the part of the line after Brigade pulled out the Canadians. It's called Happy Valley, sir.'

'But where are the horses, for God's sake?'

'All sent down to the rear, sir. There's no horses left, sir. No men, either.'

Arch returned to the tender and drove on. He passed those stables where the Indian bearers had polished their horses until they glowed like old furniture. But the loose-boxes were empty of grooms and animals now, and only the neat rows of polishing rags, and the name of each trooper in brass above his stall, betrayed the memory of any brilliance which latterly shone there. There was an ominous presence about those abandoned stables and their tidiness which caused Arch grave unease.

The gentle countryside he remembered around the château was illusory, and quickly yielded to angular and deformed contours. How swiftly everything had changed. As he drove past, the valley surrendered to a scarred underworld, disfigured and dishonoured. The forest of Elincourt was stricken, leafless, much of it on fire. What had once been villages were abandoned dunghills of rubble with a shell-scarred track scored through the middle. What had been market towns with churches, houses, shops, inns, were now no more than ruined causeways, even the last stones being torn down to make barricades. A village church was reduced to a mound of bricks. The motor-vehicle took Arch as far as Albert, or what remained of it, with the mocking statue of the ruined Virgin hanging absurdly from the belfry tower. At Albert he left the vehicle and walked up the white, chalk-spattered road which led to Bapaume, and then over the reserve trenches, past the Tara line to the artillery batteries. Gunners, stripped to the waist and blackened by cordite smoke, nourished the guns in a never-ending feast, from ammunition pile to breech-block, while the Number Ones wrenched back the screw and the empty shell-case hissed out, sizzling to the ground. A dazed gun-layer dressing a splinter wound in his hand pointed left-handed: 'Yorkshire Dragoons, down there, mate – Frankfurt trench – keep your head down . . . it's bloody murder down there.'

'How is it?' Arch called out.

'We're winning, mate. Winning all along.'

Under the discord of the guns, misdirected by shrieking orderlies, gas-sergeants, frightened, bewildered sentries, across a network of trenches, Arch eventually found the remnants of the Strathcona Squad buried in a funk-hole and, crouched under his tin hat, his brother Chas. His once joyful face with its wrinkled smile, that familiar grin, was crocky and hopeless. He had turned overnight into an old, old man. He walked with difficulty, not limping, but as if every movement was shifting an insupportable weight.

'Arch . . . ? Is it?'

'Oh, Chas, thank God for you.' And he scuttled, bent double, along the duckboards, pressing past cowering soldiers.

'I'm feeling a bit crook, dear old boy – but, Christ, it's good to see you.'

Formerly so reserved, with that kind of eager shyness so popular among the girls, Arch this time felt his brother fall across his own shoulders, a dead weight as he dropped into his arms.

Arch stood holding up his brother, comforting him. Chas was virtually a cot-case. He could not help but imagine, vividly, the stricken face of Father-Sir at this distortion of his beloved eldest son.

'Hold on, old fellow, don't break down now . . .'

'We've had the most dreadful show,' he said, and his voice was husky and tense, as if fearing to be overheard.

A horse-sergeant, ducking under the parapet, ordered the remainder of his platoon to fall back in a rush.

'Come out! YDs!'

Chas with great difficulty hitched himself upright.

'Come up to Brigade HQ. We're dug out in Mametz Wood. We'd best go up by Happy Valley. Here, you'll need this.'

The horse-sergeant pressed a steel helmet into his grip and Arch, instinctively ducking as he emerged from the protection of the sandbagged gun-battery, took his brother by the hand and led him. Back through a junction of discoloured trenches they dodged and ducked, snaking their way to the rear. The YDs were being relieved by the Glasgow Tramways. They had finished their stint in the line. The earth had been churned up until there was no blade of grass to be seen. Chalk soil in ugly heaps had been defaced by stains of yellow and green bile, where the vapours of high-explosive shells had burst into splinters. And the smell, the smell of dead bodies, that *black smell* ... The trenches were patched and battered, the timbers were shredded, and tangled heaps of barbed wire, broken-barrelled rifles, rusty machine-guns, discarded clothing, overcoats mud-drenched, boots, steel helmets pierced by shell spikes, lay in ghastly confusion all over the place. In a lull, Chas whispered hoarsely to his brother: 'Have you brought a gas-mask, Arch?' He had forgotten it.

'Never mind, we'll get through all right. We got quite a whiff of it last night. It's mainly the weepy stuff – sort of chlorine gas. Best cure is pee on your flannel. I had to keep taking my mask off last night, to show the sepoys not to be scared of it, and I got a lungful. Doesn't do too much harm. It gets into the eyes and blinds you for a while, that's all.'

They were able to talk a little more clearly in the Mametz dug-out. Chas was breathing rapidly, but in shallow gusts.

'What happened, Chas? I was in the air yesterday all

through the day. It's a fearful shambles, isn't it? The bombardment never cut the wire through. Did you get shot up?'

'Staff told our chaps the wire was pierced at High Wood. This was where they were holding us for the big breakthrough. One of your people signalled that he'd spotted the Huns evacuating the place. He probably spotted a ration-party . . .'

'But I thought you were held in reserve.'

'We were meant to wait for the big breakthrough. We were all lined up in splendid order – my God, that was a sight, Arch, believe me! – oh, to hell with *that* – the assault misfired right down the line, the Hun climbed out of his trenches, ready to counter. Brigade ordered our lot to stop up the gaps. The command came down the line. Dismount!'

'Dismount?'

'They led the horses back to base and marched us up the line, just as we were.'

They had reached the Contalmaison crossroads, and turned east towards High Wood, at the very point where the Canadian Seventh Infantry had made so gallant an effort to break out the day before.

'Keep well down behind this bank – the Hun is holding the top of the hill up there, they know every inch of the road, and if you as much as twitch a muscle, all hell breaks loose.'

They crouched low for a moment, then edged forward cautiously. Chas continued his account.

'Brigade attacked Pozières, some 2,000 strong. Sacrifice Division, they call them. When they came out, there were a mere 600 of them left. The Anzac boys have come in support there. We were hanging about in reserve, then we got off our horses and they marched us forward, just as we were – in breeches and spurs, off the road, into the reserve trenches, through our own shells, and into the advance trenches. They call us the "broken spur" battalion.' Chas sighed, as if sucking the air: 'We've lost seven

278

of our officers, and 113 other ranks. And the horses came off worst of the lot. Over a couple of hundred of our best animals are gone and no end of draft-horses.'

'And the Doghra Lancers?'

Chas, still whispering, seemed to shake with helpless rage.

'Shot to pieces. Went into a dreadful funk. They're as poor as crows. They don't know how to fire a gun. For God's sake, man, they've never been off a horse in their lives. They don't know what the earth is, they've never stood on it. Their subahdar, a magnificent fellow, led them into some sort of half-crazy charge, and yelling their war-cry, raising their sabres, they ran on foot straight into crossfire at Mametz Wood. Ah! There the howitzers are again . . . Keep low . . . Look for a funk-hole.'

'Have they come back?' Arch was still thinking of the Doghras.

'Five or six got out. There's nothing left. Machine-gun fodder.'

A sequence of high-screaming shells pitched into the north-west corner of Mametz Wood, uprooting a plantation of shattered tree-stumps.

Arch and Chas cowered until the crumps ended.

'We'd best wait for it to pass over. No good walking into that stuff, while it's about, as we've got to get through that way. We're working ration-parties today. Someone's got to do it. The division we relieved had a far worse time of it than we did. The Fritzies went right through the lot. Talk at railhead says we're going to be relieved tomorrow. Come on, let's push on now. The Hun is extremely precise with his little hates. He's given it all he's going to for now. Don't for God's sake step off the duck-boards.'

And, bent at the double, running in that ungainly and uncomfortable position, the two brothers managed to make ground and reach what passed for Brigade Head-quarters.

'Something of a pig-sty, I'm afraid, but it's the best we can do.'

The familiar voice was that of the commanding officer of the Yorkshire Dragoons, whom Arch remembered before so languidly passing the port as it went round the white table. The rumble of the bombardment persisted outside. Arch also remembered their conversation about the break-away.

'Lord Adversane – Captain Gendron, sir, Flying Corps.'

'Good of you to lend support, Gendron. We're winning all along here.' It sounded a courageous, but vain, boast to Arch, as he looked about him.

In strict contrast to the dismal surroundings, the colonel and his reduced Staff had managed to preserve a little of their former discipline but, beneath the elegance, the tell-tale signs of exhaustion and collapse peered out. The walls ran with condensation, and underfoot a puddle of slime sucked at their boots. Still dressed as cavalry commanders they looked ill-at-ease in their present surroundings. Two of the Indian officers, ashen in spite of their colour, without turbans, one fearfully disfigured with stained bandages, sat haplessly on the same bunk, their eyes grey and lustreless. The air smelt foul and musty, of rotten food, of wounds, and flies buzzed angrily around.

'We just have to make the best of things,' said Lord Adversane. And, with a tender gesture to the dejected Indians, 'The Sikhs in particular have taken a terrible beating. But, when it comes round again to our turn to hand the stuff out, I don't doubt for a second that the Hun will soon run back with a kukri up his backside.' The colonel appeared to be encouraging himself. 'I insist on all ranks having a daily shave if humanly possible – in spite of artillery barrage, or what have you. Going over the top with an unshaven chin is not a terribly decent thing to do. I always say once you let yourself go under, the men will go next.'

He stood proudly determined, looking a little ridiculous in his breeches and spurs, gas-mask on chest, helmet a little tilted at a jaunty angle to reassert his own confidence. He glanced around, almost perkily.

'Jolly little place, wouldn't you say? A primus stove and a petrol can will work wonders, you'll see. You come back here in a few days' time, and we'll have the regimental silver out. Let's make a toast to it.'

And, drawing out his silver flask, he filled up the outstretched tin mugs. When it came to the loyal toast, thirty feet under the ground, in that dripping chamber, with the thunder of gunfire overhead, each officer stood alert and to attention, Chas and Arch with them. And, when it came to their turn to drink, Arch observed that the Sikhs downed their mugs with the rest, only this time it was not water.

Arch embraced his brother at the fire-step just beyond the trench. Chas patted his back.

'God bless you, dear old fellow! Heaven protect brother Arthur.'

'Remember, Chas – all the luck of the Irish,' he said.

Chas smiled. 'Look there,' he pointed in the direction of the setting sun, 'the Kilties,' and dodged back to the dug-outs. There was a whine of pipes. The Tyneside Scottish – the Fusiliers – the Glasgow Boys Brigade – and the 'Black Buttoned Bastards': towards him, from the west winding up the hill, marched the long columns of the Brigade in relief. They were passing by in platoons every hundred yards. Two regular battalions of First Brigade, Cameron Highlanders, in front, with pipers and the Black Watch. The Rifle Brigade had already moved up to Thiepval, to support the Bapaume Road, and behind them the Rat-Catchers, and the Glasgow Tramways Battalion, marching steadfastly to Frankfurt Trench, where in October they would make their grave – the last battle on the Somme. The no-surrender boys. They wore their scars in their very tread. A dozen times they had formed and re-formed. Ranks thinning, grouped and regrouped. Been attacked, and counter-attacked.

Their spirit was undismayed. None could march as these men marched. While they trooped past him, songless, their eyes severely to the front, Arch stood by himself at the side of the road and, for reasons he could never analyse or interpret later, held his right arm rigid in salute.

CHAPTER TWENTY-ONE

November, 1916

My dearest Dazzle, my only love . . .

By the time you receive this, our new show will have opened in London – the mixture much as before, called *Our Boys!* and, as usual, all the Boys are Us Girls from Number Seventeen, and there's more of Mr Chancellor than anything else. He does know how to look after us. I don't know how to write this to you, Arch, and so I can't even try to break it gently, but when you come over next on rest, I think it would be better if you didn't come to see your Mysie any more. The thing is, I get so lonely and desperate without you, so miserable when you desert me each time, I've decided I can't go on with it. Please forgive me for not explaining more or a little better, but I just don't know what to say to you. It wd be even worse trying to tell you to your sweet face, so I have taken the coward's way out. I have always felt very lonely all my life – perhaps it is because I never had a father – I don't know . . . If it helped, and I don't suppose anything will, it doesn't help me much, all I can say is, it seems worse to love you and make love with you the way we do, and then lose you, than not to have you at all. I can't really explain any better than that, and feel very lonely and low right now. Sometimes a girl just can't go on. My friend Flee has told me she felt the same once about a boy, and it nearly killed her. So, there's the two of us now. After the war, perhaps we might do better, if there is an after.

I think it was last time at the Goodbye Gate that did it, I don't feel I can put up with any more farewells.

It cannot be easy for you to find a way to forgive me,

but I have to ask you to try. It is the best I can do, I just seem too scared and lonely to do better. The revue is a misery, especially as we have to try to cheer people up, who don't want cheering up these days. In saying good-bye, I know I will never find a finer boy, for all my life. You were always captain of my heart.

All my poor love, Mysie.

Arch felt his shoulders and back ache, with a sudden and persistent pain. He longed to cry, but found he couldn't.

What on earth to do? His head was not blank, so much, as in a traditional kind of funk. He actually couldn't focus on what he should do. Thank heaven, he had no immediate order to fly on patrol for a few days. Arch was battle-weary and had been having head-pains in the air, on one occasion a serious black-out at 7,000 feet. Inexplicably out of breath at times. He would fly to Boulogne that very day, he decided, take a second machine home to Dover, and arrive at Victoria the same evening. In that way, he would be able to meet Mysie as soon as her performance ended – she would be overjoyed to see him. All their troubles would be wiped away, like the summer storm it undoubtedly was, and her reassurances would turn to caresses and in turn into protests of love. That was it, he thought, and felt a thousand times more cheered up – she was *testing* him. She needed reassurance. Mysie hated his departures at the Goodbye Gate. Suddenly she had lost heart. He knew women, understood their gentle hearts, how easy it was to crush them. Now he had found out the explanation of Mysie's otherwise mysterious letter, he felt a revival of his lost spirits. He wasn't sure he didn't feel even better now than before, at the happy prospect of witnessing her face light up like the sunflower it was, unexpectedly seeing him outside the stage door.

Back at the Hay, the lamps died just as he pushed his way through to a stall seat. Without seeing her at once, he knew Mysie was on stage somewhere; he felt her familiar presence of light and freshness, as she entered the place. His eyes found her in an uneven line of girl-sentries, typically looking the wrong way. Arch may have wished to forget all about her – everything – but found his memory, to torment him, preserved the sweet-hearted moments of their life together, and worse, prompted the funny times when they'd shared in laughter – foolish things – Mysie, bored, counting the bald heads in the front stalls, Mysie, wilfully kicking her toes to the left, when the rest of the chorus line kicked to the right, Mysie, provocative, mischievously exposing a beautiful naked breast behind Chancellor's back.

But now, he wondered. Who else was sitting 'out front', as her colleagues put it? Everything around her, also, seemed to parody the sheer unworthiness of the flipperty revue: *Our Boys* they called it – a thing of bits and pieces, vulgar chicanery of the worst kind, stared at with a kind of bored astonishment by a house half-full of sleeping soldiers and ageing civilians. Chancellor's 'front-cloth number', as he used to describe it, even by the old manager's hideous values was blindingly dreadful, the more so to the youthful veteran of Bloody April, and the autumnal gunfights the month before over the Somme.

We like a scarlet tunic, and perhaps an evening suit –
But what are they to khaki, to bandolier and boot . . .
You heard the call and answered it and signed on there and then,
We love you now you're troopers, while before you were just men.

Dear God in heaven! *Just* men? Barely. Had some of these slackers stood by and watched the scarecrows and debris hobbling out of Sanctuary Wood, Plugstreet and Jesus Farm? Men who fought like wolves and disappeared in front of you, as if dropping into hell. Of farms and valleys and craters won, and entire battalions lost. Counties even. The Hertfordshires, the East Surreys, the West

Kents. What became of the East Lancashires? The cheerful names were now a litany of despair: Hell-Fire Corner, Battersea Farm, the Fish-Hook, Half-Way House.

Unable to face the prospect of Chancellor's recruiting song after the curtain flapped dustily down, and determined to capture Mysie at the stage door, Arch swung his legs off the seat of the chair in front, and gasped thankfully at the fresh evening air outside. He passed the blustering posters on his left-hand side, and ducked down the alley between the theatres, composed of second-hand furniture stalls, and he noticed with dismay, pawnbrokers, where formerly there had been oyster-shops and tea-rooms.

Even Fenge, his old friend at the stage door, who had kept Arch entertained by the hour, with cups of tea, and back-stage gossip, feeding the theatre-dog, Chant, with shared tit-bits, appeared to wish to prevent him going behind the scenes.

'Oh no, sir, on Mr Chancellor's strict instructions, sir, nobody allowed back-stage while the show is on.' In order not to offend the flustered old man, Arch forbore to insist.

'Try The Volunteer, sir,' said the stage-door-keeper, in a final effort to help, 'most of the company have left by now.' Of course, the old actor-manager's habitual 'Codpiece and Plackett.' Why didn't he think of it himself.

He pushed his way through the public bar of The Volunteer, at least that seemed as cheerful and crowded as he remembered, and the potmen, although newcomers, waved him forward to a corner table. But of Mysie there was no sign, and sitting beside his half-pint of Best Boys, Arch wondered miserably to himself how next to proceed.

A familiar voice broke into his reverie first of all — it was unmistakable in its timbre, and also its theme. A voice well accustomed to project itself to a large darkened auditorium and command respect — ill-suited to the intimate cosiness of a public bar.

286

'Heaven preserve me,' the voice was heard to complain, 'from a timid artiste . . . It's like a puritanical tart . . . ' There was a guffaw.

'Oh, Mr Chancellor, how true, how true,' and Arch felt sure he recognized the sycophantic tones of Fickling, the 'low-comedy merchant' he had met at Railway Cottages. The manager bent over his pint of 'huffcap' was surrounded by most of the usual gang, a couple of regulars armed with tankards, a soubrette or two, but not Mysie, he noticed, nor her friend Flee, and, to his surprise, a naval cadet (almost a fresh version of himself) and, on benches behind, a gathering of the younger, more impressionable members of his company. Arch rose to his feet to join the friendly old party, and to ask him to help him find the whereabouts of his girl. He knew the old-stager would not let him down, he had always been of the kindliest. He arrived at the table, and waited for Chancellor to conclude his peroration before his admirers, not wishing to interrupt. He knew better than to break in upon the old man's monologue in flood-tide.

'To respect your customers, to recognize deep down in your heart a sympathy for them as men and women, and to be filled with a desire to bless and benefit them – even if it be only a desire to make two grins grow where there was only a frown before . . . Well, that is the formula of success.'

Now the old man had drawn breath, pulling hard on a good two inches of his beer, Arch felt it appropriate to break into their convivial group. The actor-manager looked up smilingly, but with an air of mystification:

'Forgive me, but do I know you, sir?' Arch was astonished, and quite incapable of speech. Had he confused the genial, arch-browed figure before him? Impossible. There was the unmistakable wig-line, the shabby stains of spirit-gum, the carmine lips, still in their curled-up grin.

'It's Captain Gendron, Mr Chancellor, from 10th Squadron, you remember me, Mysie's young man, you

287

must remember . . . ' His voice trailed awkwardly – he was beginning to lose confidence, the actor-manager was looking at him so expectantly, but uncomprehending. Politely, he half-rose to his feet, extending his right hand towards Arch as if to welcome him formally:

'It is always the greatest pleasure for us theatricals to make the acquaintance of our eminent aviators!' Then, addressing the admiring beer-guzzlers around him, 'I'd be out there in France with the rest of the lads, you know, if it wasn't for the old leg!'

'Of course you would,' piped up Fickling, 'and what a loss you'd be to the home front. Mr Bottomley said in the House you were worth a battalion.'

'Let me invite you, sir, all the same, to partake of our modest hospitality.' And calling to the potman, 'Octave, bring me some owls' water . . . !' But before it could arrive, Arch rushed from the bar, crashing flat-footedly into the customers as he left. To take his girl away by the back door, while he was defending the front, like a burglar in the night . . . a new and terrible betrayal dawned on him.

Of Mysie there was no sign. Perhaps she was still sitting in the theatre. As he shoved the outside door of The Volunteer open to the pavements, he staggered at full tilt into the shoulder of a tall man, in long scarf and wide-brimmed hat, and, with muffled apology only, almost swallowed his own words when he recognized beneath the hat brim the nervy features of the person he most despised in all the world, Wilbraham. Rage flowed thickly into his mouth, the taste and texture of blood. Gripping the actor by collar and tie, he jerked him bodily against the railings until he felt the young fellow's shoulders collapse. It lasted barely ten seconds, and the taller man slid heavily and helplessly to the ground, blood pouring freely from the corner of his mouth. The hat went flying, and the scarf wound round one of the iron railings, until it looked ready to strangle him. Arch had not bargained on quite so extreme a conclusion, or so hopeless a defence, and for a second or two truly wondered if he had indeed killed his adversary. Wilbraham, overtaken by the suddenness and the dark, in a fog as to what was actually happening to him, assumed he was being battered by a vagrant, or worse, a drunk soldier, as he had a vague sense or smell of a khaki uniform. The disordered shape in front of his eyes was shouting and yelling at him something about 'Mysie', Mysie, one of the chorus girls from the theatre, but he could not imagine why. He barely knew the girl. Perhaps it was a drunken showman, or something, he couldn't work out what was happening, and concentrated on regaining his breath.

Wilbraham felt a dreadful weariness flood over him. He was always like this these days. Doctors told him that his asthmatic condition was worsening ever since he'd taken up helping out as day-nurse at Guys. They warned him he was doing too much for his fragile strength, but when the healthy men were doing so much, he thought it was the least he could contribute. And this was not the first time soldiers had picked on him just because he wore civilian clothes. Life was unfair to him.

He still felt very unclear as to what was happening. The soldier who first of all knocked him up, was now wiping the blood from his mouth with a handkerchief. Presumably to rob him, he thought. Not that he had anything worth taking on him. Slowly, however, he began to retrieve his senses, all scattered by the force and fury of the attack. He *did* recognize the man – it was the flying officer, he remembered him clearly now, what was he called? – Arch, Arch Gendron, that's right . . . A decent chap, he thought, and kind to that poor lost girl. So many of those soubrettes ended up with the wrong fellow, and drifted about London. You used to see them, especially in the war, hanging on the arms of this officer and that officer, he'd seen it so often. Melissa Bingham was that sort of girl, a drifter, never really attached to any one thing, no prospects, no ambition, no talent. A lot of them ended up in Chancellor's vaudeville. Like himself, really, when he came to think of it. The pain in his mouth and the taste of the blood brought him round. There must have been a misunderstanding somewhere – Arch Gendron must have mistaken him for somebody else. Some soldier's quarrel. What on earth was he jabbering about now? Still on Mysie? Mysie and *him*?

'You arse, Gendron,' he replied, as his breathing continued again naturally, and his asthmatic crisis lessened, 'you absolute bloody arse. All this stuff about Mysie Bingham. What have I ever had to do with her . . .? She's a friend of mine, that's all. She's one of the company, that's all she is to me. All she ever could be. Look to Chancellor, if you want to know who's robbed you of your girl. Ask Chancellor, that's all!'

Again, the weariness to death flooded over him. That was all it had been about. A rotten soldier's quarrel. It was too bad. Life was always unfair to him. His asthma doomed him for a start. Too sick to fight. He never got the right parts, he never got the girls.

'Christ, Wilbraham, I'm sorry! I thought, you see . . . well . . . you know, Mysie and you on the stage . . . '

'I don't care what you thought. Just ask Chancellor. Dear God in heaven, Gendron, you soldiers! You're as thick as pigs the whole lot of you.'

And brushing away all the young captain's efforts to help the actor to his feet, and rearrange his scarf, and retrieve his wide-brimmed hat, Wilbraham steadied himself at the railings, and limped gingerly down the backstreet behind the Hay, towards St Martin's-in-the-Fields. Arch stood shouting out apologies, confused and ashamed. How was it possible in any world, for the youthful and fragile Mysie to seek protection beneath the jaded arm of the ludicrous Chancellor? It was unthinkable.

Wretchedly he walked back, drawn by a magnet, to The Volunteer. From inside the bar, he heard the clumsy chorus of one of the music-hall songs Mysie used to sing herself to cheer him up:

Half-past kissing time, and time to kiss again,
For time is always on the move, and ne'er will still remain;
No matter what the hour is, you may rely on this –
It's always half-past kissing time, and always time to kiss.

He looked round the public bar one final time, just in case Mysie had slipped in from a back room, but he knew in his heart she could not be there. His eye fell on the dreadful Chancellor, slumped over his beer: going down-hill by now, he thought consolingly to himself. It wouldn't be past the old faker to consider a front-line tour in France, they were often turning up safely behind artillery batteries, in some château requisitioned as a nursing station. He knew the sort well. On a 'cheering-up' mission, patriotic and safe and vile.

But when Arch pressed his face to the glass in fury, he suddenly saw the crumpled old stager puffing the froth off his beer – his 'owl's water', his 'old whoreson' – and sickened by his own injustice towards the wronged and wretched Wilbraham, all the rage burned out of him. He meant no harm, for Christ's sake. Nor did Wilbraham.

That was the trouble with Chancellor, he thought, as the genial, collapsed face, with its upturned eyebrows and tea-stained hair craned enquiringly round towards him. There was something *nice* about him; ridiculous cer-tainly, contemptible probably, indecent without a doubt, but all the same, at the end of the day, something fundamentally nice.

How could he have considered – he, the opponent of Manfred and Lothar – how could he have even enter-tained the idea for a second of brutalizing the sickly Wilbraham, and murdering (for he had wanted to) the absurd Chancellor? Righteous indignation was always one's favourite emotion.

Arch stood patiently below the dark windows and the

291

net curtains of dressing-room Number Seventeen where all those months ago – it seemed like a century – he had first entered the captivating world of Mysie and her friends of the Little Theatre in the Hay.

There was almost a sense of relief when he reached the evening's Station of the Cross and, in his heart, a true well-spring of exultation at the prospect that all roads now led unsparingly to France.

CHAPTER TWENTY-TWO

Into Battle

The machines lay separated in various corners of the airfield, in the expectation of enemy attack, each one surrounded by a small knot of ground crew and mechanics. There stood the Biff, the famous British two-seater. Bickerton was already in place, notching his twin-Vickers diligently into position, screwing them down. He was helped by his two armourers, one of whom loaded the extra magazines and drums of Buckingham and tracer into the cunning compartments the observer had had welded on to the side of the machine, 'a Bickerton touch' as it was called. Arch waited by the side of his machine, listening, and struggling into his large wool-lined leather coat. He was accustomed to swinging changes of temperature from his nights out under the Southern Cross, desperate heats and frozen chills. But this was the moment, *now*, he always felt, the checking, rechecking, listening, thinking, looking, sensing. Goggles in hand, as he wound his scarf round and round, he looked up, one last, private time into the indifferent sky. Everything about him was shapes, blurred and clumsy and indistinct; and, as he looked upward, trying to peer within it, to work something out in the impenetrable gloom of the November dawn, mist and darkness swayed around him and the drizzle wetted his forehead. It looked to him too humid for icing up, unless, at 7,000 feet . . . ? And too cold for the sky to break into anything more promising than what he had already discovered, a vast, boiling, upturned sea, in which the fronds of tree-branches, like an unearthly seaweed, were just beginning to etch their pattern. And silence, again, as the sergeant mechanics finished their tuning. Maddeningly he felt a familiar twinge of discomfort from a malignant tooth. Must remember to visit the quack on his return.

He scrambled over his head the little kidskin mask, with the loose sphere cut around for his forehead and eyes (he had invented it himself) and after that, his wool balaclava, which had stood him in such good stead minding the guns out at Vange, and finally his tough wolfskin helmet, with fur-lined ear muffs. His gauntlets he still held as he stretched on the white cotton inner gloves.

Handing his walking-stick to the sergeant mechanic to put behind the pilot's seat, he climbed up on the hub of the petrol tank, and slid into his cockpit.

Behind him, Bickerton was still occupied with the attachment of his guns, and the stowing of his ammunition. He noticed, as he turned round in his seat, the observer hitting at the mounting with the large two-pound axe he always carried for fear of his guns jamming. Diviani was there to assist him, as always, into the complicated shoulder- and leg-straps. As he strapped him in, just before the pilot tucked the flaps over his ears, he gripped his right shoulder: 'All the luck of the Irish, sir,' and there was nothing, just the man and his machine, and the silence about them, and darkness ahead of them. Automatically, he checked rudder-bar, control-column, front and rear ailerons, rigging, instrument panel, throttle and pressure pump, gun sights, photographic-lens sights and, in the little tidy-hole behind his seat, his prisoner-of-war satchel with his shaving tackle and underpants, socks and pyjamas, miniature set of Shakespeare and Sweet Afton cigarettes. He placed his goggles over his eyes, and his gauntlets over his white inner gloves. Already turning over their engines, Arch was grateful to see his fighter escort in position on each side. Two youngsters, fresh from flying-school in Andover.

He signalled with his left arm, and saw with some

satisfaction the station commander standing at the edge of the field, Bedlingtons at his heels. The major fired one Very light. He acknowledged the signal.

'All set, Mr Gendron?' asked Diviani, standing with hands on the propeller.

'Set.'

'Ignition switch off, Mr Gendron?'

'Ignition off.' Two mechanics held the wings down.

'Suck in, Mr Gendron, sir.'

'Suck in.'

Then that tense moment of listening, pilot and mechanic, for the correct mix of air and petrol vapour, as the slow propeller chunk-chunk-chunk-chunked around. Then, Diviani stepped back, took a quick look round to ensure the others were not behind him, and, putting his weight against the top fin of the propeller, swung it with all his force anticlockwise against the compression.

'Contact, Mr Gendron, sir?'

'Contact!' Arch flicked both switches, pulled the throttle back half-way, and the air was filled with blue fumes.

These were the first seconds Arch lived for. The turning-over was simple and short, even for a wintry morning. Diviani's Wolseley Vipers hummed and buzzed away to their satisfaction. Hand-signals and gestures signified everything in the cockpit was well, the indicators and instruments, such few as they were, registering. At a second wave, the mechanics hauled back the chocks. He revved on to the runway, with a series of short blips and burrs, and, forcing the nose down, until the speed was correct, flew upward.

Airborne, he felt the ground beneath him reel away. He never lost the exhilaration of that one wonderful moment, to him it was as if his body had broken away beneath, and let his spirit fly up unaided, on miraculous wings. There was little but hardship and brutality in his life now, but this one short moment seemed worth the rest. The controls vibrated and spun in his fingers, just as the shoulders and flanks of a good horse did, underneath his thighs and the palms of his hands. His fighter escort climbed neatly and decently above him and, in answer to Major Medlicott's second flare, all three machines straightened out at 9,000 feet.

Peering below him into the murk as if into a dark room, he saw vague aspects of shape and colour reveal themselves sparingly and with reluctance. That dark ribbon down there began to resemble a long straight road, and those subdued browns and greys and blacks were surely fields under the plough, and forests, which showed their green only in midsummer. The horizon line itself was blurred in dark mist, as was the air above them, and over to the south-east, near the muddied salient, a tunnel of darkest cloud showed signs of unlimited barrage, against a shredded sky where the sun refused to rise. A warning bang on his shoulder, causing him to turn rapidly, showed Bickerton unloosing his twin-Vickers. He waggled his wing-tips and was relieved to find the youngsters in their Camels answering alertly with hand-signals left and right below. Stut-stut-stut-stut-stut-stut-stut banged the Vickers, with both barrels, a short urgent burst answered rapidly by a few rounds from the aircraft beneath. By now the sky was lightening, and some details of the ground emerged, as ribbon farms, and tidy patterning of trenches, even stationary convoys, and the faintest hint of villages and towns below revealed themselves by the plumes of smoke from their chimneys. The mist around them amplified the drumming of their engines. Arch drew his map from its ledge-pocket, and watched for route directions. They were due to cross the lines at any moment and, as he did so, he felt that old familiar snatch in his guts. Another wag of the wings warned the others they were over enemy territory, and might expect action, either from the air above them, or from the ground 9,000 feet below. Some visible Archie a little to the east was of no account; he knew they were not flying within range, but a half-mile further on a few range-finder phosphorous exploding shells were both visible and audible, bursting below them with a rasping consumptive sound. Arch gestured with his hand to the pilots beneath him, that he was ready to drop altitude and photograph the lines below.

And then he saw *them*, low and away to the east, flying in a horizontal line, clearly hoping to cut them off as they turned.

Bugger this, he thought, and pushed his nose down. Always he remembered Captain Dyson's advice: nose down and go in hard! He never forgot it. He was not planning to come home without one photograph at least. Bickerton unslung the Vickers, and leaned over the cockpit, still in his casual landlordly attitude. That's it, Arch thought, he's just like the landlord in a corner pub. Genial. He slipped effortlessly into his combat routine. Judged how many minutes before they might engage, and looked awkwardly behind his shoulder, always the black spot, for the hidden danger of additional hostiles not accounted for.

The sky seemed empty enough. He could single out a Hun machine when it was as indeterminate as a liver spot. But to his horror, he realized suddenly that the two other pilots, both inexperienced, had not seen the enemy, and were simply flying alongside in unison, as instructed, as if they were on a civilian reconnaissance. Bickerton was yelling and swearing as the wing-men stood alongside, too high, and right in his firing-line; he gestured furiously with both arms, and received nothing but friendly waves in response.

Three Huns, Fokker sevens, and Captain Hildebrand's red Albatros above, flying apart, waiting for the straggler in the usual way. Arch fired off his Very light in desperation to warn, but it was too late. Bickerton showed his class and barked violently at the nearest hostile, but the two Sopwiths did not stand a chance. The first exploded in mid-air; the second disintegrated a thousand feet above the Sambre. A flamer. It seemed to Arch a lifetime before the Bristol answered his touch, as if imperfectly warmed up, but he pulled on the right-hand wing which was all the opportunity needed for Bickerton to take out the lone Albatros with eighteen rounds Direct maximum. Both fliers saw the pilot's head knock forward on to the dashboard. The Albatros with its lifeless cargo rode past them on the wind, unscathed, to an eerie destination.

'Christ on the Cross.'

It was everything that Arch feared. Worse, perhaps. The earth spinning away beneath him, a tug back on the stick, a sharp gulp of drawn-in breath like a diver's before his leap into cold water, and the headlong upward lunge. No time to look up, out, right and left, but these three Huns already side-stepping, down towards him out of the eye of the risen sun; it stabbed his eyes even to look at them. Arch climbed blind into it, head down, feeling the machine tremble as he banked ever more steeply, to get the vibration circulating in his bloodstream, already churning about at the sudden shock. He had not caught the 'feel' of the machine under his fingertips, he could not feel it. He cocked his ear, to isolate an alien sound, a horse-powered rag-time rhythm above his own or the toc-toc-toc-toc of Bickerton's guns. It was a consoling sound. But he held his course desperately, like a good horseman – he *was* a good horseman – sometimes he rode too fast on a curve – and tried to hold the curl on the Biff. He held, and held hard. Arch screamed, the machine screamed, the wind in his ailerons screamed. It was his impression perhaps, but he was sure he heard the twin-yoked Vickers blasting away through the air-screw as Bickerton bashed into the general shrieking and cracking around him. Punishing the clouds all round, ripping the sky apart. But, mercifully, no answering fire. 'Save me, O God: O let me be delivered from them that hate me, for the waters are come in, even unto my soul . . .'

Twenty seconds later, Arch ransacked the sky, climbing, turning tight on his wing, throwing his and Bickerton's stomachs into their throats and down to their groins in alternate jerks, not interested in bearings or direction, just forcing the Biff's wings to stretch-point, tormenting them to the final pitch. The device worked. Kicking the rudder pedals and jerking the stick, Arch flattened out at 4,000 – clutching at no more than a rag of cloud-space, which covered him for seconds, on the right-hand side a mere scribble of river-line below him through fir trees, a barren landscape to his left glance. No Spandau fire-burst pursued him. The whole crazy escapade had been far too haphazard. The Hun marksmen could not follow him, there was nothing to follow, there had been no design to it, no method, no pattern. But his two wing-men paid a high price for their negligence. Above him now, the Huns were at their exercise. Dear God in heaven, he thought, three against one, my fighter escort browned-off.

The youngsters in the Sopwiths had gone into funk, forgotten everything in the first gunburst, and done everything – or the one thing – Arch had instructed them not to do. Turn tail and present the enemy with a stationary target. Fresh from flying-school, one lesson's theory, one lesson's practical, amounting to – say – forty-eight seconds armed service didn't add up to much. Arch felt a sharp shock of triumph over his own evasive tactic, and decided to draw breath. It ought to be brutal now. The enemy recognized instantly two recruits, one veteran, and would take their own time. Arch gained speed, and took up a little height, like a fisherman paying out line, and watched through his mirror the distance between them run. No hope they would let him escape now. Arch abandoned his photographic clobber for buoyancy. He watched in front for further trouble, but the cloud was below him now, the sky, blue apart from tracer spendings, blotches, smears which already stung the nostrils, and his view clear. The sons of the morning were well set in the sky. Drawing breath, he switched off and set into a shallow dive. The three Fokker sevens were, he noticed, regrouping and trying to gain the high ground. Knowing there was, ultimately, *no* time, Arch decided to *take* time, to relax, talk, look around, reflect, and prepare. Lessons well learned from his improver at Oxford. No wing-man to count on, just himself alone. And Bickerton. Remember to let the dog see the rabbit, he thought.

'Well done, guv,' yelled Bick, as if he might have enjoyed himself. He *had* enjoyed himself. 'Handsome bit of flying.'

'Good shooting, Bick, you got that bastard in the Albie fair and square,' he called back. They were floating with the wind now.

'What do you think?' Arch shouted. 'Seven minutes? Less?'

'I'll give you six minutes, but we're going the wrong way. They're bound to come after us.'

'Sod that, I want to get back for tennis.'

'I think we can take them out, Arch. I'm nicely warmed up.'

'How's the Galway Blazer?' referring to Bickerton's twin-Vickers. He had cleared its throat effectively enough.

'Strapped up ready for go. Sixty rounds tracer. I've emptied one mag and lashed up the next. I'm digging in.'

'Good hunting, Bick. I think we can beat up a fearful. This is it, now . . . ' dipping his nose for purchase into the wind, and pressing the button.

One glance told him everything as he dove down and Diviani's well-tuned engine flared into business. The *Jägdstaffel* were conventionally spaced in a triangle, with altitude above him, approaching at probably 100, 140 upward. At his own speed they would collide nose to nose in ninety seconds. Alternate sensations of cold and heat and sweat and shiver ended instantly. The wind had brushed him further west than he had considered, during his glide, and mushroom-puffs of enemy Archie to the Bristol's left revealed the machine had edged towards German ground batteries. The central Fokker wagged his wings, and the *Dreidekkers* scattered. Arch felt nothing any more. His heart was trembling as the machine trembled, his fingers were light on the stick, he could not hear the engine, he could hear only his breathing deep, and even, and simple. In his window, the sky emptied all around him, and he noticed Bickerton's lantern jaw beneath his goggles, already grimy with black powder from the double-Vickers. He could hardly credit it, but fancied he saw Bickerton yawn. The three war-birds drove menacingly out of the sun at their murdered man. *Hals und Beinbruch!*

If he could help it, Arch was not going to involve himself in one of those circus head-and-tail free-for-alls that usually happened. There was ground to make up, and he knew the triplanes had the edge of speed. Arch, slower, could match them in manoeuvre, and relied on Diviani's genius with the Wolseley Viper to put the machine through its devastating paces, to gain altitude on the slow climb, and distance in outstretching the Fokkers nose-down, at speed, going into antics which might pull their red wings off. But, first, he had to get upstairs. Arch thrust the stick forward until he had gained 7,000 feet without great difficulty. Once he had reached his favour-ite height, he looked over, observing, as he did so, on his right hand, one of the Fokkers dropping heavily, waiting for the Biff to come out of the roll on his tail. *Two* to one, he thought, lowering the odds against himself. There was no roll in his mind.

The Biff flew level, and straight towards the enemy machines, both of which anticipated combat, and made a few dancing movements. Arch set forward, twisted the machine as if about to climb, side-stepped and went into his dive, and one of the Germans – which he immediately singled out for first blood – turned to go into a loop. That could soup it once and for all. Arch levelled off and, instead of the expected dive, jerked his stick to put the Biff's nose up, and presented Bickerton with a perfect view of the rudder. It was momentarily flat before him, like a flag in a driftless sky, as high and broad as a tithe barn-door. Plumb. He waited expecting the savage barrage from Bickerton's Vickers, but no sound came. Bickerton's guns had jammed. Shit and corruption! The Hun sailed carelessly away.

Dear God! The odds had reversed overwhelmingly. It should have been two to one. Of course, the enemy had seen as well as heard, or rather not heard, and would be climbing into position to come down on him a second time, unarmed, and this time there would be no escape. How could there be? Before one of them could get on his tail, and return the compliment by emptying a drum into his own rudder, Arch flopped his machine into a lifeless spin, broken-backed, clawing through the air, wings tearing. The wind rushed tears and cold pain up into his blanched face. Bickerton beat on the magazines with his fists: it was useless, he was a dead duck, he could not change quick-shooters at this angle. The gunner was crippled, knocked out of the fight. He might as well be dead; he was going to be dead. Richthofen's only rule was always get the observer first. Put out his eyes, and then murder the blind man, that was the heart of it.

Suspecting a ruse, realizing no shots had been exchanged, the Huns from their different approaches of the sky watched the machine drop down, down, down, and waited for it to surface from its death spin. Far away to the east, a slimy fleece of morning cloud rose from the river-line which led to the Ardennes forest, but too distant to provide shelter for the enemy machine. This time there would not be a mistake. Arch needed every foot of sky to climb into any kind of defensive position; home lines were of no purpose now, this was the final struggle.

What the hell, he thought, there's been some fun in it after all, to get as far as this. And, as for the tennis game, it was only a friendly afternoon match. He did not fear death. He did not fear the Huns. Therefore, refusing to present his tail to them – defenceless – he would fly *forward* and *at* them.

Arch climbed studiously, away from the *Dreidekkers*, now levelling off at about 12,000 and flying in precise harmony, one above the other. These were not recruits from night-school. They knew the game-plan backwards. They anticipated he would wait for them to climb on to his tail before he turned. He had to. Every second counted. They knew, also, that he would dive and drop into spin, then soar again, and this deadly pursuit would continue and continue, until the moment came when he would spin too low – for they would follow him right down – and leave it too late to flatten out, ending in a yellow explosion on the floor; or – this was the only possible alternative – roll, and push upwards in an effort to get above, a pointless manoeuvre with an empty magazine. But as the Hun machines lined up gloatingly at his tail, in a neat pattern, one, two and three, the Bristol curled up and around to face them, flying directly forward on to their propellers. Arch felt his heart thunder – he wondered whether he'd ever been happier in his life, or more terrified.

The jerk on the stick swung his guts around, and the sudden tug caused the machine to lose speed. It sagged. The air at 20,000 was too meagre for his Wolseley engine to bite into, and without warning the pram dropped like a stone, the engine stalled, and Arch found himself in a vicious, blinding spin, falling out of control, like a nightmare, unable to check or level out at all. It was accidental, but it saved their lives. Arch lost all consciousness as he spun. Bickerton found his arm numb, he had been so intent on the jammed barrel he had lost sight of the punishing altitude. The Huns pulled free, and gained height, leaning out of their cockpits to watch the collapsed stick-and-string package crumble to the ground.

As he hit the thicker air at high speed, Arch's head cleared. His hand held the stick with that mixture of care and delicacy which made him the ace he was. He did not see the ground rushing up to meet him, like a reverse avalanche, but heard the wicked screeching of the wind, and the straining ailerons about to snap. He felt the violent, tearing, livid force stretching his cheek muscles. He imagined his eyeballs sucked and wrenched out of their sockets. But he hung on and, lowering his head, as the air in his crushed skull cleared, pulled the stick only gently, and held in a dive, and then, at 2,000, even lower, hauled out, and levelled off. His entire body was vibrating as he did so, and he marvelled at the resilience of the old pram. Where he was, he could not say, or where the Fokker pilots had flown to, but for that second he was supremely alive, and the machine intact, and Bickerton with it. Where his ankle pressed against the stick, the skin was grazed and bleeding.

Arch kept just above tree-height, but he had no notion in what direction he was travelling. Ahead of him, so far away before, and only a little closer now, was that enticing film of grey cloud, low in the sky, but at least something to bury himself in, like the undergrowth for a fugitive boar. He saw the rear of his cockpit riddled with bullets, and the instruments smashed in, but Bickerton was still intact. Arch realized with sickening conviction that the Hun *knew* his tactic – the only one he had – and would be anticipating it. As if in confirmation, he saw the three Tripes had abandoned their close order, and were spread out in layers for him. If he flew directly at them and missed his mark, they would hang behind one another and blast him as he swerved from one to the other. On the other hand, the Huns had obviously been over-confident in expectation of destroying their target, their marksmanship had discernibly suffered, and the machine, though riddled by bullets and scorched by tracer, was intact, the motor, so far as he could tell, still functioning, thanks to Diviani's expertise. Bickerton, wrestling ferociously with his stubborn gun, tears of rage streaked down his cheeks by the rushing wind, swearing and brawling, presented an easy target for the relentless Spandaus.

Arch looked over his shoulder, but they were there,

high up, this time ahead of him, with continued advantage. The Fokkers had him now, as they began their banked turn. They would take him now. Him and, only as an afterthought, the machine. Up towards them, take the one in the middle, and get between them. Face the bastards head-on, nose-to-nose. He had nothing, not even his life, to lose. But it was different this time, the machine's speed seemed wrong, it had slowed down, everything was heavy and unwieldy. He was wounded, perhaps, was he? Dead? But the Hun machines seemed slow too, slow and inexorable, painfully grunting towards him, coughing and spluttering, lifting their noses first up then down. Everything seemed to be in slow motion. Under the sea. Drowning. He worried that these manifestations around him of slowness and weight were some form of having wind up. He was among them now, swerving and jerking like a puppet, their bullets were all around him. He even heard the metal spears strike various parts of the machine, and some ripped through the back of his seat and into the folds of his flying-coat. Brazil-coloured blood seeped into his boots. Every inch of air he clung to, throttling forward and back, altering speed, dodging and weaving, standing still even, bouncing the machine, in no familiar rhythm the enemy pilots could adhere to. And, while he did so, he felt his blood run cooler. Perhaps the wind up was over. Arch wheeled and flipped, ducked, circled and dived. More Spandau bullets struck within an inch of his head, around his ears, a second burst of tracer cut his instrument board to pieces, the tachometer glass fell on to his hands; the needle spun port to zero, but he remained calm, going into a one-man immelmann turn, again and again side-stepping their fire, giving them the most awkward shot in air-battle, the right-angle flight across at 140 miles an hour. But, although they raked the stricken wreck time and again, they never got their vital burst inside that vulnerable corner of soft flesh just under the wing.

Bickerton thought, Hullo, this *is* a bit of all right, and

ducked his head, involuntarily, like a small boy in a snowball fight, protecting himself behind canvas fabric, wire struts, and wooden fuselage. Impotent, his gun fixture lolling helplessly forward on his scarff mounting, he was forced to listen, as he crouched, to the guns of all three Fokkers exploding in one deafening unison. The wood and glass on his instrument board tore away in shreds, powdered, splintered, and the hot fire slashed his cheek and nose: the blood half-blinded him, and dribbled into his mouth. Their firing was badly out of control; Bickerton, even in extremity, was filled with contempt, he could thread a needle with one burst from his double-Vickers.

It was Arch's final rough magic – and he played it for all he was worth, plummeting like a stone to a cascading spin. He was flying supremely by now, flying by the soles of his feet. The Hun could strafe the heart out of you, he wouldn't make a hash of it for ever. Perhaps 4,000 feet of clear blue sky might be enough, but beneath lay cloud, so Arch kicked the rudder, took his chance, switched off, felt the flaps bend back to tearing point, and dropped like a boulder, seemingly out of control, until everything around him blotted out. Bickerton assumed his pilot to be shot dead, and that he was drifting down in an unmanned machine. His eyes closed in the dizzying, unending spin. He clung pathetically to the sides of his cockpit, as helpless as a frightened child.

'Oh, my god, the rudder's gone, falling, falling, oh, my God, the ailerons are gone, oh shit, oh God, falling, falling, the controls are gone, the pilot's dead, we're in spin, oh my God, oh dear God in heaven that's a hot bullet through me there's another dear God that's blood sliding down me cold blood oh shit help me oh mother oh sod it those guns firing fuck it fuck it oh dear Christ in heaven, falling still falling . . .'

The Hun officer in the leading triplane knew that the cloud was dangerously low-bellied, and had pulled up fast. There would probably be hills below it, trees even, river-bank. It could flatten out at 200, 250 feet. No machine could pull out from such a speed at that narrow angle. He had accurate visibility, and from 12,000 feet saw five FE Scouts at fourteen miles south-east, and wagged his wings to warn the triplane below him. The pilot had lost the Biff in cloud, and was toiling back into line. My God, thought the veteran of Boelcke's wolf-pack, if that little *schweinhund* of an observer (he sat there with his arms folded, like a schoolboy at a dull lesson, he remembered, in the thick of the fight), if that little shit-hound had got his guns unjammed at any point, all of them would be pigs-meat by now. He saw his commandant's wings wag, as he patrolled the space. The skies looked clean enough but there was a smear of mist rising from the ground which he hadn't observed before, and he climbed upstairs a further 2,000. Felt the chill through his leathers. Not too much fuel left: his model was thirstier than most. To hell with it, to hell with all of it, he thought.

Virtually empty of ammunition, the three unscathed hawk-men dropped down to thicker air, and legged it eastwards, on low ceiling, to the Jästa Staffel at Lagin-court. They felt, each of them, although unscarred, something of a defeat. The lumpy two-seater, defenceless, had held the three *Dreidekkers* at bay and deserved to escape. All the same . . .

The shit-hound. The filthy, rotten, bastard, lucky shit-pig.

Inside the impenetrable grey smoke, Arch was unable immediately to wrench himself out of the spin, but the wet cold spray acted like a sponge on his reeling senses, and he brought his numb fingers and chilled arms on to the stick, and felt with his dead, bloody feet towards the rudder. Everything, as well as the freezing fog, swirled. He had no notion, apart from the dizziness he felt inside his head, how deep the cloud extended beneath him. Arch felt bird-like, turning like a bird, floating with the caprice of the air and mist, it was protecting him, sustaining him, gently upholding him. The words of the old hymn floated somewhere into his head, he didn't know from where, from schooldays was it, from the choir, he couldn't recall . . . ?

'If I take the wings of the morning, and dwell in the uttermost parts of the sea . . .'

Then the cloud did break, at just below 500 feet. He was alone in the sky and safe. Bickerton was gone off crook, but alive, at least. No sign of the hostiles now, thank heaven. The faithful pram, its instrument panel demolished in front of him, had taken a terrible beating, and the wings were wobbly, but the engine, unscathed, flooded back into some kind of half-life, as he engaged the Wolseley Vipers, and gently and patiently bottomed out.

'Even there . . . thy right hand shall hold me . . .'

A thick, white frost covered the ground. There was no possibility of finding the airfield at Emerchicourt at this stage. Besides, he had no idea which direction to take. And very little fuel left. Arch looked eagerly for a field, any clearing where he might bring the stricken machine dumpily to earth. His hands were beginning to quiver with the delayed shock action. He did not know whether Bickerton had come through, when a huge bash on his shoulder forced him to turn. The great stubbled chin and cropped peasant head, ashen and shot about with bloodstains but still with its permanent grin, was nodding and shouting meaningless sounds, and gesturing below.

The sight, even for Arch's hawk-eye, was unprepossessing. A narrow river cut through tall banks at 200 feet, and only a short way beneath that the tops of trees, and what seemed like white escarpment on every side. And then the engines, so delicately tuned and refined by Diviani, collapsed dead as a dog, and the machine flopped forward on to its nose.

'Down there to your right, you arse, down there . . . !' screamed Bickerton. The last gasp of the controls checked the belly-flop, and Arch steadied the machine's roll, hearing unexpectedly in the whistling quietness Bickerton's urgent instructions. He felt everything suddenly growing dark. Arch bent the machine away from the river-line twenty degrees. The exhausted harness-horse needed the gentlest of touches now. Bickerton was more encouraging.

'Set her down, guv, steady as you go. See it! Hold her on your right hand . . .'

'What can I see, for God's sake . . . ?

'A field. Not much of one, but it's the only piece of flat for miles. We're in a forest or something . . .'

Arch, thinking he would be forced to pancake on top of the trees, hoped they were bushy-tops, or scrub. He had only a further twenty degrees turn at this low altitude without power. The wind sang through the struts. He was grateful to see the river bend behind him, then more trees, he couldn't recognize them, larches, or something like, and then, reversing the way he'd drifted, was surprised that Bickerton had clearly spotted a detail he had overlooked, namely a rock-strewn threadbare field, frosted over, inhospitable, but demonstrably more level than a pincushion of fir trees. He might come in on angle, he thought. No time to try to restart the engines, not enough speed up anyway, and the Biff might nosedive there and then. Better not chance it. He'd chanced enough that morning. Christ, he suddenly remembered the cloud-bank. That was more luck. It might have been a few hundred feet deep, and down to the ground. Was he wounded? His shoulder hurt, his ankle grazed, his knees were numb, but that was the ice-cold perhaps, and in his mouth . . . The controls demanded fierce reaction, without the air to hold them up. Kick, jerk, kick, back again, flap, flap, will they support the last few furlongs? There was a ridge of stone wall he hurdled over by inches . . . Christ, were the pram-wheels still intact? He'd know soon enough.

He concentrated on the last moments. Not end here,

please God! His mouth hurt. Tasted of somebody's blood. Dropping the final few inches, and *bounce*, a screech again, the machine wrenching wickedly round on its left-hand side. More hard rudder again. But this time Arch floated it in so slowly, there was little danger of a severe tilt now. He remembered the days he'd entered the 'slow bicycle race' with Apples at Port Meadow, and they'd flopped into the wind together, managing to land on their field *backwards*. He mastered that. So . . . stationary then. No ground-swell, just mist floating. His jaw hurting again, to remind him. Christ. After all that. As his propeller swung whistling to a dead stop, and the inert Biff, like an out-of-breath swimmer, haggard and washed up on the beach, lay there, Arch discovered he still felt a slight twinge of toothache. He leaned back, and closed his eyes.

That the old sandbag was upright at all was completely absurd. Now his body began shivering all over. First knees and fingers, next wrists and shoulders, then all the rest of him, convulsively like a fit, vibrating like the machinery of Diviani's engines at their height, as if they were extracting reprisal. He trembled and trembled and trembled. Heard whimpering. Whose voice was it? Was it his voice? His breathing slowly subsided, calmed down. Through his nose now. Shoulders released, and he lay back again. He felt the most terrible bone-ache. In the quiet machine, within the mist, Bickerton and Arch rested. Neck uncomfortable, blood all over his scarf. Mysie's emblem. Blood in his boots too. His cold fingers warmed by the wetness around his collar. Shoulder pains, cruel. A sharp sting told him it was a surface wound. Not yet clotting. Light red to look at, not that fatal burgundy. Felt for it again, with finger and thumb, traced his way by the damp blood, and withdrew a wood splinter. The Spandaus had flattened the back of his seat, and virtually severed the canvas belt. He had bent forward over the controls. His landing had been crushingly bumpy and rattling. The tyres were shot through, he saw on inspection, as he got awkwardly out of the cockpit, and slithered down the wing. One aileron was swinging crazily, on the other side, nearly unstrung. The starboard wing-spar was peppered disastrously. The propeller had bullet-holes through it, the rotary-engine was dented, the fuselage splintered by eighty or more holes. The nacelle was totally beaten up, but appeared mysteriously to have deflected some of the worst. The tracer had left ugly brown marks on the fuselage, but the speed of the death-dive could have extinguished the flames. Arch had a memory of fire at one stage, remembered he smelt it even. The tail-fin had caught a lot of combat-fire, and its grey metal shone brightly beneath the blotched paint. The elevators were almost inoperable, and the tail-skid shot off. It was perfectly possible for experts to explain how, in spite of everything, a skilful pilot could manoeuvre the stricken machine into a 'controlled crash' in the middle of a field, but the truth was, the achievement was nothing short of the very best of Irish luck, or the hopelessly miraculous.

All this time, while Arch painfully extricated himself from the ruined cockpit, and examined the stricken machine, abandoned like a broken toy, small and defenceless in the middle of the stone field, while he soothed his limbs and dabbed at the flesh wound on his cheek, Bickerton – head backwards, eyes closed, face brimming with gluey blood – slept.

PART SIX

Blood of the earth —
The Blood of men,
Oozes from the same furrow,
Spills from the same heart.

CHAPTER TWENTY-THREE

Belgodère

No birds sang. Of that he was certain. Arch thought he heard a shotgun fired somewhere in the valley behind the fir trees, but could not be positive. It seemed to be an empty quarter, uninhabited, in the line of retreat from another salient. Dogs barking, perhaps? He couldn't be sure. There was still a light mist shifting lazily about, and the faintest hint of wind. The screen which had protected them was just dispersing. Arch removed his goggles, stained and flecked with oil from the leaking pipe, and looked carefully around him. It appeared they had landed the machine on a plateau raised far above the finger of a ridge of hills, pine woods all around, and in a field of recent cultivation. Large bitten rocks protruded at its centre, but previously the land about must have been under the plough. It lay neglected now.

For a while neither man spoke. Bickerton remained motionless in the fragments of his cockpit, his head forced back against the shattered cowling. Wherever it was they had landed, certainly they were a long way from human habitation; there was a stillness, and even a curious unease, about the place. Part abandoned, yet in part cultivated, at some time anyway, the evidence of human occupation, but remote, hostile, intractable. There was dried blood on Arch's collar, and the sickly taste of blood in the back of his throat. Bickerton broke the silence under his breath:

'What a pair of balls . . .'

Darkness was closing about them, in the way of October mist there was also an inescapable feeling of being overlooked, but a cautious glance round revealed nothing.

'I've got to piddle to break my neck,' swore Bickerton grimly.

Arch had no idea whether they were behind or between German lines. The latest troop movements were difficult enough to follow, and secretive; the actual demarcation lines of enemy and Allied ground to the far east were blurred. Bickerton, revived, had jumped to the ground, and was pissing against the side of the machine. The familiar splashing sound was almost a reassurance. The observer's cheeks and ears were blood-covered, and he had wrapped his gun-rag around the wound, staunching it as best he could.

'Christ, Bick!' Arch broke the silence between them. 'Those bastard guns jammed at the moment we most wanted them. I was right at the end of my rope there . . .'

'You did well to get us out of that, sir. I never thought we'd make it. Jesus Christ! That knocked the shit out of me. And, when you dived down, I blacked out. I thought the wings were going to tear off.'

He had never blacked out before. Bickerton had never experienced such terror.

'All thanks to Diviani, the engine kept going. Good old Div. Worth an extra stripe to him. But it was good luck, mostly.'

'I still can't fathom it. Those bastard Vickers – that's never happened to me before . . . even the hammer couldn't budge the bastards. I'd checked through every round myself. It must have been double-feed.'

'That was love or luck, I suppose,' observed Arch. 'Some of the canvas here is ripped off, and the struts have fairly well had it – there's tracer all over the cockpit, and bullet-holes into everything, but we've been lucky too, let's face it. They missed the tank. My God, Bickerton, but I'm astonished they missed us so much. Look at the cockpit, it's in fragments. They must have

318

been as funked as we were, all we've got is scratches.' He shook his head in disbelief. 'Diviani made good.'

'God bless him,' added Bickerton.

'We were as dead as maggots if they'd only shot straight.'

The observer finished his piddle, and tucked himself in. His fingers trembled at the buttons.

'Do you think we ought to burn up the machine?' Bickerton asked. He felt for the cap on the fuel-tank.

'Hold your horses, Bick, old fellow; you never know,' Arch warned. 'We might be able to make our way back. Better to find out which side we've landed on first. I've no idea where we are . . . no idea, whatsoever. No man's land somewhere, I suppose . . . it certainly looks a bit like no man's land.'

Bickerton pointed towards a break in the stones, forced by wind or possibly man-made, at the far edge of the field. His customary nerve was returning to him.

'This seems like it may lead to a sort of track.'

Arch agreed. 'In any case, I'm getting cold, and hungry. I could do with a Scotch too, if there's a Mess about. How about you?' And seeing his observer steady himself with his left hand, while he comforted the wrapped wound across his cheek, Arch, deeply concerned, ran up to him. 'We've got to get a field-dressing on that scratch of yours, Bick, old fellow; are you sure you can make it?'

'I can make it all right,' replied the observer. Arch ignored the blood filling his collar.

The two men followed the ridge of the plateau towards what looked like an accidental division in the stone wall, but when they reached it there was a second track beyond, hardly more enticing than the one they were already walking on. It appeared to take them in the direction of yet a third and lower stone wall, a better proposition than anything else offered to them. This in turn led firmly to an unmistakable cart-track, where the countless wheel-ridges bit into a stony and difficult surface. For several moments they continued their walk in

319

silence, sensing the dark beginning to close in on them, bringing with it a thin mist. Both men were anxious to find any kind of shelter ahead of them, before darkness fell, and they were left on this biting, exposed plateau.

'This is nowhere leading to nowhere, if you ask me,' grumbled Bickerton into his boots.

A broken gate, consisting more or less of two rusted iron bed-heads, wound about with thorn branches, presented little resistance to their progress; it seemed to notify ownership rather than to deter trespassers. Then, suddenly, in front of them, up till then hidden by barriers of gorse and branches, they discerned in the thickening mist the outline of a tall stone building – a shelter for goats perhaps, much of it in a condition approaching ruin.

'Over there, Bickerton ... We could dig in, over there.'

At least these stone walls, however inhospitable, would offer some kind of security through the day. In the darkness they could explore further, work out their whereabouts, forage for food, and friendly 'locals'. But, as they approached yet another gate with a modest lifting of spirits, they were appalled to find themselves confronted by three men carrying shotguns standing in their path.

Bickerton cursed his discarded Vickers and Arch instantly regretted not having drawn his service revolver from under his leather flying-coat, not that they would have had much prospect of success against three shotguns. The next minute, each of them recognized that not only were these men not regulars in the Hun army, they were clearly not soldiers of any army, being far too old for one thing, and dressed in the characteristic black corduroys worn everywhere by the local peasants. So it was without too much apprehension they lifted their hands, and in response to a grudging jerk of the head from the eldest of the three – a ferocious-looking fellow with a grey and white stubbled beard and a matchstick in his teeth – marched before their captors in the direction demanded of them.

'*Aviateurs anglais*,' Arch began to say optimistically, but a double-barrelled shotgun in his spine forced him on.

As they advanced, both men examined the granite shape ahead of them as well as the appearance of the men who held them in check. The grey rocks which sheltered left and right of the pathway were reflected – the high walls of what appeared to be a gaunt and isolated farmhouse. It was already difficult to be certain in this mist which drifted in bandages around them. At one corner it stood tall and austere; along the side ran a gallery, one storey high, and at the far end of it what seemed, in the confusion of mist and shadows, high-roofed and angular, some kind of chapel. The windows were narrow and, at this dead hour, already shuttered. Not a fissure of light escaped, and the men leading them found their path more by instinct and old custom than by oil-lamp. As they approached the building, a parade of dogs barked from the gallery, and the two fliers could discern the silhouettes of five or six hounds of various sizes, ages and breeds, darting backwards and forwards unwelcomingly, with hostile cries of alarm.

The peasants, each of whom was many years older and some inches shorter than their two prisoners, watched them aggressively, their shotguns cradled in their arms, and certainly cocked. They remained at a surly distance. Their escorts were not German, that was obvious. Arch knew that however off-course he might have been flying, he could not have penetrated so deep inland; nor was this part of the terrain familiar to either of them along the bitterly contested salient.

Those unadorned swampy fields around the Somme, the soldierly files of poplars, the woodlands beyond Béthune, the plain single-street villages of Picardy, and the farmlands of the Belgian frontier, were all recognizable to him, and he spoke enough French to identify local conversation, but these men were austerely taciturn.

When he attempted to explain again they were English airmen, Arch was immediately restrained by old stubble-beard, who shook his chin threateningly, and once more indicated by a twitch of his jaw and a prod of the barrel that he merely required the two men to walk forward without debate. From his leaves in Paris, Arch could manage café French. However, when they muttered among themselves, he could identify little in their language familiar to him, and realized that the peasants were speaking in a regional dialect so remote it was quite incomprehensible. In front of them, a half-hinged gate, ajar and supported by an isolated portal, bore a name cut into the slate. The single word 'Belgodère' seemed to menace them like an expected blow. They walked on, blinded now by the darkness of the freezing fog. All light had forsaken what was only the middle of the day.

A powdering of snow, yellow and dirty, lay on their hair, and Arch felt it dissolve on the thin branches of blood around his neck: again he felt pain there. An inharmonious orchestra of several different barking dogs, accompanied by curses and whistles from within, pursued them until the men turned into a courtyard. The fractured light of an oil-lamp, perched on the hub of a farm-wagon, revealed a stone-arched courtyard of impressive size, where various animals were close-tethered; at the domestic end, a bridge, low and uneven, beneath which they were forced to walk, stooping their heads. This in turn led to a vaulted granite barn, where some thirty or more cattle were roped to iron rings in the wall. The floor was pebbled, and a central gutter carried liquid yellow dung to an open cess-pit. In one corner was a pitiful fire, by which a stable-hand was crouching, disturbed in the business of milking. He looked up momentarily, and after establishing the presence of strangers of no probable importance to him continued his task. In a further shed, by the same lamp-light, the steaming dark bulk of two huge groaning oxen. The yard smelt of a mixture of animal manure and of milk, both sweet, rather sickly odours.

A long, low-ceilinged room abutted on to the farm itself, and the patrol walked their men through the cow-byre and up worn stone steps into a kitchen, whose fire flickered warmly, and which smelt of burnt boiled coffee. At first glance, Arch imagined he could count four women, and at least two more men, one sitting so far into the corner of the chimney that he seemed to be almost on fire. Another very old, dwarfish man crouched on a straw stool, smoking a pipe. From the shadow came the even tick of a wooden-frame grandfather clock, with a decorated balance. There was no effort to make room either for the newcomers or for the peasants, as they entered, although a slight angling of some of the shotguns seemed to indicate that the intruders might be regarded with a little less than hostility.

'Dig in, Captain,' proposed Bickerton.

When Arch began to speak, one of the younger men – himself not many years short of sixty – gestured roughly to two chairs by the table, and after some muttered instructions to the women next to the chimney (their exchange was more like argument) two bowls of flat, black liquid were pushed unceremoniously before them. It tasted of earth and acorns, flavoured with coffee-grounds, and was sugared by a dark brown substance which had been stirred in with a thick wooden spoon. But it was hot and not unfriendly. Bickerton muttered it had been brewed from oak-apples. The faces staring through them were austere, unyielding, but not so pitiless as had seemed at first. With a kind of respect the man with the pitted beard spoke first to the grandfather in the old-fashioned duck's-nest grate, and he in turn addressed himself with similar respect to a woman turned aside from the strangers. Arch could vaguely determine 'bagarreurs', 'étrangers', 'alleymans', little else. Everything was conducted in this same guttural patois, always in an undertone, of which neither he nor Bickerton was able to hear, let alone decipher, a sentence. Bickerton, who at his most expansive seldom showed a tendency to talk, concentrated on his hot drink, but stole a reassuring wink with his one good eye which seemed to

323

indicate he was not over-worred about their forthcoming destiny. Clearly, 'dig in' was his advice. Arch felt apprehensive now, but not threatened. He could not work out whether these peasants were collaborators – could they be? – few ever were in this region. Where on earth had they landed? Perhaps they were in Alsace? There was something reassuring about the stone walls, the stoked-up fire, the stalled beasts, the lounging dogs, and finally the solidity of these peasants into whose calloused hands they had fallen. But whenever Arch tried to speak, to explain, to gesture, the spokesman of the group, the pepper-beard, pointed roughly to the bowls, and grunted, '*Manges*', one of the very few words spoken aloud they were able to recognize. So, obediently, they bent down and fed.

'This is another of those thinking-out jobs, Captain,' said Bickerton, and he too relapsed into silence.

When they had finished their gruel, as if waiting for this moment of formality, Arch pushed away his stool. Gesturing towards himself and his observer, he said in the best French he could manage: '*Nous sommes les aviateurs britanniques, les compatriotes du Capitaine Guinemer.*'

'*Et Tavera, célèbre bagarreur français,*' added Bickerton.

Surely even here they had heard of Tavera, the famous 'top du top'.

It was the woman, her back until that moment towards them, who suddenly turned and asked, in perfectly gentle classroom French: '*Vous êtes donc les prisonniers échappés, ou descendus en avion à cause du manque d'essence, ou d'une bagarre en plein ciel . . .?*' She was younger by far than the rest of them.

'*Descendus à cause du brouillard après le combat . . .*'

Arch reddened, looked down, and pushed the tin mug at arm's length. There was a substantial silence. One of the dogs made a deep growling sound in the back of its throat. He felt all eyes turn on him. Even the little dwarfish character had taken his pipe out, for a better look. The stubble man removed his match.

The woman asked, in English: 'So you are Englishmen?'

'Why, yes,' answered Arch, defiantly. 'I am English, although I have come all the way from Australia. But I fight for the Allied army, for France, if you like. My companion is as English as we presume you are French. We hope, like yourselves, we are all fighting for the same side, for our God, and for the same freedom.'

The woman took a moment to consider this, perhaps translating it to herself.

'Then it is just as well, and everything will be all right. If you had been German airmen, I do not think you would have been very fortunate, nor so welcome. This farm is called Belgodère. *Soyez bienvenus.*'

Arch was about to reply when, with a gesture, the woman turned away from the two fliers, and speaking earnestly, this time half in French, relapsing sometimes into the patois, she explained to the family gathered around their nationality and identity, accompanied by frequent gestures in their direction.

That this brought about a change of atmosphere would be an exaggeration, but certainly there was a detectable alteration in tone, and the shotguns were half-broken, and the cartridges clicked out by experienced thumbs. Faces turned from the fire. The dog still growled. The ancient grandfather came forward, unbuttoned their flying-coats, and examined their uniforms diligently, appearing to be impressed by the ribbons at Arch's breast, and the service stripe on Bickerton's sleeve. When it was established definitely they were indeed British fliers, the old man extended his two rough-etched hands to each in turn, taking first their right hand in his, and then their left hand. This gesture of acceptance led to an exchange of comments from one to the other, in which the word '*anglais*' could be frequently heard; and also '*bagarreurs*' and '*amis*'. In turn each member of the family approached and shook hands, silently, formally, the women at the rear just

325

nodding. This was accompanied by grudging smiles and grins and even winks, and in the case of the youngest, he of the beard, a harsh thump on the back.

They were all of one family. Each man who came forward presented himself, copying the grandfather, shaking the hand of each newcomer in turn, both before muttering his own name, and after it. The room which had seemed desolate a moment ago was suddenly overcrowded. At first Arch and Bickerton could vaguely assume identities – the peasants resembled such similar shapes, uniformly dressed, even men and women looked alike. Only much later did their appearance grow and personalities emerge. The grandfather, Le Vieux, who called himself Old Xavier, was over ninety, and then came his three sons, all men in their fifties and sixties – Ignace, Toussaint and Pascal. The little bent man – not crippled in any way, but the one who had sat apart, by himself – came last, pulling off his cap with a flourish, and from him there emanated a rank smell of goat, and his eyes were alternately blue and brown, with a yellow bar in them, and oddly circular, like those of the animals of whom he had special care. Without his cap, he looked much younger than before. Not one of the family, but enclosed in its protection, he was called Gorgonus, and resembling a stunted, energetic and – even at first rough glance – sly man, it seemed appropriate that he should go by the nickname – from the rest of the farmhouse – of Le Rapide. As for the women, they were not presented at all by name, but hung back in a shy, smiling cluster by the fireplace, and were dismissed by Old Xavier collectively as *'les femmes, les filles, les femmes, quoi . . .'* accompanied by an imprecise gesture of his hand, and some head-shrugging. The names of the strangers posed more difficulty and not a little opportunity for humour – the observer they christened Bikkytun, the pilot turned into Capitaine easily enough (he was automatically regarded as the leader, being the spokesman), or, occasionally, Arche.

Space was made for the two new guests by the fire, more sour coffee poured, and the younger women began to put spoons out on the large wooden table. For the first time it was possible for the fliers to take notice of everything around them. This, together with the questions Arch was able to put to the peasants, the answers they gave, through the translations provided by the youngest of the four women, began slowly to account for the extraordinary picture which had begun to assemble in their minds. And, for the next hour, they sat in front of a crude but solid meal, some stewed rabbit-legs, chestnuts boiled in their skins, and goat cheese with black bread, as ordinary and fortifying as the somewhat grudging welcome they had received in the kitchen of the old farm.

'Now this *is* a bit of goose,' said Bickerton.

The woman who spoke in English addressed them.

'We must clean these wounds of yours. Fortunately they seem to be only on the surface – just the skin is broken.'

She shyly led forward a stout woman, who carried a pudding bowl of warm water.

'This is La Grosse.'

Of herself, she explained simply: 'My name is Hortense.' And she softened the congealed pits on his neck and cheek, and soaked off the dried blood from a basin on her lap. Bickerton stripped to the waist before the fire, where the fat woman carefully wiped clean his wounds, bandaging them afterwards with strips of an old linen shirt. There was nothing serious which merited a doctor's attention; the farm-women were anyway accustomed to accidents of this nature, and cleansed and bound the observer's shoulder securely, not before Arch had noticed the bruised and yellow discolouring all round. There had been no significant loss of blood from either of them, only bruising, splinters and shavings from the instrument board that had pierced the skin. Bickerton winced a little when the splinters were drawn out.

'How are you feeling, Bick, old chap? Can you stand it?'

'Handsome,' came the characteristic reply. 'Not dead yet, at any rate.'

'Dig in, Bickerton, old chap,' said Arch, to encourage him.

'That's exactly what I am doing, Arch,' he said, using the Christian name for the first time. 'Digging in!'

It became clear that, after the air-battle, Arch had followed the river-line in quite the opposite direction to his own lines, owing to his defective compass, before the mist rose up and obscured their view of the ground altogether. He and Bickerton, who now dozed gently, the nose of a hound on his thigh, were now fifty kilometres or more behind the German lines, lost in a region far from the usual lines of supply to the front. Flying blind, Arch had succeeded in taking the machine way beyond the Ypres Salient, way behind the splintered wilderness, to a remote and unfamiliar terrain in the Ardennes, a plateau beside the forest. It was an area of rough, inhospitable, forbidding countryside, whose peasants scraped the rudest of livings from a thin-blooded scrub which yielded little, and demanded unending toil by man and beast. It was said the crows themselves flew upside down to ignore the poverty below. The area had been isolated for centuries by its unapproachable position, the grudging product of its rocky soil, the harshness in the extremes of climate, and the suspicious nature of its people, culturally and linguistically divided from the rest of the country. The people of this craggy area worked the land to their best advantage, farming in barren strips among the forest, barely subsisting, but surviving nevertheless, with a certain degree of pride, against so many obstacles. They travelled little outside their own region, not often beyond their own acres, and spoke their own language, farmed with their own stubborn techniques, remaining intolerant to strangers, and interbred among themselves. Hortense, who had travelled once as far as Paris, was called 'the Parisian'. Some of them had never left the frontiers of their own farm. The flooded tributaries of the Meuse cut them off on their northern arch, the coalfields of Flanders in the east, and to the south the boundaries of Germany's lowland states divided the men and women of the Ardennes from the outside world, allowing these reclusive families to create a pattern of life which had been barely disturbed since the Middle Ages. In the war it was disputed territory. And it was on one of these rugged stretches, which inadvertently had served as an emergency airfield, that the two men had descended.

Belgodère itself was more remote than the remainder of a wilderness already isolated enough, standing quite by itself, at the highest point above the plateau, ten kilometres by road from the nearest community, a slate village called Corbeille, or a shorter, more treacherous, clamber down the hillside along goat-tracks. For seven centuries Belgodère had stood as a farm and it had neither altered nor improved. Its obdurate stone walls neither prospered nor shrank with the passing of time or fortune. It was by now a substantial half-abandoned building, with large sections of it uninhabited except by dogs or beasts, the family clinging together under the main central fireplace which had been erected in the thirteenth century by the Maresquier, a clan chieftain, original ancestor of the family who farmed there still, the Maresquiers. The family hearth was comfortable and compact. Six bedrooms for all led off the large kitchen, where the family stayed winter and summer, and the fire had burned for a hundred years, without once being extinguished. Outside this sanctuary long stone-walled corridors, which the two fliers had seen during their approach, contained the animals. There were goats, pigs and oxen, as well as the cows they had seen being milked, and stalls for farm-carts and harrows. Everything was confined under the one roof, wherever there was a roof. Few barns or cow-houses stood beyond the restrictions of Belgodère itself, and the farmhouse protected family, cattle and forage within its tough, granite boundaries.

All of this the two men came to learn gradually in the days which followed, by their own discoveries, and also because the younger woman, Hortense, who had addressed them in English on that first evening, was able to communicate with them. She had been the language teacher in the one school in the nearest village. Before 1914, it had been an extensive parish of more than three hundred labourers – now reduced to eighty-seven. Hortense had married into the family, and came originally from Corbeille, where her father had the smith's forge. The school at Casta had educated her well before she retreated to Corbeille as a child might into a convent. She it was who explained to Arch and to Bickerton the distance they must have flown accidentally, and told them of the remoteness of the farm they had found, and a little of its past. She explained to them the nature of the handful of inhabitants, whose life was, from ancient times, so extreme. Centuries ago, Belgodère had been fortified, might even have stood as outpost for the Fourth Legion in the Gallic Wars. Pascal behind the plough had frequently turned up broken pottery and gold coins from Roman times, and the plateau itself, with its unimpeded views of the country beyond on all sides, presented an ideal vantage point. Doubtless the outworks had served for generations as a sentinel, guarding the south-eastern entrance of the Ardennes, had sheltered or defended against Roman, Goth and Gaul, and witnessed many savage encounters between them. Later, however, the original advantages of its precarious position in those ancient times had resulted in the estate standing on the wrong edge of progress. The central thrust of the advance in industry, in rural life, everywhere else, had passed Belgodère by in its own isolation, and, a short period of prosperity apart, when the fortified farmhouse became in the seventeenth century the seigneurial demesne of the Maresquiers, it had been an uneven struggle to wrench any kind of livelihood, however meagre, out of the soil. The stone mansion continued as a farm solely because in

330

local memory the buildings had always been one; and, as each new generation handed the property down to the one below, the Maresquiers in turn, the young ones, married and brought up their children to work there, without rebelling against the tradition. Belgodère had become for them, for centuries, like an axiom of religion, neither to be questioned, nor criticized, frequently hated and feared, but ever in authority. Fortunes declined and the demesnes of Malentendu and Carthagéne with them, but Belgodère did not decline. It endured as implacably as those who sheltered within its walls, and the walls themselves presented their obdurate face to whatever bitter weather and wind might try to shake it. If the Maresquier family spoke of pride, it was the pride of those stone walls, and rocks and boulders outside, it was the pride of throttling from those barren fields the merest existence. It was the pride of ignorance and endurance, and of unending, back-breaking, unrewarded work. To belong to the Ardennes was an honour of distinction; to belong to Belgodère, the highest form of benediction. It was an aristocracy of servitude, an élite of drudgery.

Of these things, though, the two young fliers knew nothing at this time, but came to know gradually, by talking by the hearth with Hortense, the schoolteacher, in her broken and forgotten English, and with the men, stumbling in their own halting French. It was a surprise, for example, to uncover in Old Xavier and his clan this awareness of their unknown way of life, even as if they themselves recognized that it was backward and out of touch; it was a surprise too to find that, although the inhabitants in Belgodère were ignorant of any other form of life, they were equally uninterested in experiencing such a thing, as if it were something they already knew and had rejected. To some extent their isolation had protected them spiritually from the conflict raging some thirty miles to their west, they did not know what exactly was going on. But not exclusively protected. This accounted for the fact that there were no young men at

Belgodère, and that the village of Corbeille was, in Xavier's words, 'a village of children and the very old'.

The head of the family was the great-grandfather, Old Xavier, now over ninety years of age. His wife had died ten years before, and her daguerreotype (with dress and shawl painted over a gentle blue, taken one afternoon in the engraver's studio in Saint-Cyriac) stood above the chimney, the only adornment. Every morning he walked stiffly down to his place in the chimney, and stood in front of it. It was a moment of privacy, and respect, which the family observed. The old lady had dominated the household while she was alive, with her rigid severity, and determination to pursue well-tried paths. She despised the Maresquiers' name and remained, as she had ever been, Madame Framboise. This had hardly made for domestic ease within the farm, nor within the marriage, but she had the advantage of bringing with her on her wedding day the substantial dowry of all the land to the east of Belgodère, fertile grazing ground for the goats, which had been the ambition of the men of the farm for several hundred years, and the recognition of this piece of good fortune was not to be thrown away. Madame Framboise was a poor farmer's daughter, and she was his last child. She represented the last acres of good grazing. However, perhaps the undisguised hunger of generations of the Maresquiers for the property had bred in Madame Framboise a defensive obstinacy; and, knowing her price, she was determined that her new family should never cease to pay it. She was respected for her inheritance, admired for her discipline, esteemed for her aloneness, commended for her sacrifice, but feared as a woman. Perhaps, in his silent act of homage every morning, Old Xavier rendered symbolically that acknowledgement. Her severe influence continued long after she was dead. To keep the pasturage together, her three sons had taken a vow before the priest of Saint-Cyriac never to remarry.

The senior woman in the household, a seniority of years only of course (the youngest male child had greater authority), was Tante Fanny, who was only two years younger than her brother, Old Xavier. The Maresquiers, noted for the longevity, had mourned the death of the youngest sister in her seventies, a few years before, as something of a phenomenon, it had been an event of such unlikeliness. Tante Fanny sat generally in her own arm-chair on the other side of the chimney from Old Xavier, winter and summer, before the fire. She spoke little, and stared from behind her tired, pouched eyes. So much of the labour and grief was laid on the shoulders of the women at Belgodère that, in spite of their great capacity for long life, the wrinkling, wearing down, ageing process appeared to take a far greater toll of their countenances than of the men's. Her cheeks were lined and furrowed like a ploughed field, and the colour of the eyes were pale and limp. A few grey hairs hung over her upper lip, which was itself greyish in colour, and drawn down at the edges. Childless, unmarried, she was nevertheless the only warmth and love of the house, and the men of the family had known her knee better than their mother's, and the widows knew her shoulder better than the poor priest's. Tante Fanny had absorbed so much grief, it had become almost her profession, no less real for its frequency, no less painful for all its compassion.

The only other unmarried woman of the farm was known by her nickname rather than the name with which she had once been christened. Formerly Catherine, a young cousin of Grandfather Xavier and Tante Fanny, she was dubbed La Grosse, having grown immensely fat in her young years and, if anything, slightly fatter as she aged. She was still in her middle years. She it was who had bathed Bickerton's wounds. She it was who knelt before Arch and washed the blood from his feet. Covered in black at every season, her shapelessness increased; she remained an unfathomable bundle. Her place was most correctly standing by the table, waiting on the men. She had been taken into the farm at sixteen, having given birth to an illegitimate child, which she had had by a servant in the house she worked for in the village of Corbeille. The old lady had insisted, for the family's sake, that La Grosse would be harboured at Belgodère away from the scene of her shame. But it was more a gesture of punishment than tenderness, for La Grosse, even in her mature years, was never granted the rights of the grown-of-age, and she waited on the members of the farm from the day of her arrival. The child was taken to an orphanage held by the Carmelites in the nearest town, forty kilometres away, nor did the mother ever visit the convent. It had been rumoured the child also was a servant in the nuns' refectory. The shame of the Maresquiers was ignored, but not condoned.

'She was once a servant to a family in the village,' was the old lady's rational comment, 'why should she not now be a servant for her own family?'

Catherine could not be called unhappy, having never been especially happy, and she sat for long periods of time, when not waiting on the men, apparently lost in the reflection of her own thoughts. In fact, during those empty hours, she was not thinking of anything, having blotted out memory and the past. Encouraging her own fatness, she was always in the kitchen, and as nobody reproached her, her life was content enough, divided between work and rest and gratification. The period of work was what she expected from her life, the rare moments of rest she treasured, the finishing of scraps her pleasure; her imagination never went beyond that.

The second generation of Maresquiers were the three men who had confronted the fliers earlier with shotguns. These were the sons of Old Xavier and Madame Framboise, the eldest Ignace, then Toussaint, and Pascal. There was also Gorgonus the goatherd, and poor little Bastien, who was simple and short-statured. He was called 'Half-a-Brain' by the family. Bastien had been milking the *brébis* when the procession passed him by, interrupting his industry without curiosity for a mere second. He made no appearance that first evening, although the two men came to know him with friendly intimacy later on. But between this older generation and the unexplained presence of the three young women (the small children were in bed in the loft, all tucked under the same sacking stuffed with straw) there was a wide and discernible gap. Arch had noticed it at once, and understood the reason. Of course, these were the wives of the grandsons, the able-bodied, the strong, the vigorous, the inheritors. And they were all at war. Those left behind, for all of their strength and tenacity, were indeed, as Old Xavier had bitterly declared, 'the children, the very aged'.

The wife of Ignace had died while giving birth to their third son – Camille – who was with the artillery around the salient at Noyou. Toussaint had never married, he despised women, and the wife of Pascal had run away shortly after the marriage. He had taken a girl from the town, whom he had courted diligently for six years. But there was family opposition. She had been a good-looking woman, called Thomasine, and she worked as a kitchen-maid in the convent. Their courtship had been long, as the Maresquiers had resisted her, Old Xavier's wife especially, because she brought no dowry. A woman without land, Madame Framboise asserted, was worse than barren. And with pride, Thomasine had refused to be married into a family where her poverty was treated with disrespect.

'I will not belong to a family where the parents are claws against me,' she asserted defiantly.

Eventually, Pascal had threatened to kill himself if his mother did not give permission for the marriage, and forced her to sit down and write to the young woman a letter of welcome and reconciliation. The letter was signed and presented by hand. The marriage was completed at the end of the year, but the resentment glowered. Thomasine was a slight, pretty, happy creature, who sang as she worked. Madame Framboise called her 'the goose'. Used to the cheerful labours of convent life, and the kind Sisters of Mercy, Thomasine found

335

release in the natural life on the farm, but the cruel silences of the grandmother, and the timid displeasure of the rest of the clan, wore away her spirit and her sweetness. Pascal found that, in spite of himself, the resentment of his family was a greater force than any joy he might feel from his attractive, smiling wife; and, although nothing was ever mentioned between them, it was no surprise when Thomasine one morning left the farm, taking nothing with her, and quite simply disappeared. Pascal, pride offended to the very roots, swore revenge and oiled his shotgun, but the rest of the family determined that his wife should be allowed to go without hindrance, and that Pascal should be forced to remain at Belgodère. A wife, at best, can only become as close as a sister; a man would call her 'sister'. Once again, the opposition was too great and overpowered him. He replaced his shotgun on the hooks above the chimney, under the picture of the grandmother, and continued working at the farm. Thomasine's name was never mentioned. The final word was from Xavier's formidable wife: 'She came to us with nothing, she gave us nothing, she stole nothing from us, she left with nothing, we have lost nothing.'

And the matter ended there. Pascal, the third son, 'the sore tooth' of the family, was a reserved, cheerless man, incapable of much delight, but as hardened to the unfair blows life gave him as the boughs and boulders were to the wind. Because of this division of the land, all three brothers mutually vowed to remain as they were, widowed or unmarried. In this way, none of the precious grazing would ever leave the family until all three brothers had died. 'After that,' they would say, 'is another affair . . .'

Of the younger women, each was married to one of the three sons of Ignace. Berthe was the heavily pregnant wife of Camille, the artilleryman. Every week, as she fattened, she worried more for news of her husband at Noyou. Hortense was the wife of François, or Fan-Fan, who had enlisted in the cavalry, and Cécéline was the wife of Ambroise, a prisoner of the Germans since 1914, captured in the very first month of the war. Cécéline and Berthe were two sisters who married two brothers, both from the village of Corbeille, and well received by the grandmother, because they had been sensibly educated by the nuns; and Hortense because she was a teacher and, most important of all, because her dowry came from the excellent blacksmith's forge her father owned in Corbeille.

Ambroise had always been the best loved of his family – the one who had a way with horses, the youngest, a singer of magical improvised songs, which had surely won over the heart of Cécéline, when they first met at the fête of Saint-Cyriac. The feast-day had been celebrated in the cloisters of the Dominicans. During *Tenebrae*, while the women sat in front on the pews, and the men stood half-defiantly at the back, Ambroise alone, while the candles one by one darted out, had stared fiercely at her bowed head in prayer, desiring her, even then, right there during the Eucharist. A picture of him brightened the shadows above the fireplace, in gay military dress, smiling, taken on leave by the army photographer. Beside it was the symbol of crossed flags of all the Allies. His expression was cheerful, conceited, chin upturned, eyes excited. He was a trooper in the cavalry, with the insignia on his sleeve. But, at the Battle of the Marne, his squadron had been overrun when the French Cavalry Brigade advanced across the river at Châlons. He had been sighted at the head of his column, always an eager horseman, and clearly seen cantering into the forest at Argonne. There had been some kind of ambush. A squadron of Uhlans advanced on the far flank, machine-gun fire from an emplacement scattered the reserves, and Ambroise was not seen or heard from again. Posted as 'missing', so early on in the war which all the soldiers said was sure to end before the leaves fell from the trees, his September death could not be considered. Not such youth, not such energy, nor such a singing voice. The cavalry officer had written to the widow:

> We do not accept his death. You must not accept it either. He was seen, splendidly alive, riding into the wood. One day that wood will be retaken by our cavalry, and Ambroise and his companions will ride out of it again, of that you may be sure. Only the evening before, behind the lines, we had all enjoyed a sing-song by the bonfire. He sang some of his own poems, with which he used to delight us, and then some of the lovely old songs of the Ardennes, which he sang with such expression that a group of officers, returning from their Mess, overheard, and hung back on purpose to listen. We believe Cavalier Ambroise is taken prisoner, and inspiring the spirits of our men behind the German lines with those wonderful ancient songs . . .

This spirit Grandfather Xavier firmly believed. The favourite, the darling of his heart, Old Xavier refused absolutely to acknowledge any suggestion of the death of his favoured grandchild. The hope of his family, adored husband, and admired horseman, there was never any question that he should one day return to Belgodère in as cheerful a spirit as the day he departed. And so, full of confidence, the old man, each Thursday, took the cart, and the cart-horse, and set off down the untidy track many miles beyond Corbeille. There, there was a junction of two railway lines. One led east, and trainloads of young prisoners-of-war in khaki, sheepskin coat and rolled 'barda' could be seen standing in the corridors, taking their last glimpse, yearning many of them, of their homeland and the countryside they knew. The other transports led westwards, towards the Salient and the trenches, and these held mute groups of determined men in field-grey with *Stahlhelme* and *Pickelhauben*, far more numerous than those going in the opposite direction. For they were the human supplies to fill the gaps in the long uneven line which slithered from the flooded lowlands of the River Yser across the flat, desolate fenlands of the Ypres Salient, the industrial slag-heaps of Artois, along the tortuous river-line of the Aisne, and ended against the Swiss frontier at the mountainous Vosges. And once a week there were the wounded, the gassed, the reprieved prisoners of war, covered, covered in mud from head to foot, hungry-looking faces, swathed in grey cotton-wool bandages. Every Thursday at this junction, La Croisée, in a bare clearing between the two valleys, an ancient fir plantation and a ruined mill signifying the spot, Old Xavier would wait with his cart, and watch for the solitary train which passed that way. He would scan their haggard, worn-out faces as they flicked past, in the hopes of recognizing his own blood. And, his optimism undiminished, he would drive slowly back all those miles, determined to return to La Croisée the next week at the same time.

'They tell me my boy is missing. But he will come back. I know it. He will come back.' And he would mutter defiantly to himself: '*Il reviendra. Il reviendra.*' Like a refrain. '*Il reviendra.*'

So this was the besieged remnant of the Maresquiers, custodians of Belgodère, and of its ancient, arrogant way of life – although all the secrets belonging to the place and its people were unknown then to Arch and Bickerton, who sat at the rough table, eating a potage of chestnuts and beans, flavoured with rabbit flesh. They ate with wooden spoons, and the soup was poured out of the black pot it came from, into crude holes cut into the table. And when they had scooped as much as they could manage, learning from Gorgonus, who watched them feasting with an extra envy, they sopped the black hunks of bread in front of them with eau-de-vie, and scraped the hollows clean, and sucked the alcohol-dough. An added rapport was established by an exchange of Bickerton's refined army-issue cigarettes for the fat, coarse 'Boyards Caporals' with yellow papers accepted from Toussaint.

339

Bickerton showed the admiring group a weal across his cigarette case made by a subdued Spandau bullet. A cask of brackish wine had already been disposed of when, at the end of their meal, with the ceremonious air of one who introduces a great rarity, Old Xavier brought out a small bottle of colourless alcohol, with pickled grey grapes inside it, which Bickerton promptly announced could have flown the machine back to Béthune. A goat's-milk cheese, smelling of goat's hairs, was put before them, tangy and peppered.

'*Attention! Ça pique! C'est piquant!*' said Gorgonus.

And Old Xavier added: '*Un fromage comme ça, ça se respecte!*' A cheese like that, you will have to pay your respects to. It stings, like a hornet.

'*C'est l'essence*,' laughed Gorgonus, '*pour l'engin!*', referring to the enraged colourless spirit, the home-brewed quetsche.

La Grosse cleared the fragments which remained and shooed the crumbs down for the dogs, and Hortense translated for them the arrangements for where the fliers should sleep for the night. A ladder which appeared to lead into a hole in the roof was in reality the only way to reach the granary. There they would find sacks and straw and could be comfortable as well as warm. And it was perhaps the most intimate sign of their acceptance by Belgodère, that the family – one by one – reverted to their habitual silence facing the fire, Old Xavier spitting drily into the ashes with a sharp hiss, and tapping the hearth-stone with his pointed stick, the men in a circle round him, soundless, arms folded heavily, and the women working on their shawls, with rapid noiseless movements of their large knitting-needles, and the only sound emanating from Gorgonus – as was customary – set back from the fireside circle, on his joint-stool, hissing through his teeth a suppressed goatish sound. Suddenly, he turned to the fliers at the table. The hot fire penetrating their bones, the rabbit stew, the eau-de-vie which made their brain swim, the deep, deep feeling of exhaustion within them overwhelmed their bodies. It was not merely a survival from yet another dreadful day which appeased them, everything they had lived with, week after week, month after month, had suddenly vanished. They had escaped from the battle with no dishonour. The miracle everybody along the line from the North Sea to the Vosges had prayed for, and longed for, and never believed, had reached them, uniquely, and no one else. It had *stopped*. Gorgonus, at the best of times, needed an interpreter, even among the family, he spoke no French, and his version of Ardennois was very much his own creation. Hortense turned in her chair to translate: 'Gorgonus says that Old Xavier will kill the pig to celebrate your arrival in Belgodère. They have never seen an English soldier. Gorgonus has never seen anyone outside Belgodère.'

But the two men were already fast asleep on their arms.

In the darkness, away from the warm familiarity and comfortable smells of the kitchen, miles out in the forest, a cautious dirt-fox set out on his snuffling trail for a vixen, or to ambush one of the wood's smaller night-creatures. He had been driven from the empty hay-barns of Petit-Grain. The first brushes of snow at that altitude had taken away much of his habitual food, there was not a granary rat to be had, and he felt driven down to the arms of man on his scavenging expeditions. The berries he tasted were bitter, and rooting around the stumps of trees produced little but a sour fungus . . .

Arch had not been wrong about hearing shotguns, just after he crash-landed at Belgodère. And the barking dogs belonged to Pascal, his '*chiens rapporteurs*', cross-breeds with spaniel in them; Dick, and his mother, the dun bitch Cléa, old now and toothless but tenacious. The men had tracked down the day before, in the late afternoon, a wild boar, and the dogs had run it out of the lower slopes of the forest, coaxed it to open ground, and through the

341

scrub by the river-line where the guns could have a good clear shot at it. Then the machine had crashed, and disturbed the hunt at the wrong moment, when Ignace claimed he had winged it, and the men wanted to return to pick up the traces. Ignace swore he had seen a spray of blood, new and bright, show up red against the pine leaves. The three peasants – joined now by Bickerton and '*le Capitaine*' well muffled up in goatskin jerkins over their uniforms – side-stepped their way down the sheer mountain, descending the plateau of drained Belgodère, to the valley of the little Chouette, a narrow river, fed by the forest-slopes of the Ardennes. Only the farmers carried their shotguns; Arch was loaded with cartridge-belts and Bickerton with the sacking. Once they had arrived at the bottom, hoarse and sweating, the men soon picked up the traces, and the hounds fed on the scent hungrily. Lank, scrawny buggers they were too, thought Arch as he slithered and slewed down the pine-cushioned scrag, vaulting a tree-trunk here, and side-stepping a fir-tree stump there, manoeuvring as he would in the air, but without the keen spear of danger. This was sheer fun, without the panic. The dogs, with their scarred mugs, and flea-ranged flanks, veterans of countless rat and boar chases, had found the scent in the flattened bracken, and Gorgonus, old and agile, leaping like some breed of goat, was pointing to a fresh trace of blood. There was little to choose between the half-breed dogs and the figure of the stunted man, vanishing and reappearing between the firs. Then they were out in the quag, and yesterday's mist came down to swallow them up, until they could only communicate by guttural cries. Belgodère, reflected Arch, was so high, it remained clear above the habitual seasonal mist. Now, they were ducking around in an unfamiliar slob land, often up to their thighs. This was flow country, soggy and damp underfoot.

'Keep the cartridges up, Arch,' called Bickerton.

But the dogs held on to the scent; it must have been

342

new-sown, that morning, luck really, as damp air and mist tend to disperse the tang.

They had risen early, or rather had their rising forced upon them, by Gorgonus throwing a bucket of icy water over them with a shriek of delight.

'You bastard!' swore Bickerton quietly, looking round for something to hurl at his attacker. Arch blearily flattened his wet hair with his hands, and rubbed at his eyes. Light edged under a gap in the door and through a trickle in the shutters. The old goat was making curious disfigured gestures with his mouth and hands, and muttering away: '*Manges, manges, manges.*'

'Who's this – some kind of loony-bin merchant?' asked Bickerton irritably.

'Wants us to drink something, I think, Bickerton.'

'Drink something! I'm not woken up yet – not with this cot-case about!'

Gorgonus hustled about energetically, and came back from the fire with a metal pot of black stewy liquid, and set it on the table with two wood bowls as large as soup-plates. Then he returned with a large hunk of yellow bread made from chestnut flour, threw it on the table, opened his clasp-knife and plunged it in.

'*Manges – manges – manges* . . .' And he patted Bickerton fondly on the back, as a father would try to ease a child with a fit of croup.

'Friendly but insane,' laughed Bickerton, and winked at the short figure. 'He's a cot-case . . .!'

Gorgonus, by way of reply, whistled back to them, like a thrush.

The hot black liquid he placed in the centre of the table was by no means the coffee they were imagining – their china bowls contained a sort of gruelly paste, liquefied and hot and mercifully sweetened, tasting of chicory. Its brackishness shocked them as they drank it down. What was disconcerting about Gorgonus was his flat eyes, with a yellow bar in the centre. He had an animal look. When he bustled about – he was a hard worker, even inside the house – he accompanied his urgent sharp movements with staccato outbursts and meaningless grunts, belches and short fart-like noises, which issued from the back of his throat. Nothing could dissuade Bickerton from the notion that he had escaped from a lunatic asylum nearby – at best a 'character', at worst a cot-case.

Pascal had thrown open the vast double-doors, wide enough for a carriage to drive through – in the ancient, grand Maresquier days, they did – and light poured through, the fire rearing up in the sudden draught. Toussaint stood behind him carrying the shotguns.

'*Le sanglier*,' he explained. '*La chasse. Il le faut. Eh, Capitaine, eh . . .!*'

'*Et les Boches . . .?*' enquired Arch, indicating the telltale shotguns.

'*Ils sont trop loin – trop loin*,' replied Ignace, pointing vaguely eastward.

'*Et les femmes?*' Arch asked of Pascal, the more communicative.

'*En bas – elles descendent pour l'eau. En bas*,' he gestured firmly downwards with his hand.

'*Rien dans le village?*'

'*Elles descendents à la fontaine. Ici, il n'y a rien. En bas. En bas.*'

Even among themselves the Maresquiers had the habit of gesturing first, and only employing language as a later resort. Arch watched Pascal arm the pockets of his black cord waistcoat with his clasp-knife, and pipe and tobacco, and salt, and struggle into a bulky jacket also made of black cord which buttoned up to the neck. Then he wound a check scarf round his throat, and pulled a cap with ear-flaps over his cropped head. All the while, his lips twitched and jerked at the matchstick he kept between his teeth. Gorgonus and Toussaint both draped coarse brown sacking with hoods over their heads (Toussaint was dressed in the identical peasant black cord as his brother), resembling, Arch thought, engravings he had seen in schoolbooks of coal-miners in the previous century.

It was, as he later discovered, traditional in that part of the Ardennes: the natives wore these clothes for generations and handed them on. It was not a country where things were discarded. The shepherds slept out in their sacking hoods: once, Toussaint told them much later, he had woken up in the fields on a February morning, to find himself covered in white snow, but buried warm within his sack.

Clattering beneath the arch which held a remnant of the long-forgotten aristocratic entry to Belgodère, Arch and Bickerton were able to study more precisely their surroundings, the architecture of the farm about them. While he arranged around his neck and shoulders the several bandoliers of cartridges which Pascal slung at him, Bickerton observed how very remote the farm was, and thought with some satisfaction that Germans and British alike would take a lot of time to scour them away from their new refuge. Even with a restricted view through the damp mist, he could see that the farm stood entirely isolated with steep scarps on each side cascading to the valley a long way below. Tracks and stone paths there were in plenty, but nothing whatever resembling a road which could be travelled by the toughest motor-vehicle. Behind them the first foothills of the impassable Ardennes forest stretched away to the east, and scrub and marshland further to the west. It was an inhospitable landscape, a place of anonymity, aridity, and silence. The people who lived there – as harsh and agile as the beasts they appeared to tend – were not on the road *to* anywhere. Where the ravine dropped to the west, thought Bickerton, and the farm receded behind them in the wet, icy mist, you might imagine a hostile sea pounding and heaving: if anywhere was the end of land, it was Belgodère.

This threadbare, lunar landscape presented a very different picture to Arch, accustomed to the vast scale of South Australia and its immense sheep-stations. Everything was impoverished, barren, austere. And, like

Bickerton, he felt the absence of Flying Corps life, the comradeship, the terror, the parades, the dawn patrols.

So, as the assiduous Dick and Cléa picked up the smell and the blood of the *marcassin*, and as Gorgonus, giving vent again to guttural animal cries of exultation, splashed through the moor-bog, Arch enjoyed the pleasure of the chase.

In his inexperience, however, Arch had no inkling of the sheer malignancy of the *marcassin*. This tough wild boar, leathery and quilled like a porcupine, with a hide sharp and stiffened by mud, had already received one barrel of shot in his left flank, and had gone to ground in the salt-marshes. The scent that dawn was patchy, but the half-breed got a lungful first, and Dick's tail shot up, a lean mud-coloured dog, with a nose as accurate as an arrow. A screech-owl rose up and betrayed the boar; Toussaint crouched to get in line for a shot. No suggestion of taking stations here. Bickerton ran up beside Pascal ready to reload. All three of the peasants fired both barrels into the impenetrable scrub, and the resonant mist gathered the explosion and re-echoed it in all directions. This was what Arch had heard the afternoon before, after the crash.

Bickerton shouted: 'They haven't the first idea about it here . . .' He realized that the boar might thread his way through them at the moment they were reloading.

The dogs checked, they were puzzling the scent out to no avail: the beast was near, but unnervingly taciturn, tired but cunning. It gave the men their chance to reload: nervily Toussaint fired again at nothing, into the scrub. It was a wasted bluff: the furze did not stir, the retrievers, silent and foxed, had lost the line. Pascal yelled at Toussaint to fire his second barrel, but again nothing budged. The dogs' tails dropped.

'Elle est juste là, la bête, juste là, dans le fourré . . .'

'Yes, and he's not coming out, I'll bet,' smiled Bickerton, handing Toussaint new cartridges. Arch was anxious about his observer.

346

'For God's sake, don't get caught between the hounds and their fire, Bickerton; they've no idea about stations. Just dig in.'

Then the pale bitch got her nose right down, and came on to the scent which was warm enough still, although the wild boar must be getting colder.

'*Attendez . . . attendez, Toussaint,*' called out Arch urgently. '*Gardez votre feu.*'

Toussaint obeyed.

There was an abrupt surging only twenty yards from where the two peasants eagerly leant forward, and the furze seemed to scatter left to right. The dogs owned to the scent and got a good whiff of it again and the *marcassin* reared up in front of them, tearing through Dick's thigh with a flashing tusk. Arch was astounded, he thought he'd never seen anything quite so fierce and so fast – the razor-back was at them, driving into them as directly as a torpedo, low on the ground, squint-eyed, flaked in blood, mulberry and bright red, and two stubby dreadful uprising tusks. The hounds at his heels dropped their noses down and pushed him hard, this time with an impatient and intermittent whimper, ever four paces behind. Where the tense silence had once been was now a huge roar, and the earth seemed truly to vibrate. The beast presented a narrow target as all the shotguns exploded at once, and the dogs were dangerously close behind on the burning scent. The peasants fired inaccurately and excitedly, and failed miserably to kill, although Pascal's second barrel winged the boar's left shoulder. Gorgonus had fired first, and missed twice, lurching his gun-stock upwards against his shoulder, in his anxiety triggering both barrels at once. Bickerton seized the carbine, broke open the steaming breech, while the boar levelled his wicked head towards him through the under-brush. Only one barrel did for him.

'Let the dog see the rabbit,' he muttered, with enviable calm.

Arch watched, as if in slow motion, while the observer

loaded, snatched the barrel shut, lifted the gun-bore, tucked in the wooden haunch, and fired in one flowing movement. He took no aim at all, and the boar – at a mere five yards, tangled in the scrub and furze – somersaulted cleanly, carried forward a further eight feet by his own fierce momentum. It was so small suddenly.

Bickerton back on form, Arch thought contentedly to himself.

Pascal whistled through his matchstick, Gorgonus grunted, and Toussaint shoved back his corduroy cap. Bickerton felt a little better towards the disastrous previous afternoon, but all he said was: 'Well, at least it didn't jam that bloody time.'

Arch held the sacking open for the dead weight to be shovelled in. It took the strength of two men to lift the creature. Pascal took Dick's torn body, ended his struggling and yelping with a single shot, and threw him in the stream.

It was hard work lifting the animal back up through the scrub and furze, and over fallen trunks, and around awkward stumps with such a dead weight on their shoulders. Several times they halted, changed loads, breathing heavily as the moisture drained out of them. Few birds sang in the monotonous forest, and even they petered out entirely as the men's footsteps thankfully sought out the cobbled paths back to Belgodère. Gorgonus alone seemed unimpressed by the climb, and once carried the sacked boar across his neck without any reduction in his customary agility. But, as they climbed higher, in spite of all their exertion, and the additional load of dead boar, shotguns and spare cartridge-belts, a clinging wet mist penetrated their goatskins and, when they climbed into the stone kitchen, where the women were working, they felt grateful for the wood fire. The six men stamped their feet to restore circulation, and scraped away the mud around the edges of their boots. Chilblains tingled and buzzed. The morning was still bitterly cold.

As they entered the communal stone hall, the women

348

around the table immediately vacated their chairs, where they had been peeling boiled chestnuts and heaping them into a large saucepan. After the sudden German advance in the autumn of 1914, most of the local farms had been stripped of everything edible, except sweet chestnuts, and even those . . . Wordlessly the men sat in the recently abandoned chairs, and La Grosse, at once knowing their need, poured out the dark chicory, which had pickled a further few hours in the grate. Like the fire which had burned for a hundred years, the coffee was permanently nursed in the embers. They broke the thick blocks of brown sugar-cane into their bowls, while La Grosse bent over each man, and Ignace followed her round with a bottle of colourless liquid, a well-ripened eau-de-vie, with a faint flavour of almonds as it burnt in the throat. Seeing the other men mix it into their coffee, Arch and Bickerton did the same with relish.

'Now this *is* a bit of all right!' said Bickerton, winking his one eye, while the men solemnly lifted their bowls to the successful marksman.

'*Le quetsche!*' they muttered, pouring the stuff down in a flourish.

The women, standing behind the men's chairs, leant forward from time to time, to hand over thick haunches of bread and a tangy cured bacon inside it, peppery and spiced, or to refill their coffee bowls. All the time, the dead boar was splayed across one end of the wood table, its filmy grey eye upturned; although Arch and the observer found it hard to ignore, the other hunters carried on with their eating unconcerned.

As if it were a personal prize, when he entered the door-way Gorgonus had carried the boar directly up to Old Xavier, seated as he always was by the fire, pipe in hand. His nod of approval seemed to be accepted as a signal, and only after that had the men advanced to their traditional places at the table. The death of a wild boar was an unusual occurrence, it was explained later – and I can't say I'm surprised, thought Bickerton, if that's the way they shoot.

349

At a command from Old Xavier, La Grosse waddled forward from the darkness carrying a dish of hard, bony pastry, obviously intended as some delicacy, which the men dipped into the remnants of their coffee and eau-de-vie. It tasted sweet and dry, like shortbread, reminding Arch of his experiences out back soaking damper in the old roo-shooters' battered tin saucepans, where nothing mattered provided one was tired enough, and hungry enough. For a minute, he wondered how the good old 10th Squadron would be getting on, wondered, too, whether the squadron might be concerned about them; and realized that this was the first time he had thought about such a thing for a full night and day. Missing, supposed killed, he imagined, and dwelt for a further moment on the image of their names being dutifully rubbed out from the blackboard of patrol duties, and erased from the tennis competitions, a glass raised to them at night in the Mess, and not much more. He hoped he might count on Diviani's grief, though even he, perhaps, would be more troubled by the loss of his famous engines. It was not much in the way of a valediction. Bickerton must have been thinking about one and the same thing. He picked up his bowl in his large hand, and announced: 'Here's to the memory of a skilful flier, and his gallant observer, who fought to a standstill in the skies, and flopped out somewhere over Charleville.'

'And lived to make a joke about it.'

'Too true, mate. And, from now on, let's forget it.'

'Good show, Bick! Exactly what was in my mind.'

Gorgonus came in in his shirt-sleeves, carrying two iron pails which he banged together: '*Au boulot! Au boulot! Demain on tue le cochon . . . le boudin . . . le petit sal . . . les rillettes.*'

Gorgonus wound his feet and ankles round about in long strips of rag, and tied them firmly with cord, then over that he pulled on a horny pair of nailed boots. Old Xavier took from the back of the door a vilely stained brown apron and carefully tucked it around his corduroys.

Their boots clanged against the stone flags as they trooped outside, in file, almost with the regular tread of foot-soldiers. Winter kept its scaly grip up on Belgodère, hard and black and acid.

Tante Fanny was outside already, a black sack of hessian about her head to keep the cold off, working what the people of Belgodère called her 'oat-pickles'. She was bent down to the ground spreading a mixture of old boiled oats with mashed thorn-apple and cut-up leaves of rue out beyond the stone porch. The starlings, already fluffed up in the cold and inflated like little puff-balls, hopped about enquiringly, pecked for a few seconds at the confection and staggered over dead. Then Tante Fanny gathered them while they were still warm into her pannier, and brought them into the larder. But, before she prepared them for cooking, always prudent and mindful of waste, she slit their little gizzards apart with her penknife, and emptied the oatmeal out on to a piece of cloth so that she could use it a second time.

'No point in wasting good wholesome pickles,' she muttered grimly, before setting out her bait to tempt the starlings again.

But they enjoyed these tasty mouthfuls at night over the fire, crunching them in their mouths whole, just like hot chestnuts, brittle bones and all, or pounded into a soft mush with myrtle-berries, as a luxurious paste. When the men finished their food, they pushed the bench back with their iron-shod boots, and the women who had been standing patiently behind came forward now and cleared the table and mopped out the holes in the wood where the food had been. Scraps went to the pig in the yard, and crumbs to the dogs under the table, if there were crumbs or scraps. Nothing was thrown away at Belgodère. La Grosse brought the bowl of coarse sugar-lumps, and Xavier alone had the privilege of pouring out the final thumbful of quetsche to each man in turn. This was called the '*adieux*'.

But, this evening, Hortense stood behind Bickerton's

351

stool, arms folded loosely, opposite Arch, and, although she remained still furtively in shadow, Arch could see the side of her cheek and her nose beside the fall of her black cowl. Her mouth seemed prominent and its corners turned downward, as if spoilt, and he felt her eyes on him in some unexpressed accusation. When he looked up, and caught her eyes fixed on him, she would not look away. Brown, with an ochreous stain in the whites surrounding them. The dogs ran to the chink of wind under the door, snuffling, yelping, excited by something outside. The silent, morose Pascal, who always wore his black jacket over his shoulders in the house and kept his black hat on his head at table, went for his shotgun, but Old Xavier at the fireside forbade him.

'*C'est rien. C'est monsieur le renard.*'

And Gorgonus explained to Bickerton in dumb-show by miming hurriedly the cross-legged patter of the fox, and the weight of his brush behind. So the second evening ended in grins and nods of the head, with the dogs whimpering excitedly and shoving their wet noses as far under the door as they were able.

Every morning of his life, Grandfather Xavier sat down to the table with his bowl in front of him. He took out his clasp-knife, and set it carefully to the bowl's right-hand side. True he was old now, and bent at the shoulders where before he had been upright, and his sight was going, but in his great days Old Xavier had been the strongest man in the region, the hardiest, and drank the most. His neighbours would never call him 'poor' in his old age, as they did 'poor old Julien' at Werpes. He wore check cloth slippers on his feet, which because of a painful form of shingles made him complain of being 'on fire', but every morning of every day he took his place at the head of the table, cutting the bread for the men with his stubby clasp-knife as was his right. Nobody was certain, but the Maresquiers reckoned his age to be about ninety, perhaps more. Only memory knew for sure, there were no written records kept. His bowl in front of him was the only one used at Belgodère, and it was of white china, with a single dark blue ring around the inside. First he took the bread, which La Grosse baked every Saturday for the week's supply, and holding it against his waistcoat buttons, sliced with care a firm crust off the end of it, sawing his stub-bladed knife methodically towards him. This crust he broke into several smaller hunks, and dropped them one by one into the bowl. Next, he would rise slowly to his feet – the other men never tired of watching this morning ritual – and, from the corner of the well-tempered chestnut kitchen-dresser which stood against the stone, took the unlabelled bottle of colourless eau-de-vie to the table. He poured a hefty measure right up to the blue marking line. Then he would recork the flask, put it back on the dresser, return again to the table, sit, and painstakingly sup each soaked crust through his teeth, as fiercely as if it were a fig. At the end, he would wipe the inside of the bowl clean with a final fresh crust which he left to one side and dry, for the exact purpose. At supper he would observe the same custom, with the addition of three white heads of onion, which he slowly chewed. Very rarely he might be tempted to try a little meat, salt pork for instance, or wild boar in season, well marinated in thyme and a good Argonne, but this fiery diet had fortified him winter and summer for many years, and his good health could be attributed to it. The Maresquiers swore Old Xavier had never suffered a day's bad health in bed, and never would until that day in the future which he would decide to be his final one. His own father had been the same, 'Le Cocagne', Hortense told the two strangers, and kept up to the end, until one night suddenly he announced, 'I've had enough,' to the family before the dying fire, 'That's it, I'm going to bed with a shovel,' and turned his face to the wall for ever. People said of him, 'He was a man among men', '*un homme parmis les hommes*'. Old Xavier was a veteran himself, but liked to reminisce about the lines of battle in the Peninsular War which his father told him all about, and

353

how he had seen a man's head, neatly lopped by a rattle of grape-shot, roll along the top of the trenches just like a leather ball. Le Cocagne played his part. He had taken his place in the line with Marshal Soult from Salamanca to Toulouse – one of the Old Trousers brigade.

Above Belgodère, following the road-which-ascends, as the villagers call it, half of its life spent hidden in wet cloud, a haphazard stack of rocks unveils the ancient stone town of Corbeille, encircled by ruined walls. A short dirt-fox, with a patched mask, drags its brush along uneven stones.

Then it was the morning when Old Xavier traditionally slaughtered his pig. November was the proper month, and Wednesday, Toussaint, the ordained day.

There was a doomed feeling, and a kind of edgy tension in the air. The pig due to be slaughtered was an old friend of the family, never more so than in the past ten weeks, when it had been swollen to bursting with all available scraps and some food that the family themselves, and the dogs certainly, had eyed with envy. Hard enough to bear the carcass of the wild boar up from the valley below Belgodère, it was out of the question to haul the bulk of a dead sow up to the kitchen, and so the creature had been quartered in improbable style in the farm buildings themselves, and pampered with the leavings of the house, cabbage leaves, the parsnip and turnip mops, dark brown potato-leavings. 'All the sweeter for the knife,' the local saying was, 'the richer the forage, the richer the pudding . . .'

Old Xavier was the executioner, by tradition, just as he was favoured for cutting the bread, and he stood apart, summing up the slaughtered pig, gently stropping a long-bladed knife against the worn stone on the outside door. The women of Belgodère already stood in a line carrying large pudding basins for the blood. It was part of the tradition that they should watch the cutting of their own pig's throat.

'Makes me think of us, up there, with my bastard guns,' said Bickerton beside him, nodding to the sky. It was true. There was something helpless about the pig in the corner, and the women with bowls, and the man with his knife. 'A sitting pig,' said Bickerton glumly, 'poor old stick.' And his one good eye was filmed with moisture.

Without twin-Spandaus to defend itself from every kind of indignity and brutality, the beast was quickly subdued. It wriggled and squealed, but could not escape. Old Xavier still watched and evenly sharpened his long blade, while Toussaint and Ignace between them held the snout captive; Pascal wrapped a coarse rope firmly around it, so that the squealing, which had increased to frenzied proportions, was suffocated. Arch noticed how the intensity still remained, but the noise diminished – it was like a cornet with a cushion crammed into the horn, stifled and strangled. Then the men wound ropes around the four frantic legs, and pulled outwards, until the beast sprawled incontinent and drunk. Excrement lay all over the ground, the men slithered in it. Bickerton tied his scarf over his nostrils and mouth; the slime was green and stank of terror. The men were quite silent, they knew their way in this exercise, they were all tradesmen. Pascal handed Arch his end of rope to make a fourth. The pig's weight had fallen forward, between its trotters, it could no longer control itself, too heavy for those short flailing struts. Still without speaking, Grandfather Xavier moved forward a few paces, not looking at the animal, but checking studiously, in the thin light, the knife-edge, reminding the flier, with his reflective, almost pious air, of a priest about to offer the sacrament, and then – an astonishing thing – knelt beside the supplicant and cradled its head. He put the knife gently on the ground. Bickerton held the cord attached to the snout, and at a sign from Pascal, only a short approving nod, as if to say 'now', pulled backward respectfully. Old Xavier gentled the beast's contorted throat, and the white underside ceased to strain. There was a moment of complete silence in the courtyard, and the cry began again, more strangled than ever, as Old Xavier rose up and took his knife. Toussaint yelled urgently '*Vas-y! Vas-y!* Bickey-tonn', and obediently, without instruction, the observer gave a sudden haul upwards on the snout-cord, up shone the white throat for a grisly second, this was like a fish-leap, and balancing neatly on the soles of his feet Xavier inserted the needle-tip of the knife. A faint thread of blood spurted out, and the pig's cry on its solitary sustained note bubbled and crackled. Arch's own blood swam and buzzed in his eyeballs.

'*A toi, Berthe . . .*' said a voice. '*Doucement . . .*'

The women knew at once, by the altered, cracked-trumpet note, that it was the moment to come forward with their basins, which they held, each of them, in their grey check aprons. Berthe leant forward the first, capturing the thread of blood as it sank from the pig's neck. The muffled gasp came and went now like an organ-pipe whose stop has jammed, and Old Xavier knelt beside his granddaughter and, taking one of the quivering feet gently in his harsh hand, helped the creature to die. The image of the priest persisted, the scene was like a benediction now.

'*Cécéline, c'est à toi, maint'nant,*' whispered Ignace, '*mais doucement, toujours.*'

The fountain spilt over, and was taken up eagerly in Cécéline's earthen bowl, the old man and his granddaughter bowed over the slit throat, with the submissiveness of penitents, each one comforted at the altar rail, one bowl replacing another. Hortense stirred the warm ruby gruel, as it trickled in, down to the joints of her fingers, and added salt, so that the blood would not curdle. A soft steam arose about it, a gentle haze. Hortense looked up once to where Arch stood, and gestured with her head for him to relax the hind-leg rope. He nodded and slowly released the cord; no answering tug now, no twitch; the bristling body lay flattened on the stone flags, beached like a mountainous fish, only the upturned sacrificial throat still in its pose of obsequies. Hortense continued to look at Arch, while she stirred with her fingers. She had a light scar across her underlip. She looked younger than he had first assumed. He noticed how the corners of her mouth turned down. From nervousness, almost like a cold shiver, he smiled, but the woman did not return his smile. The intermittent cries from the pig were softer now, and even. Now it was the sound a child makes in the summer, blowing through blades of grass between his hands, a sweet sound.

'Do you think it takes as long as this for a soldier to die?' asked Hortense. Her gaze was so steadfast and unflinching.

'Tssss!' warned Old Xavier, as if she were interrupting the silence of a sacrament.

'*Doucement. Tout doucement . . .*'

The rasping breath had lowered to a whisper by now, the pig's life was a sigh. And after that silence.

The pig was upended, amid much swearing, on to a firm tripod of bean-poles. There was only a faint dripping into the bowl by now.

Arch felt the cold mist reach his fingers. Berthe replaced Hortense and the girl climbed clumsily to her feet, balancing a full bowl, supporting her weight with a wet, blood-gloved hand. The care she took, the clumsiness, Arch suspected she was pregnant under that bulky, shapeless apron. Her forearms were red with the blood of the dead pig. Smoke from the bonfire of half-burnt wood blew across their faces. Then he saw that Gorgonus had re-emerged holding a touch of gorse in his hand, flaming and smoking. And he began a half-crouching, half-limping, ancestral dance, lunging from moment to moment at the swinging pig-corpse, burning and singeing the beast's white skin, and darting back from it, like a terrier, for fear that it should lash out at him. It seemed to the two airmen that he was tormenting the dead creature as in some half-buried retaliation. All the time he kept up his croaking and grunting rhythm. The women stood, the men squatted, watching this odd, spiky dance, as the sweet-scented gorse sparked and fizzed, and mixed with the acid tang of singeing bristle.

The pinkness of the pig's flesh slowly charred to black. Old Xavier, his eyes fixed on the beast, gestured with his left hand, a fussy, urging gesture. Pascal, Ignace and Toussaint drew their penknives from their deep waistcoat pockets and, each taking a corner of the corpse, began the task of scraping at the coarse bristles, blackened and crisp from the flare of Gorgonus's torch. When they touched the skin from time to time, to steady themselves, or their knives, their fingers started back sharply, stung by the burnt fat. Gorgonus lunged forward again with the fire-branch, and the scrapers followed him, close to the burnt scar, to get a clean, sharp strip. Blade followed flame, and the bristles and outer layer of skin fell away, as easily as fish-scales.

All four men grunted and swore, and even sang, in a low jerky rhythm as they bent to their work, and Gorgonus continued his eerie, staccato dance between the fire and smoke and ash. A curtain of wood-smoke parted and, eager to turn from the spectacle, to relieve his eyes for a moment from the sight of the pig, Arch found that Hortense, alone among the women, was not watching, but looking at him. He smiled, but she did not smile back; she remained looking towards him, as if beyond him, in the direction of the overcast light outside the courtyard.

Old Xavier stepped forward and, drawing his red handkerchief from his worn corduroys, wrapped it firmly around one of the pig's trotters and, with a quick sideways jerking movement, snapped it off, then with the claw of his clasp-knife tore out the red-hot blackened nails. This drew a muffled grunt of approval from the peasants, and appeared to signify the conclusion of the first part of the business. The oppressive weight of the beast, faintly braised by now, trembled on its hook. It was no longer pig, but had become a bundle of inanimate

charred meat, appetizing and worthy of Gorgonus's ceremonial dance.

La Grosse shuffled slowly forward bearing a large dish of
chestnut biscuits, which she set on the table inside the kitchen, and the men's iron-soled boots rattled back again on
the flagged floor. Behind her, Cécéline took up the tin pot of
burning coffee from the fire, and poured it into six wooden
bowls. All this was done in silence.

'*Et maintenant, on mange . . . On casse la croûte . . .*'

'Drinking, more like,' said Bickerton, glad all the same
for the break, and he sat on one of the stools waiting eagerly
for the diet they had already grown used to, the brackish
coffee and quetsche and crumbling, tasteless biscuit.

'Handsome,' he announced, with relish.

Stifled half in low cloud, the morning at Corbeille begins
raw and wet, long after the mist has risen in the valley. The
dirt-fox debates with itself whether or not to desert the
security of the stone village, and squeezes under the
draughty crack of a barn door. Its mask and pads are
damp, and there has been nothing to forage. A thin dog
tied on a string sees him at a distance and barks, rebelling
against the strain of the leash, front legs in the air. But the
fox neither increases pace, nor wastes a look behind. He
squats against a stable-post, leaving contemptuously a
dank stink behind.

'Ambroise . . . Ambroise . . .' calls a woman's voice,
from inside the cold walls, while her husband chops firewood in the yard. The village is shuttered and apart, like a
prison. The fox slinks by, belly on ground, his decision
made up. He will descend to the plateau. The winter hunger
gnaws at his skin too keenly – worse than his craving for a
vixen in the spring.

'The water of life,' translated Hortense, while Ignace
moved from shoulder to shoulder around the table pouring each a measure.

'*Le quetsche,*' he announced with pride.

The men nodded in satisfaction and approval, and patted their chests.

'*C'est bon pour le rhume . . . cela fait du chaud contre la grippe . . .*'

'*Eau-de-village,*' explained Old Xavier, grimly, as if it was poison.

As Hortense stooped over the blood, which the women had spilt into a large cauldron, Arch saw faint drops of sweat gather just beneath her eyes, and the light from the fire caught in them, and brightened her intent gaze. As she pulled back to lift the heavy liquid weight, almost more than she could bear, he saw her strong breasts braced under the strain; and, when the pail was supported again by the iron hook, and she relaxed, he watched while she pressed the flat of her back with her fist and felt her pumping heart with the other hand. Some dark hair brushed up from her neck fell back, and the sheer strength of her, the disarray, the bulky weight, suggested a rough contrast to her faintness. Once, when she found the weight of a second iron pail too great to raise on to the hook suspended from the chimney, Arch rose quickly to help her, but Berthe and La Grosse pushed him aside, offended, and all three together lifted the handle on to the waiting irons. Breathing deeply Hortense stepped a pace back from the fire, and wiped the sweat from her cheeks with her apron, and in a faintly coquettish gesture stroked her errant hair into place. For the first time, the effort made her smile, but privately, to herself. La Grosse went round again with the quetsche and stirred the dregs of the acrid coffee, and then silently the men returned, refreshed, to their labours.

Old Xavier paused a moment, confronting the hanging carcass, as if in prayer, and, steadying its slow spin with his left hand, inserted his penknife blade-deep. The folds of pig-flesh slowly shaved away at each side, behind his knife, and laid bare the entrails. Tucked away behind the fat, the viscera sat in polite layers, as if labelled ready for plucking. A faint steam emerged as the skin unpeeled for,

360

though the outside skin had cooled, the kidneys, liver and lights were still gently simmering. Xavier hooked out the spleen with a short, circular jab, and regarded the small green purse with dislike . . . The yard-dog stepped forward, tail wagging expectantly, but it did not go to him. Cécéline and La Grosse held each end of a wooden tray, and in a few moments, following the precise swipes, jabs, switches, and slits Old Xavier's penknife made, the pig-sides collapsed like a cave and a mound of steaming, pale entrails glistened between the women's shoulders. Dark kidneys and lights glimmered together, like jewels, lungs, plucks and tripes in clusters of crystal, and at last the opaque heart. As the women supported their heavy cargo back into the kitchen, the heap of flesh seemed alive, as if a magician might restore the living animal from the assembly of steaming organs they carried. The men turned away from their task, folding their penknives, and replacing them deep inside their waistcoat pockets.

Now it was the women's chance, and they folded their sleeves and hitched their check aprons, in the race, as the day descended, against decay. As soon as Old Xavier had sawn through the head, La Grosse bore it proudly, as if it was her personal trophy, into the kitchen and set it inside a black pot to simmer and stew overnight. Its glazed eyes appeared to stare with a dignified contempt over the proceedings. Gorgonus bent over the severed head, and chattered to it, like a comrade, inviting rebuke. Patted it once, familiarly, on the crown, with the inflated bladder Xavier scooped out for him with a sharp thumbnail.

For hours then, and all through the rest of the afternoon and late into the night, the women worked with basins of blood, and cauldrons of chopped pig. They salted the lard for the rest of the winter; pickled the tongue; the trotters were boiled, the head went on the simmer; the liver was chopped and minced, the ribs were fried; the haunches and hams smoked up the chimney trough, and the lumps of flesh casseroled. While the women sweated and lifted and stirred and seasoned and smelt, the men would nod their approval and make the strange pecking gesture with their second and third fingers and thumb, towards their mouth. It meant winter rations to them. Outside in the yard, the morose figure of Pascal had taken over from Old Xavier. He hacked and sawed away on the chopping-block, piling up the meat at one side, as the pyramid of ham bones and thigh bones gathered in greedy mounds. And, from the outhouses to the kitchen and back again, the Maresquier women bore these basins of blood, basins of brawn, basins of lights and basins of boudin, unwearyingly and without respite.

'You'd think there was more blasted pig in those bowls than when it was alive,' said Bickerton, 'you begin to wonder where it all squashed in.'

'I don't care if I never see another pig as long as I live,' Arch answered, 'I'm sick to the skin of it.'

But, by the end of the night, the work was finished, or rather the work of demolition was finished; the cooking and pickling and stewing and stirring and simmering proceeded; by the parchment glow of oil-lamps, the men dipped into the basins in the wood, silent and tired together, smelling of burnt pork. Arch could see how its fragrance had tunnelled deep into their working-clothes and, looking round at them, with their stubbled chins, and left-over waistcoats and corduroy jackets, realized that Bickerton and he now resembled farmers, not fliers.

Old Xavier gravely dipped his crusts into the eau-de-vie, and chewed at his cloves of onion as usual. La Grosse came behind them with a stewing-pot of kidney-bean soup, with cabbage, a bay leaf, and a piece of bacon fat. Afterwards, Cécéline walked round to serve strips of stewed pork, with whole onions and turnip-heads. The fire barely touched them at the table, but they were warmed inside their skins by the grub, which tasted gluey and fatty and good. And the women of Belgodère stood behind, placidly, waiting to prod forward hunks of bread, or pour their wine; no longer resentful and austere as on

362

the first evening, this time they were grinning and chuckling openly as if participating in a shared joke. And,
heated in their brains by the wine, and in their bellies by
the nourishing soup, the two newcomers began laughing
too. It was the best evening yet. They began slowly to
understand things.

About Ambroise who had been taken prisoner in the
early days of 'quatorze'. About François too, now defending the ramparts of Verdun. François was the grandson
who seethed under the repression of Belgodère, and the
weight of the Maresquiers, and longed – once the war
ended – to move away with Hortense to Corbeille, above
them in the mountains. There he could feel himself
breathe, free of the farm, free of the weight of his
brothers, free of the suffocating plateau, and there Hortense could teach the children. She could read Italian and
English. She preferred the company of mountain people.
François was convinced it would be easier for both of
them to breathe at Corbeille. He ached to smell the
mountain-pines. It was Hortense who explained they
wanted to make something of both their lives. They had
been so far unlucky with children of their own. Fan-Fan
was the middle son, and as healthy as his grandfather.
Cécéline had two already, and Berthe's children were
growing nicely. But they . . .? François, when at home,
blamed the constriction of life at Belgodère, and the
unhealthy climate of the plateau, surrounded by cold
mists, and prey to sudden upsurges of storm. And, while
he stubbornly guarded the mud-escarpments of Old
Confusion under the coils of barbed wire, he thought
longingly of such a time and brooded and schemed. All of
this Hortense was able to explain, in the quieter hours,
when she and Arch could talk together, and the Maresquier men slept.

Of the three Maresquier sons, Toussaint, the ox-man,
was most full of pride, and he had never married, although
there had been stories long ago of a girl from Corbeille
who caught his eye in church. But nothing came of it, and

363

he went back to his oxen. He knew his age, he was fifty-seven, too old for the military. 'Toussaint ploughs a lonely furrow', the others used to say, but he was cheerful enough and good-hearted. Of Xavier's three sons, only Pascal sat apart, and worked apart, often walking forwards and backwards in his own company, or seated at a corner of the rocks staring moodily out at the featureless plateau. He was morose, the village said, even before his wife had deserted him thirty years before, but he had grown worse, the way people do. The story was she had run away with some itinerant crop-picker in the bad days, and set up house far off on the frontier. But Pascal could never find them, and it burned into his heart. Pascal was always the first to stretch up to the three heavy shotguns which hung in parallel racks above the fire. Even after thirty years, he was known as 'the abandoned' and the humiliation still smarted. He was the most grudging towards the two interlopers, and seldom acknowledged their greeting. But even he had been known to smile when, after the table had been wiped down, Gorgonus stood on a small stool and, with much prompting from the other men, sang a long, vulgar song called 'La Bicyclette', which made the men laugh, and the women in the shadows blush and giggle. Then the fire collapsed, and the women went to the beds they shared with their children, and the men took the oil-lamps and blew them out; and, while Bickerton sprawled in his usual place, Hortense remained to sweet-pickle the best brawn, which was her task.

*

Franzie, country-born, knowing all the ways of the Wienerwald, and its large fertile plain, spelt out the ways of trapping a fox to Xaverl, who was town-bred.

'*Du machst es schweigend, Xaverl, und sorgfältig . . .*'

'You do it with silence, Xaverl, and you do it with care . . . You see, Xaverl, you have to get more cunning than the fox, so, *be* the fox. But it's no good with poison, because you kill too many innocents, stray dogs, wild cats, rabbits . . .'

The two Uhlans were trotting smartly along a cart-track, leaving the protection of the forest shade for an isolated plateau which stretched endlessly ahead. Sabres clattered against slack stirrup-irons, and their carbines were loosely slung as they were many kilometres into security behind the lines. Only when the Tramontane wind turned in the direction of Corbeille, could they hear, ears pinned, the far-off crump and pound of front-line artillery. Xaverl still felt nostalgia for the front and the companionship of his regiment, the smell of the stables in the early morning – but Franzie was exultant to be so free, and stuck his boots outward on their foot-rests, for the sheer hell of it. No horse-sergeants to drill them and bully them, no officers moaning about their field-dress, and thousand upon thousand of kilometres of wild country to range around in. This was the life! This was soldiering! Their function was to keep a check on the outlying farms and villages behind the lines, make an inventory of forage and commandeer carts and cattle – to requisition farm-horses, cobs and chargers, and to keep one eye open for scroungers. Only last week they'd come across one poor bedraggled specimen cowering in the rocks, half-starved, threadbare like a scarecrow, reduced to grubbing for parsnips in the fields. He seemed almost grateful to be picked up, and the two young Uhlans, mindful of their own discipline, had not found the heart to turn him in, where he would have been arbitrarily shot in a corner of the barrack-square without trial of any kind. After a brief discussion among themselves – Xaverl was not hard-hearted – they let the ragged creature try to find his own way home. Franzie gave him a mouthful of sausage. He was reminded of a hard-hunted fox, on its last legs, and at heart felt the same sympathy for such a fugitive.

Spotting the bones and feathers of a ptarmigan by the side of the track, he vaulted excitedly off his saddle: his intuition was proved correct.

'You see, Xaverl, I told you, old sharp-ears is around

here somewhere, I swore I heard him whistling, and barking in the night. This is his larder, I *know* it is.'

'But how can you tell?'

'I know these things. I can tell as easily from the noises in the air, Xaverl, as the way the kite hovers in the current, the run of the hare, the flight of the partridge, the flapping of the rooks. I can tell whether he's hunting wildfowl in the furrow or rodents in the plain – all I do is set my traps and wait. But you have to have patience.'

He was never happier. 'Look, Xaverl, I'll show you. It's easy as blinking . . .'

And keenly, like the child he still was, the enthusiastic country boy unbuttoned his cumbersome belt, and drew out of his field-grey jerkin the delicate, lethal cunning-wire he always wore next to his vest. Xaverl, rather more impatiently, watched, and thought scornfully of the leaden-footed local hobnails he had encountered on horseback, staring open-jawed, and of how little they understood of the wild. His friend, Franzie, was mustard to them. He had pluck. How otherwise could this forest be so strewn with wildlife and carrion? Franzie busied himself setting the cunning-wire under the leaves. Xaverl, close to his clumsy grey horse, prepared to wait. He thought enviously of his regiment somewhere in action, and wondered how they were making good along the Somme.

*

The dying wood-ash bubbled and cracked on the stones. Bickerton, lying beside it under the goatskins and on top of his old flying-coat, mouth open, mumbled and snored, stirring at times, sighing and groaning in the uneasy rhythm of the kindling. Just like a dog dreaming of rabbit-holes. Sometimes he turned strenuously and grumbled, still wrestling with his jammed machinery, dreaming the battle. And, while Bickerton fidgeted in his sleep, Arch sat at the table, and murmured in a low voice to Hortense, in order not to wake him. She looked anxiously at the restless figure on the stones.

'He seems so unhappy like that. Not sleeping at all.'

'No, don't wake him. He often does that.'

'He looks as if he will wake up at any second.'

Much of the time Hortense was silent, concentrating on basting the ham in the basin before her with a mixture of sugar, cloves and vinegar-wine. There was no paraffin-lamp at this hour, only an oil-wick burning, so the corners of the farmhouse kitchen stayed largely in shadow, and Arch could barely see her face.

And that was how he began to ask about her life in Belgodère, and how she came there.

'I live at the farm because I married a Maresquier. I was glad to come here. Glad to marry into Les Mares-quiers. I feel safe here, I feel protected behind these stone walls.'

'But how did you come here, Hortense? There is no town anywhere near Belgodère. No village even.'

'No, I lived in a poorer farm than this one, you know. Even its name does not hope for much. Petit-Grain. Five, six kilometres from here, if you take the walk up by the old convent. Behind the hill, beyond Corbeille. You don't talk of distances, but of the hours it takes you, and for Petit-Grain you must count two hours at least.'

'And your mother and father owned the farm a long time?'

'Their parents and grandparents and a long way behind them too, for generations. Just like the Maresquiers: where could they go? For hundreds of years, they have always lived here. It is so poor here . . .'

Hortense turned her head away as one of the briar-logs collapsed and caught fire, a tall yellow flame vaulting up the chimney-corner, shadowing and illuminating one side of her face. Arch leaned forward while she was distracted and saw details of her which had remained hidden. Her skin was so very pale and soft, he felt an immediate urge to touch it, to brush it with the back of his hand, the soft skin on her face and throat – by comparison to her hands which were large, even mannish, with squat, plain

367

thumbs, and reddened by the abrasive touch of the vinegar.

'. . . the people are so very poor, the soil, you see for yourself, it is stone everywhere. Stumps of trees everywhere. There are not even any rich people; they live a long way away. So we are used to it. Nothing grows much, and what does grow, we eat. We sell very little. When a child is born, either here, or in Corbeille, it is never time for a celebration. If it is a boy, well then, it will grow up and work in the family; but if it is a girl, it is a time of mourning. My father and mother buried three and saved three, I was the sixth child, the youngest, we were a small family, three living and three dead . . .'

By now Hortense had stopped stirring the vinegar, and sat quietly, looking towards the chimney, wiping her fingers on her apron. Her brown-eyed gaze was still: Arch had never captured her before in a moment of repose. She grew stiller, as if asleep, her hands folded in her lap, and turned her stare towards him. He observed a faint bump on the left side of her pointed nose, the tiniest of flaws which emphasized the simple lines of everything else, nose, cheeks, lips, chin, brow, and he spoke in an undertone.

'I think you are a beautiful woman. You have always been beautiful. Especially when you were a young child in your own home, before you came down the hill to Belgodère to marry, before you became a part of this stone family.'

Her brown stare never faltered, she gazed at him unsmilingly.

'You can't eat beauty with a spoon. You know what they say.'

'The women in this house, Hortense, are beasts of the field. They work in the fields, gather the stones, fetch the water and stand behind the chairs while the men sit at table.'

'The men work harder.'

'The men are stronger. They are equipped for it.'

368

'They die before the women.'

'The women can only eat what the men leave behind.'

'Yes, I know. I know we do. What more do we deserve? I told you, Capitaine . . . a time for mourning.'

There was a silence disturbed only by Bickerton's snoring. Hortense took up her kitchen-knife and chopped at a hard slab of brown sugar-cane. She broke off twigs of dried herbs and threw the branches into the dying fire. Arch, with another of the knives, chipped the rosemary and myrtle into small pieces. Hortense smiled for the first time. He remembered how seldom he had ever seen her smile.

'You shouldn't be helping me, you know, this isn't intended to be your work.'

'I see you doing enough men's work in the day.' Arch pulled the earthenware crock towards him, and added the herb vinegar for the sweet-pickle and pork.

'Oh, we're used to it at Belgodère.' Her voice was quite resigned. 'It's the way we live here.'

'But the men earn good wages, surely. It's a prosperous farm.'

'We earn nothing here. The men earn nothing but their crust of bread. There's nothing to earn. Working is our way of life. What we plough, we eat . . .'

'But what you harvest, you sell. Like the farms in my country . . .' He was uncomprehending. 'You take the produce to the market each week, on market-day, and *sell* . . .'

'We *don't* sell. We don't sell. We eat. Corn for the bread. Chestnuts for flour. Pig for meat. Roots in the winter. Roots for the beasts, roots for us. And we exchange. Flour for a plough. Eggs for wine. Potatoes for cockerels. How else do you think we manage, any of us around here? In Corbeille, it's no different – and at Petit-Grain, it was worse . . . When the Germans arrived, they took what little there was. A handful of scraps saved for the dogs we warmed up for ourselves.'

The tiny wick flickered like a glow-worm in the damp

369

and drowned in the oil. Only the dance from the fire lit them and their shadows danced in reply against the wall. Hortense sunk her chin in the well of her hand.

'The men work in the fields, or with the beasts. The women work for the men. We have to survive, or at least the family does. When you come into Belgodère – and all of us women, Cécéline, La Grosse, myself, we are all strangers, we all come from *outside* – you marry the family, not the man.'

'So where did you come from, really? You didn't learn to speak English at Petit-Grain.'

'No, I didn't. It's simple, really. My mother came a long way away, from Normandy, in a little place called Olivier, a barge-stop on the river. Her father owned the auberge. When I was sixteen, she wanted me to see something of the world that was not the world of Petit-Grain: I think she didn't want me to work in the fields all my life, which all the others did. She wanted me to stand on my own feet: I don't know why, perhaps because I was the last, although only a girl. So I went back to Olivier. I could not imagine anything so difficult, so far. All the time, I cried. And my letters home were miserable. But, in the end, I liked it – and my grandparents were kind, and sent me to school. Three years I stayed, and then I was put to work in the house of an English family who lived there in the manoir . . . and I learned from them, English. Hearing it all day, it was not so very difficult. And they, of course, did not speak French.'

'Nothing?'

'Not a word, naturally. The English cannot speak other languages.'

'But they lived there.'

'Well, they were a large family and always talking with each other all day . . . so I was their lady's maid, and that way I learned the language quite easily – I lived in their house . . .'

Hortense smelt and approved the vinegar and herbs.

'And Olivier had a small school. They asked me to help there, and teach the children, which I did, for a year, and stayed with the family still. Not just English, but everything, even their catechism and history.'

'Why should you ever leave?'

'In the winter of 1910 a terrible thing happened in Petit-Grain – there was a dreadful cattle-sickness, *la varicelle*, they called it, swinepox, and my father lost all his cattle and his oxen, and my brother all his pigs, even the horses were weakened: it was pitiful – they died where they stood, in harness sometimes – everybody suffered. *La varicelle* spread. The village was destitute. Belgodère also. All the region. And so I came home to help – the English family were very good, and helped us with money.'

'And then?'

'It was the most terrible winter of my life – and I had left such happiness behind in Olivier; but I could not go back. François Maresquier had no quarrel with Petit-Grain, and my sister had married a Maresquier cousin in Corbeille, and so we met, you know how it goes, and then in the summer we married. Well, Fan-Fan needed a wife. He was alone up here, and it was hard.'

Again that fleeting smile, almost an afterthought.

'So you fell in love . . .'

'Oh love, I don't know about that. You know, it isn't always possible to have all these things.' She looked across at him where he sat, hunched forward, in shade. 'And it isn't always so very bad. Not in the summer, at least . . .'

Hortense crumbled more sugar into rough powder; it looked like earth, as she stirred it into the vinegar with her fingers, and the sourness rose up to their nostrils, mingled with the scent of sweet wood burning, stinging their eyes.

The old farmhouse clock with its decorated brass-face – 'Le Mercier: Horlogier', an ornate pendulum, wound in metal flowers – struck eleven with faint iron-strikes, but

Bickerton hardly stirred. Hortense looked up anxiously. There was a short pause before it struck eleven notes again.

'The Angelus,' she said, tidying up the table in the dim light, making a furtive benediction.

Their eyes were accustomed to the shadows by now. She lifted the large side of pork, dosed and marinated in the soused vinegar and herbs – its pungent mixture attacked his nose again, brought a teasing blink to his eyes.

'And Camille beats his wife. Ignace told me. Boasted about it, to Bickerton and me in the fields.'

'I don't deny that. In this farm, in this region, nobody is any different. We work and bear our children and then go back to work. You spoke of Camille to me. I know Camille. It is true, he does beat his wife, and she cries. But nothing changes. Berthe is his wife. What can we do to change that? She has his children.'

'Then if he doesn't like her, why marry in the first place?'

'I asked him that one day. "I only took her so she could work," he told me. That was his answer. One day, outside in the court, she was crying, it was so cold. Not because he beat her, or hit her with his fists, she was just cold, and it made her cry. "If you are cold, work harder. That'll warm you up." That's all he said. Well, what can we do? My husband, well, he's at the Front now, but he doesn't beat me. Why should I protest about somebody else's husband? Besides, Camille is at the war. And François. Like Ambroise. '*Prisonnier de guerre*", they tell us. Old Xavier thinks he's coming back. You hear him. Every Thursday. All the time, he says: "I'll go to meet my boy Ambroise at the station. He's coming back." The train which comes once a week from the front line and stops for water at the Carrefour. "I'll saddle up the horse and cart: Ambroise, he's coming back. My grandson." He isn't coming back.'

'*Not* coming back?'

'He's dead. I'm sure of it. We have heard nothing from him. So what becomes of Cécéline? She has two children. Babies. She has a family. They will grow up and work in their time, but they won't starve. That sort of woman is respected. At Belgodère, she is safe. None of Old Xavier's sons will ever marry. They do not want to divide the land.'

'You have no children, Hortense.'

She paused for a moment, drying for a final time, her fingers on the black apron which smelt of vinegar. In the quietness, wood-ash and Bickerton sighed in unison.

'No. No. I can't hold a child. The women have a sort of contempt for me. They think it's a special reward, because I can write, and because I'm a teacher. As if God deprives me in a justified way. They feel they have revenge over me. It's curious, perhaps they're right. I have a husband and no children. Cécéline, now, has children and no husband. Nobody liked Ambroise in the farm. Not his brothers, or their wives. Only Old Xavier loved him – Ambroise was his favourite. That's why he waits for him. Cécéline doesn't wait for him.'

She took the heavy basin in her arms, holding it firmly and confidently like a mother, and rose to her feet. As she faced him, hiding the faint glow, she disappeared into silhouette, taking the warmth and light away.

'The men work and die. Some live a long time, like Old Xavier. Or Gorgonus. He's like the beasts. Some die young. Some are hardly born. Some are not born. As for us, in the village, you know, up there in Corbeille, when a woman dies the men don't mourn her. They don't wear black. Not for a woman. There's a burial, of course. There's a priest. The wife is buried with the family. But no Sung Mass, and no procession to the *cimetière*. And, when they ring the church-bells in Corbeille, in Saint-Cyriac, the bells which toll are just the small ones.'

She laughed, and walked into the greater darkness of the larder, and across the court, to the unknown rooms beyond.

373

'Just the little bells, which sound like tin. Almost as if they cost money . . .'

And she had gone, taking the last of the light from the rooms.

Arch remained hunched at the fire for a long, long time, shrouded in his coat, thinking to himself, before crawling into his place by the side of the fire. He listened to the draught probing for weak gaps under the doors and against the shutters, until the noises outside and the clock's complacent tick and the stirring hearth and Bickerton's easy breathing eased him to sleep, and he dreamed of Hortense's dark brown eyes staring out of the white of her skin as if refuting an accusation. And above the fire, in equal reproach, the pig's sightless head, missing ears, eyes, and tongue, sat in the brine simmering and bubbling throughout the night.

The old fox had regained his stronghold in the town, and sat forward, ears flicking back and forth and to the side, jaw slightly open – panting – vigilant – aware of every sound, of every movement without sound as well. He was aware of the snail by the corner of the water-butt; he was aware of the rat opening its eyes in the safety of the ordure. Around his watchfulness the wet forest dripped and stank, the dead bracken had rotted before the frost, and the husks of horse chestnuts exuded a secret poison of their own. The two Uhlans had made themselves comfortable the way all good soldiers should: for all the decreasing temperature of the night, Xaverl with resourcefulness had found out a stone shepherd-hut, and Franzie had lit a sparking wood fire in the black corner: there were even pans and kettles left thoughtfully by the shepherds for later travellers, and they cooked their rations, crouched above the blaze, eyes pricking with smoke, and washing down the pumpernickel and West-phalian sausage with their last bottle of beer. Xaverl slept at ease, while Franzie, untroubled, sat out double watch until dawn, and caught a glimpse of the dirt-fox he was waiting for, just at first light.

*

The next morning Gorgonus elbowed aside the tall double-door and, while new light streamed through, stabbing the dust and ash of the night before, once again he doused the young men lying before the fire with a pail of freezing water, slivers of ice still floating round on its surface. Then he cackled with idiot-laughter to himself. Arch was so instantaneously stunned by the explosion of water, sunlight, bright, cold air, the pail clattering to the ground, and Gorgonus's hysterical contractions, he felt himself stumbling inside some terrible dream. Bickerton by contrast, sat like a man unconscious, a concussed fighter, his head bowed in his hands, the water still dripping down his hair in an icy fringe. It was not a popular pleasantry of Gorgonus. He did not understand their unmuffled oaths; but certainly he understood the tone.

'Jesus God! What an oaf . . .' mumbled Bickerton bitterly.

'A total, bloody, downright imbecile,' added Arch, 'I could just gut him.'

'That bastard, Gorgonus . . . I'll bloody murder him.'

But, though they nursed feelings of vengeance, they were powerless to do anything else except wake themselves up; which they did, blinking, and falteringly climbing to their feet – and brushing away the worst of the water: in reality, it had been thrown with such exuberant delight, it had barely penetrated their shirts and trousers.

'*Café, café, café, café, café, café* . . .' repeated Gorgonus, to make amends, as he balanced the black sauce-pot which had been stewing all night. Bickerton kicked the sluggish logs into renewed activity, and the heat emerged directly the sparks crackled and wound upward. A penetrating draught swept down from the chimney-vent and blew the dust up. They were beginning to accustom themselves to these cold mornings when the face of frost

375

lay on stony fields outside. Arch recollected the austere comment of Camille: 'If you are cold, work harder.' Besides, he noticed, none of the other men of Belgodère complained about it, so why should they? The Maresquiers were a family made of stone.

Old Xavier and the other men and the dogs joined them at the table. They brought the cold air about their heavy clothes inside with them. With no Hortense to help with the translation – the women had been up an hour or so and were out fetching water from the wells at Corbeille – the peasants relapsed into their usual gruff taciturnity, other than an unsmiling handshake before sitting down. But Arch and Bickerton were used to that also. They secretly enjoyed it. Toussaint grunted '*les boeufs*' by way of explanation for the day's work. Bickerton had no idea what it meant, and replied with his all-purpose nod. 'God knows what they want us to do now.'

The peasants took up their hessian sacks, and trooped out, followed by Bickerton and Arch.

It was an unemphatic dawn, misty because the sun was pressing to come through. The Maresquier women were returning with water buckets balanced on their heads. Arch waved, but the small, stately procession passed without recognition. The men paid no attention to their women, crossing their path like sentries, exchanging patrols in silence.

The six men trudged across the yard towards one of the larger outbuildings, constructed from the same indistinguishable stone, which Arch had previously overlooked. Passing some cow-sheds in the corner, he saw the concealed machine where they had wheeled it the day before, its nose and propeller peeping out from the straw bales round about. A few lank chickens perched among the struts, and around the undercarriage bedraggled bantams scratched and stalked.

'*L'engin! L'engin!*' repeated Gorgonus with delight, pointing at the Biff in the haystack.

'You want to watch out for him, Arch, he ain't well,' said Bickerton. As if the observer had not yet noticed, Gorgonus came up to him, and pulled his sleeve.

'*L'engin, Bickytonne.*'

'I'll "*engin*" you one of these days, my friend. You aren't well, Gorgonus,' he yelled after him. 'You are a cot-case.'

But this insult was wasted on the goat-man, who rounded up his herd with brrs, growls, and hiccoughs, and stones for the stragglers. It came as some surprise to them to stop after passing the iron gates, and to turn into a large bouverie, or succession of adjoining low-roofed stalls. It was the smell which hit them first, so ripe as to make them almost sick in their stomachs, a smell coupled with a coarse, muggy heat, wet and sweet.

'*Voilà* . . .' Pascal repeated softly the only words he had spoken since they had left the comfort of the kitchen: '*Les bêtes* . . .'

Bickerton nodded in recognition. And there, in the murk, and among the dungy, acidic, straw-packed smell, they saw the oxen: two huge, stationary, fuming, low-headed, leather-muzzled, black Welsh, beads of froth at their nostrils.

'*Les boeufs, les boeufs* . . . *egh! egh!*' grunted Gorgonus, nodding his head.

'*Flore*,' pointed Toussaint – he was the ox-man – indicating one of the vast black bulks, swaying and blowing softly to itself, like a man on his fingertips. '*Et Turc*,' indicating the other. They were so heavy and black but for all their size, there was no violence in these gigantic preternatural beasts. They surpassed creation, with their long branch of brown horn, its black fringe between, and the resentful groan that bubbled somewhere deep inside their gorges.

Toussaint, as ox-man, hauled at their chains, while Pascal held the dogs behind at a distance, coaxing the vast hulks out of their stalls and into the yard. And all the time he kept up a monotonous and unbroken mutter, chiming in unison with the rumbles and groans emitted by the oxen themselves, as if they were sharing a profound and intense conversation. Then, at last, they stood outside, perspiring in the freezing air, beasts as well as men, a cloud of vapour all around them as if the very effort of walking ten paces had covered them, thick and restless as a hive of bees.

Arch and Bickerton, close by the stable door, watched while Pascal and Ignace harnessed up the oxen; Toussaint caressed the mulish, ferocious heads, and Old Xavier himself walked across to the yard carrying wooden buckets of water on the yoke. It was impossible for the young fliers to distinguish between the beasts, but Turc and Flore seemed accustomed to working in a familiar pattern, and pawed the cobbled ground distractedly until the chains hooked them comfortingly together. Turc was the lead-bull, and Flore the hinder, the thill. Toussaint, all the while, spoke to them, as if to a young child.

'Húe, Turc . . . tsé, tsé, tsé . . . Flore.'

Gorgonus thrust a hay-fork into the men's hands and, by simple, incisive gestures, demonstrated how to muck out the manure, and stack it outside in the yard. While the ox-men went about their unhurried task of feeding and watering the oxen, Toussaint never departed from his flow of encouragement and reassurance, all the time in a guttural, caressing undertone, and the bullocks grumbling, sighing, puffing, snorting and pawing. Camille had been right about work keeping out the cold: the stack of smoking mixen soon stood shoulder-high, and the rich golden peaty crusts drained away in the gutters, before the ox-men were ready to draw to the fields, where they should attach the plough. And both Arch and Bickerton were thick and clammy with sweat. 'You'll make a good little dung-spreader, Captain,' winked Bickerton. The procession of six men and two beasts leaving the bouverie at an undertaker's pace, descended with a sort of slow-march step, rhythmical and majestic, down the stone path: in order, Pascal, Toussaint, Turc and Flore, behind walked Ignace, Arch and Bickerton together, and Gorgonus.

They looked out at a seven-acre field, more of a barricade, or a quarry; in England, Bickerton mused to himself, you wouldn't honour it with the title of even a field, more some kind of scrub, or waste-ground; you couldn't graze cattle on it, or farm it, you'd let it out loose for a few pence for the chickens to scratch over. Pascal handed over two pails to the newcomers, and with the merest nod directed them towards the bulls' heads, to gather the stones in the earth in front of them. The ox-man harnessed up the oxen with a ploughshare and placed the coulter in position, and, with Arch and Bickerton before them like an advance guard, sharing with Pascal the labour of stone-cropping, the ungainly cortège lurched forward at Toussaint's urging, with a strong, steady pull.

'*Húe! Húe! Turc, vas-y . . . doucement, Flore, doucement, sois sage, Turc, sois sage, maintenant . . . avance . . . avance . . .*'

Still the monologue kept on. Nor did it cease all day, while the oxen plodded forward, and the two men bent double their backs, and grubbed for the stones, and Gorgonus bore away the full pails; Toussaint murmured into their ears at the head, with Pascal at the tall, and Ignace trudged beside, with a long hazel-goad as tall as a tall man. It was old ground that had received its share of hack and hew before this, but the harsh roots had taken tenacious hold following the cropping, and the harvest of stones was as prodigal as ever – this would be the work of generations to come, not just a single season. The earth was scratchy at best, even when stone-cropped there were thin pickings. Its colour was the dull brown of a rat, and it had no smell or life inside like the raw meat of Sussex earth.

But Tousssaint, the ox-man, ploughed on determinedly with his fervent commands, almost a kind of prayer.

'*Turc, húe, húe . . . tsé, tsé, tsé, Flore, tsé . . .*'

And if one of them straightened his back, or blew on a knuckle, Gorgonus would call: '*Capitaine, húe!*' or '*Bick-*

379

ytonne, marches', as if the men too were oxen to be goaded on.

Bickerton worked ahead purposefully, and filled his pail before the others, giving himself time to turn and watch and rest his back. Harnessed in their collars and traces, he could see – he knew how to farm – the oxen's dead-steady pull plough deep into the furrow, and their great hooves with a screwing tread pulverize the intractable earth into a fine sooty tilth to make the 'season'. He was impressed to discover – far from it being, as he assumed, ineffectual and primitive – how the old Ardennes wooden plough accommodated itself to the turnings and twistings of the furrow, guided by Pascal at the plough-handles, and jacking round at the headland. Up to the end of the field and back again, what they called at home a 'went', turned eighteen inches, and both of the men, unfamiliar in their trade, found the labour gentler than they had feared, and, steadying their pace in imitation of the peasants, took on themselves the slow impassive rhythm of the bullocks' swaying tread. The ploughed earth clawed at their boots, and sucked them in, but they adapted cheerfully to a steady, rambling pace. Every four 'wents', as regular as a watch, the little group would stop and light their cigarettes, complete their smoke, and return to the trail.

Arch, used to the frenetic tug of eager horses, and the drive and noise and dust and heat of sheep-running, could not contemplate anything more placid, more lethargic than this, but let his step fall in beside the plodding movement of the oxen-team. The work never ceased its imperturbable rhythm. Wanting to relieve himself at one point, Arch had only to follow the example of Ignace, at the head, who simply unbuttoned his trousers flap and pissed in a wavering stream as he walked along, not missing a pace. In the afternoon he could have sworn he caught the ox-man himself, Toussaint, one foot in the furrow, one on the blade of the ploughshare, eyes closed, fast asleep. He considered how ox-man and ox-span had

380

trodden down this earth with the same, impassive, patient tread, neither hurried nor scurried, for a thousand years. Human waves rolling monotonously upon the unbroken shore.

For the first time since their crash, Arch became – quite suddenly – aware of a secretive and austere beauty, of tree, stone, furrow, and sky: of grey, and dun, and wet, and cry of unseen bird, and flap of unwatched wing. Ignace, at the team's headland, completing the 'went', sang to himself, in a quiet undertone, an unhappy but tuneful song. There were no words for it. His tune changed its course, rather like an insignificant stream, in a melancholy and indecisive manner, but always slow, always quiet, and somehow private, in the middle of that seven-acre field, and under that vast grey expanse of sky.

'*Dia, Flore . . . Turc . . . dia! dia! Reposes.*' There was a drowsiness about his refrain, like a Sunday morning liturgy.

Only once did the ox-man call a halt, and that was at midday for food, which the half-brained farmboy, protesting, brought them in a wrapped cloth, with a dark bottle of red wine to drink. The dying sun had frozen to a sharp, thin strip. The two bullocks stayed in harness, but Gorgonus set down in front of them a bucket of water, which the beasts supped through their bits: Arch noticed how gently they rested their muzzles on the surface of the water, making no motion with their tongues, sucking without a ripple. Pascal handed the grey bread to Ignace who, as the senior, cut it towards his belly with his clasp-knife. The snow-wind whipped at their exposed faces like stinging nettles. These were the days of the ice-saints, when the shepherds huddled under their hoods, and their dogs burrowed in a heap at their boots.

The lumps of ham, spiced with pepper, helped the gluey bread go down, and the two young men, who had not eaten since dawn, welcomed the respite. Although the peasants ate in familiar silence, as the bottle went round with the bread there was a sense of sharing the

381

welcome benefits, as well as the hardships, of life between them. Gorgonus, who always accompanied every action, however small, with his own sequence of elaborate gestures, tapped the foreigners on their chests, and made a pecking sign towards his mouth, with his closed fingers.

'*Manges . . . manges . . .*' and the men grinned in reply, their fury at the morning's rude awakening forgotten.

'They work well, these English,' muttered Pascal.

'Put them to the plough. They'll soon get the hang of it,' said Ignace.

It was agreed that the two Englishmen should lead the oxen and press on the plough, once the beasts were yoked again in file. Toussaint kept on with his shouting words of consolation and encouragement, but now it was Bickerton's turn to add his own: 'Hey, Turc, hey!' or 'Get on with yer, boy, get on . . .' or 'Over, boy, over . . .' and, as the bullocks so obviously responded to the sound and not to the sense, it seemed to serve as well. Arch had had so much experience with sheep-running and horses in the station at the Jericho it was not long before both men, for all their unfamiliarity with the bulk and lethargy of these beasts, were serving and toiling like veterans, to the wonder of the peasants.

And so the work went on, stone-gathering, murmuring, ploughing, trudging alongside the plough, through the afternoon until the light dimmed. The men walked their ten miles; the ploughed earth yielded up its two acres. Sometimes Bickerton held the shafts, and Arch carried the goad, and sometimes in reverse, with Bickerton in front at the head, and Arch pressing down on the furrow and the plough-ails behind with all his strength. As the thin sun declined, the cold penetrated their jerkins, and they were grateful when the beasts were unharnessed, and the ploughshare hauled to the protection of the hedges. Exposed all day to the snow-wind their blood felt on fire, and their cheeks and ears shrill with frost.

Back to the cow-house they walked, the beasts as sure-footed as ever, tirelessly treading forward, the men, shoulders slumped by now, aching behind the knees, and taut around the backs of the thighs, summoning up some last reserve of strength to spread out the bedding of straw. Toussaint shouldered the stoop of hay, and forked down gorse and sartage for the floor. Old Xavier met them with the dogs and a rushlight to guide their homeward path, and the eyes of the cross-breeds were small red darting gems burning in the darkness, captured in the lantern's gleam. Arch could read the wintry landscape in the stars above their heads. Orion stalking across from the east, with the moon sharp and frosty before the seasonal fogs closed in. From the mysterious fir trees above them, the only sound was the sharp cry and squeal of little-owls and the churning of the eve-jar.

And once the anxious whistle of a fox.

Perhaps the very best moment of the day was when they sat together silently in the shippons, listening to the bullocks grunt and belch and munch and chew, while the paraffin lamp swung in the rafters, and lit up their faces. The wind nagged at the sacking over the windows. Even then the work was not entirely finished, as the peasants cleaned the harness, wiped the brass, and oiled the chains, but it was a restful, sitting-down labour, and the contented sounds of the cattle about them added to their repose. Sometimes the oxen stamped their hooves on the muffled straw. The men were in a row together, the cloud of their breath mingling with the smoke and steam from Turc and Flore, the sweet, dungy smell, Bickerton and Pascal warming their hands on the muzzles of the dogs, which laid their jaws on their laps. Bickerton's lazy eyelid quivered into a near-grin. 'You know what I like about this ox-work, Arch? No think-ing out to bother about.'

Even La Grosse and Hortense and Cécéline inside the house were all grins and chuckles when they stood behind the men's benches and served their food, hot rabbit stew, and chestnuts, and turnips, washed down with brackish red wine, that heated up the throat and belly, and made them drowsy. Old Xavier and Tante Fanny remained as sentinels in the hearth. As they collapsed into sleep that night before the fire at Belgodère after their third day, Arch recalled, almost with a pleasurable smile, that neither he nor Bickerton had addressed more than a few dozen words to one another the whole time, and had probably spoken more to the oxen. He had never been so tired, not even jackerooing on the sheep-station, and he fell asleep in a confused dream of saddling oxen for the stockmen, and driving them across the dry-scrub of the Jericho.

And that was the way life went on at Belgodère. For all the days which followed, Bickerton and Arch stayed on as brothers to the oxen. Milching, dunging, feeding, watering, harnessing, ploughing, treading, turning, rambling, gathering, unloosing, returning, homing, stabling. Turning and following the furrow, day after day, gleaning, stoning, at a steady rambling rate until the two seven-acre fields spread out parallel lines of gleaming trenches. Clouds of black birds scavenged behind for the grubs recently released beneath the boulders. Piled-up baskets of stones formed a cairn at the corner of the field reminding Arch of the great stack of white bones at the Jericho accumulated over the years by the roo-shooters. That sand, these stones, that heat, this cold, there was little to choose, he thought ruefully.

Bickerton and Arch loosed their aches and pains by sheer repetition, rose early in the cold, stripped in the open air and doused themselves with water, which Hortense and Cécéline charitably warmed, towelled themselves down before replacing their night vests and woollen pants, which they tucked under their layers of leather and hessian to shield themselves. In spite of it all, they felt fit and strong, probably never stronger. Their frayed nerves – the scars of battle – healed completely, and the hunger which was never entirely appeased by their diet of vegetables and chestnuts was an agreeable hunger, and they looked and felt like young farm-labourers, relishing the fierce strength of their shoulders, and the tight muscles developing in their bodies. They slept dreamlessly and well, rose early, lay down early, and of all that outside world, the grim rituals of dawn patrol which threatened and menaced from afar, they remembered little and cared less.

'To hell with that,' was Bickerton's phrase, and Arch went along with it. 'Hey, you're getting on well with that Schoolie.' But Arch refused to answer him.

The only work they were spared by the Maresquiers was goatherding, as that was the special franchise of Gorgonus, but sometimes they walked out with him as he pranced from rock to rock, chucking stones after his beasts, fizzling and calling to them, sometimes by name, and answering their bleat or cry. The goat-man knew their ways, and knew their track, and followed them unerringly.

One afternoon, it was the fourth or fifth day, out in the open pasture with Gorgonus, while they shared (as they often used to by now) the rye-bread and goat-cheese at the side of his stone hut, Gorgonus held up a warning finger. The wind had turned slightly and blew a little more strongly from the north-east. A sound traversed the field, a sound apart from, and lower than, the dribbling bleat of goats, or the faint cry of the fieldfare, or even the soft squelch of wet soil as the men shifted their weight uneasily. It was a curious sound, and it came from far away. A noise or what? A flapping shutter in the wind, or the furtive thump of wings in an empty room? Or sometimes a sound which gave the impression that the earth shook beneath them, although it was the sound and not the earth which shook. Gorgonus held his finger in the air still, rather melodramatically, like an old-time engraving of a terrified monk in a doorway.

'*Le canon.*' He repeated dramatically: '*Le canon.*'

'Do you hear that, Captain?' said Bickerton.

'I hear it, Bick, I hear it.'

'*C'est le vent. Le vent qui apporte le canon. Le canon qui vient avec le vent.*' The idea of the two thoughts appeared to bemuse Gorgonus.

Even his goats pricked their ears up, and stayed their incessant grazing. That strange impression of the earth trembling under them; the earth so harshly composed of stones, boulders, rocks, it seemed to them so obdurate and firm. And then, hurling a pebble at an errant goat, '*Ai-eee! Tsé! Tsé! Tsé! Ugh! Agh! Agh!*' Gorgonus was off, perching from rock to rock, and the wind seemed to alter course again, and the solemn vibrating at their feet ceased.

'You know,' said Bickerton slowly, hands in pockets, beard jutting, 'I suppose one day we'll have to go back . . .'

'Yes, Bick, I suppose we will.'

'But not yet, eh?' winked Bickerton.

'Not while there's ploughing to be done.'

After they had eaten well one night, Pascal and Ignace turned their chairs about and sat in a circle round the fire. Toussaint, the ox-man, whistling as he did so in a stealthy undertone, chiselled away at the handle he was making for a new goad. Gorgonus was smoking his pipe. Old Xavier, having sopped up his last crust of eau-de-vie, walked over to the hearth, beckoning both Arch and Bickerton to join them in the circle. Then he sank into his familiar corner opposite Tante Fanny and beneath the racked shotguns, one above the other, and took out his pipe and a wrinkled wallet of black shag.

'Grandfather is in the mood to tell some of his stories,' explained Hortense, and the women also picked up stools and sat them just beyond the circle of light. Tunnelling into his leather tobacco pouch to pack firm the short, stubby bowl, Old Xavier leant forward right into the centre of the fire, and picked up between thumb and third

386

finger a smouldering ember, and, keeping it close to his nose and cheeks, drew in the fire. And only when the cinder ceased to glow, and turned black in his fingers, and the smoke rose and fell in even waves from his pipe, Old Xavier chucked it back into the grate, worrying the cinder-smut off his finger-ends.

'*A cette époque-là, après la guerre contre la Prusse, de mille-huit-cent-soixante-dix à soixante-onze, la vie à Belgodère a changé totalement . . .*'

As he paused in his speech, taking time to draw on the pipe or, for emphasis, gesture carefully with his hand, it was a simple matter for Hortense to translate the gist of what he had to say.

'It was during the Prussian war of 1870–71 that life up here at Belgodère completely changed . . . Before then it was a time of prosperity for all. It was a golden age. After that it was nothing but *la misère* . . . All the fields were cultivated – there were terraces as far as the eye could see. Each farmer had teams of beeves, at Belgodère we had six teams of working oxen: at Corbeille, they had a dozen. Maybe even more. The fields were rich and black in soil, even the crows were well fed: the scarecrows were fattened out and wore fancy clothes. One might be dressed in the cassock of the curé; one had a waistcoat of velour. The harvest of potatoes and beetroot was good, and the pork-meat every October was exchanged for wine from the Argonne. It was a golden age. Men were merry by the fireside, and songs were sung, and the children slept long at night. The good fathers from the monastery at Hornac were welcome at the fireside and sang Masses for the living as for the dead. But . . . after Sedan, shame. *La honte. La misère.* Humiliation and wretchedness. The men were taken off the land and the land went to ruin. When they returned home their hearts had been defeated also. Stones gathered in the fields, unharvested. The crows no longer followed the plough but picked out the eyes of the young lambs. The oxen fell in their stalls, their legs too frail to hold up their vast bulk. The potatoes burned in their stacks, the beetroots stank in their roots. The countryside starved. The vacheries and the bouveries crumbled. The scarecrow and the priest were one and the same, shrivelled up and threadbare – who could say which one was monk and which was scarecrow?'

Hortense had leant herself against the old man's knees. Ambroise was his best-loved grandson, but she was his favourite girl. He called her affectionately 'mignonette', and sat there talking of the past, of the good days before the bad days, squeezing on his pipe. The three sons sat about him feeling the warm hand of the fire, the two newcomers also listened attentively. Hortense sat by his knees, Berthe and Cécéline in the shadows on stools behind, and, leaning against the distant edge of the table, the remainder of the daily loaf in her arms, La Grosse, and highest of all, on one of the beams which led to the invisible shadowy arches of the roof, Gorgonus had scrambled to a position of eminence.

Old Xavier was well warmed by now, and began to tell them the stories he had heard from his father, the famous 'Cocagne', and his uncle, Aurélien, who was one of the 'old red bricks' in the terrible November march from the ice-banks of the Beresina to the Vistula, who had seen the nails drop from the fingers of the Imperial Guard, who had witnessed sentries standing upright against the wind frozen into blocks of ice, muskets still at the alert, that same Chasseur Aurélien who had shot his horse, to sleep inside the warm carcass, and ate with relish rats toasted on the end of a bayonet at Wilna. The old chasseur had in his day drunk a cake of frozen horse's blood from his knapsack.

As for Cocagne, that man among men . . .

Cocagne, he told them, had witnessed with his own eyes the most terrible of sights, a babe in arms, child of a cantinière, dead on its mother's breast, the white milk frozen to the child's lips. That was after Moskwa. He

388

had witnessed the Imperial Guard fighting with bayonets, over the possession of a corpse.

'Ask him if his old father ever saw the emperor,' Bickerton prompted Hortense. They were talking of times a hundred years ago.

'*Once* – he saw him once,' said Old Xavier, 'yes, Cocagne did, wrapped up in furs in his sledge after the Battle of Krasnoë, the tears on his cheeks as bright as icicles, while they gave a broken-handed salute. Yes, he saw the emperor that one mournful time, with Prince Eugène and King Murat in cloaks, by his side.'

Xavier bent forward, confidentially, forefinger to nose-tip.

'Cocagne was a *somebody*.'

He paused, and tapped the last few cinders out of his pipe into the fire. Hortense turned to Bickerton and said in a serious, low voice: 'And now they want one of you to tell them a story. They have told me to change your words into words they can understand, but they want to hear your voice. Can you do such a thing? Up here at Belgodère, far from the village, we do not get the chance to listen to many stories.'

Bickerton shrugged, and looked down at his clasped hands. He knew how to sing, and play the spoons, but stories he could not tell. Arch looked at Hortense and saw much deeper into her eyes than he had reached before. He had long ago forgotten many of the stories he had learned from the roo-shooters at the Jericho, he wished he could recollect them now, and here it was always so cold, and there it was always so hot – 'hot as hot', the Irish jackeroos used to swear, 'it's all hot as hell', but he remembered faintly some of the strange stories they had told him, taken from the blackfellas. He tried to remember them now; the upturned faces of the Maresquiers, trapped in the shadows, were as expectant as children's.

'This may not be easy to put into your own words, Hortense, for these men to catch hold of, but you must tell them these are the stories I heard from the blackfellas in the heartland of my own country, which is a million kilometres away from Belgodère, and is as hot as this is freezing cold, and impossible for them to understand.' Old Xavier, with his pipe-hand, made a small gesture to encourage him.

The men leant forward intently, as he began, haltingly at first, but, allowing gaps for Hortense to follow him, he gained in confidence.

'Their beliefs are strange, and difficult for us to follow,' Arch said. 'Life is a harsh and painful business for them. The land is bare and brown and lifeless. In the sun's glare, the sheep lie panting for a little air, the birds flutter open-winged on the branch, their beaks gape, horses stand head to tail in the draught of their hair, a man loses his shadow beneath his feet, and night is very little cooler than the day. Winds are great flatteners and a herd of cattle might be swept away entirely by a solitary blow.'

Arch saw that he held their attention, and so he continued.

'But these blackfellas who live out in the sandstone desert, and have lived there for many centuries, always the same, believe there was another Time, a better Time, long before, when the earth was not famished by the sun. When there was no night, but only a kind-hearted day. These were the Times of their Ancestors, who lived in the Dreamtime . . .' He waited for her to explain the word carefully, and repeated it. 'The Dreamtime.' The men and the women behind nodded. They understood. 'Les jours des rêves.'

'And the Dreamtime was the Time when their Ancestors lived, and they were spirit-people. And the daylight was the glorious brightness of one of these Ancestors, who filled the sky and the earth with flowers and trees and fertile rivers, not stunted and wilted and blackened as they are now. These blackfellas say the Sun is one of their spirit-people, a human being, who was misunderstood, and badly treated, and he withdrew from the

390

family in great sadness, and became a god, and in his sorrow made the setting sun. Do you want me to go on?'

He paused to see whether they understood his story.

'*C'est curieux, Capitaine,*' said Old Xavier, '*mais nous aussi, nous comprenons les Ancêtres.*'

Hortense nodded gently, and the faces stared at him with a new kind of wonder. They loved this strange story, told them by this strange man who fell from the sky. Old Xavier spoke for all of them:

'Every word, we are able to understand. Captain, you must speak on – *c'est un pays des rêves . . . l'autre-fois . . . les chimères.*'

'For a long time, there was no sun, before this Ancestor, but there were the moon and the stars, and the stars were fires, and the haze around the moon was the smoke which the spirits of the dead lit as they travelled alone through the sky. And when the world of Dream needed light, because the sky was low down – so low a man could not walk upright in it – the spirit-people made the sun from one of their fires. Each new morning they arouse it, and keep it at its height, until it begins to die away in the evening, when the spirit-people cover the blazing branches with clouds, except for a handful they allow to burn still into the night, which they keep for the next morning.'

He stopped, but Old Xavier, so absorbed he had not relit his pipe, asked Hortense to request him to tell them more about the sun and the stars. And Arch recalled the tales he had heard from Crusoe and Foxy, north of the Never Never, and days spent fishing for salt-water crocodiles and flatheads.

'You must tell Grandfather Xavier, all this I learnt from the blackfellas, and they did not tell me much more, but this I can remember – the Pleiades are seven sisters, the Milky Way is a waterfall, Orion the Dog-star wears two boys at his Sword and his Belt. The comets' tails are huge families of spirit-people so thirsty they drink up entire rivers into the clouds, and meteors mean death.

The Southern Cross is a spirit-tree, but that too is a reminder of the first coming of Death, and there are Mad Stars, and Laughing Stars.'

The little watchful group smiled at the idea of such a thing.

'Oh, yes,' continued Arch, 'Venus is the Laughing Star. A man who told a rude joke and who has gone on laughing at it ever since. He's a rude old man, that Venus, that Laughing Star, these dark people say. They swear by him. And they say no man can live without his shadow. I cannot remember anything more they told me.'

*

Were they watching the fox? Was the fox watching them? It was so difficult to tell. Franzie had been the first to see him, dirty and bedraggled though he was, just skulking along the edges of the scrub the way foxes do, but not proud and golden and tail-high the way he had hunted them a hundred times in the forest of his boyhood. He remembered only too well the time he and his sister had discovered the cubs outside the earth, when the hunters had passed by, and how he had smuggled one back under his blouse, and Hannerle had nursed it secretly with milk from a dropper. They had brought it up without anybody knowing, except of course old Engstrandt, the gardener, and kept it away from the house, behind the asparagus-beds, in an ancient glass-frame for warmth's sake and released it out to the deepest, darkest corner of the woods. Hannerle, as expected, had stolen back to that assignation below the branches, so dark no light stole through, hoping to see the fox again, even once, at a distance, but she never did or, if it returned, they were not there to see it.

But this was a poor specimen, pursued and harried by local hunting dogs, he supposed, shot at by the scavenging, impoverished farmers of the area, a rough, thread-bare, desolate region, whose peasants, resentful and semi-starved, refused the superior knowledge of husbandry they could offer, and faced their German generosity with sullenness and silence. Brutal, too, he had observed. He had seen a woman harnessed to the plough, bent forward over the traces. Primitives! Hobnails! There was the fox nailed to the barn doors in the stone-croft which stood apart in the valley. A loathsome parody of the crucifixion. Few birds sang inside the leafy woods, as the peasants limed them in traps and ground their meagre two-pfennigs of flesh into a sort of crude paste mixed with chestnuts; they dug roots out of the ground which they ate raw, and drank a moisture made from crushed acorns, and boiled chestnuts instead of potatoes for their starch, and left their new-born daughters in icy rooms, unfed, for some kind of traditional test of survival. He had witnessed a gibbet of magpies, ravens, crows, herons, hawks, outside a farmyard. How unlike the cheerful prodigality of the farmers he knew and worked with in Saxony: the robust village-festivals during the *must* season, the intoxicating weddings and head-spinning harvest-homes. The grins that greeted you at every door, the flowers pressed into your hatband and sabre-holster, the cornflowers that in autumn the village girls had twined about his spurs and round his stirrups. The entire regiment had floated away down the dusty streets blossoming like a garden.

Still, in spite of the inhospitable character of these barbaric people, it was their duty, as honest Germans, when on patrol, to fraternize, and share with them their prosperity and advantages, and to create friendships where none existed before. There was certainly little else for them to do. He, and his old friend Xaverl – thank heaven they had kept together since their basic training – had patrolled the region for months now, and even so still found themselves uncovering corners of this desperate, uncivilized region which knew little of the outside world. No newspapers ever reached them. Most of the labourers were born, married, worked and died in the same village: many of them had not even visited the village next to their own lower down or higher up the mountain, and one crofter, admittedly an old man, and his wife, with nothing but chickens and a solitary pig, and a wretched scrap of garden yielding artichokes and parsnips, did not even know there was a war being fought. He had heard the thunder of the guns, and put it down to an exceptional season of storms. It was hard to decipher that depth of ignorance. They farmed as their ancient forefathers had farmed: they failed to rotate their crops; they were entirely ignorant of fertilizing their fields; they worked one field in five, letting the others produce forage for their beasts, and rushes for their roofs; they performed their ordures in the open air, or in the streams from which they drew their water; they lived in cabins and stone-huts like savages in North America, and sometimes one village spoke in a language which could scarcely be interpreted by their neighbours a few miles deeper into the forest.

But Franzie, who wrote and lived only for poetry and the open air, found a peculiar exhilaration about it, and wrote enthusiastic letters to his mother and to Hannerle at home. And they, of course, were grateful he had not been drafted to the Western Front, from where already serious reports of losses had been arriving. Their much-adored nephew, Attila, on the Hungarian side of the family, had been mortally wounded at Mouse-Trap Farm, and nobody knew what became of their neighbour's son, Reinholt, but they had all read his fearful letter home, passed from hand to anxious hand: 'You cannot imagine the frightful torments I have undergone . . . crawling in and out of raging gunfire, seeking for a bolthole: you do not know what Flanders means, the trenches of hell . . . you can never know . . . it means blood and scraps of human bodies and desperate courage and faithfulness unto death . . .'

Xaverl longed to return to action, and hated his wasted days on horse-patrol behind the lines: he had not volunteered for the pride and dignity of an Uhlan regiment to be relegated cruelly to behind-the-line patrol duties. You might as well be in the cookhouse, or with the officers' servants: he felt it an acute disgrace, and craved to return to those joyful days in September 1914, riding through the fields at a steady hand-canter in the morning mists which floated across the River Marne, and infiltrating the enemy patrols, and pursuing the straggler with the lance and sabre across country: that was proper sport, those misty skirmishes at dawn, or better still, at dusk, when there was frequently the chance for a stolen kill on an infantryman malingering along the river-banks. He remembered the evening his Uhlan troop rode unawares upon an entire platoon of Worcesters bathing naked in the river, and shot them where they were, before they could swim to the bank, and then swerved back before the machine-guns could cut them down in a swathe; he savoured the thrill of riding back through the late fields of cornflowers, dusty and hot. A fine open warfare, fast-paced, and stealthy, over the hedges and along the dust tracks, like the finest steeplechase. Kill or be killed, that was the spirit. Xaverl sat moodily apart, chucking stones at a bottle on a wall. Franzie hissed to him to cease. With his binoculars he had spotted the dirt-fox skirting the scrub, and beckoned his companion over to him for a glimpse. They both watched its circuitous and secretive route from scrub, across a field where oxen were at toil, camouflaged successfully against the dun earth, until it merged with the gorse and the granite. The wind appeared to turn, and brought with it a few perilous flecks of snow that melted on the troopers' grey capes as soon as they alighted. The Uhlans led their horses on the greasy stone steps and followed the fox's path to the ploughed fields far below on the plain.

*

'Gorgonus wants to show you his library,' said Hortense mysteriously one morning when the rain was too mon-otonous for ploughing to be done. 'Slicing through turds,' was how Toussaint laconically explained it.

The two men had finished cleaning out the shippons,

and the feeding was over. In their few days working together, it was Bickerton who had struck up the closest friendship with Gorgonus, sharing with him his midday grub, crouching back on his haunches, and cutting off the pickled slice of cheese, which he always described as his 'little bit of pork'. And Gorgonus enjoyed the comradeship, returning the compliment by prompting Bickerton to 'dig in' to the dark wine (which, Arch swore, tasted like rusty pen-nibs) and stabbing with his penknife over and over again; '*il faut respecter, il faut respecter*', pointing to the cheese. The two men communicated happily together, often by signs, were often seen chuckling together and, when the rest of the Maresquiers found Gorgonus hard to fathom, then Old Xavier himself would look to Bickerton to interpret to Arch, Arch to Hortense, and thus round in full circle.

So it was about this time, accompanying his brisk gait with furtive, suspicious gestures, to ensure nobody else followed them, Gorgonus led them through the courtyard, and away into a series of stone passages and dismantled cloisters hidden behind the main hearth of Belgodère. The unused rooms of the old manor were shuttered and cut off from the liveable quarters, but they had been occupied once, even so long as a hundred years before, and gave the appearance of having been abandoned in haste. Arch assumed it had been built originally as a fortified house, and some of the dismembered walls were blackened and scorched, where it had been presumably put to fire. Perhaps as long ago as the Goth invasions. Nettles and brambles throttled the rusted iron railings. A ruined stairway took careful negotiation under Gorgonus's encouragement. But they were able to pick their way through the treacherous rubble to a gallery above, not unlike the triforium of a cathedral. Stooping beneath a low archway, perilously balanced, Gorgonus prompting all the time with grunts and imprecations, they found themselves in a secret chamber, easily overlooked, where the yellowing plaster had mouldered away leaving patches of disfigured red brick. Beyond this, stack upon stack of old books, mostly open, in clusters, their bindings rotting, frequently covered by fungus, even green spawn, hundreds and hundreds of them, some crazily tilting in precarious shelves, some face-down and half-chewed as if they had been plundered by a raiding party of enraged schoolchildren.

'*Tiens, tiens! Attention! Attention!*'

This was Gorgonus's library, his '*bibliothèque*', as Hortense shyly explained, and the goatherd stood proudly by, gesturing vaguely at the mess before him, as if marvelling at the treasures of the Vatican.

'This is a bit of goose, Gorgonus,' smiled Bickerton, crouching on his haunches to salvage a seventeenth-century volume, half-eaten away by rats.

'What is the story of this room?' Arch wondered, gazing round at the strips of silk which clustered from the walls, like fluttering bright banners. In the middle of the room sat a large, squat, black metal trunk, or clothes-box, full of manuscripts and yellow decayed paper which disintegrated and flaked off in his fingers. A hatbox, the shape of a tricorne, contained what looked like title deeds, estate papers, heaped in confusion, discoloured, and redolent with a frightful damp smell. There were some old brown family photographs, already difficult to decipher, a man in naval uniform, a wedding-party in front of a church, groups of retainers in some kind of livery, a row of gardeners bearing rakes, and a pleasing château whose elegant lawns flowed gently down to a lake. One page of a letter bore the signature of a king, another of a general to the emperor.

A silence came over them, and the two men felt stirred by the desolation and the memories. Something was uneasy within the room, as if a fearful crime had been committed there. Or something abandoned and forgotten for eternity. There was an unseen inhabitant in the *grenier*, something indecipherable stirred in the nest of a dark corner. Rat's piss and mouse dirt fouled the air. And

Gorgonus, oddest of librarians, stood in the middle of the disarray, showing off his collection with pride, whistling and tut-tutting to himself at the impossible scale of the task ahead of him. As if he, Gorgonus, who could not read, and could barely talk, were to have at some time to bind and catalogue and analyse the entire mouldering collection. But it was enough he should have valued their friendship and their confidence to share with them his marvellous secret. It was an occasion of special pride for him.

'So this is Gorgonus's library?' wondered Arch to Hortense. She had visited the shrine before, of course, with the goat-man, in the winter, when he nourished his sick goats there, and they too had played their part in the random destruction. Candles stood in the stone alcoves, gnawed by rats like rinds of cheese.

There was one corner, however, of the vaulted ceiling which retained a trace of earlier grace: a lovers' knot in stucco, with faint streaks of blue and darkened gold upon it. Straw scattered about everywhere, but on the panel of a shutter, which protected one half of a window, was enamelled the ghostly image of a lady, half her face smiling, beckoning, the other half faded into the seam. It was as if an atrocity had been committed to one side of her face. And everywhere, mixed into the straw, hundreds and hundreds of books, Arch easily could recognize, in old French, German, Italian, Latin. Some in an indecipherable language of flourishes and serifs. Hortense, her hands tucked into her armpits, for warmth, explained.

'The library belonged to an old priest who used to live here. He was a very famous man, and played the organ in the cathedral at Amiens. They say he was even the composer of his own music, and he came to Belgodère to spend his last days with his family. He was an uncle of Old Xavier, I believe . . .'

The dull, leaden sound of a hollow bell came from a distant room. Gorgonus shook his head, and gestured that it was the wind beating on a forgotten casing somewhere among the ruined staircases and collapsed galleries far away.

'This old father,' Hortense continued, 'tried to help Gorgonus to read and write, and brought him up with the family. He left him his library in his will, out of affection for him, but as you see the poor fellow cannot understand a word written down. He could not master a single letter of the alphabet. I have seen him standing there among his books, pretending to recite from them. Gorgonus is the guardian, and he cannot understand a word of it. So, everything gets more and more ruined. What can we do about it, in any case? Now the war is all around us, who is interested in a roomful of old books?'

Suddenly, without warning, Arch felt his legs tremble beneath him, felt for a handhold on the bare wall, and at the same time Bickerton sat clumsily down. There came a threatening rumble deep, deep down, as if from the dungeons of the fortress. Arch thought for a moment they had stumbled unawares on a corner of the ruins above some underground passages which was about to collapse, but Gorgonus – as if accustomed to the sensation – was standing in the centre, finger uplifted in a gesture of warning. Then the two young men realized it was not the sound of masonry capsizing, but rather a faraway grumble of thunder.

'Le train,' explained Gorgonus, 'le train de Charleville . . . le train. Attention!'

But, as Hortense watched their faces drain of colour, the men knew better: it was not at all the sound of a distant railway-engine, it was without question the bombardment reawakening like a violent beast disturbed, hundreds of miles away on the Salient. And now it had reached them, found them out. Even the earth shook, even the stones of Belgodère. And they knew they would have to return. Soon.

One Saturday evening – was it Saturday? – as promised, the boy they all called 'Half-a-Brain' showed them the way through the trees to Corbeille. From below, the crown on the hill resembled nothing more impressive than another scattering of rocks. These rocks, however, concealed the walls and terraces of a village whose foundations were built in the ancient past. The two young men in their goatskins, nothing like soldiers now, clambered eagerly in their hobnailed boots behind Half-a-Brain up the path towards Corbeille. After following several disguised goat-tracks which led to dead-ends, they corrected their route and, passing the ruined cloisters of Hornac, a deserted convent, on their left hand, saw rising above them the flinty outposts of a small commune. Corbeille was hacked out of the very rockface itself, its eyeless houses wedged in between cuts in the rocks, and presenting to the grey sky a blank, featureless appearance, with no warmth of welcome or light to invite. Its sparse inhabitants were renowned for their hostility to visitors, inbred and resentful. The young had gone to war, leaving the very old and children behind. As if to compensate for the unfairness with which destiny decreed their isolation in so exiled a place, so cruel an environment, the people of Corbeille faced the world with a double portion of pride and rage. As the rocks swung above them, ever about to cascade on top of them, Arch and Bickerton managed to spy out a narrow crevice, into which the goat-track seemed to wriggle and eventually disappear, and they made their way towards this gap. Once past the outlying scarp, the path was a little more certain of itself, and wound past stable-traps, and even house doors, all of which were firmly bolted against any visitor. And yet, even so, Arch had the distinct impression that their every step was witnessed, and that behind the shuttered windows exact note was taken of their progress, was even perhaps soundlessly communicated, like a patrol filtering incautiously through a network of silent spies into an ambush.

The rock path was dirty. The debris of decades had been shovelled out of back doors and left to rot. Animal manure, black bottles, many of them broken, countless single shoes, bones of chicken, carcasses of rabbit, the entire fur and skeleton of a cat, wine-barrels, the remnants of furniture which had not ended up as firewood, a discarded iron gate, abandoned clothing, an iron bed-end and, oddly, a large mechanical piano with its keys ripped apart. Stacks of chopped logs stood before each stable door, and domestic mules and asses were tethered, snorting and stamping as the strangers passed them. Some stumbled free, as far as their chained forelegs would allow. Thin spirals of smoke floated upwards from concealed chimneys or more likely, thought Arch, from sheer holes in the roof. Sometimes a shutter swung open and banged back against a broken window. These were the abandoned houses. The entire impression of the village was unfriendly, ill kept and ruinously poor. Xavier had warned them:

'*Là-haut, c'est la misère . . .*'

An old man astride his mule, on an uncomfortably strapped wooden frame for the transport of logs, prodding the stubborn beast forward with his heel, passed them. Bickerton and Arch backed to the wall of a subterranean passage, and bent their heads. 'Half-a-Brain' was running on ahead. The driver was greybearded and wore black corduroys with a wide red sash tied round his waist. The long jacket and its draped back was so exposed to rain and sun it was quite grey in places, and patches of later corduroy, salvaged from other clothes in the family, stood out in severe contrast. He carried with him an umbrella, and they also noticed a shotgun. Bickerton nodded amiably at the wrinkled bearded face in the way he had seen Old Grandfather Xavier do at Belgodère, a grudging, unsmiling upward jerk of the chin, but received nothing by way of reply. The old peasant kicked harder into the sides of his mule, and continued stubbornly on his route down the hill. It was as if the two strangers had been invisible, neither man nor animal acknowledged their existence.

It could even be said that, for all its diminutive scale, balanced as it was on the utmost spur of a mountain, Corbeille, once penetrated, might give an invader the impression of a substantial colony; the passages, tunnels and tracks spread out in every direction, on every angle, and walls and rocks yielded to intricate alleyways of more wall and rock, resembling the earthworks of a fortified town, with ramparts and redoubts. In the past, of course, in the ancient past, this was exactly what the town had been, an inland fastness against barbarian invaders, Goth and Jute and Hun; before them, the eastern Mongol. Its stony embrasures had held out against relentless assaults, vigorous against fire and starvation, as the community had its own limitless resources of fuel and victuals stacked away in subterranean cellars. For this reason the doorways were hewn out of granite, and there was a minimum of narrow windows. Time passed, and the military necessity grew less demanding, but the village people of Corbeille themselves preserved a traditional antagonism towards the world outside, seldom venturing out of their own houses, or even beyond the family circle. It was a system which worked for them. Besides, the summers were so wet, and the winters so fierce, that most of their time they spent – when not grinding for existence in the fields – around their own meagre fires. They lived, virtually, as troglodytes, and had done so for centuries. It gave them their craggy, reserved natures, and permitted them the privilege of isolation; they withheld friendship until they could be so sure of it as to entrust their lives to such a man. History told of a betrayal by an ally within, and a merciless massacre. That had been their past – all outsiders were hostile, all visitors were destructive, and, although times had changed, for five hundreds years they had not softened.

The arms held by the family of Damaris, to whom the earldom anciently belonged, boasted the one word 'Fortitudini'. Green eagle, red claws on silver, three boars' heads and chevron, and carved above the fireplace at Carthagéne: *'De bon valour servir le Roy'*.

It was difficult for suspicious people to cast aside the habit. Even the closer villages disliked the Corbeillards and avoided them, except for rare – very rare – marriages and funerals, and sometimes serious family disputes continued through many generations resulting in accidents in the forests, or among the goatherds, with shot-guns, or knife-wounds, and one of the family forced from the security of his home, to live a nomadic life out on the mountains in the stone shippons; very few lived for longer than a brief matter of years, the life was brutish, exposed, so hounded, so unsafe, and legends grew up about them, and songs were sung in their memory. A pitiless exile curiously dignified their crimes and this provided their music of nostalgia and close-cherished grief.

It was the alien, guttural cry of such a lament which drifted in gusts to his ear as Arch sought out the obscure paths to the bottle-house from Half-a-Brain's incoherent directions. He scurried ahead of them like a rat. The voice was male, and yet the sound was untypical of a man's, as in tone it was high, melancholy, and frequently ornate. Small tugs of wind at the corners brought the sound closer, and Bickerton and Arch stopped walking for a moment to listen. It drew attention to their destination. House-front and rockface were indistinguishable, and Arch, unsteady on his feet from both pathway and wind, edged himself awkwardly down a narrow and tormented alleyway, under a vaulted tunnel, by means of one hand pressed against the wall, rather like a sentry parting the heavy boughs of trees. As both men stepped forward, aware also that the sky had darkened since they reached the outskirts of the village, a doorway in the rock – up to then totally obscure – opened suddenly, and a minute, white-haired woman, bent double, dressed in shapeless black, beckoned them in sharply. They stepped inside and saw at the same time where the singing had issued from.

Les Cinq Billards. This was the famous bottle-house, Corbeille's only bar. As the music was still progressing, they remained where they were at the back of a small, unlit stone room, where the shadows of a few oil-lamps created the only relief in a circle of utter blackness.

It was a dwarf who stood in front of them, with hair cropped round his ears, holding under his elbows some goatskin bagpipes. In contrast to the disdain only minutes before of the old man on his beast, both strangers recognized they were the object of exceptional, but by no means unfriendly, curiosity. As his eyes swept carefully round the room, Arch observed no less than some dozen men, all dressed identically (just like the Maresquiers) in black corduroy, their jackets propped on their shoulders – never worn through the arms – all of them sitting on low benches, or stools, in almost identical posture, elbows on knees, with harsh heavy hands folded loosely. Several were bearded, and most of them had three or four days' grey stubble on their chins. Their cheekbones were prominent, and the skin flared by constant exposure to the wind. It was as if their flesh was of a darker texture than most other Frenchmen's, for these were the inhabitants of the Ardennes, and their faces were layered in coarse, burnt tones. Arch noticed this smell in the room, quite sweet and heady, of long-haired animals, largely of goat. He suspected the presence of Gorgonus. Dogs lay under the stools, nervy, obedient, darting looks from their foxy eyes. They were the guardians of the long-haired mountain goats which gave most men of Corbeille their living. If one of them chose to lurch beyond his master's chair, the occupant, with a kick or uplifted hand, above all with a sharp cry, would threaten the animal back, and it cowered on its belly to the former position of stealth, and remained there, looking anxiously for some sign of approval or forgiveness from its master.

Most of these men were short of stature, stunted and misshapen, resembling more a dwarfish than a human race, smaller in height than the family at the farm, although, just as there, no young men could be seen. All of them in the trenches, leaving the villages deprived for miles about but for the oldest grandfathers and women and small children. Xavier had warned him: '*les vieux . . . les gosses*'.

In the low-ceilinged room behind there were several women standing, wearing long black dresses and black shawls, as if in communal mourning, and from time to time they filled the men's glasses, or pressed forward with stodgy-looking biscuits. Two glasses were put into their hands as the song proceeded and the customary colourless wine was poured, just as had happened every evening since their arrival at Belgodère. There was a trace of smoked wood about it, and it chafed their throats. There was some sort of celebration in progress, a feast-day perhaps, the benediction of the pigs. In one corner sat a priest, as fierce and wind-burnt as the rest of the company, who waved them over. As the voices rose above the general monotony of talk, Arch noticed he spoke in the same patois, with the jagged staccato accents of all the rest. This was the same Franciscan from Saint-Cyriac, who had once warned Old Xavier he had water on the knee. But the old man stubbornly refused to hear of it. 'I've never drunk water in my life,' he insisted.

Just as at Belgodère, the women here served the men. If they sat at all, they would retire by themselves to the back of the hall, and squat on lower stools, which had doubtless come from the church. They only occasionally spoke to one another, one cowled head bent towards the next, but seldom with laughter, or even a smile.

More of the colourless liquid was passed around. Arch saw that, far from sipping it, as wine, the Ardennes peasants nourished it in their hand a second, warmed it, and swallowed it in a gulp.

'This isn't alcohol,' said Bickerton, 'this is snake-bite stuff.'

When Arch and Bickerton did the same, they quickly began to feel an intense warmth, a shiver followed by a

405

deep intake of breath, and a subtly growing sympathy with the singers and their song. Four men stood close to one another, almost formally in the centre of the room, arms around each other's shoulders. There were two tenors, a drone, and a bass. At first they tuned their voices in a wild, almost inhuman cry or wail, and then the eldest began a lament for a lost companion who had been forced to exile himself in the forest after one of the countless family feuds in the village.

The song developed into a seething turbulence of sound and melody, and even discord. It had the intense passion of a dance. This was at the heart of their music, a carefully explored ingredient of destruction. And this gave their song part of its depth and much of its pain. More watery liqueur flowed, and then more songs of an uneven, robust nature replaced the lament. The dwarf played on the bagpipes with his elbows. Some choruses were boisterous and self-evidently – by means of gesture and expression – coarse. The old women broke belatedly into grins, clapping their hands, and slapping the cheeks of their husbands with mock indignation. The priest pretended to be shocked, blocked his ears with his hands, but was smiling to himself. Arch and Bickerton felt themselves uplifted by the combination of fire, music and strong alcohol, content to sit quietly beside the chimney, enjoying the shadows which excluded them. The harsh work of the last days had both strengthened and fatigued their muscles, and for the first time they felt deep inside their bones a tender peace-able unwinding, at tune with the earth they struggled against, and which brought them, for their greater strug-gle, a greater peace. And the music soothed the poison inside them. It was a gentleness they shared.

Over the wood-ash fire, the women were now scorching large chunks of kid, and passed them round on wooden skewers, wrapped inside thick wedges of bread soaked in fat. These burnt the lips and tongue at first, but tasted sweet. They ate potatoes out of the ashes, bouncing them as they baked from hand to hand.

'Makes a change from the good old grease and kidney beans,' said Arch.

Bickerton's reply was short and to the point; nor did it interfere with his chewing.

'I'm digging in.'

When the fire dropped, someone at hand would throw another large log on top and treadle it into place with a rough heel. Sparks mingled and clattered like fireworks, and the dogs started up in a daze, only to settle themselves again, accompanied by further cries and blows. The pale alcohol was frequently passed round. The dwarf danced in the centre of the room by himself. When it came to their turn to sing, as they knew eventually it would, Arch and Bickerton stood on a couple of stools that were set up for them, and sang 'Tipperary' (the only song they both knew), which was approved with hearty cheers for an encore; so they sang it all through again, and some of the better singers in the room, the quartet for example, joined in with them, and created their strange harmonies, struggling with the unfamiliar sounds. At ten o'clock, almost at a signal, most of the men, wrapped up in their goatskins, and calling their dogs and, some of them, their wives, who followed mutely with the same obedience as they had shown all evening, stepped out into the night.

When all but a circle about the fire had gone, the door opened, more gently this time, as if caused by a draught, and Hortense stood transfigured, in the traditional black, draped in a black shawl.

'Where are the *bagarreurs*? Where's Half-a-Brain? My God, are you drunk – all of you drunk already? – at Corbeille there's always trouble and drinking . . .'

Even the few last stragglers in the room, some of them swaying and clumsy, seemed to be overtaken by a respect and the women's cowled heads bent mutually together again, as at the exchange of whispered confidences. They resembled a conference of Poor Clares.

'*Les femmes de Belgodère*,' Arch could hear the old

crones muttering, with a rare feeling of awe. Bickerton felt the deceptive clear alcohol getting a grip of his brain, and sat down to clear his senses.

Hortense gave no greeting to the room, nor acknowledged the silence. She walked across to where the two men were sitting by the fire. She gestured urgently.

'Old Xavier has sent me up to collect you, he wants you out with the oxen in the morning. It will mean an early start, and a long day. He wants them to be driven to Carthagène. You must come at once.'

The fire inside their heads was so strong that, once outside in the wind, they found it hard to hold their footing as they blundered sightlessly down the rocky pathway. Hortense pushed them in front of her in irritation, just like a teacher in charge of unruly children. Occasionally one or the other of them lurched into the wall. Bickerton fell sprawling in a heap of laughter, and Hortense was forced to clutch Arch's hand harshly to guide him. Even so, they could not help but grin at the pathetic efforts of Bickerton to make any progress at all; each time he clambered back on to his feet, they appeared to betray him immediately. Where the path was too steep and sharp, he attempted to walk crab-fashion, half on his backside, to make any kind of progress at all. Arch and Hortense half-supported him downhill until they reached Belgodère itself, and then, finding the going easier, supported him to the granary loft, where he collapsed and blundered into a drowning sleep.

'Oh, my God, if we should wake Old Xavier at this hour . . .'

A dog disturbed in the yard below began barking, and Hortense and Arch were forced to lower their voices and communicate in muffled whispers. It added a note of conspiracy to the scene, made the two of them partners in some illicit, childish adventure. The breakneck descent had braced his spirits and Arch whispered about the song he had heard the men sing in the bar, and Hortense nodded her head in recognition. He even attempted quietly to whistle the harmony, but she knew it at once, and stopped him with a warning finger.

She lit the oil-lamp from the candle.

'Oh, my God, I've drunk too much tonight. My head's turning round,' complained Arch.

'What do you expect,' said Hortense without sympathy, 'that stuff is strong enough to drive your machine.'

Arch fell back on the rough oat-sacks, hand behind his head, propping forward, so that he could watch better the lamp shadows rise and flow about her broad cheeks. It was as if he had never looked at this woman before. Not closely. Her mouth was full and large, and she had something of a stone-carving about her. Half-smiling, when he was not looking.

'Hortense,' he repeated her name to himself. Hortense. It suited her so well.

But she shook her head imperceptibly, and her grave expression returned. She bent to adjust the oil-lamp and a huge shadow swallowed up the rafters above him. As she eased herself back on her haunches, Arch saw how carelessly her hair was brushed upwards and captured in a ribbon. As she bent forward into the oil-light, Arch lightly extended his hand, and stroked away a careless strand.

'Ah, no . . . no . . . please, no . . .' she said, and leant back again, looking down shyly, rather like a child scolded for some small misdemeanour. But she made no attempt to leave. The oil-lamp spat and popped. Arch closed his eyes, and lay back further. On the other side of the granary, sprawled on his heap of straw, Bickerton was snoring lightly; the sacking creaked as he stirred.

'He'll be sorry for all this in the morning,' whispered Arch, eyes still closed. Then the wood-smoke, the candle-light, his fuddled brain, all overwhelmed him and he dropped into unconsciousness, as deep as the sea.

As he dozed, the fear of falling woke him harshly. For a long time he lay thinking of the airfield, and felt within him the familiar rising of his body, and the earth falling

409

away beneath his feet. His body responded to the familiar prodding of the ailerons, and that exact moment in suspense before the machine reacted to the rudder, and the well-remembered bouncing sensation as the ground left the machine and the first airstreams hoisted the extended wings. His body shivered slightly, and he slept on. The shudder of the machine's roar, as the noise and pressure struck his eardrums, that instinctive watering of the eyes while the twisted air lashed them, struck him in his sleep – and that sense, later on, of flattening out, as if dozing on the fat underside of cloud. Into his head from far off crept an almost forgotten echo of a hardly learnt psalm. How could he have remembered that? He was a schoolboy – he saw sunlight on the bark of gum trees, a flashing parrot's wing, and heard a voice intoning slee-pily, so sleepily:

If I climb into heaven, thou art there: if I go down to hell, thou art there also.
If I take the wings of the morning . . .

He had been down to hell all right – he and Bickerton – down to the uttermost corner of hell.

Arch fell then into a mixture of dreamtime and wake-fulness, and as he sank down, even half-recognizing the sensation, he felt a gentle weight lay across him, pro-tecting him, and seeking his protection. There was the faintest smell of sweat in his nostrils, and something light seemed to touch his cheek. His eyes opened, and he knew he was neither sleeping nor dreaming. Bickerton still snored from the dark wall, but there was this even pressure across his breast, restricting his breath. He welcomed its warmth, which rose and fell in unison with him. It was Hortense who had sunk stealthily across him. She lay there, her arms round his shoulders, quiet like a child, for all of the night until through gaps in the granary roof, where a few tiles had been dislodged in winter gales, a ray of the morning edged through.

410

Arch could not imagine anything quite so still, nor such lightness. The easing away of her body at some time barely disturbed him. Then he must have lapsed into unconsciousness again. Later, at five a.m., all the dogs of the farm seemed to leap out of his brain barking, and, shaking a disgruntled Bickerton out of sleep, on to the granary floor, Arch emerged from the barn into early light, where Toussaint and Ignace, harness in hand, stood prepared to lead out the oxen.

Gorgonus walked into the courtyard with two bowls of hot chestnut gruel to fortify them, and to the hilarity of the Maresquiers, Bickerton, ashen-faced, was sick in the corner, by the pump.

*

'*Er ist da, Herr Fuchs. Er ist da!*' called out Franz, exultantly: '*Ich wusste wohl, dass ich ihn abfangen kann . . . !*' 'There he is! Mr Fox. There he is! I knew I'd catch him out . . . !'

And, sure enough, there lay the dirt-fox, only just that minute dead, and still quite warm, smaller now than it had seemed before, and contorted on the path. Franzie's wires had done the job, but the strugglings had only just finished as the two troopers rode into the clearing of pine trees. There was a great blood-sweated scar across its shoulders where the dirt-fox had jerked its mask and teeth back to tear and grapple at the unseen, unfelt 'thing' which imprisoned him in its metallic vice. For a second, Franzie stood above it, and felt an overwhelming shame. It was such a little and poor stunted thing, mediocre in colour, and dirty, dirty. A poor shrivelled dirt-fox.

'See, Xaverl, he's still warm! Warm as the sun! Feel him . . .'

'Nothing to eat here,' muttered Xaverl grumpily.

The older boy was too fastidious for these farm tricks. He dismounted and, taking the two bridles tethered their horses to a sapling. Next he rolled a cigarette in his fingers from the little tin pouch his mother had given him last *Dreikönigsnacht*, and kept watch. In his heart he

411

faintly despised the gamekeeper's work fumbling around in the gristle, Franzie up to his wrists in blood, already at work with a sharp knife. After a few draws on his thin tobacco, he had had enough of even that, it was as bitter in his mouth as bay leaves, and he walked away to listen to the silence inside the pine trees. He watched them defensively, suspicious that they concealed the shadows of advancing men. He balanced his carbine on his knees.

'You never know, deserters and cowards hole out any place, these days, even in a wilderness like this one.'

Franzie took off his grey field-jacket and hooked it on to a gorse bush; this was going to be hot work. Flaying-knife in hand, he quickly unloosened the snare-loop around the dirt-fox's wrung neck, and his fingers and nails were quickly stained in the darker blood from the dead animal. Standing upright, he braced his shoulders and ripped the warm, almost pulsing carcass from stem to stern, right down the spine, and there was a sharp crack – something like a rifle-shot. Xaverl under the trees turned sharply, for a second in doubt, as the backbone split apart.

Franzie reeled back as the sudden crude smell of dung and bile flattened him, like a fist in the mouth. The ribs gaped open with a raucous grin, and in a trice, under the flaying-knife, the entrails and livers and lights spattered on to the earth. Franzie grunted with satisfaction and effort. He fumbled about inside the warm wet pocket at the centre of the slippery wallet, until he found what he was looking for, a pendulous, peeled fruit. Kidneys like little seaweed grapes. He hooked them out and shook them violently on to the gravel at his feet, and a few wintry flies buzzed above them like sentries.

'Now if it had been a decent-sized rabbit, there'd have been a tasty stew out of it: mix in a few turnips and swedes. Parsnips. Dumplings.' His mind raced back to the Wienerwald.

'It's miserable out here, for the good God's sake, Franzie,' muttered Xaverl, 'I could do with some warm food inside me in a warm kitchen. Couldn't you?'

Franzie wiped his hands and wrists along the grass in the lightly fallen snow.

'You remember where we saw the oxen at plough yesterday? There's an old stone farmhouse down there too. Must be somebody working it. I saw smoke from the stack.'

'Usual low-brained beasts,' said Xaverl, 'the Ardennais. I hate their guts.'

'Surly-looking stone-pickers, sure enough,' answered Franzie, drying his arms and face on the back of his saddle-blanket, 'but there'll be a fire in the place. Some bread and pork too, most like.'

'Think of people who pick stones for a living, and eat raw mangolds.'

Xaverl dropped his field-glasses back on to his chest, and stumped back to the horses, which stood with meek, bowed heads among the trees. They closed their eyelids against the first flakes of snow that year.

'I could do with some warm food down me, and just the sight of a decent fire-grate wouldn't be bad,' answered Franz.

'Some pickles and beer would go down well, what do you say, Franz? Eh, old sweat? What d'you say? We've been out in the weather for a week, now. Shall we ride down?'

The flayed skin, a shabby little thing by now, was roped on to the saddle, and the troopers remounted. The snow, falling heavily, was already obscuring the scuffed-up ground. Very little sign of both struggle and snare – easily forgotten. Franz took out his worn report book. In the back of it were several fumbled and crossed-out lines of his blunt-fingered verse. He thought there might be the promise of a poem about this death of the small dirt-fox, and made a short note of it.

'Usual low-brained peasants,' muttered Xaverl again, riding on, 'I hate their guts . . . Still. If there's warm, and a bit of bread and pork . . .'

'Surly bastards at the best. But a good fire is a good fire

413

after all, Xaverl. Wherever it is. We've been out in the weather for too long.'

And so, their harness jingling as lightly as a sleigh-bell, the two Uhlans descended to the great plateau, towards the stone fortress which called itself Belgodère.

That little dirt-fox had done them a service after all.

*

'This is my promise,' said Hortense, quietly but intently, taking Arch's right hand and placing her own two hands on each side of it, 'the promise of a true Maresquier.'

'What promise?'

'A promise never to forget you,' and she took each fingertip in turn, and set it against her own, one after the other, until their hands were completely joined together.

'And you must promise never to forget me. Think of me, not always, but from time to time. That is all I ask in exchange.'

'Of course I promise.'

Stepping back one pace, Arch looked into her dark eyes that never ceased to surprise him and, to please her, repeated: 'I promise that I shall never forget you.' She nodded unsmilingly.

Then she kissed him on the mouth. It was only momentary, enough though for him to scent the peppery redolence of her brown hair under its black cowl. But, before he could take her properly in his arms, as he longed to do, and sweep back the fringe of her shawl, Bickerton surprised them both by stepping out of the shelter of a stack of winter wood. Politely, he affected to notice nothing.

'I'm digging in here all right,' said Bickerton, hoarsely, stamping in rhythm, perking up his circulation, 'even though I could cheerfully murder a man for a pint of warm beer. I've got head-staggers today all right! That local crippler gives me stomach-gripes.'

'Keep going, Bick.' Arch was relieved that it was not the ox-man, Toussaint, or the morose Pascal. Still in the half-light, and partly framed by the rush-lantern, Arch

414

saw his observer's arm pointed upwards, directly above their heads.

'There's Orion, right over us – you see, the two arms – and there's Orion's belt. Now – take two notches down on Orion's belt, and there's Sirius. You see it, *there*.'

And he took Hortense's head to the level of his arm, lining up her eye as if along the barrel of a gun. After his grub, and his beer, and his twin-Vickers, Bickerton loved his stars best. The Plough was far from clear in the mists, but he could discern Venus winking crudely at him, the second planet blackfellas call the Laughing Star, for ever chuckling at a rude story told among the Gods.

'There's Jack and his Wagon, dipping down,' he laughed.

'Every six times, Venus flashes once red,' explained Bickerton, 'so watch! Watch her carefully – there she goes – one red.'

'And over there?' asked the girl. 'So close?'

'The belle-star, Betelgeuse. Look at her now. Do you see?' And he called upwards: 'You bright, flaming bastard!' and stumbled down the path.

'Listen!' commanded Hortense when they were alone again. The ice in the air crackled on pathway, branch, and stone wall.

'Listen . . . !' said Hortense a second time, more urgently, her eyes glistening like hoar-rime, 'listen carefully . . . ! Listen like a fox!'

She turned to him expectantly, nodding: 'Now do you hear it? Toussaint calls it the whisper of the stars!'

And indeed there seemed to be a feverish crackle all about the sky.

'It must be the wind from the mountain catching the pines somewhere further up,' said Arch, more prosaically.

'The wind of Belgodère,' whispered Hortense. 'Old Father Xavier swears it brings down blood with it.'

But she was smiling with a kind of private mockery, and this time Arch was able to fold her completely within his arms, his heavy leather flying-jacket about her shoulders.

Her kisses were stronger than anything he could give her, until not a single corner of his face, neck, or hair, or throat, was left unscathed. Just as suddenly, the storm subsided and, without a further word, Hortense ran down the track to Belgodère, and Arch closed his eyes against the frozen air.

Bickerton was at his best with a child in his arms, or bouncing it up and down on his knees. By this time, the observer was, in his own favoured expression, thoroughly 'dug in'. In the language of signs, not a word exchanged between them, Bickerton had reached an 'understanding' with La Grosse.

It was the feast of poor Saint Cyriac; and Arch had fairly well dug in too. The companionable Sweet Aftons had long ago been smoked out, but they had been replaced by the no less welcome, and infinitely coarser, Spanish 'jaunes', and Arch had successfully cultivated the art, imitated from Toussaint, of balancing the dog-end on his lower lip at the same time as talking. In their black corduroy, and heavy black sabots, and fringe of brown stubble around their chins, both fliers looked to the letter as if they had worked the ground in the Ardennes for all the days of their life.

So Bickerton sat facing the fire, with Old Xavier and Tante Fanny each side of him, bucking the older of Berthe's two young boys to the old music-hall tune of 'K-K-K-*Katie*'. The little chap, with his cropped mangold head, grinned and bumped his bum awkwardly in an effort to follow the rhythm, breaking out in feasts of gurgling laughter, applauded by the old lady. Sometimes, with that childish trust in protective hands about him, he'd launch himself recklessly off the observer's knees and faint backwards into space, chuckling and confident that Bickerton's saucer of hands would shovel him safely back again to his former, precarious position. This was a game which looked like going on for eternity, according to the child's unbounded energy, and Bickerton's patient willingness to repeat the manoeuvre. Old Xavier tugged away at his stubborn pipe, and Tante Fanny clapped her hands in front of her face as each chorus reached its triumphant conclusion:

> When the m-moon shines
> Over the cow-shed,
> I'll be waiting at the k-k-k-kitchen door!

Over in the corner, near the grandfather clock, Arch was learning to play at 'fingers' with Gorgonus, and making a wretched job of it to the goat-man's delight. The women busied themselves in the larders at the back, strung with pork sausage in rows, like clothes-lines, clattering with pudding crocks and china basins full of the harvest of the previous week's slaughter.

To celebrate a saint's day with a feast is in order, especially when the saint is poor, and this the only feast day in the year. Even at Belgodère.

When the table was cleared of a rich pork supper, unsmiling and as morose as ever, Pascal circulated with the famous 'eau-de-village', wasting first a valuable tear — *une larme* — to swill out the tell-tale purple dregs of Argonne wine. Then, the sugar-cane was produced, and the glasses filled once again with the tell-tale 'water of life', as Hortense called it. From the larder Berthe produced, rather like an overworked priest with additional sacred wafers, a dish piled high with traditional hand-baked biscuits, and they circulated also, without hope of denial. Refusal was counted a cardinal insult.

'*Allons, manges, Capitaine! Manges, Bickerton! Allez-y, les gosses!*'

And the children came to the table for the sweet things and banged spoons against the benches, clamoured to drink the inoffensive-looking spirits (and were rejected), were spoilt by uncles and lumps of sugar, and this added to the general noise of feasting and ecstasy. Saint Cyriac, poor as he was, would surely have approved the thoroughness with which the Maresquiers, habitually so austere, celebrated his feast-day.

Then Cécéline, shyly, unbuttoned the dark front of her dress, and put her little daughter to her breast, and she lay there like a bee in the lubricious stamen of a full white flower. Until that moment, the little child had stirred fretfully and with irritation – unsympathetic to the happiness all around – the small bandy legs criss-crossing, the feeble but impertinent arms and wrists doodled in the air. However, when her lips enfolded the moist, inflamed bud which pushed into the already sucking mouth, a most astonishing repose crept over the unresting limbs, and flowed across the entire body, and beyond – it affected the tenderly exposed mother, and then all about. The warmth, the generosity, the sweetness of this suckling emanated outwards like a wave, or an old song – softening all that was exposed to its powers. At moments the drowsy eyes of the child opened and fluttered in a colourless, filmy way, and the inebriated and over-large head regarded sluggishly these fierce toilers against an obstinate soil, and an unyielding harvest. And in their turn, they too, ox-like and chipped out of stone, were gentled by the fragility of a crumpled child drinking at the fountain of its mother. The harsh, murderous exterior of two war-battered fliers weakened at the prospect of such timid grace. Everybody watched in silence as Cécéline fed, her outstretched fingers supporting the child's onion-like head. Gorgonus gave faint animal sounds from the back of his throat, expressions of eagerness and delight. From time to time, hands leant forward to encircle or refill the glasses of eau-de-vie. Old Xavier nodded a taciturn approval. Hortense, at the corner farthest away, was watching Arch's face, as he in turn watched the child, its mouth and chin smeared and shining with milk. La Grosse, standing behind Bickerton on the other side, where she had been urging sugar biscuits upon him, leant over him, pressing her own mountainous breasts against his back so that he could rest on her great weight, like a huge dog leaning on him, and she folded her arms round about his neck.

Tante Fanny held Berthe's oldest boy, asleep now, in her arms like a sack – Old Xavier sat with pipe unlit in his hand; Pascal hesitated, trapped momentarily between the glasses of Toussaint and of Arch, the bottle of spirit motionless in his grip. And Gorgonus wooed the child with the softest of his lullabies, the song with which he serenaded his goats in kid, until the liquid eyes rolled upwards, glazed over, and the oversized head lolled back against the luminous white globe of Cécéline's breast.

In the silence, which the people of the Ardennes call the silence of the stars, the heavy double-portals of Belgodère burst open, and the two Uhlans stood framed in the doorway. The silence remained. Gorgonus concluded his song and, placing his forefinger to his lips, whispered to the newcomers: 'Shhhhh!'

Young Franzie, with his freckled Saxon face eager and open, holding his *Pickelhaube* in the crook of his left arm, edged forward on tiptoe and he signalled to Xaverl to close the double-doors silently behind him. Outside, the November afternoon had deteriorated, and a few untidy drifts of snow, as dusty as chaff, danced behind the two troopers.

'*Attention – attention!*' warned Gorgonus. Without appearing to open his lips, he was counselling Arch and Bickerton to remain exactly as they were. Pascal placed both hands outstretched on the table, and leant his chest against its edge, for reassurance that his clasp-knife dug into him, securely in his waistcoat pocket, alongside the pipe and pouch of shag.

Franzie took stock of the situation immediately – a simple family at dinner, old men and women, babes-in-arms, babe at the breast, two or three farm-hands, possibly war-wounded, or excused-duties, but bearded and all dressed uniformly in their local relentless black cord. No fear of deserters or runaways here. He was no barbarian, he would show these illiterates how the Fatherland behaved to civilians. What was it his friend

Xaverl called them? Ah, yes, hobnails. Understandably the women had backed away but that was more from respect of men than fear of the intruders. It would have been the same in the Angeln, the women knew the meaning of the word 'respect'. No need to intimidate them, therefore, so he extended his arms in a symbolic, almost priestly, gesture of sympathy, as if giving the family his blessing.

'*Soldats allemands – n'ayez pas peur. Rien à craindre,*' said Franzie and, gesturing to Xaverl, in schoolboy French, '*Deux bons jeunes garçons!*'

'*Wir sind zwei gute deutsche Kavalleristen, und suchen nur ein bißchen heisses Essen in diese Winternacht: vor uns müssen Sie sich nicht furchten,*' said Xaverl.

Out of respect, immediately, as soon as the men had walked into the kitchen, Hortense, Berthe and La Grosse had vacated the benches and withdrawn timidly into the shadows. Cécéline, alone, remained seated, so as not to wake her child, whom she rocked almost imperceptibly in one arm. Modestly, with her free hand, she buttoned the front of her dress, grey upon white. Arch, who had been smiling only moments before at the child, felt himself incapable of any other expression; the rough intrusion, so desperately unexpected, had taken him totally by surprise. He could not think straight, his thoughts were muddled with wine. Looking across at Bickerton, he could take comfort from his observer's iron calm. With his characteristic lazy grin, his wind-worn face with its weeks of stubby growth, one eye virtually closed, his coarse fists curled on the table, not to speak of his worn-out clothes and wooden sabots, he was indistinguishable from the rest of the labourers in the kitchen. Arch hoped he too looked characteristically wind-worn, no longer the British officer, but the Ardennes peasant, low-witted and servile.

The cavalry troopers advanced towards the empty spaces on the bench, to which Old Xavier, cap in hand, gestured in welcome, and Pascal slid forward two glasses already full to the brim with eau-de-vie.

'*Pour vous rechauffer*,' said Pascal, '*et pour la fête de notre Saint-Cyriac, le pauvre.*'

'*Et pour l'amitié de tous*,' replied Franzie heartily, unbelting his sabre, which hung uncomfortably by his side. Xaverl, less hurriedly, followed suit, putting his own sabre, together with its belt, flat on the kitchen table.

Amitié, yes, he remembered that was the word. But he kept the hilt of his steel at his fingers' ends.

'Ahah!' Xaverl spoke for the first time as he drained his glass in a single gesture. '*Das Aquavit ist gut.*'

And the colourless alcohol moved round a second time. Silence, while they poured and tasted. It warmed, and helped to break the tension, and both the troopers coughed harshly at the sheer force of the drink.

'*L'essence!*' said Toussaint. '*Pour les machines.*'

'*Ah! L'alcool!*' answered Xaverl, and imitated the roar of a motor-vehicle. The bottle went round again.

'*Allez, Hortense, servez les galettes pour les soldats.*'

And Berthe, Hortense and La Grosse, like silhouettes, circled the table, bearing the traditional pastries and scraps of pork-brawn left over from the feast.

'*Du siehst, Xaverl, diese Franzosen sind überhaupt nicht so schlecht: unwissend vielleicht, aber sie sind herzlich.*' 'You see, Xaverl, these Frenchies are not so very bad after all. Ignorant, perhaps, but with a good heart.'

And Xaverl grudgingly agreed:

'Anything's better than riding outside in this weather; yes, of course, there are far worse ways of spending a Sunday.'

Now the old man had come forward, the one they had observed almost sitting in the fire itself, working at his old pipe.

'*Je vous supplie, soldats allemands, de lever vos verres à la santé de notre bien-aimé, le pauvre Saint-Cyriac.*'

421

A scraping back of benches. Following the toast th
two Uhlans presented themselves by name, formally
shaking hands first with Old Xavier.

'*Ich bin Franz, Kavallerist, und mein Kamerad ist
Xaverl. Wir haben seit Beginn des Krieges zusammen
gekämpft.*'

'*Mois, je suis le grandpère des Maresquiers – je m'ap-
pelle Xavier – le vieux, quoi. Et, la famille, quoi . . . les
femmes . . .*'

Arch and Bickerton were introduced as the husbands of
Berthe and of Hortense, both of them '*mutilés de guerre*'.
Arch, rising, made as if to indicate a wounded shoulder.
But, before he blundered on, Bickerton saved the day
with an even more dramatic gesture. Resolutely, he
remained where he was, on his side of the bench, and
pointing downwards said hoarsely: '*Les jambes, finis,
kaputt.*' And added, for good measure: '*Cambrai.*' He
shrugged.

Franz leaned over the wooden table to shake his
unknown enemy's hand in a gesture of fellowship.

'*Attention, l'engin, attention . . .*' croaked Gorgonus in
his warning voice.

'I could do with another plate of pork-flesh.'

'At home we'd have sour cabbage to match. And a full
stein of warm beer!'

'This is better than nothing!'

'Franzele! This is a lot better than nothing.'

Arch had thoroughly cleared his head. He and Bickerton could see nothing but the barn and the tell-tale
fuselage and propeller of the Biff. It was camouflaged but
how well? Certainly the two young Uhlans had missed
the machine when they rode up, but how? It was dark, or
course. Possibly they had tethered their horses just outside Belgodère's stone arch, and then tramped through,
disregarding what might lie concealed in the outbuildings. It would seem exceptionally careless, or maybe just
their good fortune. Bick raised his left eyebrow enigmati-
cally, but Arch was unable to read the signals.

It should be growing dark outside, no, it was already dark, and snow falling – the cold air rushed in as Pascal opened the windows to reach the shutters. The cavalrymen knew nothing, apparently suspected nothing, they were secure behind their own lines, and so the wisest remedy would be for the fliers to sit tight and keep their heads down. It was another example of Bickerton's philosophy, 'to dig in' – or, in his other phrase, ruminating on what the next move might be, assign the whole business to 'a thinking-out job'. Old Xavier, playing, Arch thought, very successfully the ingenuous peasant, to gain time, was now leading forward the women of Belgodère to present them also.

'*Tante Fanny, au feu, Cécéline, la petite mère.*'

'*Ja, ja,*' agreed Franzele, thinking of his red-cheeked Hertha at her milking stool in the Angeln, '*die junge Mütter.*'

Xaverl, emboldened, showing off a little in front of Hortense, unslung his carbine, lay it flat on the table and unbuttoned his jacket to his braces, which were startling red beneath the grey field-dress.

'To the end of the war,' called out Franz, lifting his glass. 'To this war's end, to the end of all wars. To comradeship.'

'To the future peace,' called out Old Xavier, 'and the return home of my beloved grandson.'

'*Kameradschaft,*' added Xaverl, rising to his feet, clinking glasses with Arch.

'But where is he? The husband?' persisted Franz.

Old Xavier gave a far-away gesture with his hand.

'*La-bas! Dans votre pays – prisonnier.*'

Franz raised his arms in a helpless but sympathetic gesture – what was the use of reproaching these poor people for their grandson's foolishness in getting himself captured? It would be more honest to sacrifice a life for one's fatherland; it was still the honourable thing for a cavalryman to do. Xaverl for one, he knew, would prefer to be worked off – as he put it – with his spurs on.

423

Then to business: Xaverl, the sterner of the two, asked the questions, and took a notebook from his breast-pocket.

'Have you seen any deserters from the German Army in this area?'

'*Non.*'

The interrogation continued, Franz attempting roughly to translate.

'Have you seen any English or French deserters?' – 'No.'

'Have you seen any suspicious movements in the last few weeks?' – 'No.'

'Any foreigners of any description? Gypsies? Travellers? Bohemians? Have any of you witnessed round about the region any unfamiliar faces? Priests? Schoolboys?'

One by one, they shook their heads. Lastly, Franz demanded: 'Have any of you ever seen around your farmhouse, or in the local villages, even in the churches, any sign of escaped prisoners of war? French, English, Belgians? Now we are all friends here, I must have your word on this. If you have, it is your duty to inform us. Including your own countrymen in uniform. You are under our rule. You must remember the penalty of harbouring enemy soldiers is one of military trial and execution by firing party.'

'They will steal your chickens, and rape your women, you know,' added Xaverl crudely. No. Arch looked at the ground between his sabots, and shook his head gravely, as if their question was an offence to the integrity or loyalty of them all. His head was icily clear by now. He hardly dared look the Maresquiers in the eye. Pascal was turning the matchstick in his mouth.

'Very good. Then everything is good between us,' said Franz by way of conclusion, as if the matter had been distasteful, and picking up his glass he signified the end of the official side of things by gesturing for a refill from Bickerton, who sat nearest the bottle.

'We have to ask these questions, you know.' Franz

conspicuously withdrew his carbine from his shoulder and propped it against his chair.

'No chance of any latrines round here, I don't suppose,' Xaverl said.

'*Attention . . . attention . . . l'engin*,' came again Gorgonus's warning voice. Perhaps, thought Arch, this fellow will just unbutton himself out in the yard, and no harm done. By now it will be too dark to see anything, least of all a machine hidden under the hay. But, hesitating a moment at the porch, and sensing the pitch-blackness outside, the tall Uhlan returned to the table, and took with him one of the large storm lanterns.

'Close the doors behind you, you idle bastard. Keep the cold out,' Franz called after him. 'Now, who's ready with a song?'

Gorgonus suddenly rose to his feet and, in his characteristic and quavery voice, began the long saga of 'La Bicyclette'. To keep the rhythm going in an easy-going way, both Toussaint and Pascal joined in the humming, while Ignace kept up a steady flat-handed beat on the table. Cécéline, blushing a little, enfolded her baby in the supports of her shawl and, stooping to kiss Old Xavier on both cheeks, departed for the rooms behind the kitchen.

It puzzled Arch that Old Xavier and all the men should appear so unconcerned. Cécéline, it was true, had disappeared, Berthe clattered in the larder, but La Grosse and Hortense were patiently wiping down the table, and Toussaint cheerfully filling not only Franz's glass but his own as well. Gorgonus was singing, somewhat blearily by now, and Pascal and Ignace crowded the German boy with a polite audience. None of them showed any awareness of the possible danger of Xaverl discovering the tell-tale machine in the corner of the cow-houses, family life carried on just the same inside the warm and friendly kitchen. How could they possibly face out the Uhlan's return? Best by doing nothing, he assumed. Live in hopes. All the same, he eyed Xaverl's menacing sabre, still in its sheath on the table, and Franz's carbine, stacked incautiously against Old Xavier's wooden armchair.

As Xaverl re-entered the kitchen, Old Xavier said quietly, laying aside the pipe:

'The red-head.'

Without a signal, without a warning sound, Pascal, matchstick in mouth just as usual, with an almost casual movement of his body – as if he was reaching for a hunk of bread, or rescuing an empty glass – gripped each of Franz's wrists, and pinioned him as fiercely as he would the back legs of a young boar.

The same second, alert, Xaverl sprang backwards in an effort to claw the carbine off his back – *'Engländer! Engländer!'* – but Bickerton and Ignace were at him in a mutual leap from their benches. The bluff was up now.

'Get a grip of that bastard, Arch, get a grip of his carbine!'

'Fumier!' swore Toussaint, lunging for the sabre in its sheath.

'Franzele!' shrieked the trooper. His friend, unaware that this could be anything other than some form of friendly rough and tumble, still sat, vaguely smiling across at Pascal, in a frozen moment of amiable silence. Silent, that is, apart from Gorgonus's song.

'Ce n'est pas un jeu, coco,' muttered Pascal, as Old Xavier, without seeming impatient, reached up above the fireplace, to lay hold of the first shotgun. He still held his pipe in the other hand.

'Oh, Gott, mein Gott, Xaverl, hilf mir.'

'Hilf mir' among the lonely pine trees and stone walls of Belgodère. As usefully cry out to God as to their granite hearts.

Arch sent the carbine which leant on the chair-back skidding away and launched himself underneath the broad table next, and clutched at the wildly kicking and plunging legs of the red-haired boy. Ignace, over in the other corner, had wrenched Xaverl's carbine away from his shoulder, sending it slithering across the stone flags,

426

while Bickerton hung glumly on to the other arm; but the Uhlan felt his right hand miraculously released and, wrenching the observer back by his hair, he succeeded in easing one of his assailants away from his body for precious seconds. His cavalry training took in close combat and, man for man, Xaverl was the match for them. His great leather boot exploded in Ignace's groin and sent him reeling into Old Xavier's precious grandfather clock, which chimed brokenly, tottered sideways an instant, before falling, smashing the glass into a thousand fragments. Bickerton lost control of the trooper's arm in the force of his swing.

'Christ's sake, Arch, don't let that bugger get at his sword . . .'

But the trooper was already there, in three simple strides, right on the table, tearing at its canvas covering. Ignace was wiped out of it, coughing up blood on the stones. Old Xavier was – as if captured in slow motion – fidgeting with the shotgun, breaking its barrel open, fingering the cartridges. Arch and Pascal were pinning Franz down, and Toussaint, the slow-witted ox-man, struggling without success to master the German carbine.

'*Hilf mir, Xaverl . . . hilf mir . . .*'

Making inarticulate grunting noises at the back of his throat, Gorgonus jumped down from the stool and pinned the Uhlan's hands as he grappled with the treacherous fastenings.

Infinitely stronger, Xaverl swung the lightweight figure from side to side, bashed it against table and wall. Bickerton judging his leap, clung to the German's writhing back, and prevented him from kicking Gorgonus's feet from beneath him. And, just when he seemed to be able to wrench himself free at last from the clutches of the goat-man, Hortense and La Grosse, combining their weight, threw themselves at the Uhlan's knees and clung there like suppliants. Gorgonus jerked away the sabre and sent it circling into the shadows. For minutes on end, it seemed, the heap of men and women wrestled and

427

swung in the centre of the room, four on top of one, but finally, like some complicated children's game, which had eventually to come to an end, the tall, sinuous figure of the Uhlan in his field-grey stumbled and toppled, and the weight of Toussaint, added to all of the others, pinioned him securely and desperately to the ground. The conflict appeared to have been going on for ever, as if both the intruders were being slowly, but eventually, stifled in the huge coil of some gigantic snake; in reality, very few minutes had passed; long enough for Old Xavier, in his patient, unhurried way, to take down the shotgun, break it open, thrust in a pair of cartridges, and snap the breech shut again.

'Hilf mir . . . Hilf mir . . .'

Pascal held the arms of Franz secure, Arch, beneath the table, imprisoned the feet. Two gigantic explosions, as ferocious as if a fire-bomb had detonated in the kitchen, left the spread-eagled remnants of the Uhlan as lifeless as a sack.

Toussaint, stealing behind the heaving body of the second trooper, strangled the life slowly out of him, with his belt.

For all that time, until the final convulsions ceased, the two women hung determinedly on to the knees, and Gorgonus and Bickerton to the arms and shoulders. Only poor Ignace sat in a heap in the corner, blood and vomit staining the front of his black corduroys.

It seemed to last for ever, the heaving and leaping and squirming. My God, thought Arch, the ingenuity and strength it takes to kill a man on the ground. In the sky . . . a few manoeuvres of the wings, a side-step or two, a careful matter of correcting the speed, and one short staccato burst. This was different, infinitely more terrible.

For months to come, Arch would dream of this, of the feeling of clutching at a man's legs, not to support him, but to pull him further, helplessly down, into the weeds of death: of the life kicking and gurgling ecstatically through them, with the eagerness of Cécéline's suckling child, he felt it in his arms, and the swift ebbing of life, just draining away, and his holding the weighty coalsack legs, and that body stretched out in some gesture of universal supplication, on the wood table, a dead thing now, an obstacle drenched in its own blood. And then the sight of Xaverl's bloated face. Their lives hadn't lasted long. Only the morning. And, worse than the sniper in the front line, or the flamer in the air, these soldiers were slaughtered among friends. Or friends they assumed they had made. Men they had exchanged cigarettes with, toasted in 'the water of life', shaken hands with, shared songs with . . . Christ on the Cross! . . . he remembered. That bastard Gorgonus and his singing . . . right the way through. Bickerton was right – 'a cot-case'. And finally, that horse.

In the dreadful silence which followed, a silence disturbed in an eerie way only by the panting of the women clinging still to Xaverl's knees, this sudden terrible shrieking and trumpeting. The horse, the white horse of Franz, rearing up, shredding its traces, and careering and clattering terror-hooved down the track from Belgodère, screaming as it fled.

Well, all that mattered now, without words being spoken, was to restore everything to the way it had been before. And so they did, Arch and Bickerton, wordlessly taking the lead from the Maresquiers and, patiently and without emotion, clearing the wreckage, and concealing the bodies. Nobody would pass this way again for months, even years. So it was necessary to clean away the men, and continue as if nothing had happened.

'And now, back to work,' said Pascal, when everything was done, 'there's a winter's work to be finished.'

Gorgonus went to his goats. Pascal and Ignace to the cattle-byre. Bickerton and Toussaint to the oxen. Arch to help Old Xavier stack and chop the winter logs.

'*Nous revenons au travail – il faut travailler. Le travail toujours. Le travail d'hiver.*'

The women lay the bodies out straight on the kitchen

429

table, washed them, and dressed them in their field-grey – Berthe darning as well as she could the torn jackets – and set under the table a saucer of salt, 'to stop them rising', Tante Fanny said, and a candle by their side, 'for company'. It was wrong to leave them alone and in the dark. The Maresquiers of Belgodère knew how to obey the proprieties and, besides, were well used to the ways of burying the dead.

The fox and Franz were killed now, and the next task was to bury the dead. Silence had fallen on the stone farmhouse of Belgodère since the intrusion of the two young German troopers the night before.

'The winters in Belgodère,' Pascal had already warned them. '*C'est la misère.*'

The first renewed sprinklings of snow outside testified to that. The aftermath of the disaster had left all of them with a kind of inward weariness, a weariness to death, and Arch felt an overwhelming sorrow for the two dead soldiers, which he had never imagined for anybody else, least of all an enemy. It was the war, of course, and every argument could be used to justify their actions; certainly, they and the Maresquiers were dead men had they weakly succumbed, or surrendered; and if Xaverl had found the way to unsheathe his sabre, or Franz to reach his gun . . . Nevertheless, he and Bickerton felt they had acted like murderers.

In the night, once again, the strange sound of thunder, like a train underground, revealed further bombardment at the front, far off. Arch sat in the window, with the shutters open, staring outwards into the dark. He sensed, in the distance and in the obscurity outside, however faint or remote, voices crying to him, reaching to him, almost in the way – he remembered now – Conrad had described to him that he had witnessed the ghosts of dead men coming from the edge of the English sea. The voices he heard were wordless and indistinct, but they were voices he knew. Voices he recognized. He would go, he answered them. He would go. Why should everything be filled with ghosts and dreams and these indistinct phantoms?

Gorgonus led the way, hopping firm-footedly from rock to rock supporting with his wiry strength the entire body of the red-head, on his shoulders. He reached the edge of a jagged scarp, and hurled the body into the gorge below, before Pascal could stop him. More cautiously, they hewed and hacked into the stone and pine-needle floor, and wedged Xaverl's weighted corpse, still in its field-grey, in between the crevasses, and dug, and trod stones on top of it.

Before the deep hole – they dug it well down, for fear the foxes or the ravenous wild boar would scrape it into the light – Toussaint, working quickly, bent forward and removed a gold ring, the fob-watch out of the breast pocket, the dull tin of cigarettes, and stripped away the belt buckle, and the tunic buttons.

'No point in being over-hasty about these things,' he explained to a disapproving Arch, 'where he's going to billet, he'll not need this stuff.' And Arch felt himself as cold and dead as the German in his grave.

'*Mais il faut partir, il le faut.*'

'*Ouais, maint'nant c'est nécessaire.*' Hortense understood Arch, whose face was white, and his eyes a sullen brown.

'Fly like hell for home, is it?'

'I'd spit my death on it,' answered Bickerton.

If it is true, as they say, we do not re-meet those we love if we do not truly wish to, so also must it have been true that Arch and Bickerton might have found their way back to Capité had they set their minds on it. The real truth was they had not wanted to, and remained at Belgodère voluntary hostages. Any time taken out of that wasting war was time gained. Once Bickerton and Arch bent themselves to the task, fearful that at any hour a second Uhlan patrol should discover the concealed machine in the cattle-byre, with Toussaint's help they stitched and

431

tinkered the stubborn Biff back into flying shape. They brought the fuel down on muleback from Corbeille, tortuously but sure-footedly; and, once patched up, not unlike a child's toy kite, caressed by the fliers, watched by a small clan of admirers from Belgodère, the machine was coaxed out of its hiding-place, filled up, wiped down, oiled, and Diviani's loyal engine hiccoughed into an exploratory life. Not at the first turn-over, nor the second, nor the tenth, or even the twentieth, but at three-thirty in the afternoon of their tenth day (was it no more than that?) at the forty-fourth strenuous swing, from Toussaint and Pascal, oil-cloths in hand, for all the world like professional artificers, the bullet-scarred propeller buzzed into whirling life. Half-a-Brain staggered back as if hit by a shell, and Gorgonus ran to the other side of the field, and hid. As he revved, Arch felt the old familiar power humming and vibrating beneath his feet, and braced his shoulders for the sudden press forward. Bickerton, by the wing, gave the excited thumbs-up, which Arch repeated, and in turn Half-a-Brain and the rest of the family copied them. It was a kind of talisman, they supposed, like a benediction or the sign of the horns, to confuse the evil eye. Bickerton jumped into the observer's seat, and unlatched his double-Vickers. There would be no nonsense about jamming this time, and he fired a burst in the direction of a clump of bedraggled wind-bent firs to the north-east, and to the delight of the men of Belgodère the branches splintered and split in shreds.

The departure had turned into more of a feast-day than a farewell. Pascal, Toussaint, Ignace and Half-a-Brain came forward and kissed each of the fliers in turn. It took a long time, and not a word was spoken, and not a bird sang. Two kisses on each cheek, the right, the left, the right again, warm and wet, the left again:

'*Good life, good health, safe return, and come back soon.*'

In the stone kitchen, the women pressed upon them sausage, a bottle of eau-de-vie in brown paper, a basin of pâté – this was from Tante Fanny – and, as a special gift from La Grosse, a fresh-baked cow-pat of chestnut bread. Bickerton was wrapped up in his winter greatcoat once again, his stubble beard giving him the face of an Arctic explorer. He had wiped goose-grease over his cheeks, and he shone. He stood almost embarrassed, tears in his eyes, his hands full of good things to eat, just like a spoilt child on Christmas morning.

Bickerton slipped his pocket-watch out of his own hand into that of La Grosse – and then, solemnly, Pascal and Toussaint took out their knives from their inside pockets and slapped them into the two fliers' hands – there was to be no refusal. When Gorgonus came out of the shadows, he held in each hand a waistcoat without arms made of wild goatskin, which he insisted wordlessly they wore, in spite of their resistance: first his friend Bikkyton, and next le Capitaine. And, after embracing them, he stepped back, and said, looking at the ground: 'Mes frères.'

Hortense was at Arch's elbow. Their thoughts remained unvoiced.

'You see, it is so little we have to give you, the people here are so poor, so very, very poor.'

Arch kissed her mouth, as dry and inexpressive as his own.

In silence, Madame Fanny, who had said nothing the entire time, moved from her place at the fire: she was a small, black figure, reaching only to the men's breast-buttons. She did not embrace them, but, as the two fliers stooped to her level, she etched upon each forehead with her thumb the Father, the Son, and the Holy Ghost.

Hortense plucked the hem of Arch's goatskin; he hung back.

'I will never forget my promise to you, Hortense, I will think of you on the morning I die.'

'Then nothing matters between us. I will love you, Arche, always. It is very easy to love somebody for ever.' Hortense stood a little apart, swathed in black clothes,

433

the darkest of brides, touching at her breast one of her cloth buttons, her other hand folded, priest-like, across her belly.

Now they stood together in a little group around the machine, and the long business of reviving the engine began. Arch felt the old, resilient energy come stumbling back after its winter slumber, there was a discernible shiver from stem to stern, and on the forty-third swing the contact struck. Next time, they would try to get off.

'Do or dare, Bick!' And the actual farewells were perfunctory. 'We'll go through on the next swing. Back like hell, Bickerton, old chap!'

'That's the spirit, sir! Chocks away!' he yelled and gestured urgently with his hands outstretched. 'Nose down – tail up!'

'The rudder's strappy but I think we're going to make it! Bail up, Bickerton!'

'Fly straight and narrow, Mr Gendron, Captain, sir!'

Hortense neither spoke, nor gestured, but remained where she stood, rooted like a finger of granite, unmoved, unflinching from tears. At first she was with Arch in the machine; as the earth dropped away from them, she felt the rudder kick to the east, and the tug of the ailerons as the wounded Biff flew one wing heavy: when Arch corrected the balance with his fingertips, Hortense felt the wind surge under the soles of her feet, the vibrations ascend the correct pitch; he throttled back, and tipped the stick forward to level off. He had flown into the sky, leaving her alone on the earth for ever.

Lazily gaining altitude in the thin air, Arch turned the machine about for one final time. There was Belgodère, standing upright and arrogant in the middle of this vast rocky plateau, suddenly diminished, which had been, so recently and for so long, a vast and impressive empire. And there in the centre of the snow-field, where Gorgonus as a boy had stood as rook-scarer and stone-gatherer, was the little family, tightly drawn around in a

434

circle, growing smaller and smaller, waving and waving until they were no more than dark seeds on a surface of white.

Watchful for any sign of hostile Huns, although he suspected the hour was too late, and the conditions too murky, Arch drove the machine dangerously low over the pine trees, following the river this time to the west. Suddenly he received a thud on his shoulder from the observer; but it was not an assailant. Bickerton had spotted, over to the north-west, motionless by a level-crossing, in a break in the forest, Old Xavier's horse and cart. Tilting the rudder gently, cautious not to be over-taken from above, Arch steered towards them, one eye still on the river-line leading back to the home lines. Of course, that was why Old Xavier had been absent from the parting at Belgodère: it was the day when he visited the level-crossing for a vain glimpse of his youngest grandson. And there he was, patiently awaiting the passing of the trains of wounded prisoners from the front line: '*Il reviendra! Il reviendra!*'

Arch flew the machine as low as he dared above the railway junction, and Old Xavier, as upright and digni-fied as ever, perched on the box seat of his old cart, one hand on the reins, lifted from his white head his worn black hat. Bickerton and Arch tried yelling above the crackle of their engine, but dared not switch off, for fear of never restarting, and, leaning half out of their shattered seats, waved one final time. Somehow the ferocity of the icy slipstream blurred and blinded Arch's vision, and he climbed, without ever looking back, into the edge of the mist above the teeming, anonymous forests of the Ard-ennes.

'*Il reviendra! Il reviendra!*'

435

PART SEVEN

I do not fear death – I fear it as little as to drink a cup of tea

NED KELLY

PART SEVEN

CHAPTER TWENTY-FOUR

Wolves to the Slaughter

'Dear God in heaven! Where on earth have you two ruffians been?'

It was Major Medlicott, for all the world like a bad actor, standing dead-still in his tracks, scratching his bald patch, as he held away his peaked cap with thumb and forefinger.

'What in hell's name have you two rascals been up to? Acting the giddy goat? Sergeant Horner, look what the wind's turned up . . .'

And it was true, standing there in their shredded goatskins, dark-faced, wind-burnt and heavily bearded, they resembled turnip-gatherers more than veteran fliers. Arch offered up some kind of explanation:

'If we could see you privately, sir, perhaps we could . . .'

'Privately! To hell with it. You've been missing ten bloody days, the Wing's worried stiff, Baring's in a blue funk, there's no word from home lines, no word from Hun lines, where the hell do you think we thought you were?'

The major had a cheerful grin, but the apparent relief of his initial greeting seemed to have given way by now to moderate irritation.

'Sergeant Horner,' called the Major again, into the shabby interior of the offices, 'come outside and see who's turned up – a pair of bloody rascals if ever there were, and looking like Cherokees, too.'

A sheaf of log-book entries in his hand, Hoppy Horner limped out and pretended to stand frozen in his tracks.

'Fucking stroll on!' he said, after an interminable pause. 'Arch Gendron and Bickerton, isn't it?'

'Of course it bloody well is,' said Arch, 'who do you think it is – Boelcke and Göring?'

Bickerton, who had withdrawn into his legendary taciturn self, leaving Arch to do the talking, volunteered: 'Captain Gendron, sir . . .' in a conciliatory tone, which infuriated Arch even more.

'That wasn't the way you talked to me at Belgodère.'

'No, sir.'

'Well then.'

Bickerton stared glumly to his front.

'Well, fucking stroll on,' said the sergeant, inventively, for a second time.

What a pair of balls! Bickerton thought to himself, hardly worth bothering to come back all this way.

'Not been skylarking, I take it, you two, eh, Bickerton?'

'We were shot down, sir,' explained Arch. The loyal Diviani and his artificer were already tinkering with the uneven revolutions of the machine's propeller, and active with oil-tins and grease-guns.

'Missing, presumed killed, the book said,' added Horner.

'A spot of unofficial leave in Paris, was it, with a couple of Empire girls . . .?'

The major was smiling good-humouredly, but his tone angered Arch, every bit as much as Horner's inane repetition of 'fucking stroll on', which seemed to be the only phrase he could find for the occasion. Arch, taking a leaf from Bickerton's book, relapsed into silence. This was hardly the homecoming either had anticipated. He remembered the desperate struggle for life in the sky, and the terrible death-battle against the Uhlans. And flying home had been nerve-racking enough.

'We were shot up by some Tripes on dawn patrol,' he muttered, 'the observer's gun jammed, the wing-men were not up to scratch and got themselves shot down, one of them was browned off in a flamer . . .'

'And we landed on this old farm, sir,' continued Bickerton, barely more eloquent than his pilot, 'an out-of-the-way, behind-the-lines sort of place, sir, we don't know where it was . . .'

And then he stammered, 'Captain Gendron saved my life. We were right out of luck.'

'All right, Bick, there's no more to say,' interrupted Arch, 'we have nothing more we want to say. We were shot down, we smashed behind the lines. God knows where. Some bloody place. We repaired the machine. We killed a couple of Hun scouts. And we came back home. Nothing more to say than that.'

The major was breathing hard, his face drained white.

'Well, the situation here is a damned sight more bloody than that – Command's in a bugger's muddle, the Hun's cutting us up in the air, they've got an Albatros or some damned thing that makes our machines look sandbagged – morale's rock bottom, it's flying murder up top, the whole business is pretty well rat-arsed if you want to know – so you can understand why 10th Squadron feels pretty huffy about you lot . . . We need every man we've got.'

There was a brief silence, disturbed only by the sound of Diviani gently restoring and soothing the Biff's worn-out engine to a steady rhythmic tone; all four men, grateful for neutral ground, cocked their ears for the harmonious sound.

'Much better,' said the major, as if sampling a tasty casserole, 'coming along nicely.'

The engine dilated quite suddenly, and the airfield was once again buzzing with the sound of larks.

'You rascals missed a treat – while you were gadding about – we took a tender down to the island of Werpes, you know, down in the mudflats. Some of the Rifle Brigade fellows had spotted a pair of avocets nesting there . . . Unlikely visitors this time of year. Marvellous sight. And the squadron bluetits are out – just look at the dear little beggars, up there on the roof, fluttering their wings . . .'

And Major Medlicott walked stealthily round the edge

441

of the verandah, stood on the balustrade and, one hand
on the drainpipe, whistled and clucked like a hen at the
guttering.

'Yes, there they are! Go to it, my little darlings . . .
that's the spirit!'

Switching his attention, just as eccentrically, he dismissed the sergeant back to his clerical offices.

'That'll do, Sergeant Horner; now listen, you two
ruffians, whatever it was you got up to, whether some
kind of rag, or spree, or what, it wasn't quite straight bat,
but we'll say not another word about it. Point taken, you
two?'

Arch and Bickerton stood looking into the middle
distance, trying to cool the red blood which mounted in
their faces. With a sense of relief Arch felt his fingers curl
around the clasp-knife Toussaint had pushed into his
hand; it calmed him. He thought about Hortense as well,
and that soothed him more. Major Medlicott had
whistled up his Bedlingtons, and they were sniffing
excitedly around his riding-boots, anticipating a walk.

'In any case, let's forget all about it, you fellows, shall
we?' he continued, with a wink at Arch. 'But you rogues
should tidy yourselves up a bit, you look like a pair of
hedgers and ditchers what with your beards and your
fur-apparatus, whatever it is. And, when you've finished
your combat reports, hand in your log-books to Horner,
and take yourselves off on a forty-eight. Horner will sign
your passes. Come along, boys,' and, with a whistle to the
dogs, he turned fast on his heel, and strode away in the
direction of the château.

Arch and Bickerton stood there a few seconds in
silence. Bickerton's blind-eye popped open alarmingly.
'Go and piss up a rope,' he mumbled under his breath,
while the major was still in earshot, 'I'll not go down on
my knees for him.'

Arch shook his head in disbelief: 'We got in a right
three and fourpence there.' He was seething with resentment, and even a kind of impotence at his personal failure

to stand up for both of them. But the words just failed to come into his brain, or tumble off his tongue. He remembered they had both been silent for too long in a world which ignored speech. But for two '*bagarreurs*' he felt they had put up a pretty poor show. Gorgonus would have been shocked by them, Half-a-Brain would have done better.

Bickerton had already started slumping his way back to the machine, his first task to dismantle the double-Vickers, which had caused so much pain in the first place. Events might have turned out very differently; not better, just different. But, as he approached the sheep which were grazing, instead of quietly skirting around them, or plodding along behind, he suddenly began clucking and yelling and whistling and leaping about in all directions. 'Brrr . . . burrrr . . .! Heh-eh-eh!' Arch saw what he was about – he was remembering Gorgonus and his goats, and indeed the observer did for a minute resemble the goat-man with his strangely multicoloured goat's eyes. At the commotion several of the squadron ran out of their tents and Hoppy Horner poked his head through the office window, shaking it in wide disbelief again as the sheep panicked, Bickerton leap-frogged about, and Arch capsized backwards in helpless laughter on the grass.

'*Hey! Bickyton, le machin, heh! Bickyton, heh! heh! heh! Prut-prut-prut!*'

Their laughter drowned out the purring of Diviani's precious engine.

Major Medlicott divided their partnership. Bickerton worked as observer to Chidiock, Risdon and Wyse, and Arch flew on as pilot to Treby, Gathercoal and 'Hap' Brown, and nothing was ever quite the same. His face took on the earthy colour of the grave and, in spite of his skills, he experienced too many white-knuckle fights to enjoy the sensation he formerly had taken for granted. He felt his back open to the enemy. He became also more and more of a hero, less and less of a flier. He knew the way to survive, though. 'He who lives and flies away' was not the motto he would have admired a month or so before. Besides, the Huns were achieving relentless air-superiority, or so he felt.

'Fly in fast, behind and below' were the orders of the day for the merciless new intake of *Jagdflieger*: 'leave the fancy manoeuves to the ones who know better.' The Fokker Tripes, Arch noticed, had more stability in the air, and possessed the subtle edge of balance between intense audacity in manoeuvre and catastrophe. In other words, his flying-intelligence or his instinct told him, all the difference between victory on the one hand, and death on the other. His old abilities of tactical dog-fighting were losing their force; superior flying skills now ended in disaster. There was even the possibilty the British and French aces, for all their brilliance, might be shot out of the sky by lesser, but more *effective*, adversaries. And still the offensive went on and the losses grew. 'Wolves to the slaughter' was the way Conrad described it.

Conrad had told him that 'the flight of the eagle should not be disturbed by the scattering of the sparrows', and, as Arch perfected his flying-technique, many a dud observer owed his life to that ability of evasion, and his impeccable sense of balance in the air. He picked up the new nickname of 'side-slip'. As often as he might, without the security of Bickerton's unerring single eye, missing his loyal off-sider, Arch would gratefully escape the howl and jungle of battle and, diving away from combat, outrace the terrifying stridor all around him – but not the fear. Terror, like a familiar friend, erupted deep inside the wall of his stomach every day now. He felt frozen at his fingertips. He had never lacked 'bottom', and was a marvel to the ashen-faced recruits which Command burdened him with in the gundeck, but to himself he was afflicted by fear night and day. And all of this, of course, was a novelty to him.

But one Monday, the worst day of his life, was the morning Bickerton was killed.

* * *

444

he scrap began unexpectedly when they went in Strutters to bomb the railway terminus at Bedenburg, and were set on by a hornet's nest of triplanes. It had been the usual business. Arch side-slipped and split-arsed a couple of aggressive passes from the Hun machines and, for once defended by an effective quick-firer, had the satisfaction of seeing a Fokker triplane lose altitude at speed and drift into a spin from which he could not recover. Noise and tracer and cordite slapped all around him – as well as concussion and a few lethal 'flaming onions'. He was accustomed to face the guns if he could and dodge them head-on – but he was surprised to see on this occasion a friendly machine racing towards him, as if to force a collision. A white ribbon of vapour pulled out behind, like a kite's tail. He pulled the stick harshly towards him, and felt his machine shudder and respond at the same moment, and was astounded to see, as the other machine passed just beneath him, flying forward on a dead-stick landing, the unmistakable sight of the British pilot, head slumped – either stunned or, more likely, shot in the face – on the instruments, and the arms hanging heavily down. And in the same image, which remained stuck inside his eyeballs for the duration of the war, his old friend, the observer, Bickerton, bolt upright in the second seat. And, as he jerked in a frenzy of terror and misery, unmindful of his shouting rear-man, who pointed urgently towards the menacing Fokkers closing in tight on his tail, Arch discerned the tell-tale furtive wisps of yellow flame, licking their tongues around the cowling of the stricken Sopwith Strutter. He did not need reminding. Trusting to his observer to warn off the needling Tripes spitting out hot tracer on to his tail, Arch throttled back, abandoned the combat, and chased after Bickerton's dead machine as soon as he had settled himself. The Sopwith was slow-moving but flying relentlessly onward in a direct line. Short tusks of fire, accompanied by two escorts of dark smoke, balanced proportionately each side of the engine. Even the engine-sound was metallic and grating, as if the propeller was striking the edge of a grindstone at each revolution.

Arch needed no education in this: he had seen a 'flamer' close-to once before, when an inept beginner had crash-landed at flying-school, in front of them, lucklessly tipping over, and spilling the 80-octane. As metal struck metal, a single spark ignited the whole contraption. In the same second, there was a flash of heat and lightning, a horrific explosion, and spars, fuselage, tail and rudder billowed high up into the sky, with the buoyancy of a hot-air balloon, before smoke engulfed it all, and the debris came spattering down. As suddenly, out of the inferno, a shape, transfigured, saintly, arms wide in benediction, slowly floated towards them. Everything moved in half-time now, the apparition wrapped in a fireball of ecstasy, calling in slow, single gasps, quite clearly and precisely, hands and legs moving in a circular crawling manner, but not like a human image at all. An 'improver' called sharply: 'Put that man out!' And then people ran up with buckets, and threw sand on this twisting, slowly wriggling shape, surrounded by yellow fire-flames at the edges and smouldering. And, of course, he recalled the same figure later, capsized on the ground, stinking of burnt fur, and orderlies and tent-wallahs running up helplessly, unrolling canvas and leaking hoses.

And now, in the air, there was Bickerton, alone, about to blaze up in his fiery cockpit, the pilot, his deliverer, slumped dead on his stick (there was no doubt about it, Arch saw blood across the temples and ears), flying obstinately into clouds and distance. The pilot was better off. On either side of the nacelle, slow flames.

'Dear God in heaven,' Arch both prayed and swore at the same time, 'put that man out.'

The machines swung close together for a precious moment, and involuntarily Arch stretched out a futile arm. He could hear vaguely his own observer hysterical and screaming above the engines, and even sense the rapnel and the high explosive still trying to ignite him from the tail, but he had no eyes for that. Afterwards, he could not be sure – that Bickerton was just sitting there with his arms folded as the smoke rose, there was no doubt – but he *thought* he saw Bickerton's head turn towards him slightly and his lips seemed to mouth: 'I'm digging in.' It was possible: with Bick anything was possible. The yellow streamers were curling higher around now, and had a hold of the insensible pilot. It was a proper 'flamer'. From the ground the stricken machine would appear like a shooting star, transcended by a fearsome beauty. Arch felt the heat, and hardly dared approach his wing a foot closer for fear of exploding his own tank. Small stubby pieces of the Sopwith looked like breaking up, and sparking outwards like Catherine wheels. And Bickerton was sitting there, arms folded, somehow at his ease, and looking dead in front, mildly curious. Arch was more terrified of the sight of his friend bubbling in a 'flamer' than of the proximity of the two machines, or the risk he was awarding his rear-man. Besides, the hostiles had given up the pursuit. The two-seaters were alone in the sky, one of them ablaze. The Hun had blinded the eyes of the Sopwith and put the second man to the torch. Arch felt himself to be flying with the dead.

His instinct was to throttle back again – his paralysed brain began to clear – and follow behind and empty his Vickers gun straight into the holocaust; perhaps that would do the trick. But . . . murder your own man? How could he do that? Murder Bickerton? The Strutter flew ahead of him now, and Arch saw quite penetratingly the paint on the fuselage, the circles and emblems of identification, quiver and flake; larger particles of the struts and spars began to dart off dangerously close, the smoke-stack started to plume. In seconds, he knew well, the dragon would explode entirely, and engulf the wings, but would propel itself blindly, weightlessly on for minutes before the engine parted from the fuselage. Without a

447

further fraction's hesitation – the whole manoeuvre ha
taken thirty seconds, not even that – Arch pushed the
button on his instruments and kept his thumb forward
until he was satisfied that nothing lived aboard that
fire-flaming wreck, and with a sudden whirlwind and
grating explosion drowned it in its screaming yellow sea.
Bickerton was the best man he ever knew. And he had
murdered him as if he were the worst of his enemies. It
was the last time he mourned the death of a young friend.
After that, the deaths of soldiers were no more to him
than pages read at the end of a book, names on stones,
lists of ranks and initials on a memorial. They were
simply incidents of conclusion faithfully recorded for the
future, and nothing, *nothing* more. It was nothing to him
anyway, for by then he had ceased to live.

CHAPTER TWENTY-FIVE

Winter and Spring, 1917

1917 with its terrible April – the days of 'flying murder', as Major Medlicott spoke of them – passed, and with it the unrewarded summer, and the autumn and winter offensives. The German Second Army still held the line firm, and remained in possession along the salient. So the next spring brought none of its customary grace or renewal. In England the appearance of brown buds exploding into waves of frothy, dancing green, the dazzle of the poplars, the flowers turning gaudy in the London parks and squares were nothing but a mockery to the passers-by, nodding with brilliant contempt. April was bitter, May hateful. Spring came and went unobserved, unworshipped. The prevailing mood of despair created on the tributaries of the Somme and Meuse spread over the Channel to The Vestry and Pall Mall. Blinds concealed barely illuminated rooms in the stone clubs about St James's. The Cavalry Club, the Artillery Club, the Officers Club, were closed until nightfall. The Inns of Court Territorials were crippled around Vimy with the Canadians. The Jewish Brigade had suffered terrible casualties at the Windmill. Arch accompanied Conrad to a memorial service at the synagogue in Curzon Street. He saw elderly and well-dressed men rolling on the ground and ritualistically tearing their clothes; the shockingly youthful father, who bore aloft in his hand the last letter from his son, crying out in an utterly devastating and un-English way, 'I give my soul to God, and my youth to my country,' filled Arch with an unfamiliar misery as cold as stone. He respected this father, and his alien muddled grief, and longed to console him. Conrad sat on the step outside and patiently held a mother's hand for an hour, but nothing did any good any more. Even the seasons appeared to have lost their power to heal.

Two letters crossed. From the Château at Bellinglise, Chas wrote to his brother:

> Letters from home brought only bad news. Father-Sir mysteriously ill in bed with something the quack calls 'Bright's disease'. And dear old Grimp is dead, just two runs short of his century.

Arch wrote to Chas from Capité with the news of Bickerton's death in a flamer.

Chas wrote back consolingly, but seemed to have recaptured some of his old 'bottom'.

> Arch, dear old boy,
> Your observer, Bickerton, had the luxury of dying with his boots on, and I don't think you can ask for anything better than that, the way things are going. There aren't many good chaps left alive now, not in our mob there aren't. I wonder whether you remember one of those interminable old Irish songs Hooley used to regale us with, back at Brontë? It came somehow into my head, when you wrote me the rotten news. Poor little sod.

>> But Bickerton muttered sadly
>> As he loaded up his gun –
>> 'Oh, what a bloody pity
>> That the bugger had to run!'

> True, I've changed the words round a little – it was about the shooting match at Stringybark Creek – but it seems to fit the style of good old Bick and will do as well as anything for his epitaph. By the way, this is your big friendly brother speaking – who's standing in for your 'off-sider' now? A sharp-shooter, I hope. What bad luck about Grimp, though – he so wanted to see his hundred runs go up on the board, and he was just two years short of it. Father-Sir wrote me at the end he kept hearing old

songs in his head, the songs of his young days, and the odd thing is he began speaking again, just before he went under. 'I don't want to let the dear boys down, God bless them all,' were his last words, according to Father-Sir. Bless his golden heart. Well, back here at Mucky Farm, we're shoring up the First Australian Division, front-line-Charlies, and wet bloody through most of the time, but as the dug-outs up here seem to have made a first-class bollocks of everything, I suppose we'll be backing up the old foot mob 'til we're all blown to buggery. Still, 'such is life', as the great man said. All the luck of the Irish, roll on big ship.

Your loving brother,
CHAS

Grimp gone. Father-Sir ill. Chas up at Mucky Farm with the plucky remains of Anzac. Where were all his friends? Where was Harry Legge? Where was brother Arthur? Where was Port? *Wo bist Du* – where are you, Bickerton? What had become of Mysie? He had left a message for her at the stage door of the Hay, but it had been returned to the Carlyle, unopened, *Address unknown, correspondent enlisted overseas.* Would he ever see anybody ever again?

CHAPTER TWENTY-SIX

The Train Station, Abbeville

They did meet once again, as it happened, Mysie and Arch, during a lull on the Western Front, at the train station, Abbeville. The soldiers, the walking wounded, had never honoured the lonely platform with the title of 'railway station', because it was not one: no sentiment attached to it, no sign identified it, for instance, there was no waiting-room, no ticket-office, no small, neat garden beside, no porters, no milk-churns, it was merely a defined space on the military map, where trains pulled in, and where trains drew out. It had no town to provide for, no history of ever having been what the ordinary foot-soldier or cavalry-man would consider a 'railway'. Abbeville was an anonymous crossroads. Troop trains used it as a port-of-call to exchange the handicapped, the incurables, the infirm, the walking cot-cases.

Arch had driven there with Conrad, to see him safely on to one of the ambulance-wagons. Conrad's wound was a courageous one, high up on his left thigh, serious enough to cripple him, and give him a strange floating walk which he dismissed mockingly.

'Why not?' he used to say, without much trace of a smile. 'I'm a poet, why shouldn't I add a Byronic glide to my other less romantic aspects?'

Arch, walking alongside him, offered practical sympathetic reassurance. It was purposeless, this bitterness. The bullet had severed his riding muscle, it was true, but the wound got him out of the front line and away from the salient, where odds were narrowing every hour. A sharp-shooter from the trenches did it.

It's a hell of a hoof for me, Gendron, from now on, I'm afraid,' he apologized.

'It doesn't hurt you too bad, old fellow, does it?'

'Well, it slows me down rather,' was Conrad's main grievance, and he leaned heavily on his walking-stick, taking the weight off for a moment. It could still pain him at intervals, in the damp, exposed air. In his basket chair at the field-station he had queried: 'A good year's worth of wound there; no more hunting now, I suppose?'

The surgeon's face wrinkled in reply, and looked at the younger man's apprehensive brown eyes; eyes now weakened by disappointment, and cruel physical disfigurement.

'Not with that leg, no, well, not for a season or so. More a question of sitting in front of the fire, taking the weight off, you know. But it'll pick up in time, you've got a jammy one.'

'You don't know me, doc, I'll soon be out on a horse's back, laying on hounds.'

'Good man,' answered the doctor, patting his shoulder, 'that's the spirit. Just keep on with the writing – and, by the way, try not to be too much of a weary Willie. Our chaps at the front want cheering up.'

And now they sat, the two close friends, in a cold spring breeze, on a bare platform at Abbeville. How long ago that morning down by the sea at Roman Landing seemed. Arch remembered his friend standing looking at the broken water as motionless as a heron. And Port was gone now, he appeared just to vanish somehow, leading his men into a wood at Ovilliers. His motto above the stone fireplace – '*Jour de ma Vie*'. The wind whipped up the bleak stalks of a forlorn cabbage crop in front of them, on the opposite side of the solitary track, as if across the tops of waves, bringing in its wake a smell both fresh and rotten. It was such a bare, comfortless platform, a cul-de-sac. In times of advance and build-up, battalions of dazed recruits were unloosed in a helpless and disorganized way on the siding and left to march their own

strength up the lines. Arch had witnessed once the arri
of a wagonload of Chinese coolies in pouring rain one
November morning when he had driven some badly
burned flying officers to the railway. The drab platform
was only distinguished by the dip at the western end of it,
in order that field-wagons could back their tail-boards
directly on to the awaiting rolling-stock, and shunt the
casualties on their stretchers into the train trestles.
Engines came and went, warning of their approach with
gloomy whistles. Even their arrival appeared hesitant and
stubborn, edging themselves uncomfortably backwards
on to the buffers, with jerks and ricochets. Their departure was equally tentative, as if to say, 'Come back, come
back.' The men waiting were cases of shell-burst, almost
all of them strangely silent and appalled. Both Conrad
and Arch were well used to such things by now. Some of
them held a hand to a part of their head, gently, as if to
ease the weight of it, all of them were very still, and
absorbed in themselves, pale and listless particularly,
motionless, unspeaking; one sat on the edge of a bench
weeping soundlessly to himself. The VADs ushered them
forward and back, attentive, like mothers. The shell-burst
cases appeared like a ward of the deaf and the dumb,
vacant, smiling, wordless. They looked bloodless and
dirty-faced, overshadowed by grey-bearded terror.

'Cracked up over there,' said Conrad. 'Poor brutes.'

This day, Captain Gendron said nothing, but watched
them choose their places in the empty carriages; for a
moment, in their stillness and slowness, the men's aching
progress reminded him of the huge black oxen at Belgodère. Sluggish to the point of death. Dirty, dirty.

'Those men along there,' muttered Conrad, 'on that
platform are not walking wounded. They're cursed –
cursed by God.'

The carriage, to which Arch assisted his friend, was
occupied already by two blind subalterns from the Royal
Horse Artillery, and their nurses; further down the
platform a fleet of field ambulances was bringing in a

...chment of fresh casualties from an advanced dressing-station, and orderlies ran to and fro calling out raucously. Some flap on, presumably. Arch was able to decipher from their cries there had been a panic up the line in the direction of Fricourt, the collapse of some show or other in the swamps, and the train's departure was to be held. The officers, their faces heavily bandaged, presented two distinct and contrasted characters, one grave, the other cheerful, one taciturn and dulled, the other talkative, even sprightly. The silent one had his entire head swathed in a turban to bind in the back of his brain. Each of them smoked once the smiling VAD had lit cigarettes for them and guided them between their lips. Arch pulled out his Sweet Aftons, and shared them with Conrad, leaving him the rest of the packet for the journey, tucking it in his top pocket.

'Well, thanks for those, some comfort anyway.'

'Promise me you'll write to let me know where I can find you, old fellow, and I'll visit you as soon as I can.'

'Oh, don't you worry about me, Gendron,' said Conrad, stretching his bad leg out in front of him to ease it, 'I'm in the pink. A-One at Lloyds.'

Friends that they were, Conrad addressed Arch always by his surname.

'When I'm back on square one, I'll be upright enough to volunteer for a wooden-top outfit,' his disparaging word for the Guards.

'How are you boys getting on?' asked Arch, hoisting Conrad's heavy angular kitbag on to the baggage-rack. It was full to the brim with his poetry-books with sharp edges – 'better that than bull-shit webbing' was Conrad's comment.

'Getting on famously,' came the reply from the cheerful head-case, as Arch leaned forward and read on the surgeon's ticket: 'Shot through the eyes. Blind.' They were on their way from the dressing-station to a permanent hospital twenty kilometres in the rear. The two Red Cross nurses smiled enthusiastically and Arch thought

again how much they resembled young mothers retur.
with their boys to boarding-school. An orderly brough
round hot tea in a bucket. Conrad declined. Arch shook
his head, pointing to the head-cases.

'Hot tea, gents? Any customers?' And the nurse handed
the cups around.

'Thank you, sister,' answered the cheerful head-case
courteously. They were always so grateful, these dying
men, thanking the nurses and the surgeons for their
wounds and handicaps with their last breath. 'God bless
you, sister. Thank you. Thank you.'

'One half of his brain came off in the bandages,'
whispered the sister, indicating the quiet one muffled in
white cotton, 'he can't speak.' And she turned back to the
head-cases, bending over them to talk in a childlike way.
Days after the battle in the swamp, the pale grey mud still
flaked on their stained khaki battledresses. They were
veterans of the celebrated Dirty Half-Hundreds. Fought
to a standstill at Fricourt, most of them suffocated in the
mud. Trenches were sandbagged with their bodies.

Conrad wanted to move out to the corridor; he was not
comfortable with the two head-cases, so they leant
against the door in privacy, facing out at the cabbage field
which ran the length of Abbeville siding. They drew on
their Aftons without talking.

'So damned polite all the time, these corpse-fatigues,'
Conrad said at last. He was disgusted by almost everything now, and needed to restore his nerves. The head-
cases, the wounded, the gassed, the shocked, grated on
him, the mutilated shapes in discoloured khaki ending in
bandages where an arm or leg was cut away; he had
reached the end, he was worked-off, or nearly.

'It's an old war, Gendron, and I'm glad I've come to the
end of it. I feel whipped-out.'

It was true, there was a whiff of something about him,
something familiar, Arch thought. Still, he spoke out:
'I'm convinced you'll be riding to hounds when the new
season starts.' He looked away from the cabbage-soil,

into Conrad's kind brown eyes: 'You see. A few months taking things easy in Nineveh, and it'll be hounds running and checking, much as usual.'

'I doubt it,' Conrad answered, 'I imagine it will have to be shooting from now on – not that I ever got much fun out of bashing away at birds all day long.' He thought of pheasants whirring out of the camouflage in the copse at the angle of Paulton's Eleven, and crashing through the branches. 'Banging away mindlessly at hundreds of grouse.' He smiled at the memory of an American hostess's affectation, insisting on pronouncing the word to rhyme with 'mousse'. 'I suppose it'll be nice to get back to Old Nineveh again,' he smiled. And, after a silence: 'Well, I don't know. Riding to me, remember, is pretty well like sky-flying to you.'

Conrad always used to talk of sky-flying, it was his manner. The last of the medics settled their stretcher-cases in the forward carriages, and to the accompaniment of the habitual shouting (back to basic training at Vange, he thought) train doors slammed noisily. They chucked their half-smoked Aftons out of the window in unison. Arch descended from the corridor and stood at the awkward gap between two carriages, and let the engine gain a short head of steam. It needed a stubborn run at it, to get the slightest momentum, gathered strength, juddered all down the rolling-stock, and then started again, very slowly, to move off. It was like an old man winding himself up to get out of his armchair. The officer in his worn and scratched leather coat half-opened the door of the carriage.

'God bless you, Conrad, old fellow,' said Arch, 'never say die.'

'Look sharp, that officer,' yelled the officious pale-haired medic.

'Fuck it on, old chap,' Conrad winked, and shouted out after him: 'Fuck it on, Arch!' It was the only time he recalled Conrad using his familiar name.

The train sailed out like a dreadful ship with an

accursed crew. The two seasons were at war, half-spring and half-winter. A dull and cold mist crossed the cabbage-field, like a sudden sea-fret, but they were a hundred miles from the sea. Watching a crow-scarer in the centre of the coarse-smelling vegetable plantation reminded Arch of Gorgonus as a young boy, ordered to stand there in the wind: what on earth would Gorgonus be doing now? he wondered. Squatting on his haunches, purring, clucking, and throwing pebbles at the goats. And Hortense? What might she be doing? Carrying water, stone-picking. They'd all be working on something at this hour at Belgodère. How everything reminded him of somewhere else, by now. A lark scaled in the furrow. Guns far, so far off, rolled against the shore with their listless reverber-ation, an unceasing, maddening sound. He was reminded of the combers on the shingle when he first saw Conrad at Roman Landing. A civilization ago. The smoke from the small, stubby engine-stack mingled, as it receded, with the faint mist around the platform. With nothing further to do, Arch watched the train disappear altogether. For once, he was reluctant to return to the airfield, and wondered whether he might visit a behind-the-lines *estaminet* to eat something before making his way, when he felt a gentle hand press against his sleeve. Turning, he saw the short figure of a nurse in front of him. The uniform seemed at first to disguise her.

'Dazzle.' Her voice was timid, there was no surprise in it.

'Mysie? You.' He was pleased to see her, but found no words to say.

'Hello, Dazzle.'

The soughing of the guns floated between them; they might have been standing within earshot of the sea.

'I thought I saw you earlier from the far end of the platform when you were with that officer. You didn't see me – we were helping to move the blind soldiers.'

'I didn't recognize you in your uniform. It is Mysie, isn't it?'

'A different Mysie, but yes, it is me.' And she held out both her hands.

'Little Mysie. So it is. Let's sit down over there, it's the only place,' and he guided her to a handcart which had recently been used to carry the worst of the stretcher-cases. Arch threw off his overcoat and set it down on the cart so that she might not stain her uniform; she seemed so white and blurred in her clothes, but on closer inspection he observed that even her apron was smirched with rusty blood and her head-scarf stained as well. She did not look the colour of her years. There was a little hand-sewn brown cardigan she wore over her uniform, for warmth's sake.

'Do you have a little time, before you go back? A few minutes, perhaps,' she asked anxiously. 'I'm out-of-hours here for a little while. There's another train-load to help out in a while or so, but nothing for a bit. Let's stay and talk, for a moment anyway.'

'Of course, Mysie. There's so much to talk about . . . Tell me what you're doing here, in Flanders? And have you left the theatre? And what about Flee? How's Apples? And old Fenge? And how's your Ma?'

The questions poured out of him. Of course there was confusion, though no bitterness, even though this was the moment of confrontation he had waited for, longed for, and even rehearsed in his thoughts over again. But now they were sitting there, like two young married people beside the beach with foreign gunfire far off. A reassuring sound from a long distance away. She had altered so much, though. There was still that mysterious haze in her eyes, and the two faint nicks quite clearly there, one above the cheekbone, one near the lip; but that 'culprit' look had gone, that marvellous expression of a child about to be found out. Gone also was that breathlessness he had cherished before, when her words tumbled and slithered in front of one another, like a youngster stumbling down a slippery slope, laughing and muddling things at the same time; and, in their place, a hesitant,

almost a studious, precision, a graver beauty. Her ha[...]
lay open peacefully in her lap.

She explained how Chancellor had taken his little
troupe on tour around the countryside, and that Wilbraham, the 'sickie', and Flee too had followed him, but after
a few months she had felt dissatisfied, and with some of
the other girls had decided to volunteer as nurses in the
field. The training part of it, in a large London hospital,
even with the late hours, and scrubbing out, and iron
discipline, bottles and bedpans, had been a kind of fun.
There wasn't a moment, she said, you could bless yourself
with. But transfer to the service hospital had been a
nightmare of hell. Both she and her girlfriend Flee had
volunteered first to nurse the French, as there had been a
greater demand among the Allies than in the English
regiments, which were better supplied. As soon as she and
her fellow-nurses arrived, they were pressed into emergency service.

'It began in the ambulance trains; they were so full,
men everywhere, in the corridors, in the lavatories, on the
baggage racks, under the seats, in the guard's van, sitting,
lying propped up against doors, stacked alongside one
another, some already dead, almost all of them dying,
crammed together in rows between the carriages, on the
joins, and shrieking out as the wheels jerked over the
points. And, what was worse, as the trains drew in, and
arrived at hospital-sidings, more wounded got on, none
were ever taken off, there had been some terrible strafing
up the line, and all the time more and more of these poor
casualties were handed along, some on the shoulders of
orderlies, and slid straight off the stretchers through the
windows. The lesser wounded, and they were few enough
– but those who could – sometimes hung on the outside
of the windows, or clutched the bars on the outer side of
the door and travelled that way. Anything to get away
from the front. And some fell on to the tracks, and rolled
down the embankments and lay there for ever.'

'And when you arrived at the advance field stations?'

things were a little better. But not much. At least the shaking and jerking stopped. There was just no end to the men. When the train did halt at a station, everybody flopped out on to the platform, and lay there gasping for air, and water, and coffee, anything, calling out for it, even the stomach wounds, and then we had to lift them all back again to continue to the next station. The Red Cross volunteers did their best, and of course there were lots of civilians helping, but Flee and I couldn't understand anything, and the men here, well, when they did speak something, we couldn't understand it, not with our stage-French, they were all talking in their jargon or dialect, they were all poor peasants, no officers, and they were trying to ask us to help them, to *help* them, to ease their pain, to move their broken legs, to lift their crushed bodies, to bind in their brains, to drug them, water them, clean them, wipe them, cradle them. The Red Cross put us in an old high school, and the wards were the empty classrooms.'

She hesitated for a moment, cleared her throat and went on.

'And, in the hospital beds, we had no room there, they were lying on the floor, in the corridors, you couldn't even find a lavatory, we put them in head to toe, two to a bed, sometimes three, and the smell, the green, sick smell of gangrene where the surgeons struggled to keep up, but they couldn't keep up. How could they? They were operating in their sleep, standing up. And, of course, it was winter when we first arrived and no heating, no wood, no coal, the gas was half-frozen and only a tiny little spike of gas came through, and so we were grateful enough to sleep on the straw, and huddle together whenever we could. I hated that terrible, terrible school. If there had been wood, or a little pail of coal each evening, if we could have kept them warm, lit a fire for them, given them a hot drink, covered them in blankets, we could have saved some of them, just one or two perhaps, but there was nothing. Nothing whatever we

461

could do for them. There was one basin for the wh…
ward, and one awful pail, the surgeons used it for swabs,
so we couldn't even wash them. Not even when they were
drenched in "the whites". And the army blankets already
there were covered in filthy blood, and suppurations, and
lice, and soldiers' sick, and dressings, and we couldn't
even clean them: but just to heap one of those vile, filthy,
sodden blankets on top of them, to cover their heads, or
their gangrenous wounds, was comfort enough. Perhaps
they just wanted to hide. They were ashamed of their
pain, and their filthy wounds – they were like lepers,
unclean . . . And do you know something else, though,
worst of all . . . Never once in all that time did a single
voice rise up in anger or rage.'

Her hand inside his was cold and hard and lifeless, like
a file.

'They didn't even complain. Not of cold, of thirst, of
pain, of agony. But always it was "Thank you, Missie,
I'm sorry to ask you, do you think you could move me,
would it be too much trouble to give me a piqure, do you
mind changing this saturated bandage, when you next
return could you ease my bedsores", docile as a whipped
dog, "thank you for folding my shattered arms, *thank*
you for turning me away from my shrapnel-filled back,
thank you, sweet sister, for bandaging my blindness, for
holding in my brains, thank you, Missie, for helping me
to die . . ." Oh, Dazzle, Dazzle, how could these things
be . . .? Never once a word of anger, or revenge. But,
"Sister, help me to die" – the French priests were good –
they were peasants as well – "Father, help me die, pray
for me to die . . ." – "I'm here, my son, I'm here, your
father is here, praying for you . . ." – "I want to die,
Father, please God, let me die . . ."'

And she curled her face into his shoulder, her tears
soaking his chin, and tickling his neck, at first warm, and
then cold. He felt them under his shirt. Mysie had not
wept like this for months. She could not go on. Like an
ineffectual priest, Arch felt he could only *listen* to her

462

outpouring of confession, there was nothing he could think of to console her, and little he could usefully say. He let her rush along headlong, it was best for her. He tried to warm her hand in his own – to transfuse her cold blood with a small part of his own warmth.

'That was the only good thing, when they died, and all that terrible pain came to an end for them. Their stiffened bodies were a relief. That dreadful schoolhouse is printed on my brain, not as a hospital for the wounded, but a torture house of unending and unrelieved pain. I have seen men, before they died, go raving mad with pain. Mad.'

'But something you did, Mysie, of course you did: I've seen those hospitals too, I've seen my brother Chas knocked up with shell-burst, and Conrad this afternoon, in a ward of people, their legs and arms all smashed up, their faces shot, or a whiff of gas in their lungs. He's in a train now with a couple of blindies – one's got his brains hanging out. But those nurses are like angels, for God's sake, and they do save lives, they *do*.'

She spoke softly, and calmly, the tears still splashing regularly on to his hands.

'It was a second battle for us. Sometimes, yes, sometimes I suppose, we managed. Doing the little thing, perhaps, at the right moment. Trying not to leave those things not done, piqures, medicines, bandages, hot water bottles when we could dredge up some hot water.'

He thought of the row of silent shell-stunned troopers he had just seen, scuffing with their heels on the grit. Of their stillness, how *still* they were, preparing themselves quietly for the end of a great event. And that look of 'dirt' in their skin, which was not the good dirt of soil, or gunsmoke, but of death itself. The dirt of 'working off', the bloodless, grey-blotched, green-pussed appearance. An unwashed rotting look. Cursed, as Conrad said, by God. And smelling of black.

Her furious storm subsided a little, rather in the way of a child crying itself finally to sleep.

'And were you in that schoolhouse for a long time: was trying to recall which battle it had been. Aroun(Verdun, he assumed, where he heard the Frenchies had been punished so terribly. He had been told vaguely of mutinies, in the area of Devil's Wood and Fricourt.

'It seemed to go on for ever. It was all battle, battle, battle. We took the shifts in turns of four. Four by day. Four by night. And when the casualties came in, and things got too much for the night shift, the other girls would get up and dress and help on, so sometimes we'd do thirty-six hours non-stop. We fought the battle all over again, in the ward, patching up, amputating, bleeding. The guns carried on in the salient all night long, night after night, like a thunderstorm – it made your head throb – and the stretchers kept coming in, just when you got through one batch then the next lot would come in. And the next after that. We were so exhausted nothing mattered. I can't believe we were much use: just ghosts really, cutting bandages, washing dressings, sterilizing and, worst of all, cutting through uniforms which were stitched into the wounds by the shrapnel and splinters. Patches and buttons and lanyards through a man's arms once. Some idiot or other told us to try to save the uniforms, as there was a shortage of materials, but to hell with it . . .'

'Good for you, Mysie . . .'

'Oh, there were dozens of foolish orders, but we never paid any attention. One night we had a great tough peasant boy who'd tried to shoot himself through the mouth, God knows how or why, he was tough enough – and he came in with his brains all matted up in his hair, and the bullet stuck in his head some place. And the chief medic was commanded to operate on him, to draw out the bullet, and we propped him up so the sentries could put him on trial, and shoot him properly through the head a week later. He used to tear off his head-dressings at nights so he'd bleed out – and next day we'd have to bandage him up again. Some sort of example for everybody, the major said. Otherwise there would be an epidemic of "self-inflicted"

464

ning through the entire Western Front. One of the generals addressed us all: a contagious disease, suicide. Can you imagine such a thing, men who are so afraid of being killed, they would rather kill themselves, and fire a bullet through their head with their big toe. Imagine it. All those things. It was all so pitiful. Wasted, filthy, pitiful.'

'Did you stick it out for long?'

'Yes, I stuck it out. For a very long time. And so did Flee. She never budged. Not her. What! Until we were as filthy and lice-ridden and exhausted and as starved as the men were. As pitiful too. But not in pain, like they were. Then they took us out of the wards. For a bit anyway.'

'Thank God for it.'

'Yes, I do thank him. I don't think, now, anything is as terrible as their pain.'

Her eyes were clear now and dry, behind their haze, and the tears on her cheek had dried also. For the first time, she could look at the face of somebody she loved. At first, she thought, he's changed, oh! he's aged, his hair's dusty and lifeless. There was a yellow tinge to the colour of his eyeball, and a dark smudge beneath; his ugly bitten fingers and grey skin shocked her, she recalled only too perfectly the black-brown eyes before, those eyes of a dark man in a fair face, surrounded by such a glorious flop of hair. He reached out very, very gently, for fear of frightening her, and just spread the inside of his fingers over her wrist. She, just as gently, turned her hand, so that the two palms lay together, touching, but not clasping; breathing, but not holding; together, but not entwined.

She had altered too, they had both altered for the bad. On the station platform: that marvellous rascal look was quite lost, and her hair greasy and twisted, hair that had been so soft and floating and fair like a baby's under water. The child had gone from her.

'Why, Mysie?' He had not meant to mention it, but had already done so.

She thought for a long time, and in obedience, beh⟨ ⟩
the lines, the guns stopped. The strafing was over. Th⟨ ⟩
barrage had lifted for the day.

'Why? Well, it wasn't Chancellor, of course.'

'I suppose I guessed that.'

'It wasn't poor Wilbraham either.'

'No, that I knew.'

'You knew?'

'It makes no sense, Mysie, none of it. How could you
have fallen out of love so fast as that? Even still, it makes
no sense.'

'I never fell out of love, dearest . . .' Mysie looked up
the line. She thought for a moment, and when she
answered spoke unhesitatingly. 'I was so much in love
with you, I didn't ever know what love was. You know
that wasn't it. There I've said it now. I don't suppose
either of us wanted to talk about it much, but . . .'

'Then why?'

Mysie cast a look along the empty platform and saw,
far beyond it, the tell-tale smudge of smoke of the next
ambulance train arriving.

'We haven't so very much time left together.'

The drivers and orderlies, hanging about, drew on the
remnants of their cigarettes with a greater ardour. Mysie
enclosed his hand between both of hers, and pressed her
cold lips to it.

'You see, I wanted you so much, my happiest moment,
my only happiness was to give myself to you – not just to
kiss you, or be caressed, or feel you, or be undressed by
you, but just give my body to you entirely and deeply
until there was no part of me spared for myself.'

'Why?' he repeated. She would not answer. 'You owe
me that, Mysie. *Please*. Why?'

'It was a kind of death, the worst kind of death;
because you wake up, and nothing has changed, and you
feel such a dreadful loss, that absence just before waking
up, it's like a pain: you long, oh, how you long for
everything to be different, but absolutely nothing ever is

466

rent, although day follows day, and night follows
ght. All exactly the same, unchanged . . .'

'Why didn't you come back then? The smallest word
would have been enough . . . the smallest sign.'

'I don't know why. I suppose I never did love you. Not
properly. Oh, Dazzle, my dear, I wanted you, and I
missed you when you weren't next to me, and above all I
longed for you when you weren't making love to me. But
I didn't really and truly love you. There was something so
implacable about you. Your eyes, for no reason, would
go all dead, even then – and I would feel so shut out . . .'

'You never said anything to me, Mysie, you might have
done . . .'

'I know. I just never said. And you never knew how
shut out I felt. I wanted to invade your thoughts, just as
you invaded every part of me until there was nothing left
that wasn't laid waste and flattened. You were not a man
to me, but a hero. A conqueror. You were my lover, and
my murderer. All I could do was escape. I never left you,
dearest of my heart: I fled.'

There was nothing Arch could say, besides he no more
understood what Mysie was trying to explain than he
could attempt to make sense of Conrad's poetry. It made
no sense, in any case. So he remained silent, and replaced
his hands on his lap.

'I'm trying to, but I cannot understand . . .'

'You had to *suffer*, Dazzle. And you had to find out,
above all, how much you had the power to make other
people suffer.'

The ambulance train wailed up the line. Empty rolling-
stock coming in to be filled.

Waiting for trains, he remembered. Once, ages ago,
they had spent together a happy forty-eight-hour rest at a
Bath hotel, and changed trains at Bristol Docks – and, the
next morning, they had waited together for a connection
in the chilly refreshment room on the platform and she
had been so busy looking at him, and stroking and kissing
and reassuring him, his train had steamed in empty to the

467

terminus, waited for ten minutes, filled up with pass
gers and mail and cold water, and steamed out again
while they just sat there transfixed. He wondered, simply
speaking aloud his thoughts:

'It's funny – I feel it too. This getting old thing. But I
can't explain it. I wish Conrad was here – he might do
something to put a finger on it, he has a way with words.
Before, I used to think there were children, and old people
and, in between, *us* with everything. The young. We did
everything, paid for everything, built everything, enjoyed
everything. And I suppose I thought that was how it
would go on. For ever. We'd get to be twenty-three or
twenty-four, and stop at that, not growing any older. But
after all, perhaps being young is just for one year, and
perhaps it is behind us already. One single, living year.'

'Life is only the morning, Dazzle, for the likes of you
and me.'

The rest was lost in a clamour of wheels, piston-rods,
orderlies and sergeant-majors. Another section of the line
had crumbled against the push. This time, a bell rattled
coarsely down the line, and the rails in front of them
hummed. The ambulance train was about to come in: the
orderlies trod out their cigarettes. A tremor of ghastly
preparation shivered over the platform. Two hardened
stretcher-bearers grinned as they passed on the trot:
'Make way for the sickies,' and, without meaning it, Arch
grinned weakly back at them.

'Hurry along, Bingham – your detachment is coming
in,' called out an officious matron, her cowl and pointed
wings flapping in a breeze of authority. Mysie stood, and
in her starch, tiny though she was, towered above him,
Arch had grown so thin and slumped. She spoke with the
formality of a novice repeating her catechism, one hand
clasped in the other. There was so little time left, she
knew; and she stood before him, serious and pale, like a
schoolmistress.

'It's not true, Dazzle, none of it. Everything that I said

468

ore. I shall never know why I deserted you. Perhaps I was afraid – I was always fearful, even as a girl, and I still am. Perhaps I couldn't bear to see you changed – disfigured, maimed, cut, pierced, torn, the way I see these boys – not you – I couldn't bear it. But you were always the only man I ever loved – I'll never love anybody so much again. Not like that. It would kill me to love again like that.'

And a look of such indescribable sadness came over her face, almost like terror, it tore his heart out by the roots.

'Corpse-fatigues, stand by,' yelled a medic-corporal, as the train approached.

There returned to Arch, quite spontaneously, the memory of an April night, it must have been a hundred years ago, and a cabmen's shelter, and the reflection of spray-blossom overhead in a haze of gas-light, and a smell of cab-leather, pot-pourri, and infinite spring. ''Ere, guv' – either kiss the girl or don't kiss 'er – I've got me flars to load up . . .' Then the rattle of spoked wheels through a London park. 'All my poor love,' he thought, 'adieu, adieu, adieu.' The jarvey in a distant spring.

The steam from the rolling-stock consumed her, and for one second Mysie's slight figure with her silken hair stood as a ghost on the platform, reserved, upright in her starched uniform, and then she disappeared. As fugitive as ever. From the mysterious sea-fret, a harsh command: 'Hurry along now, Bingham – look sharp – there are no more trains to Plugstreet,' and she was gone, and then the train was gone.

Hurry along – look sharp . . .

At first he would have sworn Mysie was standing there still, wrapped in her brown cardigan. Then, for a prolonged minute as the transport left, Arch felt one thrilling sensation of liberty, and delight. A glimpse of freedom he had never felt before. But, as the smoke dispersed along the length of the platform, with the noise of the iron wheels complaining over the rails, and that familiar scent left behind (as evocative to him as castor oil and new-mown

469

grass) of cinders and anthracite in the back of his thr[...]
he felt all his poor love rise up inside him. All the love i[n]
the world he had ever felt, all he could feel, accumulated
and there was nowhere for it to flow; and, as his eyes
blurred, the dreary platform swayed before him, and he
felt a succession of dreadful cold and hot sweats. Arch
was so weak, he had to sit, and the weight of his tears
shook his entire body as he sank back on the cart, head to
the sky, crying his eyes out. Dear God in heaven – all of
his love was departing on that train, and he would never
see Mysie again. Not ever, ever, ever, ever. He felt as cold
and dead as Bickerton. All his happiness fled with her,
and the wagon-load of walking dead and, in a vision (but
so transparent he could almost hear himself speak to
them), one by one, there came a roll-call of all the young
men he had known, laughed and fought with, and loved
and murdered. It was a fearful epiphany of Death.

'Jerker' James, in his first half-hour at Mons, smashed up
in training, Merrell on instruction-course, Lord Lucas
also killed. Little Tangent crashed (engine failure over
Festubert), archied at 5,000 feet, Captains Woodley and
Skilbeck, bosom-buddies at Peckwater, both in Herbies,
punctured by shrapnel at 12,000 feet. His pal, Sisley,
from basic training as long ago as Inns of Court, emascu-
lated, shooting up the trenches, poor old Porky and
'Chalk' White, buried the same day. Great-Williams
disappeared, no one knows where, in fluff above Lilliers,
'Shine' Smith, a bullet clear through his head at 9,000
feet, 'a beautiful death', Tom Weekes, Hen King and Bill
Otter, with their observers, the first days of April 1917,
all from the dear old 10th, a bad week for two-seaters.
The colonials he had known, and played tennis doubles
with at Capité, Dampier and Barr, tangled wings above
Béthune and went down like hell. That week, they buried
poor little Crow (in bloody April) after he pancaked on
his own bomb. Even Arch's Little Brighton pal, Ogg the
inventor ('the Ogg Special') lied his rotten health into the

al Ulsters and fell down at the first rush 'over the bags' on the Somme. Likewise their German chauffeur, Goerstler, at Greasy Farm. Harry Legge years ago in no man's land, just earth's goodness now; Bickerton, perhaps the bravest of them all, his old pal, Bick of Belgodère, the lover of La Grosse, inventor of the lethal twin-Vickers, shot down in a flamer in his goatskins, nobody knows where. Apple Crumbleby disappeared one day in a single burst above Corbeau. Chute mortelle. Laidlaw drove into the ground on a dead-stick landing. 'Shaky' Drakey died at Mons, Chesney caught a whiff of gas with the Fighting Half-Hundreds. At Ovilliers Arthur Portarlington, leading from in front, was struck in the mouth by shell-splinters. Pride of the 'wooden-tops', his staff-sergeant caught him going a second time over the top to retrieve his pince-nez. Tusky Powell and the McKenzie boys, missing somewhere in Shrapnell Valley. And of his school chums from Brighton Grammar – the home side, the Old Timers bicycle team, the nets bowlers against the Trumble brothers, the elegant, bright dancers of Brontë, that line of chaps with long legs either side the saddle, slumped over their horses' necks (more grooms than officers, the adjutant said), slouch-hats pulled down over their brows – of all those boys whose sacred sepia likeness Arch held constantly tucked between the pages of a love-letter from Mysie, not one left alive. Their names, irrelevant now. All worked off with the 1st Australian Light Horse in the assault on Lone Pine. 'Up the hill' their war-cry. Up the hill. Not a single man, of all his radiant schoolfriends, left alive.

And that was his last meeting with Mysie. At the train station, Abbeville. Roll on, big ship.

471

CHAPTER TWENTY-SEVEN

A Funeral in the Forest

All Conrad ever asked for was a poor man's pagan burial, somewhere near where he had spent his hunting holidays, in the loneliness of the countryside; in attendance, perhaps, a few dear friends. And of course, in those bitter days before the final build-up to the *Kaiserschlacht* of 1918, a pagan burial was precisely what he did not receive. Arch felt that he had somehow betrayed his great friend's trust, but he could hardly be blamed. He was not family, or county, and never aspired to that 'closed circle' in which Conrad's people moved – after all, he thought, if something rotten happened to work off Chas, himself, or brother Arthur, he was fairly certain Father-Sir would have something to say if a whole crowd of beery officers turned up and ordered things around, even if they had marched through hell together. At least Conrad was assured of quietness, and Arch attended the simple country funeral in the plain Victorian church of St Cuthman, which stood by itself in a clearing in the Forest.

Anticipating the terrible eventuality in his typical and straightforward way, Conrad had left Arch some scribbled instructions as to the sort of affair he would have liked:

> perhaps a reading of one or two of my favourite pieces, the sort of thing I've had in the old top-pocket, you know, Arch, what I mean, Tichbourne's elegy, Nun Appleton, Edward's short poem about the dead ploughboy. Drummer Hodge, of course. *That* particularly. And ask Honeywood or Ives to Blow for Home. My own days

carrying the horn for the Ancient Southdown seem golden to me now I remember them – that was the best bit of huntable ground in the south of England. Didn't someone say once, remembering happiness is better than happiness itself? Something like that. Anyway, that's what I think, dear old chap, writing to you not very optimistically from a cot, in, I don't know, some bloody place, my head's not too great this morning. If it turns out for the worst, and it might, I suppose somebody better tell Chevalier and poor old Ascapard, how Lordy got a bullet in the face. It'll probably have to be you, Arch, volunteering for corpse-fatigues again. The odd thing is, until this splinter business cropped up, I always thought I was a true duration-man – but if I am to wash away – and I don't want to be permanently "on the stick" like Siberry and Midge Jones – just a – *above everything else* – non C of E lament, without a whole lot of smells and bells, but something *decent*, and *short*, and *pagan*. Dump me in a neat hole in the open air somewhere forest-side around Iping, and if there is a last wish at all . . .

Arch had spoken to the family rector, who seemed decent enough, and he agreed to perform Conrad's last request.

It had always been Conrad's intention, long before he had even said it privately (and without his nose down a brandy bottle) to Arch at the Carlyle Club one night, 'to end up terribly neat and tidy', which was his own way of speaking of his death. Out in the front line preferably, using slang he had learnt from one of Arch's Anzac chums, 'up the digger', and not to let down his men. But, ironically, far from neat and tidy, the whole thing ended up in a mess, with a botched-up scratch turning ugly, and the shell-splinter which seemed so inoffensive at the start (why would he refuse to have it dressed? – there and then? – at the field station? – because he insisted on getting the patrol back to Plugstreet – that was the death of him) turned black and gangrenous, and then –

although nursed and bathed and cooled among the sheets in the great house at Old Nineveh – he began t spit white broth, as if in convulsions over a former attack of stink; the village locum swore it was harking back to that time he got a whiff of gas. His lungs were lined with it, the quack confirmed. His last words to the nurse, holding her in his tight grip, shouting in her face every filthy obscenity he knew – 'Back like hell, boys! Back like hell . . . !' And then just rolling over into a dead faint: 'I don't care a bugger – but so long as my boys don't get killed.'

The very next morning Canon Dodimead drove over from Brockenhurst, with his little box containing the sacred phials and funeral-bands. Bending over the wooden cot, where Conrad lay, by now quiet and at his ease: 'Would you like to make your final confession?' he murmured.

'*NO*. No, thank you.'

Canon Dodimead tried again and, kneeling, spoke in his dove-like tones:

'Would you accept the last sacraments, and the absolution of sin? The reconciliation of God, and his Church?'

But Conrad, for all his exhaustion of the spirit, was quite lucid, and spoke with an unerring politeness, and loudly too.

'No. Thank you. No.'

So the thwarted canon had no option but to rise from his knees, pack up his sacramental clobber and withdraw, his errand of absolution unfulfilled.

And so, there was Arch, the only service officer in uniform, sitting by himself in the last pew. He felt the damp rise up from the flagstones under his riding-boots. The church was half-empty – all funerals these days were poorly attended – but he was grateful to see a healthy proportion of local tenants from the Nineveh estate, and people who worked in the big house itself. At least *he* would have liked that. Cramped uncomfortably between the furs and veils of the Southdown gentry, he saw also the red raw faces and sometimes hands of the hunt ants, Nim Ives and Billy, wearing with a peculiar respect their bottle-green livery, and Cornet Honeywood, the Master, carrying Conrad's whip and hunting-horn. These must be the local buck-hounds, ridden over all that way to be in at the 'death' in a way. Craning round, he looked anxiously for a sight of Captain Chevalier. But he did see, in an empty pew ahead of him, the slumped figure of a short-backed, rather plebeian man, with a balding head, and a taller woman beside him covered in veils and nets, and recognized from the *Illustrated News* the poet Hardy, looking full of misery, and defeated in his place. Sorley was there too, and the young Grenfell boy, and von Zehnder, but still no sign of Captain Chevalier. Smarter-dressed, more upright, in velvet-collared overcoats, their silk hats beside them, sombre, book-faced men, Arch assumed there sat a row of literary celebrities, they appeared incongruously mixed up with a handful of Staff officers holding black melon bowlers. He smiled to himself, recalling his friend's affectionate nickname for the aristocratic Guards – 'wooden-tops'. Watching the row of hats, he saw it was not misplaced.

Conrad's misgivings about the hymns were unfounded. In fact they were both appropriate, and oddly affecting. First came the Processional accompanying the plain pale wood coffin. The stirring tune and defiant words of old Jimmy Bode's evangelical anthem came sliding back into Arch's head, like a long-remembered promise – of course, he recognized it from Sundays spent perspiring, stiff-collared and grey-stockinged, in St Andrew's.

> O Jesus I have promised
> To serve Thee to the end –

was solid enough, but how the little forest church shook when it came to

> I shall not fear the battle . . .

No, by God, nobody could say that of Conrad. Fear Battle! What!

Then there was a reading – 'my house has m̄
mansions' – 'he fleeth, as it were, a shadow' – 'to
everything there is a season' – 'the last enemy that shall be
destroyed is death' – and then the small congregation
shuffled to its feet and sang quietly, almost to themselves,
'We blossom and flourish, as leaves on the tree, and
wither and perish . . .' And very loudly they recited the
words of '*Jerusalem*'. He remembered Bickerton in his
chariot of fire. Oh, these English, thought Arch to
himself, these English with their slow sad songs, –
whatever will become of them? They are so hopeless, and
their grief contains such courage . . . A few more inau-
dible prayers followed. Then it was the rector again,
climbing the wooden pulpit.

'He hunted,' said the old vicar, who wore his Military
Cross proudly pinned to his white surplice, 'he hunted the
Hun with the same vigour as the warrantable hart, and
that could never be despised.'

Surprisingly, Canon Hawkshaw, a snow-haired major
from the Hampshires, was far from the blood and guts
school of army padres he'd met (with the same contempt
as Conrad) behind the lines, or on the home front – what
was the name of that bugger who talked about wanting
the men 'sweet, clean, and ready to die . . .'? Far from it,
he was gentle and compassionate towards the living, and
regretful 'so passionate a songster was so speedily cut off'
– and, instead of a biblical text, spoke from the pulpit
Conrad's best-known poem.

The rector took from the inside cover of his prayer
book a piece of boy's exercise paper, quite small, and
folded into four.

'These lines', he said, while he painstakingly unfolded
it, 'were written to commemorate the death in action on a
summer's day of an ordinary foot-soldier in Conrad's
platoon. He told me himself, he had been talking to this
man over a mug of tea half an hour earlier, on Pip Ridge;
he had to check through the things the poor fellow had in
his pockets. Known to almost all of you, I am sure, it is

ed "The Sunbather" and', he added, holding up the
exercise sheet, 'this is Conrad's own copy.'

> Was I to believe him dead
> Or sleeping, outspread in the sun,
> Hand just resting beneath his head
> Covered in sand, his shirt undone?
>
> This slackness looked the same
> As sleep; had he been thinking
> Of death when it quietly came
> To him while he was drinking?
>
> Or had this bondsman ever thought
> Of death, of lying there, struck
> Before the whine or the report,
> Before he had time to duck?
>
> Death came first before its warning
> Swiftly to the sunburnt man;
> Whose jaw hangs open, almost breathing,
> Feeling where the wind ran
>
> To other mouths. Soft is the cry
> That speaks for him, for here down dropped
> Already nothing but the name they called him
> by,
> A gun, a watch that stopped . . .
>
> Here on the scarp where the sun drenches
> A man died as if resting
> After a childhood in the trenches,
> Who never minded living.

Hawkshaw was one of those 'old school' parsons, born
and bred about Iping, who knew the Forest rides like his
own well-thumbed Book of Morning Prayer.

  'Our friend Conrad', he said, 'belonged to an England
you cannot kill. As we all remember, from his childhood,

he hunted with the Ancient Southdown. He was on that ancient line of huntsmen and warriors and land owners and farmers, whose forebears fought as archers at Agincourt. The Purdues, Pour Dieu, tradition claims, was their cry. We know the Romans marched this way to their station at Alfolfdean. Later, the tribes of Eallha: custodians of the strolling acres for a hundred miles each side of Conrad's ancient and proud home of Old Nineveh; it should be proclaimed the family of Purdue belonged to the land – the land did not belong to them – it was held in trust and passed on. When Conrad went into battle, it was for more than merely the *name* of England that he fought, but for its farmhouses, its harvests, its bouveries and bergeries, the majestic Forest rides, the four-square, plain Forest churches, like our own beloved St Cuthman's, the English language itself, our hodden and eloquent poetry, redolent of the spirit and soil of the land. His epitaph comes not from the Bible, or commonplace school prayers – for his short span, I will read to you from a work whose passion, and unswerving confidence in Nature, whose own peculiar music, is close to the Conrad we love, and mourn:

> He comes with western winds, with evening's
> wandering airs,
> With that clear dusk of heaven that brings the thickest
> stars:
> Winds take a pensive tone and stars a tender fire,
> And visions rise and change, which kill me with desire –

'Conrad's last wish was that he should be laid to rest, not in the noble family monument which has commemorated the Purdues for generations, but in the coverts he loved best, hid in as a boy, and hunted in as a man. And his last wish shall be observed:

> Deaf is that ear that caught the opening sound
> Dumb is the tongue that cheered the hills around –
> Unpleasing truth! Death hunts us from our birth
> In view, and men, like foxes, take to earth.'

d then, with a simple unforced dignity, the rector drew the family into the Forest which lay outside the brick church, and followed the coffin to a space some quarter of a mile distant which had already been cleared, and Arch followed behind, but within earshot. Only a handful of people stood around in a half-circle, as Conrad's body was lowered into prime Forest soil, the flag of the Diehards wrapped around him, and his spurs and velvet cap and hunting-horn placed gently on the top. Then the rector said, in a quiet, still voice, and there seemed to be no sound of birds around, not the merest flick of a leaf:

'Conrad's last words contained one request, which we are here to see dutifully carried out, and in good heart. He had always asked that his body could be lain in the open air, out of consecrated ground, here in the Forest of Iping, in a place where, he said, and I would like you to hear his own words, "where the light twinkling feet of hounds may sometimes pass over my grave".'

Scarlet in the face, perhaps with exertion, Nim Ives, his loyal hunt-servant, wound the horn for Home, while the nervous hounds panted and whimpered at the grave's edge. And, deep, deep inside the heart of the woods, a green woodpecker added his keen yaffle to the clamours around his monument. So Conrad got his pagan funeral after all.

CHAPTER TWENTY-EIGHT

Captain Chevalier at Home

'Before we talk, would you care to have a look at the *figures*?' asked General Ascapard, when Arch called on him a few days later. The housekeeper who opened the door to him had taken the liberty of warning him that the general 'was not entirely himself these days' but he was unprepared for the shock. The plume of bright, white hair was tragically reduced, and even the hawk-like bead in the solitary eye seemed dimmed. He had, in a very few months, Arch thought, aged considerably. Captain Chevalier had warned him also to be prepared for some changes, but even he had underestimated the self-evident deterioration. The iron-ramrod frame had actually caved in like a tunnel, and the figure in front of him, greeting him at the doorway to his 'den', was like his old grandfather, and in bedroom slippers and plaid dressing-gown too. The 'figures' he referred to were lead toy soldiers, of which he had a large collection.

The visit to Captain Chevalier had been something of a puzzle to him also.

'Don't talk to me about Conrad,' said the young elegant figure, now in the top-boots and silver epaulettes of the Hussars. 'I did my mourning yesterday.'

In his narrow sitting-room in Sheffield Terrace, furnished by curious-looking pictures and a few pieces of white furniture, overlooking the gardens of an old rectory, a second officer, rather scruffy, lounged in braces and breeches, with his feet on one arm of the sofa.

'What do you feel like this time of the morning, Arch, do you want a tankard of "the boy"?'

In fact at that minute Arch thought fondly of what Chancellor used to call 'a handful of beer', and could have downed a pint of Best Boys with eagerness, but suspected it was not quite the thing at that hour in the morning. He remembered the general's old trick at Roman Landing, and thought he would make use of it.

'Well, what day of the week is it?'

'Wednesday, I think.'

'If it's Wednesday, then I'll have some of that champagne.'

'Entertain one another while I bring up another bottle – you know Captain Gendron, sir, he used to be a perfectly sane officer in King's Troop and then went mad and joined the Flying Corps.'

The officer propped up lazily on the sofa smiled as Chevalier wandered off in the direction of the pantry. Arch could not make out his rank.

'I say, this war's a bugger, isn't it?' asked the prone figure after a little pause. Arch thought there was something familiar about his face, but failed to place him. The Carlyle, probably, or even one of those weekends down at Port's. Wasn't sure he cared for him much, he seemed to be ordering him around, as well as Captain Chevalier.

'I must say –' began the aloof officer, 'oh, give me one of your cigarettes, will you?' gesturing towards Arch's recently opened packet of Sweet Aftons, '– so many friends seem to have gone off. Decent chaps, nearly all of them. Both sides too. All these dreadful losses in France. Senseless when you think of it. And now Conrad. That's one of the worst things to ever happen in this bloody war; worth the loss of an entire regiment, Dinkie Bamborough told me.'

Arch felt a little taken aback to be lighting his cigarette while this nonchalant officer lolled at his ease on the sofa, actually bending down to do it.

'Thanks so much – I must say these are damn good – feels like a proper cigarette in the lungs, instead of those dreadful blond things they seem to give me.'

481

Possibly, Arch thought to himself, the explanation was they *had* met, *did* know each other, and he'd forgotten where and when – would it have been when he was with Chas, and the Yorkshire Dragoons after the Somme? Perhaps that was it. There was something hoveringly familiar about this chap, and something curiously 'shining' about him that set him apart. But his speech wasn't apart at all, in fact he spoke with a quaint half-Cockney intonation, like somebody brought up in the stable-yard. Curious chap. Couldn't place him at all. Arch thoroughly wished Captain Chevalier would come back.

'I liked Conrad very much. Most people did, who met him or spent time in his company,' he answered, to keep the conversation ticking over until the champagne arrived, and he could get on his way. If they already knew all about Conrad's death, why on earth had he been delegated to tell people, he wondered? It all seemed a waste of his time. 'But, in reality, I hardly knew him. He just wasn't around long enough to get to know.'

'Friend of his out on the huntin' field, were you?' the young man asked politely for once.

'No, not really. The only hunting I ever did was Hun-hunting.'

'Oh yes, of course, you're Flying Corps, aren't you? I approve of that.'

'Do you now?' said Arch, somewhat stonily. He'd had enough of this sofa-wallah. Sod him, he thought. Bickerton would have a few words to say to his face. He remembered countless knife-edge air-battles, and Bickerton and himself fighting out like *bagarreurs*, and considered the prospect of this indolent bugger's 'approval', impertinent, some upper-class oaf in braces and breeches, lying on his back smoking one of his precious Aftons.

Happily, Captain Chevalier arrived back brandishing the champagne in a white napkin.

'So sorry to have kept you both waiting, but there's absolutely nobody about – God knows where my batman's gone off to, scrounging about as usual, I suppose –

482

way, this is good and cool. I've tried it – it's quite eat. Pink's Least Disgusting, I call it. Here, Arch.' And then to the idle officer on the chaise-longue: 'Prince?'

Chevalier held out a silver tankard of ice-cold foaming fizz.

'Hah! Goes down well!' said the nonchalant officer. Perhaps he was Chevalier's staff officer. It was irritating the man wasn't wearing his jacket.

'Arch, old feller, you'll have to go down and tell Ascapard,' began Captain Chevalier, but Arch's eye was taken by an idle trooper engaging a passing nursemaid in banter just outside the garden gate. From the couple, and the pram in front of them, his eye wandered coolly over to the car parked in the street behind them and, following the lines of a smooth well-made Daimler, camouflaged in customary field-brown, saw to his dismay the tell-tale fleur-de-lys painted on the door.

Of course! The face that stared at him out of a hundred popular cigarette-cards. He was even to be uncovered in packets of Sweet Aftons. But the yellow hair was brighter than the colour on the cheap cardboard. He was daintier too than Arch had previously imagined. It must have been the smallness of stature that deceived him, and the voice, of course. Wouldn't Father-Sir be bucked! – and he'd made such a hash of it. But an extra sense warned him the worst thing he could do would be to start bowing and sirring all over the place. Obviously the chap had come incognito and wanted to remain that way. Lucky escape, though. He was on the edge of saying something in fairly healthy terms. But Chevalier was still addressing him about Andrew Ascapard:

'Honestly, we've all been thinking about it – it's going to break the old dug-out's heart, and I can't go, and Prince *won't* go –'

'No, absolutely –'

'So it will just have to be you. You'll do it well, if you shape up to it.'

'Then I suppose I'll have to.'

483

'Good old fellow,' said Chevalier, topping him u[p]
knew you'd say "yes". He's a bit of a shipwreck by now,
but *do* visit.' Arch nodded unenthusiastically.

'By the way, how's that splendid tall brother of yours,
whatsisname, Chas? Still with the "wooden-tops"?'

'He's having a terrible time dismounted with a Dragoon regiment in the front line. All part of Haig's great
"breakthrough" strategy.'

'I don't think that's going to work, do you think,
Prince? I mean who's going to be left, even when this
miraculous so-called gap in the centre does appear?'

'I've got a crowd of school pals who are out with the
Australian Light Horse. There's strong talk of them
breaking through and storming up the Balkans.'

'I'm afraid that's one of Winston's not very good, and
terribly costly, and never quite thought-through ideas,'
interjected Chevalier. 'That's over, Arch. You're out of
touch, up in the air-waves, they've come home.'

'Home, are they?' said Arch excitedly.

'Well, not home exactly. More a matter of France. Or,
as Andrew would have it, Franz.'

How on earth did Captain Chevalier know everything?

The young man with bright hair (yes, there really was
something shining about him, thought Arch), the fellow
of immediate promise, swung his stockinged feet off the
sofa arm, and walked over rather suddenly to the champagne bottle and filled all three glasses, ending with his
own:

'It's everything which follows preoccupies me a great
deal more. Particularly *me*,' and here he broke into a
most endearing crooked smile. 'You can imagine. It seems
self-evident, whoever wins now, that the old tired-out,
worked-off concepts have gone. After this battle, it
doesn't seem to me to be a matter of preparing for a
so-called truce or peace, or even enjoying it, but that the
whole of civilized life as we know it, or have experienced
it, will have to be thought about all over again from the
beginning. You can be sure of that. Not so bad an idea,

...er, what! Oh damn!' noticing his cigarette had gone out, 'will you light this for me again, please?'

'Don't bring all that up again, Prince — we had all this out before at poor old Portarlington's place in the Manhood. You were there, Arch, you remember. That fake priest, and Andrew Ascapard in a towering rage, as usual.'

'We talked about it most of one evening, sir.'

'Yes, but probably not in the same way,' said the younger man, fitting his newly lit cigarette somewhat incongruously into a short bakelite holder. 'I mean, you and I, Captain, I should imagine we're about the same age, aren't we? If there's any fresh thinking to be done, I assume it's us that'll be the ones to do it. As I said before, this war's a bugger. A pointless bugger too. Still, I wish I was in it, somehow, instead of going to parties and benefits, and investitures, and wearing a whole lot of faintly inappropriate clothes . . .'

'We each do what we can,' said Chevalier rather impertinently, and Arch thought he detected a twinge of irritation in the other man's cheek. 'According to our abilities.'

'Well . . . perhaps. But I believe there will have to be changes made. I mean, things can't continue like *this*', and the prince expressed with his eyes a gesture vaguely in the direction of the world in the street outside where his driver was flattering the nursemaid — 'or like this,' with which he made an accompanying movement of his right hand, cigarette-holder carefully poised, to include himself.

'No, of course not, Prince,' replied Chevalier, instantly checking himself with a faint uplifted motion of his eyebrows to give Arch the *congé* he'd been looking for.

'Well, off to see the general, I suppose,' said Arch, collecting cap and gloves, 'I can't stooge around here for ever.'

'Don't be surprised if you find a change in the poor old bird,' said Chevalier, returned to normal high spirits,

485

'he's taken the recent casualty lists terribly to heart. I shrunk somehow. Anyway, thanks madly, tickled pink and that sort of thing. Let me know how you get on.'

'Oh, don't bother about all of that, for God's sake,' smiled the man of immediate promise, as Arch looked all set to give him a correct salute, 'I say, Chev, I'd no idea the Flying Corps boys looked so smart in their get-up! And,' walking over to shake hands, 'I've enjoyed our little talk, Captain. Who was your improver at Oxford? I assume you were trained there.'

'Captain Dyson, sir.'

'I thought he might have been. Smith-Barry's crowd? Port Meadow and that sort of thing? Birdy Boyd-Rochford has the chore of looking after me, and he took me up with him on one of those Farman Shorthorn brutes. Marvellous stuff. Don't let Chev hear me, but that's exactly what I should love to do. Chev knows how to *think* Cavalry, but my impression is the future might be in flying. In any case, good luck, always. Adieu, adieu, adieu.'

And, as he extended his hand warmly, Arch replied:

'If it's not impertinent, sir, all the luck of the Irish.'

'So you've come down all this way to have a look at the *figures* . . .'

The brief meeting at Chevalier's had brought him down to Ascapard's country place. As the two of them stood together in his cold, rather formal summer-room with its glass roof, and unhappy plants, facing the table-top of several hundred lead soldiers, Arch could hear from somewhere the sound of children playing with high-pitched voices.

'Good of you to visit an old soldier,' said the general. 'We're pretty well bogged down here with everything, as you see.' Arch assumed, from the look of things, he was watching a set-piece battle of Napoleonic vintage.

'It's the terrible winter-war in Sebastopol, quite honestly. Lord Lucan totally bottled up – desperation

486

...ading all round – energies drained, morale at low
...b, supplies limited. Trying to find a way round the
terrible war of attrition. The King doesn't see any resolu-
tion, nor do I.'

'Captain Chevalier suggested I should come and see
you, sir. I'm the bearer of unhappy news.'

'I hope this isn't too cold for you, young fellow; most
of you young chaps have got plenty of warm blood in you
yet; it's us old'uns are the ones who feel the damp.
Always did. Even in India. Told by some medicine-man
out there, it's the sign of a long life. Damned uncomfortable one. Look at that crowd of "figures" down there,' he
interrupted himself, to point out a column of toy horse-
men, the size of Arch's fingers, galloping into a column of
Russian artillery.

'Lord Cardigan's cherry-bums. The whole lot blown to
buggery.'

'General, sir, I was sent to explain to you that our great
friend Conrad is dead. He was buried at Iping on
Wednesday.'

The general looked at him with watery eyes, and took
his hand. For a terrible second Arch feared the general
was going to fold in two directly in front of him, just like
a soft paper bag. But in fact he took the flier's right hand
with his own left one – the old fellow was quite correct,
he felt as cold as a pane of glass – and led him to another,
smaller table and began transferring from it tidy rows of
brand-new lead soldiers representing old-fashioned
Infantry regiments of a century before.

'The old foot-mob will just have to carry the burden,
that's the only remedy. The way they always do. Hold the
line firm until the armies regroup. Then counter-attack,
bluff the flank there, make a pincer over here, bring field
gunners up to here, fill the gaps. Listen, don't worry
unduly, young man, take a look round, will you.'

Arch could see only nests of short tables with various
regiments in attendance, waiting to be allocated to various parts of the miniature battlefield, and beneath them

pile upon pile of scarlet and black toy soldier boxes, brown wrapping paper.

'No, not on the field of battle. There's devastation there. Carnage. The whiff of grape-shot, the stink of cordite . . . No, look higher. Over there, for instance, Above the table, for instance.'

Arch looked where he was told. He saw a series of what he assumed must be paintings, hung round with dark scarves. He was totally mystified. He looked to the general, shaking his head in puzzlement.

'Mirrors. All draped down. Cover the surfaces of anything that shines brightly or reflects. The least thing we can do for the boys – mourn them. Old native custom in the Sudan.'

Arch sat in the inappropriate summer basket chair offered to him, and smoked while the general unwrapped with immense patience a further brown paper package obviously containing miniature reinforcements. He tried again:

'Conrad received a splinter in his thigh, high up, and it seemed to go wrong for him. He was shipped back home, but it went gangrenous and he died. The Prince of Wales thought I should tell you personally.'

Drawing the slender, enticing, scarlet cardboard box from the wrapping paper, the general studied the written information on the side.

'Royal Horse Artillery in Action. Field Guns, Mules and Limbers. It will help reinforce the centre.' And, with equal care, he began the complicated business of removing the 'figures' one by one, and setting them in place on the field of battle.

'There's a terrible feeling before an action like this, never during it – in action you enter another dimension – a terrible feeling of imagined dread. These young men, look at them where they stand, trembling with death. You feel like hell before the battle. Your bowels turn to iced water. Not during the action, mind, you can get through it, charge about shouting out, expose yourself to bullets, invite them. Afterwards of course, you feel it, you get the shock, and you start to tremble, and shake from head to stern. But the General Staff — I know because they told me — they used to think it was an accepted thing in *this* war, they used to think that the more battle-action you got, the tougher you got. But I told them that wasn't true. You talk to me of a young man with a whiff of gas in his lungs, for instance. Or a bit of a splinter in his leg. For instance. Now I knew a doc who was in the Royal Fusiliers, like some of these chaps here' — and he indicated a corner of helmeted figures, their rifles extended in front of them, all in the identical posture — 'and he told me the most valiant of front-liners, down in the dug-outs, would say, "Well, doc, I've . . . I've got a little bit of a temperature, or a bit of tooth-ache, and I'd like to go back for a bit." And this doctor told me, at the risk of his own authority, he'd send them back. Because he knew courage was expendable. You only had so much. Like capital. And, once it was gone, it had gone for good.'

Arch thought it best under the circumstances to stand quietly by himself and study the 'figures' so perfectly sculpted and painted, crouching, lying, charging with such classical uniformity.

'Of course,' General Ascapard was continuing, 'in a war, a deadly war of attrition between two cousin nations, bleeding each other white, like the Greek city-states, you know, it's hard to see things any other way. In 1915, the Germans tried to do something funny at Christmas-time, like they did the year before, but eleven o'clock at night, right across the Western Front, our guns opened up, and blew them all to bits. We never held any anger against the Germans, not really. But it isn't a question of gaining ground. Look at the "figures" — it isn't a question of fighting for the gain of a few yards of ground, but of knocking the other man out. When you box in the ring, you don't pursue your man all over the Albert Hall and half-way across London, hitting him

489

when you can; you battle it out in the ring. And th[...]
what these armies have got to do. Hence the "figures" . .[...]
What we have here is the vast set-piece battle of a corner
of the Flanders Plain, a little place called Passchendaele.
The two armies. One as brave and steadfast as the
other . . . just battering each other to death. Draw the
enemy into the net, batter away, and destroy. See whose
supply of courage spends first.'

He bent forward quickly and snatched up a lead soldier
from the German army, amongst the cluster of staff
officers behind a little sandbag enclosure.

'Here he is – Crown Prince Willie. Nice man. Decent
chap. What the Alleyman calls "*praktikalisch*" – decent
chap. We guy him in the papers, Little Willie sort-of-thing
but I knew him quite well in days gone by. Decent chap.
"*Praktikalisch*." Good general. Troops love him. Gave
them all a Christmas gift of a meerschaum pipe. Generous
to a fault.'

Arch felt he had had enough of this by now, and
collected his swagger-stick and leather coat from the
basket chair.

'General, sir, I came to visit you to inform you of
Conrad's death of wounds, and his burial at Iping. And
now I must return to my Wing in Tangmere . . .'

But the general had already interrupted him.

'Oh, it's only afterwards you begin to grieve. The grief
and the anger follow after. Dead, fresh-killed men on the
battlefield, worked-off young chaps are part of normal
life, of every day. Look here,' pointing to the vast wooden
trestle table which dipped under the weight of its leaden
armies, marching back and forth.

'Look at the new drafts of young cadets in Germany
marching forward to fill the empty spaces. My God, those
cornfields in Franz and on the Somme will harvest the
most tremendous crops for years to come! Do you know,
in those massed attacks in the summer of 1914, they came
across the fields of Ypres in waves so dense you couldn't
help but hit anybody with your rifle just pointing vaguely

...he right direction. And the rifle stock got so hot with
...ring, the grease on the wooden cover used to run down
on to your fingers like pork fat. Cartridge after cartridge
after cartridge. Look here!' And the general lifted up his
right index finger where a faint scar still showed.

'All the grease ran down to here, and the end of my
finger sweated up out to here, a huge blister. Where the
boiling fat had run down. And then, on Christmas Day,
mass attacks of young German boys, sixteen years of age,
arm in arm, one rifle shared between three, singing their
songs. I remember old Maréchal Guérain there, just
standing on the parapet, before the fusillade, nodding his
head. "Keep it going boys, keep it going, your race is
nearly run."'

'Do you have any message for Captain Chevalier,
General? He seemed most anxious I should reach you,
and give you the news about poor Conrad.'

'Ahah! You're on your way, are you? Well, we'll say
goodbye to the figures...' And the general turned
towards the trestle table, and formally saluted them,
before leading the way through to the hall. All the rooms
were empty, Arch observed as he strolled along behind.
Just carpets and chairs and curtained windows, and
mirrors, draped with scarves.

'Good luck on your return to the fields of Franz,' said
the old man, in the hall.

The general was waylaid by his housekeeper who
seemed to have been lying in wait for him, and gently but
forcibly she escorted him to another of his basket-chairs,
in another long, shaded room devoid of furniture, other
than tables and armchairs. No flowers even, or photographs, or pictures on the walls. The housekeeper tucked
the rug she was carrying on her arm round his legs.

'There can be no possible doubt that the British Forces
in Franz have won themselves imperishable glory. But
"*proximus ardet Ucalegon*". The army needs men, men
and yet more men...'

The grey-haired woman, who went about her business

491

in a peculiar kind of silence, as if deprived of spee[ch]
indicated by a sequence of gestures that the young
flying-officer should take his leave, without ceremony,
which he proceeded to do, giving the same kind of
indifferent salute he would, on the peak of his cap, to a
dilatory sentry. He felt the general was no more aware of
his departure than he had been of his presence. The whole
visit was a fiasco.

The general stopped him with an uplifted hand. 'I
wonder,' he said, 'I wonder how they'd be, facing cold
steel.'

Slowly Arch made his way down the curled drive past
the rhododendron bushes. It came to him like a revelation.

My God, he thought to himself. So that was all it was.
What keeps this great old war going on for year after year
after year after year. Lonely old men, mad, in empty
rooms.

But, as the motherly housekeeper tucked the rug around
the old warrior's knees, General Ascapard murmured, as
much to himself as anyone in the room with him: 'That
young man has the flower of death in his mouth.'

He was not as mad as all that.

CHAPTER TWENTY-NINE

Eastward Ho! 1918

When he returned to Béthune, Arch found himself transferred to single-seaters and placed in command of a squadron with his own faithful Zweidekker, a Sopwith Snipe.

No contention about the seasons now. One May morning, after his unexpected meeting with Mysie at Abbeville, an entire year to the day after he saw, with his own shocked eyes, his friend, Bickerton, browned off, and one week to the day after he had sat in the church for Conrad, Arch awoke with a renewed sense of expectation and hope. This war could not last forever, it had gone on long enough, must almost have worked itself off, and he felt confident he might just as well see it out. Brother Chas was alive, and still in the saddle, so on this particular May morning he observed all his familiar rituals with an obsessive care. He remembered an old saying of Hortense at Belgodère: 'As long as the month of May.' Often she came into his thoughts: he kept his part of the promise of the Maresquiers.

First his extra-precise dressing, next the exhilarating smell of castor oil and fresh-mown grass, and then the airfield falling away underneath. His reaching upwards to the heavens specified for Arch his love of the earth. How much more he wanted than just his share. And so he continued, steering eastward, part in cloud and part in the bouncy light-blue atmosphere, as the brown earth below fell back, and he wriggled his spine comfortably inside the chair of his machine. His 'Office', they called it back in the old 10th. As he strained against the wood and metal struts behind him, stretching his legs out to the rudders, he felt, as in a dream, his body quite dist... disappear inside the machine. It was as if he was the one to bounce along on top of the sheep-backed clouds, while the brackish pulse of fuel circled round and round his own veins. There was good dense air close to the ground: some of the time he dropped heavily like a stone, but at other times he soared towards the eye of the sun with the unforced grace of a buzzard. Thinner air up there, tightening the heart, a feeling of release. A sharpness in his lungs.

In his dream that night, his latest dream, he had succeeded in fulfilling a missing corner of the jigsaw pattern of his days down at Roman Landing and set in place the last little wooden figure to compose the picture. Out of the corner of his eye, just on the edge of things, he was able to see what he had, until that moment in his sleep, altogether missed, during his winter walk with Conrad. How on earth could he have ignored it? It was translucid. The two of them, Conrad and he, necks stuck into their collars, bareheaded, pacing along. The rain slanting across horizontally. Hounds far in front, worrying over a tired scent. And an old man, at the handles of his plough, a couple of heavy horses up front, bent forward, and an old wife leading the horses' heads patiently across the furrows. And, still in his dream, a love vaster than death. Yes, of course, death was as strong as love. Could he be dreaming still? Hortense of Belgodère, for no reason, drifted into his thoughts.

What was Hortense doing now? he wondered. Standing motionless, perhaps, as he had last seen her, timidly holding the cloth button at her breast.

He surged the engine like a flood for the fun of it, and spun, for the sheer hell of it, upwards and outwards over all the earthbound things of the world: the fields, grass, gunfire, impenetrable grey armies crawling studiously across earthworks, advancing cavalry, the stone walls of contempt; nothing in the universe restricted him, nothing could move swiftly enough to imprison him, or disfigure him. He knew enough about the fox to imitate his ways.

owed his life to the ingenuity of the fox, and was damned if he'd ever hunt a fox again.

'I'll spit my death on it!' he chuckled to himself, in memory of Bickerton.

Was not great God in awe of him – Arch – as he looped and spun as he had done for a thousand years? Was he not a kestrel, a wind-storm, a hymn of derision? How splendid and grand he felt now, swerving eastward, into the sun, remote, apart. Arch felt at one with everything, with the sky and its servant, the earth, with flecks of cloud, with the glitter of pebbles under the ice, and they were at one with him. He *was* the wind. A kind of unearthly love in life, now, at this moment, flowed through him more than ever before. More than he conceived possible in his heart. Perhaps, he thought, he should marry Maddy McKay and settle down in one of those pretty little houses behind The Vestry. There were worse things to do, and he felt he deserved something of a rest after three years *hard* in the front line. A quiet life might be the answer, now the war was virtually at an end.

Arch looked downwards to where Picardy and the earthworks lay below.

The black day of the German forces was soon to dawn. All along the old front line the Württemberg Division and the East Prussians were to tremble on the very edge of their coveted break-through, recoil for an instant, and roll back with the entire Second German Army to Berlin. The length of the Amiens Salient, everything was to end. The *Jagdgeschwäder* of Oberleutnant Göring was to scatter its blood and brains like rain over the Somme. The Supreme Command's will to go on fighting would collapse; the empire yield to the humiliation of *Einkreisung* – the Encirclement.

Arch remembered his mother. Walking away from him towards the gardens, turning suddenly – he thought for a moment she recognized him. He noticed exactly the mysterious damp Australian light which reflected through the leaves upon the bark of the grey gum trees, an

495

unearthly colour. How much longer they seemed to [...] the gardens of Brontë, there seemed no end to them, stretching away, the bougainvillaea, arches of lime, espaliered apricots and nectarines, how could he have forgotten the nectarines! Melons, mangoes and the wrinkled old quince, an ancient fruit, and the greeny-grey hiding-places ripe for children's adventures. Chas always said, climb right up inside the heart of the tree so that the world moves with you, as the tree moves. Groves of shadow and enticing perfume, languishing as far as the stringy-bark glades and hoopoe cries; and the Dreamtime, and remote blue hills . . . The pale swamps of Gretta; the droughty ranges of Jericho.

For the sheer zest of it all, he looped his machine skilfully in a circle around God. The world was filled with such unimaginable beauty. Such joy! And he flew eagerly, leaving the morning behind him. His true dominion was the sublime.

Three small specks, mere traces of dust, emerged from out of the sun. Arch felt a light breeze on his cheeks, flying as fast as he dared, further east, the sunrise on his temples, warming his hair. His fingertips on the stick. The Snipe caught the sun twice, and winked.

A mere thumbprint of brightness then, falling out of the air; a plume of whiteness floating behind, crumbling, softening, dispersing.

'O God, *my* God . . .!'

Into battle then, at the end, the big ship he sought so ardently and for so long; reaching out towards further light . . . reaching, reaching. Out of darkness, into light. Imperishable, like the planets. Inextinguishable. Like the stars.

THE END